Bleeding H

"A compelling, adroitly crafted novel of
ond chance at happiness. [Gyllenhaal's] l
life while shining a light on the darkest s
evocative prose is psychologically astute
is one of our finest novelists of the heart.
—Carol Goodman, author o

"A tale of betrayal, greed, and murder v
through the gardens she describes so poet
also handily highlights a contemporary s
in every corner, as well as creates female characters with heart and ambition. . . . Fans of Jodi Picoult and Chris Bohjalian, this book's for you!"
—Holly Robinson, author of *The Wishing Hill* and *Beach Plum Island*

"Full of intrigue and heart, Liza Gyllenhaal's new novel is sure to leave
you feeling as if you've taken a stroll through your favorite flower garden
and found that strength was in full bloom."
—Jennifer Scott, author of *The Sister Season*

A Place for Us

"As timely as today's headlines, as eternal as familial love, this is a dazzling
novel of the joys and perils of parenthood and the desperation of adoles-
cents striving to belong and struggling to grow up. Gyllenhaal has written
a lyrical, psychologically astute, heart-stoppingly suspenseful novel about
what it means to be part of a family."
—Ellen Feldman, author of *Next to Love*

continued . . .

Written by today's freshest new talents and selected by New American
Library, NAL Accent novels touch on subjects close to a woman's heart,
from friendship to family to finding our place in the world. The Conversation
Guides included in each book are intended to enrich the individual reading
experience, as well as encourage us to explore these topics together—
because books, and life, are meant for sharing.

Visit us online at penguin.com.

"Gyllenhaal's novel is a snapshot of a family and a community in crisis. It is a thought-provoking, all-too-familiar story of young people attempting to navigate the often treacherous road to adulthood and adults attempting to parent on an equally dangerous path."   —*Booklist*

"Very compassionate and realistic. A very compelling, gripping story from the start to the last page."   —My Book Addiction Reviews

"A powerful story about grudges, secrets, and family loyalty."
                                                    —*RT Book Reviews*

"[With] a timely, ripped-from-the-headlines story, this book will get readers thinking even after the last page is finished."
                              —*News and Sentinel* (Parkersburg, WV)

So Near

"Unexpected, jarring, and beautiful. . . . Gyllenhaal doesn't just invite us to follow a story from the sidelines. She grabs our arms and yanks us right into the center of an emotional whirlwind. . . . Gyllenhaal demonstrates a deft hand at lyrical writing that subtly balances metaphors, philosophical realizations, and the realistic complexity of emotions."
                                                    —*Berkshire Eagle*

"Intriguing . . . a real page-turner!"   —*Publishers Weekly*

"Gyllenhaal plumbs the complexity of human emotions in this wonderful novel. With sensitivity and compassion, she creates characters that will pull at your heart on their journey through grief. I loved reading *So Near*, a truly believable and compelling story."
                        —Katherine Davis, author of *A Slender Thread*

Local Knowledge

"A bighearted debut."   —*Miami Herald*

"This is a book to savor. . . . Selling real estate is the surface story, but as you peel back the layers throughout the chapters you realize it is about family relationships, old friends, and new friends."
                                                    —*Publishers Weekly*

ALSO BY LIZA GYLLENHAAL

A Place for Us
So Near
Local Knowledge

Bleeding Heart

LIZA GYLLENHAAL

NAL Accent
Published by the Penguin Group
Penguin Group (USA) LLC, 375 Hudson Street,
New York, New York 10014

USA | Canada | UK | Ireland | Australia | New Zealand | India | South Africa | China
penguin.com
A Penguin Random House Company

First published by NAL Accent, an imprint of New American Library,
a division of Penguin Group (USA) LLC

First Printing, November 2014

NAL
ACCENT   REGISTERED TRADEMARK—MARCA REGISTRADA

LIBRARY OF CONGRESS CATALOGING-IN-PUBLICATION DATA:

Gyllenhaal, Liza.
Bleeding heart / Liza Gyllenhaal.
p. cm
ISBN 978-0-451-46670-9 (paperback)
I. Title.
PS3607.Y53B58 2014
813'.6—dc23   2014015574

Printed in the United States of America
1 3 5 7 9 10 8 6 4 2

Set in Sabon   •   Designed by Elke Sigal

For W.E.B.

Bleeding Heart

Part One

1

"*C*heater! Cheater! Cheater!"

I stopped on the pathway leading out to the barn to listen to the male cardinal's repeated cry. He and the missus lived in the stand of hemlocks behind the house and spent their days alternately foraging under the kitchen bird feeders and reminding me over and over again of my folly. *Cheater!* Most ornithologists identify the call as *cheer, cheer, cheer* or *birdie, birdie, birdie.* But I knew better. The soundstage effect of the snow muffled the bird's cry, but I still heard the warning clearly. *Don't forget! You must never forget!*

Not that I could even if I wanted to. It would be like forgetting that I'd lost an arm or a leg. The source of the pain was gone, but its throbbing absence would always be with me. For, in fact, I had been cheated. Something *had* been taken from me. Many things, actually. Trust. Security. Identity. The wonderful complacency of marriage and motherhood. Of knowing exactly where I stood in the world. And that the sun would come up again over the sugar maples bordering our old Westchester property. The Hyatt house on the corner. I could still see it all so clearly in my mind's eye! My daughters, bent dutifully over their cereal bowls at the kitchen table. Richard, flapping open the *Wall Street Journal.* The row of African violets on the windowsill. All of it gone now. Swept away—no, cruelly severed. Without warning. Or recourse. Or even—and this was the worst of it, really—explanation.

❧

"You got a call from the Mackenzie residence," Mara said as I came into the office, stamping the snow off my boots. Last night's unexpected late-winter storm had dumped another six inches on the Berkshire Hills of Massachusetts. The thrill of January's sun-dazzled snowscapes was long gone. It was mid-March, after all. Daffodils were blooming in other parts of the country.

"What?" I asked, shedding my duffle coat and hanging it on the wall rack next to Mara's oversized parka.

"The Mackenzie residence," she said again. "That big new place on the mountain. The one you and Mrs. Boyland were talking about last week."

I'm always a little taken aback when I realize that my self-effacing assistant, Mara, might actually be listening in on my telephone conversations. I guess it's hard not to overhear each other in the winter when I close off most of the old barn to save on heat, and Mara and I are forced to share the small front office. I know I should probably just shut down Green Acres altogether during the off-season. But a nagging fear that I'll somehow lose momentum and slip back into the abyss keeps me at my desk. Just as her need to provide for her son, Danny, keeps Mara, a single parent, at hers. Both of us, in the dead of winter, frittering away time on the Internet. And, in my case, talking on the phone, frequently to Gwen Boyland.

"I'm guessing two million when all is said and done," Gwen

had told me the week before. My closest friend in Woodhaven, Gwen takes endless pleasure in talking about money. What things cost. How much people are worth. Lately she's become obsessed, as have many others in town, with calculating the final tally for the glass and steel monolith on Powell Mountain that's been under construction for the past two years. Since the recession hit, building in our area has fallen way off. This was one of the few new homes to go up in ages—and certainly the biggest.

"Todd told me they had to tear out all the marble in the bathrooms because the owner thought it was too pink," I'd said to Gwen. Todd Franey, who works for Green Acres during the summer, picks up odd construction jobs the rest of the year and had been a dogsbody for the tile installer. A sweet-natured local boy, he was dumbstruck over the waste of money and materials. "He told me the marble had all been custom cut, so the owner had to eat the cost. It must have been thousands of dollars."

"I happen to know it was almost twenty thousand," Gwen had said. Before she took over as executive director of the Woodhaven Historical Society, Gwen worked as a real estate broker, and she still maintains a wide-ranging network of contacts in that world. "That's a drop in the bucket for someone like Graham Mackenzie. The man has got to be worth hundreds of millions of dollars."

"Todd said he's putting in some kind of fancy landing pad," I'd told her.

"Oh, folks are going to love that!" Gwen said. "The griping I've heard about that damned helicopter!"

I'd heard the sound myself from time to time, though only as a distant irritant. But I knew that people who lived closer to Powell Mountain swore the noise of Mackenzie's swirling blades overhead was interrupting their sleep patterns and destroying their sense of rural repose. When I'd summered in Woodhaven with my family as a girl, Powell Mountain, which rises eleven hundred feet over the northern edge of town, was a wilderness of hemlocks and birches, limestone outcroppings, deer paths, and cascading brooks. It wasn't until after 9/11, when the Berkshires were hit by a sudden growth spurt, that anyone seriously considered building there. After all, it would take a ridiculous amount of money to clear the heavily wooded mountainside, cut in switchbacks, and lay down the necessary power and water lines. But by the time I moved up to Woodhaven from Westchester five years ago, a half dozen millionaires—all loosely affiliated through business dealings—had divvied up the 125-acre property and started erecting enormous trophy homes. Graham Mackenzie was building his place on the last and biggest parcel. It was on the very top of the mountain and had panoramic views of three states.

"Where did he get all his money?" I asked.

"I've been Googling him. He's very big in hydrofracking. His MKZEnergy is the third-largest natural gas producer in the country. The stock price has been almost doubling every year for the last four years."

"I'd ask you why this matters," I said, "but I'm afraid I already know." My dear friend is not a gold digger in any traditional sense of the word. She doesn't yearn to be draped in minks or to be sunbathing on a yacht in Monte Carlo. Her ambitions are far more focused and hardheaded than that. At this point, I think Gwen would do just about anything to raise the funds necessary to restore Bridgewater House. Built in 1751, it's the oldest standing residence in Woodhaven, and its renovation is the main reason Gwen was hired as the full-time executive director of the Woodhaven Historical Society. Since the announcement of the start of the capital campaign last summer to return the structure to its former glory, Gwen has been relentlessly running down every loose piece of change in the area.

"It makes me crazy that I can't make inroads into that millionaires' row up there," Gwen said. "They throw all their money at Tanglewood and at Shakespeare & Company and totally ignore this historic gem nestled right here in the heart—"

"I've already heard your sales pitch," I reminded her. "Save it for Mackenzie. But I wouldn't put much hope in someone who rips apart the earth for a living."

"Oh, right, unlike Andrew Carnegie and Henry Frick and those other robber barons."

But no matter how Gwen tried to justify it, I was still uncomfortable with what felt to me like her growing desperation about meeting the Bridgewater fund-raising goal. I knew all too well what the campaign meant to her career. Though she tried to put a good face on it, her midlife shift into the not-for-profit sector had resulted from a series of dead-end jobs in the for-profit one. This in many ways was Gwen's last chance to turn her luck around. We're both in our late forties now. We'd both been forced to make drastic reductions in our lifestyles and expectations over the past several years. Our options were narrowing. But I believed I was coming to terms with the setbacks I'd experienced. Bitterness welled up in the back of my throat only occasionally now, and the old outrage that had once dominated my waking hours had finally slackened. Green Acres had turned a decent profit for three years running, and I believed I was finally starting to get my life back on track. I wasn't so sure about Gwen.

"And what did the Mackenzie residence want?" I asked Mara as I sat down at my desk and swiveled my chair in her direction. Though I'd suggested she set up her workstation next to mine in front of the large sunny windows that looked out on the herb garden and greenhouse, Mara had elected to stay in the back of the room near the sliding doors that opened to the rest of the barn. She'd angled her desk so that the back of her computer was facing me, blocking her body and the screen from view. It seemed to me that Mara made a concerted effort to avoid any kind of attention. Though she'd been working for me for more than a year now, I knew very little about her personal life except for the fact that she was raising an adorable toddler on her own. In the beginning, I found her guarded to the point of being rude. But just as I'd become dependent on her quiet efficiency, I'd grown used to her curt and wary manner.

"Don't know," she said, getting up and walking across the room to hand me a yellow sticky note upon which she'd written in her loopy schoolgirl hand a local number and "Eleanor—housekeeper." "You're supposed to call back."

I made a cup of tea and sorted through the mail, which was mostly catalogs from nursery wholesalers and garden supply companies. My mind was on the message, though. And what it probably meant. Why else would someone contact a landscaping firm? Like everyone else in Woodhaven, I'd watched Mackenzie's house taking shape on the mountaintop, the late-afternoon sun blazing across its row of windows. Most people thought it was a monstrosity, but I found its clean, forceful lines intriguing. It was way too big, of course, more fortress than home. But I also recognized that it was modern in the best sense of the word—unexpected and visually compelling. There were very few vantage points in Woodhaven where, looking north, you could miss catching sight of the sprawling edifice. I'd wondered in passing what sort of landscaping Mackenzie had in mind. It wasn't going to be easy. That kind of bold, in-your-face architecture demanded an equally aggressive garden design. Specimen trees and shrubs. Grasses, perhaps. Lots of stonework.

I played with the sticky note, curling the glued edge inward with my index finger. It was harmless enough to tinker with ideas, but I knew I could never work for someone like Mackenzie— someone who despoiled the land for profit. When my life had imploded seven years ago this past September, the world around me turned to ash. For months on end, nothing gave me pleasure. It was only after I left Westchester and moved up to Woodhaven that my depression slowly started to lift. The old white clapboard Colonial that had been my family's summerhouse for generations became my refuge, the long-neglected gardens my salvation.

Working almost nonstop those first few months, I uprooted the brambles that had imprisoned my grandmother's peonies. I pruned back and rejuvenated my mother's roses. I restored the fencing around my father's old vegetable garden and dug up and replanted whatever herbs had not been colonized by weeds. My daughters and friends believed that I began to find new purpose in life when I went back to school to get my horticultural degree and then started Green Acres. But the truth was I'd already found it. By then I'd lost all faith in human beings. It was the boundless, selfless beauty of the natural world that led me back to the land of the living.

"I said you'd return her call this morning," Mara said, interrupting my thoughts. I glanced up at the wall clock. It was a little past noon.

"You did?" It was unlike Mara to make such a promise. Early on, we'd settled on a clear-cut division of labor. I handled sales, client contact, and design. She took care of the billing and scheduling. Though I'd hired her as my assistant, I soon realized that she was more than my equal in terms of organization and efficiency. I'd learned to say she worked *with*—not *for*—me. We were both careful about observing each other's boundaries. I would never take it upon myself to speak for her, and this was the first time that I could remember her doing so for me.

"Yeah, well . . . ," Mara said from behind her computer terminal, "I got the feeling the housekeeper really wants to talk to you."

"But I can't work for this Mackenzie person. Do you know what hydrofracking is?"

Mara leaned around her desk, her gray-green eyes taking me in with an intensity that I often found disconcerting. Mara was hardly out of her teens, but she had the world-weary, unyielding stare of someone several decades older.

"Sure," she said. "I know what it is."

"And you don't think it's a danger to the environment?"

"Maybe," she said. "But so are a lot of other things." Despite her impassive expression, her tone was subtly wheedling. For whatever reason, she wanted me to return the phone call. She wanted me to meet with Mackenzie.

Then she added: "Don't you kind of wonder what that place looks like on the inside?"

"Is that what this is all about?" I said with a laugh. "Crass curiosity?" Mara's answering grin—such a rare sight!—reminded me of how young she still was. Young and struggling to keep her head above water. She rotated the same jeans and sweatshirts week after week. I suspected that any extra money she made went directly into caring for Danny. That Mara would be eager to learn about the interior trappings of some millionaire's house touched and saddened me. She acted so tough and self-sufficient. But, of course, like the rest of us, it was just an act.

"I guess it would be unprofessional of me not to return the call," I said.

I was doing this for Mara, I told myself. But in fact, my pulse quickened as I reached for the phone. I had to admit that I was curious, too. And something else. Something more complicated. Green Acres was still basically a start-up. There were half a dozen bigger and far better established landscaping firms in the area. Mackenzie was probably seeing them all. But, still, he'd heard of me. I was on the list. Word was getting around. The fact that he was even considering Green Acres allowed me to feel something I don't often get to experience these days: pride.

Though I still would never work for the son of a bitch.

2

I used to be such a nice person. Personable, obliging. My husband, Richard, once jokingly told me after a particularly dull dinner with a business associate of his that I "suffered fools too gladly." He was right, of course. And prescient in ways I couldn't possibly have imagined at the time. But the truth is, for most of my life, I liked being liked. I'd been raised to be polite and well mannered. But I think it was also in my DNA. So it still surprises me how much my personality was altered by what happened. How quickly my anger can flare these days! I think that many of the people who once formed Richard's and my circle in Westchester would hardly recognize me now. I've become so demanding. I won't tolerate sloppiness, and I hate being kept waiting. Which is why I almost didn't meet Graham Mackenzie after all.

"He'll be with you in just a minute," Mackenzie's housekeeper, Eleanor, had assured me as we crossed the enormous sun-filled space that appeared to serve as Mackenzie's combined dining area and living room. If Mara was expecting opulent Trump-style furnishings and outsized pieces of art, she was going to be disappointed. Someone with restrained, if extremely expensive, taste had decorated what I could see of the downstairs. A small herd of dove gray Italian leather sectionals grazed on a Tibetan carpet the size of a meadow. Eleanor, who didn't divulge her last name, appeared to be equally understated. If she had any misgivings about being a black woman who was required to wear a uniform, she didn't show it. In fact, she seemed to take a proprietary pleasure in welcoming me to Mackenzie's home.

"Can I bring you some coffee or tea?" she asked as she led me to the far end of the room, with its wall of windows overlooking Woodhaven, the valley, and the hills rolling back to the Catskills in the distance. The whole front section of the house was cantilevered out over the side of the mountain, making me feel as though I was suspended in midair with the world literally at my feet.

"No, thanks, I'm fine," I said. After Eleanor excused herself, I was left on my own to revel in the prospect below. The countryside was still covered in snow, though I noticed that several of the ponds in the area were starting to thaw. The late-afternoon sun glinted off the dam that regulated Heron Lake west of town. From where I stood, the distant meandering course of the Housatonic River looked like a hose looping through a garden.

On my way up the mountain earlier I had, on impulse, lowered the car window to take in a few deep breaths of the chill March air. I'd felt so cooped up over the winter! I couldn't wait to dig my fingers into the soil again. It's hard to explain to those who used to know me best, but probably my deepest sense of connection these days is with nature. I'm most alive when I'm outdoors. I think my two daughters view it as some kind of retreat on my part—a need to distance myself from people. But, in fact, it feels to me as though I'm actually in touch with something larger, more embracing— and, yes, more important—than humanity.

I'd missed gardening these past four months with almost the same kind of ache I used to feel when Richard was away on business trips. There was an emptiness in my life right now—just as there had once been an empty space in our bed. As the minutes went by, though, my reflective mood slowly morphed into annoyance. I glanced at my watch and realized that I'd been waiting almost three-quarters of an hour. What the hell was taking Mackenzie so long? I'd seen enough of the house to be able to report back to Mara. And even if Mackenzie deigned to offer me the job, I wasn't going to take it. So what was the point of waiting around for the man to put in an appearance?

I did, however, feel I owed Eleanor the courtesy of telling her I was leaving. I walked back across the living room trying to remember which corridor—three different ones fed off the two-story entranceway—she had taken when she left me earlier. I heard a voice behind a door to the right of the entrance and stopped in front of it. I couldn't make out what was being said, but the hostile tone was clear enough. This wasn't soft-spoken Eleanor. It was an alpha male in full bullying mode.

I realized to whom I was listening, of course, even before the door opened—forcing me to stumble backward—and Mackenzie appeared. He was well over six feet tall, with a substantial belly, a dramatic mane of receding silvery hair, and a flushed, pockmarked complexion. His eyes were a pale, glaucous blue that looked almost milky in contrast with the high color of his skin.

"What the hell are you doing?" he said.

"Nothing," I told him, straightening to my full five feet four inches. I was furious that he'd thought I was eavesdropping. "I was looking for Eleanor. Please let her know I couldn't wait any longer."

"Ah—" he said, exhaling. "You're the landscape designer?"

"Yes, I'm Alice Hyatt. I own Green Acres. And I had an appointment with you," I added, attempting to move around him, "about an hour ago."

"I'm sorry," he said, extending both arms to block my departure. "I was on an important business call that ran long. Listen, you're here now—so you might as well stay. Give me a chance to make it up to you?" He added, smiling, "I promise you won't regret it."

The smile lit up his face and transformed his whole physical presence. A few moments ago, he'd been rigid with anger. Now he leaned toward me, literally bent on winning me over.

"No," I said, deciding we'd already wasted enough of each other's time. "I might as well tell you I'm here under false pretenses."

"Oh?"

"I only came because a coworker wanted to know what you've done with the inside of this place."

"Really?" he said, starting to laugh. Then he kept on laughing— a rolling roar that filled the hallway. "I love it! Is everybody talking about it? Do they all hate it? I bet they think it's too big and modern."

"It's not universally admired," I admitted.

"Ah, well, fuck them," he said pleasantly enough. "Come on, let's have a drink. You can tell me what you have against working for me." He took off down the hall, and I had no choice but to follow him. No, that's not true. I could easily have walked in the other direction and out the front door, but the fact is that Graham Mackenzie's frankness disarmed me. I'd prepared myself for the kind of buttoned-up, self-satisfied CEO that I used to run into when I accompanied my husband to business functions. Mackenzie, clearly, was cut from different cloth. Besides, I was ready for a drink myself.

We came to a stop in front of the windows and that million-dollar view again. It was nearly five o'clock. A voluminous cloud bank drifted over the sun, smearing bright reds and pinks and oranges across the darkening horizon. I took the glass of wine he offered and a seat on one of the couches facing the windows. He folded himself into an Eames chair angled in my direction and crossed his long legs on the leather ottoman.

"So?" he said. "What's the problem? Is it the incline? I've already heard that it's going to be a challenge. But most of your colleagues think it's doable."

"I take it you're seeing everybody? Halderson's? Maggione?"

"And Coldwater, too. I also looked into some of the bigger outfits in Connecticut, but, I don't know, I feel like I just keep seeing the same ideas. Don't get me wrong—everyone's work is great. Very professional. But it all looks the same. And then I remembered the enormous limestone outcropping at Sal's place. I was there for a fund-raiser last summer, and saw that some crazy person had turned that incredible eyesore into this wonderful wall of ferns and dangling trillium and little waterfalls."

I felt my face flush with pleasure. Though Sal Lombardi, a Green Acres client who was one of Mackenzie's neighbors down the mountain, had been far more impressed with the fairly standard perennial border I designed to complement his newly installed Olympic pool, I felt the wall garden Mackenzie had admired was, in fact, my most creative and successful effort to date.

"So I called him," Mackenzie said, "and asked him who the fuck had come up with that."

I raised my hand.

"Bingo! I did a little digging around—forgive the pun—and found out that you're the new kid on the block. Scrappy. And opinionated as hell, Sal told me. Which I like."

I was tempted to smile. It felt good to be singled out by someone who could afford to buy whatever took his fancy. At the same time I knew he was playing me. It was clear that Mackenzie was a deal-maker, and he was trying to close on something he wanted. I was enjoying our conversation, but I knew I had to be careful not to antagonize him.

"It's not the incline," I said. "That would be a challenge, but it comes with the territory around here. Have you ever been to Naumkeag in Stockbridge?"

"Love the place. And the whole Margaret Choate–Fletcher Steele collaboration. I want that, too, by the way. Someone who's open to ideas. Who'll be willing to listen to me and work with me."

"You're aware that it took Fletcher Steele more than three decades to put in the gardens at Naumkeag and, even then, he never felt they were really finished?"

"What great garden ever is?" Mackenzie said, taking me in over the rim of his wineglass. "But I don't have that kind of time. I'll want the whole thing designed and installed by the end of June."

"That's a tall order. I'm sure it can be done," I said, hesitating before I took the plunge. "But not by me."

"Okay, let's hear it. What's the problem?"

"I'm opposed to fracking," I told him.

He looked at me for a moment without saying anything. But I sensed some kind of disconnect. He could have been looking through me. His opaque gaze made it difficult to know for certain where he was focusing.

"So?" he asked. "What's that got to do with this?"

"You make your living destroying the land," I told him. "I make mine trying to beautify it."

"Oh, what total bullshit!" he said, though his tone remained cordial, even amused. "That sounds to me like something you rehearsed on the way over. What do you really know about hydro-fracking besides what you read in the *New York Times* and listen to on NPR?"

"That's a little condescending, don't you think?"

"Come on—I asked you a question."

"Okay. I know it's bad for the environment."

"So is driving a car. And I don't think you walked up here."

"Yes, but my Subaru doesn't pollute the groundwater and sicken livestock."

"Neither does hydrofracking when it's done right. Which is how my company does it. In fact, I can make a very strong case that fracking—when handled correctly—actually has the potential to help *save* this planet from global warming. But I didn't invite you here to debate the pros and cons of clean-air energy. I wanted to talk to you about this property. About this project. I'm looking for something on par with Naumkeag and the rest—but contemporary and truly innovative. That's why I built this house, frankly. From the beginning I saw it as primarily the backdrop for the landscape design. I realize this is going to sound grandiose, but the fact is I want you to create the most beautiful garden in the Berkshires for me."

He had gotten up from the sofa and was pacing in front of the windows, which had blackened with nightfall and now mirrored his movements.

"I don't care what it costs. I'm willing to pay whatever it takes. But what I'm hoping for is something totally unexpected and unique. Like what you did for Sal. Only on a much grander scale. Don't worry about being able to handle it. Bring me a plan that I love—and I'll make sure you get the resources you need to make it a reality."

"I just don't think so," I said. "Listen, I'm sure you can make a very persuasive case for fracking, but I'm never going to buy it. And I've reached a point in my life where things like this matter."

"What? Things like principles?" he said, shaking his head before he abruptly crossed the room to retrieve the wine bottle.

"Yes, principles," I replied, nodding when he held the bottle up in the air in front of me. He refilled my glass.

"You know," he said, sitting back down, "I often find that when people start talking about their principles, it's an indication that they're just not all that up on their facts. It's easy to see things in absolutes when you don't know the details. No important issue I can think of is that clear-cut. Good or bad. What I do for a living has allowed thousands of families to stay on their land—to keep their hopes and dreams alive. That's what I think about when I fall asleep at night. And I sleep pretty damned well."

"That's great, but the decision still looks black-and-white to me."

"Okay, I think I'm about to make it a little bit grayer. I'm going to tell you something that I haven't shared with any of the others. It's not something I like to publicize, because I know that people would be all over me if they knew."

He got up from the chair again and stretched. I began to realize how physically restless he was. He hadn't stayed in one position for more than a few minutes the whole time I'd been in his company.

"I've established a charity in my name," he went on. "It's called the Mackenzie Project. Its mission is to save and protect endangered horticultural spaces, particularly historic arboretums and gardens. As I said, it's not something I want the general public in on, but I hope your knowing about it will make you realize that I, too, am trying—how did you put it?—'to beautify nature.' And I'll tell you what I'll do if we end up working together on this. I'll put into my charity dollar for dollar what I pay out to you, earmarked for this region."

"That's incredibly generous of you," I said.

"Maybe. But I also think it's probably the only way I'm going to persuade you to work for me."

I stared up at him, suddenly unsure of myself. How could I turn down such a magnanimous offer? I could already think of half a dozen historic—and now neglected—gardens in the area that could be resurrected by an infusion of cash from Mackenzie's charity.

But who was this man? All I knew for certain was that he had somehow recognized in me what I'd come to believe about myself: I had a natural talent for what I did. In fact, deep down I knew that I was capable of far more than most of my traditional-minded clients wanted. Oh, to create something truly original! And to have all the money in the world to implement it! Mackenzie was right: getting this commission would establish my professional reputation. But what a huge project it was going to be. For the first time, I wondered if Mackenzie wasn't perhaps putting too much faith in me. What if it was misplaced? What if I couldn't come up with a design as spectacular as the one he envisioned? The most beautiful garden in the Berkshires? All of a sudden it seemed an impossible challenge.

It was then, of course, that I realized I'd already decided to take it on.

3

❦

I first met Gwen Boyland at a sleep-away camp in western Massachusetts when we were both thirteen years old. Though my family summered in Woodhaven, we were essentially city folk. Riverside Park on the Upper West Side of Manhattan was my backyard. The closest I'd ever come to a run-in with wildlife was a neighbor's German shepherd that had somehow slipped the leash. So the weekend we went on a "wilderness trek" up on the mountain, foraging for kindling and cooking out over an open fire, felt like high adventure to me. For Gwen, who'd been raised on a farm in the Berkshires and had once helped pull a calf feetfirst out of a breech birth, a couple of nights in a tent was pretty tame stuff.

Up until then I'd had no direct contact with Gwen, though I'd been keenly aware of her existence. It was hard not to be. She was starting to develop physically, and she thought nothing of walking around our cabin stark naked, her enviable breasts roosting like little doves between her upper arms. She had older sisters and seemed to know everything there was to know about things that remained painful mysteries to the slow starter I was at that time:

the difference between Tampax and Kotex, French-kissing, and how to tell when a boy had a hard-on.

"He puts his hands in his pockets," she whispered to the circle of girls who'd inched their sleeping bags around her after lights-out. Our counselors were still sitting beside the fire, luxuriating in some much-needed adult time. "And he kind of balls up his fists so the front of his pants puff out. It's a dead giveaway."

"Has a boy ever done that to you?" Ada Sawyers asked in an awestruck tone. A year younger than us, Ada followed Gwen around like a puppy.

"No, but I've seen it a million times with my sisters' boy-friends," Gwen said.

"Quiet in there!" one of the counselors called from outside. "Not another word out of any of you until morning."

I had a hard time getting to sleep that night. I wasn't accustomed to curling up on the bare ground. It was chilly and lumpy and it felt odd not having a bed or bunk to help demarcate my space from that of my fellow campers. Ada, who was a restless sleeper, kept turning over and falling against me. At one point, her flailing right arm landed like a dead branch in my lap.

"Hey!" I hissed, giving her a little shove.

"You awake?" Gwen whispered next to me in the dark.

"Yeah," I said. "Are you?"

"What do *you* think?" Gwen said, though not unkindly. I'd noticed that for all her worldliness and bravado, she never acted mean or superior. "I got to pee so bad my teeth ache."

"Me, too," I said, realizing for the first time that that was another reason I hadn't been able to drift off. We'd carried canteens with us on the hike up to the campsite and had stopped frequently to swill the warm, metallic-tasting water. We'd had lemonade with dinner and hot cocoa with dessert. One of the counselors had left a plastic bucket by the tent's entry flap for us to relieve ourselves in during the night, but, for me at least, the very idea of piddling away in front of everybody was mortifying. I'd rather die first.

"Come on," Gwen said, sitting up in her sleeping bag. "I'm going outside."

"But—" We'd been instructed to stay in the tent, I was going to remind her. We were out in the woods, in the middle of nowhere, miles from civilization and emergency medical care. But before I had a chance to put any of these worries into words, Gwen had already slipped out into the night. My bursting bladder won out over my better judgment, and I followed her.

The cooking fire had burned down to embers, and the campground was awash in a ghostly sheen. The sliver of moon that hung like a stage prop above the tree line was outshone by the main attraction of the evening—a brilliant, dancing panoply of stars. Gwen and I stopped and stared up into the night sky for a minute or two as our eyes adjusted to the darkness. The woods were alive with sound. Insects hummed like an old refrigerator. And there was something else—a low, rough, raggedy roar—that sent a shiver through me.

"Did you hear *that*?" I whispered urgently to Gwen.

"That," she said, grabbing a handful of napkins from the picnic table that was stacked with our supplies, "is the sound of somebody snoring."

We followed the hiking trail back down the mountain about fifteen yards before squatting a few feet apart in the underbrush. Brambles pulled at my nightgown and weeds tickled my backside, but I was finally able to pee.

"You okay?" Gwen asked as I rejoined her with my nightgown bunched up around my waist.

"I'm not a very good aim."

"Let's find some paper towels," Gwen said, heading back up the path again. It was only when we started to rummage around on the supply table that we noticed someone had been there before us. Boxes of cereal had been torn apart and Cheerios scattered on the ground like confetti. Bags of corn chips had been slashed open and pulverized. Our super-saver plastic tub of trail mix was gone.

"What—?" Gwen said, looking up from the mess and around the campsite. Neither one of us had seen the bear earlier because he was so big and black and quietly preoccupied. He was sitting on the ground not far from our tent, the tub of trail mix between his legs, shoveling the stuff into his mouth with both paws. A low, rough— and now I realized—contented growl escaped from his maw between bites.

"Oh, God!" I cried. "Oh, my God!"

The bear looked up from his little picnic.

"Shhhhh!" Gwen hissed, holding my arm as I tried to bolt. "Don't move a muscle. Don't say another word."

"What's going on?" one of the counselors called out.

"Stay where you are!" Gwen called. "There's a bear out here. He's feeding. If we leave him alone, he'll go away when he's done."

Like the rest of us, the counselors seemed to hold Gwen in special regard. They quickly came to realize that she knew as much, if not more, than they did about the wild. Just that afternoon, one of them had asked her if a group of mushrooms we'd passed was edible, and Gwen had responded after quick examination: "Only if you want to kill yourself." So now, though we could hear a certain amount of stirring from inside the tents, no one emerged. And Gwen and I stood stock-still, watching the bear devour the tub of trail mix for what seemed like hours.

He'd ripped a hole in the hard plastic and was getting at the nuts and seeds through the side of the tub. When it was almost empty, he turned the thing upside down and dumped the remaining mix into his mouth, his enormous pink tongue lapping around the raggedy hole searching for one last sunflower seed or chocolate-covered raisin. Then, with a sigh of regret, he tossed the empty tub into the bushes and lumbered to his feet. He started toward us. At the time he looked about ten feet tall, though I later learned he couldn't have been more than six.

"Oh, God!" I cried.

"Be quiet and put your hands in the air," Gwen said matter-of-factly.

"Is he going to eat us?" I whimpered.

"Bears are herbivores," Gwen whispered back. "He's probably just after more trail mix. We're slowly—very slowly—going to start to back away from the picnic table, okay? Keep your hands above your head and your mouth shut. Just do what I do."

Perhaps it was Gwen's calm and seemingly disinterested response to the bear's approach, or maybe he remembered that he'd already pillaged the best of our goodies. In any case, he stopped in his tracks as we began our forward-facing retreat. He sniffed the air, turning his head slowly from side to side, let out a huge yawn, and then, with almost balletic grace, pirouetted around and lumbered off into the woods.

❦

Questions were raised about what we were doing outside when we'd been expressly told not to leave our tent, but Gwen's level-headed handling of the bear "attack"—as it quickly became known—mitigated any disciplinary action. Somehow, undeservedly, my star rose with Gwen's after the incident. Upon our return to the main camp, word spread quickly about our adventure. Older girls who'd looked right through me until then suddenly knew my name. And, most important and wonderful for me, Gwen Boyland and I became friends.

Initially, I worried that she was too sophisticated and popular for our closeness to last for very long. But I learned over the course of the next few weeks that Gwen, too, had her weaknesses. Ones that, happily for me, tended to be counterbalanced by my strengths. Where she was impulsive, I was strategic. When she tended to get bored or restless, I demonstrated inner resources and initiative. We helped smooth each other's unfinished edges. And our backgrounds were different enough for each of us to consider the other special and somewhat exotic. For the next half a dozen summers we were inseparable. The Boyland Dairy farm was only three miles outside of Woodhaven, so we saw each other whenever my family was in "the country."

College changed all that. I went to Brown. Gwen spent half a semester at Berkshire Community College before dropping out to marry a high school basketball star. It lasted less than a year and turned out to be one of her more enduring romances. The brashness that had helped her face down our bear ended up undermining her increasingly less-concerted efforts to forge any permanent relationships, just as the timidity that gripped me that same night made the security and routine of marriage so appealing. We remained friends, though, getting together whenever we could to catch up.

Things changed even more when I became a mother. I remember visiting Gwen at an apartment she was renting in Lee—in a chopped-up Victorian in desperate need of a paint job and rewiring—with Olivia in diapers and Franny in my arms. Gwen was still smoking then, and the place smelled of cigarettes and beer. The shower was running when she opened the door, and a few minutes after we'd gotten settled in the living room a man walked through with a towel wrapped around his waist.

"Behave!" Gwen had told him after he did a little jig in front of my daughters.

"You first," he shot back.

What bothered me most about the visit was not that Gwen seemed at such loose ends—I think she was working part-time for an insurance adjuster then—but that she showed so little interest in my exceptionally adorable offspring. Or my handsome, loving, and increasingly successful husband. Though, as always, she did seem to care about me.

"You still working on that horticultural degree?" she asked me when the conversation started to lag. I was having a hard time concentrating because I had to keep restraining Olivia—who was teething—from gnawing on the many inappropriate objects within her reach.

"With all of this?" I asked, exasperated as Franny began to whimper. When I was pregnant with Olivia, I'd started taking classes at the New York Botanical Garden with the hope of getting a certificate in landscape design. I remember telling Gwen at the time how excited I was by the courses—how I felt I'd finally found my calling. "No, it's just not feasible now. But I can always go back."

"Always doesn't actually last forever," she said. "Don't forget it's your life, too, Alice." I remember thinking how presumptuous it was for Gwen—who was rotating through men on a semiannual basis and changing jobs almost as often—to offer me advice. Still, despite our different lives and personalities, something kept us close. Some instinct made us reach out to each other whenever we needed to really talk and, more important, when we needed someone who would really listen.

That was the thing about Gwen. She never stopped believing in me. When everybody else was viewing me with suspicion or turning their backs, she stood firm. The moment the news hit and it became clear just how bad things were, she dropped everything in Woodhaven and came down to help me ride out the storm. It was a time when I learned all too quickly who my real friends were, and the sad truth is that most of them disappeared into the woodwork.

"Like cockroaches," Gwen had observed acidly at the height of the publicity. "Running from the glare."

Shortly after that, it was Gwen who reminded me of what I had put aside twenty years before. It was Gwen who suggested I start again. And it was she who wouldn't take no for an answer.

❦

So, naturally, it was Gwen I called first after my meeting with Graham Mackenzie.

"Wow! Good for you!" she said. "This is cause for celebration. Let me treat you to dinner at Donatello."

"Right now?" I asked. It was nearly seven thirty, and I was defrosting a turkey burger for dinner.

"I'll pick you up in ten minutes," she told me. The impulsive side of Gwen has never changed. Nor has her generous nature. What time has tempered, though, is her girlishness and unbridled sense of fun. There's a certain calculation in how she presents herself now that never used to be there. Just recently I realized she's been adding highlights to her shoulder-length auburn hair. And after the hostess at the restaurant took our coats I saw that Gwen was wearing a leather skirt that barely covered her backside. But if what she wanted was for every man in the restaurant to take notice of her progress across the room, she got it.

"Thank God, you're finally learning how to play the game a little," Gwen said after we'd ordered and I began to give her the blow-by-blow of my meeting.

"What do you mean?" I asked, pushing the bread basket across the table. My friend, who has the metabolism of a triathlete, can eat anything and still slip into a size six without wiggling. "I was totally straight with the man."

"Oh, come on!" Gwen said, buttering a slice of focaccia. "You were playing hard to get. It's the oldest trick in the book. And for good reason. It obviously works."

"A part of me is still seriously conflicted," I told her. "I hate what fracking is doing to the environment."

"Fine. Feel a little guilty as you walk away with the biggest contract of your life. I think it's great. And, no matter what you claim, I say you handled the situation beautifully."

"It's hardly a done deal. I still have to come up with designs that knock his socks off. And he knows his stuff. If he thinks a firm as well regarded as Coldwater is turning out the same old same old, then you know he's expecting something pretty sensational."

"Which is what you'll give him," Gwen said as our first courses arrived. "I have no doubt."

I talked through the whole meal about the project, all the while silently debating whether to tell Gwen about Mackenzie's not-for-profit. I'd thought of the gardens at Bridgewater House as soon as he'd mentioned the charity's mission. The gardens were extensive, historically significant, and in a sad state of disrepair, including a beautiful old nineteenth-century greenhouse that had lost half its panes and was disintegrating into a rusted skeleton. I knew that a substantial amount of Gwen's capital campaign was designated for outdoor restoration. Bridgewater House was a perfect fit for the Mackenzie Project—and a grant of that stature would no doubt help get Gwen's fund-raising efforts off the ground at last.

"So what's he like as a man?" Gwen asked over espresso and a plate of cookies. "Is he just all about making billions of buckaroonies—or does he have a soul?"

"You know, I don't think it's either-or with him. He's definitely a high-powered person. And, no matter what he claims, fracking is evil. On the other hand—" It was on the tip of my tongue to tell her about the charity and his dollar-for-dollar offer if I got the job.

"But is he someone I could hit up?" Gwen asked, cutting me off. "Would he be open to an ask, do you think?"

"Possibly," I said. From what I knew about Mackenzie, he seemed like just the kind of person Gwen should be pursuing: someone with deep pockets, big ideas, and a plus-sized ego. Why was I hesitating? It was probably just what I ended up telling Gwen: "Let me see how things go with him. He certainly knows how to make a great first impression, but let me see if he comes through." Still, something worried me about the idea. I just couldn't put my finger on it.

4

🍎

"Marmy! Marmy!" Danny shouted happily as he dragged the heavy-duty tape measure behind him up the hill. Mara had locked the mechanism before handing it over to her son to play with while we investigated the birch grove farther up the incline. But Danny had somehow managed to release it, and now a long aluminum tail rattled behind him, the yellow plastic case bouncing around at the end like a pull toy.

"Be careful, Danny!" I cried without thinking. The tape was sharp as a razor. I'd nicked myself on it often enough. He stopped in his tracks, his wide grin suddenly uncertain. I realized as soon as I said it that I shouldn't have intervened. I'd asked Mara as a favor if she could help me make a rough survey of Mackenzie's property that chilly Saturday afternoon in late March, and she'd agreed to do so if she could bring Danny along. Though she seemed so young and inexperienced, I'd come to realize that she was a super-protective and self-sufficient mother. She didn't want my advice. She'd made it pretty clear to me in the past that Danny was her business. Period. No trespassing.

"It's okay," Mara said as Danny's mouth began to quiver, "you're unbreakable. Right, bud? But your nose is totally disgusting. Get up here." Mara squatted down as Danny ran into her arms. She pulled a package of Kleenex from her parka pocket. "Blow!" she said, hugging him to her as she covered the lower half of his face with the tissue.

I enjoyed watching the two of them together. They had the same dark brown hair, in Mara's case cropped into a raggedy cap that fell slightly askew across her high, round forehead. Danny's hadn't been cut yet and it curled, cherublike, to his shoulders. When Mara was around her son, her defensive and closed-off attitude disappeared— as did the carefully maintained noncommittal expression. Seeing her with him allowed me a glimpse of a very different person— someone spontaneous and fun. I felt sad that she wouldn't allow herself to be that way around me or anyone else she came into contact with at Green Acres. Clearly, something had happened to her— a bad early marriage or relationship, I suspected—that made her such a standoffish and solitary young woman.

"Hello, down there!" Eleanor called, waving to us from the side deck. The housekeeper had greeted us cordially when we arrived and invited us in for cookies and a cup of tea when we'd finished our work. "Warm brownies just out of the oven, if anyone's interested."

"Yes!" Danny said, his face brightening again.

"You guys go ahead," I told Mara. We'd been at it for more than an hour, and the temperature was starting to drop off as the afternoon lengthened. I still had a lot of ground to cover, but Mackenzie had given me permission to walk the property whenever I wished. And I already knew that I'd need several additional visits to get all the readings I wanted. "I'm going to take some more photos before the light goes. I'll see you up there."

I watched them climb the hill, hand in hand, Danny galloping along beside his mom, obviously excited by the prospect of what awaited him in the enormous house above. I reached down to pick up the measuring tape that Danny had left on the ground. When I stood up again, I felt a rush of vertigo. The world wavered. Clouds scudding above the mountains in the distance looked suddenly ominous. A front was coming through—the forecast called for temperatures to be twenty degrees warmer by daybreak. Good news, really. Nothing to worry about. Nothing to explain my sudden uneasiness. I'd grown accustomed to being on my own outdoors. In fact, I usually cherished it. So what was this about? I wondered. But the sun was fading, and I didn't have time to chase shadows. I forced myself to shake off the willies and keep moving.

I worked quickly, framing different shots of Mackenzie's property in my viewfinder, seeing the many possibilities—and problems— that the land presented. For the most part, the gradient was at least twenty degrees, with just a few places where the slope leveled off. It began to occur to me that I was going to literally have to move the earth to create my own flat surfaces. Just how large those man-made terraces could be and how many the hillside could support would depend, I knew, on a number of variables, including underlying drainage and soil composition. I would have to bring in a landscape contractor for advice—and an environmental expert. Eventually, I'd need to consult with the EPA. I began to make a mental list of all the calls I was going to have to make on Monday morning.

By the time I started up to the house, a plan had begun to take shape in my mind. It was nothing I could even put down on paper yet. Just a sense of movement and form—like a flow of water over rock. A visual echo of the rolling mountains in the distance and the meandering course of the river through the valley.

I entered the house from the flight of stairs that led up to the side deck, and followed the sound of voices down a long hall and into a brightly lit kitchen gleaming with brushed aluminum appliances and copper utensils suspended above a butcher block island. The walls were sunflower yellow, the counters thick blue slate. The floor was covered with glazed terra-cotta tile. Despite its size and elegance, it was a working kitchen, with open shelving lined with spices and mixing bowls. At the far end of the room, a long wooden table paralleled a large fireplace. Mara was sitting on a bench facing me. Eleanor was kitty-corner to her at the end of the table with Danny on her lap. Mara and Eleanor were leaning toward each other, obviously intent on whatever they were discussing.

". . . be happy to check it out for you," Mara was saying.

"That would be great, and maybe next time we can . . . ," Eleanor began, but then, seeing me approach across the room, dropped her voice to a whisper. It struck me that the two women—who'd met for the first time that afternoon—appeared to be remarkably familiar and comfortable with each other. Especially considering that one of them was Mara. I was surprised and, yes, more than a little hurt that Danny—whom I'd yet to steal a hug from—was permitted to sit on Eleanor's lap. On the other hand, I was pleased that Mara seemed to be able to loosen up and enjoy someone else's company besides her son's.

I gladly accepted the cup of tea that Eleanor offered and took a seat opposite Mara and in front of the plate of brownies. But my presence seemed to put a damper on the easygoing atmosphere. Eleanor asked politely after my progress.

"Well, I think we managed to get a good start this afternoon. Wouldn't you say, Mara?" I asked, smiling across the table at her.

"Maybe," she said with her usual shrug.

"Mr. M told me you should have the run of the place," Eleanor said. "I'm here from nine to six or so every day but Sunday. You don't even need to check in with me, of course. But I'm happy to make you lunch or tea, if you give me a little warning."

"That's very kind of you," I said. Eleanor had a soothing, melodious voice, tinged with the singsong lilt of the Caribbean. She emanated warmth. It was hardly surprising that Mara and Danny had taken to her so quickly. I sometimes forget how formidable I can be these days. Clipped, focused, no-nonsense.

"Oh, I love to cook! As I'm sure you can tell," Eleanor said with a laugh, looking down at the gentle swells under her apron. "And I feel at such loose ends when Mr. M's away on business."

"He's away now?" I asked, though I really didn't need to. I could feel the lack of his presence in the house.

"In Europe. Then South America. The man has more frequent-flier miles than Santa Claus."

"I love Santa," Danny announced, reaching for another brownie.

"No way!" Mara said, grabbing his wrist as she swung her legs around the side of the bench. She stood up from the table. "We gotta get going."

"Let me make you and Danny a goodie bag first," Eleanor said, lifting the little guy into his mother's arms.

"You really don't—"

"You'll be doing me a favor, dearie," Eleanor replied. "Lead me not into temptation!"

❧

I made a concerted effort to be more open and engaging with Mara after that. For one thing, I needed her help—now more than ever. We'd started spring cleanup and were fielding the usual calls about improvements from our regular customers. A row of red maples down the driveway. A fenced-in vegetable garden with raised beds. A rose arbor by the pool. It suddenly seemed that all our clients had a list of things they hoped Green Acres could get to that spring. For the first time, I let Mara handle some of these inquiries while I worked at my computer on the plans for Mackenzie, my desk stacked with gardening books, magazines, and horticultural references.

I also wanted to push Mara a little. She needed to build a future for herself and her son, but she wasn't going to get anywhere if she didn't start to learn how to interact with other people first. I knew she was naturally bright and intuitive. She'd mastered the accounting software—which had taken me weeks to learn—within a couple of days of being hired. And she understood the basics of horticulture in a way that I think is unusual for most girls of her age. I knew that my own well-educated daughters, now both in their twenties, couldn't begin to tell the difference between a hemlock and a white pine. Or the best weed-and-feed for lawns in our area. Or when to prune back woody shrubs. Mara did. Some of this, it's true, she'd picked up from working at Green Acres for the last year—but by no means all. Typically, she deflected any of my questions about how she had come by such—at least for this day and age—specialized knowledge.

"That's going to have to wait," I heard her tell one client a week or two after our first site visit to Mackenzie's. "No, not because we're too busy. You gotta plant spring flowering bulbs in the fall. Yeah, that's just the way it is."

"You could have handled that with a little more finesse," I told her when she'd finished the call.

"What do you mean?"

"Sugarcoat things a little," I said, taking off my reading glasses. "Rather than saying 'That's the way it is,' you could have said something like 'We'll be happy to put this on the top of our list for you in the fall. Bulbs are a wonderful idea!' "

"That's not the way you talk," Mara said. "You don't sugar-coat anything."

"Yes, but—," I started to say, but then I had to laugh. She was right. In fact, when I thought about it, Mara sounded a lot like me on the phone. "I guess I've earned the right to be blunt. Have you ever heard the phrase 'Do what I say—not what I do'?"

"Yeah," Mara replied.

"Well, try it, okay?" I said. "By the way—what you said was absolutely correct, as you know. And that's what matters most in this business. But a nicer bedside manner couldn't hurt."

I was working halfway into the night most days now, making endless notes, drafting ideas. I contacted Phil Welling, a site contractor I'd used on other projects and had come to like and trust. We walked the Mackenzie property together as I told him about the plan that was beginning to take shape in my mind.

"It'll be a bitch to get done," he said. "But you're right. It's the only way I can see you laying in gardens without eventually losing everything to soil erosion. But how are you planning to connect the different levels?"

"Retaining walls. Stone steps with wrought-iron railings. I'm visualizing a lot of custom-made ornamentation."

"Even more reason to make sure you've built up strong, level foundations. I'm pretty sure I can make it work, but just to be safe I'd like to do some perk tests first."

"Phil—I'm on spec at this point. I can't pay you."

"Yes, I know. But the word's out that you're Mackenzie's only candidate. It's a huge score for you, Alice. It'll be the same for me if it happens—worth investing some money in up front."

It was early enough in the season for me to concentrate on the Mackenzie plans and pay Mara to pick up the slack. She contacted our regular part-timers and worked out their weekly schedules for the season. She estimated most of the special requests and sent out quotes. She was putting in a lot of overtime and bringing Danny with her on weekends. One unusually warm Saturday in early April when I had an office window cracked open, I heard their voices floating across from the greenhouse where Mara was hosing down the walls and cleaning out the seedling trays. We grew our own annuals and some of the perennials from seed that I special-ordered from heritage growers. It not only saved on cost, I found, but also cut down on disease and insect infestation.

"Do you want to see something magic?" Mara asked her son. I didn't hear his response, but it didn't take much imagination to guess what it was.

"I want you to drop this sunflower seed into that hole in the dirt. That's right. Pat it down so it's all safe and warm inside. Now sprinkle a little of this water on top. Not too much—that's good. Now, do you know what's going to happen?"

"Magic?"

"Yes, but it's not going to happen overnight. In another couple of weeks that seed is going to sprout—and it's going to start to grow just the way you are. It's going to grow all through the summer— and by the end of August it's going to be even taller than me."

"Wow."

"And you know the best part? It's going to turn into this enormous sunflower that will be made out of hundreds and hundreds of seeds just like the one you planted."

Mara was still sullen and abrupt around me most of the time. I didn't care. In many ways, I preferred that to someone who nattered on about things that meant nothing to me. She was taking on more and more, and handling the workload well. We were alike in many ways, I was beginning to realize. That afternoon, as I listened to Mara talk to Danny, I realized—not for the first time—

how much I longed to have children around me again. I missed my family. Oh, Olivia and Franny never failed to call me once or twice a week, but they were both so caught up in their own worlds—young, newly married, commuting from the suburbs to the city and their important, demanding jobs. Sometimes I suspected that they took turns checking up on me. I knew they still worried about me. And blamed me, too. Though they'd never admit that, maybe not even to themselves.

An hour or so later, I got up from my computer to stretch and walked across the backyard to the greenhouse, where Mara and Danny were bent over the utility sink, washing their hands. The seedling trays were full. I asked Danny to show me which of the sunflowers he'd planted. He looked at me nervously, worried perhaps that he'd done something wrong. Mara was constantly telling him to be quiet when he was around me in the office. I got the sense that I scared him to death. But he finally pointed to a chipped clay pot, set apart from the others in their plastic molded trays.

"Do you want to take it home with you?" I asked him, picking it up.

Danny looked from me to his mom, his gaze searching—and imploring.

"Say thanks," she told him with a nod.

"Thank you," he said gravely, taking the pot into his arms.

"Make sure it gets plenty of water and sun, okay?" I said. "And don't forget to give it a lot of love. That's where the magic comes in."

5

I thought about what Phil Welling had said. If I landed the Mackenzie project, it would be a "huge score" for him, too. The designs that were coming together in my imagination—and on the landscaping software program I was using—would require a number of subcontractors, including a stonemason and an ironworker. Why not share the spoils with artisans I liked and admired?

I consulted Gwen's cousin Nate LaSalle, a well-regarded master stonemason in the area, about the costs and feasibility of putting in the numerous walls and steps that were essential to my designs. During the last Harvest Festival at the Berkshire Botanical Garden I'd come across the unique wrought-iron work of Damon Fagels, who had a forge over in Chatham. I loved his fantastical tables and chairs with their animal feet and antlered arms, and candelabra shaped into branches and birds. He seemed excited about the prospect of creating the hand railings, wall sconces, benches, and other garden ornaments my plans were calling for. Both Damon and Nate, though, were concerned about getting everything completed by the end of June.

It was my biggest worry, too. By mid-April I had enough of my

plan ready—if not finished to the last detail—to present to Mackenzie. But when I called Eleanor to arrange for a meeting, she told
me he was still traveling. And not expected back for another couple
of days. I was in a fix. I couldn't start my work until Phil had built
the terraces and Nate had laid in at least some of the steps. In order
to get the best stock, I needed to start ordering specimen trees,
shrubs, and perennials more or less immediately. And all of this
was predicated on the assumption that Mackenzie would like and
approve my designs. A week after I first called Eleanor, still not
having heard anything from Mackenzie, I woke up in the middle of
the night in a panic. What if he'd lost interest in the project? What
if all my hard work was for nothing? And worse—what if I was
never able to put in this garden that I'd come to love? The thought
was so upsetting that I threw off the sheets, got out of bed, and
went downstairs. I made myself a cup of tea in the kitchen and then
wandered out to the living room and my laptop to click through my
presentation one more time.

It was good. No, it was better than good. Anyone who had a
serious interest in landscape design would probably be able to spot
my influences—most notably Beatrix Farrand and Gertrude Jekyll.
Farrand had designed the gardens for The Mount, Edith Wharton's
estate in nearby Lenox, but it was Farrand's plans for Dumbarton
Oaks in Georgetown that I turned to again and again when I was
thinking through how best to handle Mackenzie's sloping acres.
She'd dealt with the same problem at Dumbarton Oaks, though to
a lesser degree, and I studied her solution with care: leveled-off
areas at different elevations that formed intimate garden rooms,
each with its own unique character and focus: a fountain, a reflect-
ing pool, a walkway covered with wisteria and climbing roses. In
the end, what she'd created was an outdoor mansion—with a ceil-
ing as high as the sky.

Just as I was finally drifting back to sleep around daybreak, the computer still open on my lap, the kitchen phone rang. I ran to answer it.

"When can you get up here?" Mackenzie demanded.

"And good morning to you, too," I said, irritated that he didn't have the courtesy to apologize for the delay in getting back to me.

"Oh, honestly, Alice," he said with a laugh. "Lighten up. I'm the client here, remember? I'll be waiting."

❧

I was out of sorts from lack of sleep, and I made the mistake of drinking two cups of strong coffee to make up for it. By the time I started up Mackenzie's winding private driveway my nerves were jangling. But as I got to the top of the mountain and looked down on the hillside I'd now come to know so well, I felt myself relax. Mackenzie was right: I needed to lighten up. I had every reason to be proud of my plans. What I was about to present to Mackenzie was by far the best work of my life.

There were several cars I didn't recognize parked in front of the garages. I pulled in next to Eleanor's familiar blue Passat and carried my laptop and presentation case up to the house.

"He's in the sunroom having breakfast," Eleanor said after she greeted me at the door. "With his ex and his son."

"Won't I be interrupting?" I asked as she started to lead me down the hallway. I'd already picked up from gossip around town that Mackenzie was divorced. I wasn't surprised. I never felt a sense of family life in the house. It was more like a male bastion. A bachelor's aerie.

"I have a feeling he'll welcome that," she said. "It's not exactly a love fest this morning."

I could hear what she meant as we approached.

". . . dare you speak to your son that way."

"Because he deserves it. When I was his age—"

"Oh, man, not that again! I'm not you, okay, Dad? I'm never going to *be* you. I stopped trying to fill your shoes a long time ago."

"You're twenty years old, Lachlan. A long time ago for you means *kindergarten*, for chrissakes! Either you get a job or you go back to school. I'm not going to underwrite any more of your half-assed ideas."

The sunroom was a spacious octagon with floor-to-ceiling windows that faced southeast over the valley. Mackenzie, his ex-wife, and his son were seated at a round glass table. The former Mrs. Mackenzie was a redhead with a faultless porcelain complexion and suspiciously taut features for the mother of someone Lachlan's age. She was tall—nearly Mackenzie's height—with the upright, self-aware posture of a ballerina. She was probably beautiful, but it was hard to tell; anger had pulled her face into an unpleasant rictus.

Lachlan favored his father—the same high forehead and milky blue gaze, but his thick, wavy hair was jet-black. He wore hip dark-framed glasses and stubble across his jawline. Someone far younger and more susceptible to masculine charm than me might have considered him attractive. He seemed to be trying to project a certain go-to-hell brand of sex appeal—but to me he just seemed sullen.

"Ah, here's my meeting," Mackenzie said as Eleanor showed me in. He tossed his napkin on his plate and got up from the table.

"We're not done with this discussion," his ex said.

"Actually, we are," he replied as he walked around the table and shook my hand. "I'm sorry that you had to find us in the midst of a squabble," he went on, relieving me of my presentation case. "This is Chloe, my ex-wife, and my son, Lachlan."

Chloe glared at Mackenzie, ignoring my presence, but Lachlan looked over and gave me a nod.

"And this is Alice Hyatt," Mackenzie continued, as if the two of them actually gave a damn. "She's a landscape designer who's here to present her plans for the gardens."

Mackenzie didn't wait for a reply as he led me out of the room, though he couldn't help but hear—as clearly as I did—Lachlan's sotto voce retort: "What a fucking waste of money."

We walked down the hall to Mackenzie's home office. It was octagonal, too, a pendant of the sunroom—but darker and wood-paneled, with curved casement windows facing north into the woods. A large desk with two computers dominated the space.

"I apologize for their behavior," he said, closing the door behind us. "I can't tolerate outright rudeness, and they both know it. They fly up from Atlanta periodically to see which one of them can rile me up the most."

"I'm sorry," I said noncommittally. I wasn't there for an airing of his family's dirty laundry, and I found the subject distasteful.

"She's a bloodsucker," he went on, walking over to the window with its tranquil prospect of birches and evergreens. "That's all either of them want from me: money, money, money!"

I didn't say anything, but I was hoping he was beginning to get the venom out of his system. I didn't want his ugly mood infecting my presentation.

"They know I'm planning to cut them off entirely as soon as he turns twenty-one. It's the best thing that could happen to him, as far as I'm concerned. He's got to learn to stand on his own two feet. She's just using him to get whatever she can out of me—and then she takes a cut. It's disgusting . . . ," he said, turning around as my silence continued. "And you've obviously heard enough out of me on the subject."

"I've a lot to show you," I told him, avoiding a more honest answer. "I can give you a virtual tour on my laptop, and I also have printouts of the plans that we can go over, if you have time."

"There's nothing else I'd rather be doing, believe me. But let's see if we can't get your presentation up on one of these hi-res screens," he said, walking over to his desk and sitting down. He pulled another chair next to his and waved me over. "Okay, let's see what you've got."

❦

"There's always a lot of water running below the surface of these hills," I told him. Mackenzie had stopped me with so many questions that it had taken me more than an hour to get through the whole presentation, but we were nearing the end now. "What we discovered here, though, is pretty exciting. You see this double dotted line—east of the limestone outcropping? It represents what is basically an underground creek. I hope to redirect its course and have it come to the surface here"—I pointed to my largest terraced area, the one with the widest view of the valley— "and channel it across the garden in a low trough until it cascades over the edge in a waterfall to the pool we're going to create below."

"How far is the drop?" he asked. It was typical of his questions. He wanted facts and figures and seemed impatient if I didn't have them at my fingertips. Luckily, the ten-day delay had given me time to go over every detail in my mind.

"About forty feet," I said. "I plan to have steps leading down from over here, but I'm hoping the view will have a feeling of infinity."

"Yes," he said, staring at the screen. I'd taken a photo of the vista from approximately where I planned to site the waterfall and superimposed it on the virtual garden of ferns, irises, and hostas I proposed.

A weeping Japanese cherry dangled its whips into the channeled stream.

"That's it for the virtual tour," I said. "I have printouts of the AutoCAD plans to show you as well as photos of samples from the ironworker and the stonemason I'd like to use." I hesitated, waiting for him to say something, but he continued to stare at the last photo that I'd left up on the screen. There was the long valley with its patchwork of farms and woodland. The rise of mountains in the distance. The beams of sunlight breaking through the bank of clouds on the far horizon. What was he thinking?

"Alice," he said at last, turning in his chair toward me. For a moment I thought there were tears in his eyes, but then he threw back his head and laughed. "It's perfect! Absolutely fucking perfect! I knew you could do it."

❦

Mackenzie asked just as many questions when we went over my AutoCAD drawings with plant callouts and accompanying photos, Phil Welling's reports, and the designs for the lighting and in-ground watering systems. He obviously enjoyed drilling down into the details. He questioned some of my choices, but more, it seemed to me, out of curiosity than criticism.

"Why buddleias here? I think I would have gone with hydrangeas."

"They can take a long time to get established. You want this to be a showplace by the end of June, so I had to make some tough choices. I've called for groupings of hydrangeas up here in the sundial garden. They may not flower much this year, but they'll form a nice mass."

He glanced over my price estimates, which I'd spent endless hours assembling. I'd attached more than twenty pages of itemized lists, together with samples of Nate's and Damon's work and their own cost sheets. The grand total seemed astronomical to me, but Mackenzie didn't question a single number.

"Did you fold in your own fee for overseeing the contractors? I don't see it broken out here."

"I wasn't sure how you wanted to handle that—if you preferred to pay them directly or not."

"What—and screw you out of a markup? Alice! I thought you were a better businesswoman than that. You found them. You should get the credit—and the cut."

"Thanks," I said, though there was another reason I'd submitted their proposals separately. "But that means I'll need more of the money up front. I can't afford to—"

"I understand," Mackenzie said, reaching over and unlocking a desk drawer. He pulled out a checkbook ledger. "Shall we say half now and half on completion?"

"Fine," I said as I watched him write out in a bold, almost illegible hand the biggest check I'd ever received in my life.

"And I haven't forgotten my promise to you about the Mackenzie Project," he said, standing and stretching while I began to pull my things together. "I'll make a contribution this week. And I'd appreciate it if you gave some thought to possible recipients."

"I'll do that," I said, smiling. One came to mind more or less immediately. I felt almost light-headed with happiness as he walked me across the entranceway to the front door. He glanced down the hall toward the sunroom.

"I'm sorry if I shocked you before," he said in a lowered voice, "the way I talked about my family. I guess I just thought you knew a thing or two about unscrupulous spouses."

I stared up at him. So he knew. Of course he knew. He'd told me himself he'd done a little digging around about me. He'd talked to Sal. He'd no doubt Googled me. How many thousands of news items would he have found there, with my name buried somewhere in the fine print? Everyone in Woodhaven knew, though they never said anything. It was considered such a scandal. Such a shame. But there was something about the casual—almost cavalier—way Mackenzie brought it up that I found oddly comforting. It occurred to me that he operated in the cutthroat, mega-business world where the kind of crime Richard had committed was, if not commonplace, at least not all that unusual.

Not something that would rip a marriage right off its foundations and sweep a lifetime of dreams into oblivion.

6

❧

Richard and I always agreed that you could never really know the truth about anyone else's marriage. The newlyweds next door, for instance, who seemed so in love—*look, they're still holding hands!*—but who ended up filing for divorce within the year. Or the elderly aunt who spent a lifetime grousing about her husband and then died of a broken heart a month after his final stroke. But we knew the truth about our own marriage. After being together for nearly two decades, we were still passionate lovers and best friends.

"I hope everyone has as much fun as we do," he used to say to me as we lay together, happily spent after making love. And that's what it always felt like to us—an act of love rather than one of mere sex. Something that only got better with time and experience. Along with this—or maybe because of it—we were blessed with two pretty, kind, and intelligent daughters. And Richard's fortunes were rising at a company he loved: Lerner, Reese, and Hamilton, one of the world's leading international accounting firms. He had made senior vice president of LRH's Assurance Services Group by the time he was forty-three, specializing in something called business risk assessment, with the possibility of even greater glory to come.

"They're sending me to Hong Kong for the global conference in two weeks," he told me about a month before our twentieth wedding anniversary. "John says he wants to introduce me personally to the managing partners. I think you should come with me, Alice. We'll stop off in Paris on our way home and really celebrate."

But my daughters needed me just then. Olivia, a freshman at the University of Virginia, was in the throes of her first serious breakup, and I'd planned a tour of colleges with Franny. So we decided he should go alone, concentrate on networking and making the best possible impression, and we'd do something wonderful together when he got back. Of course, I've wondered almost every day since what would have happened if I'd thrown my parental responsibilities to the wind and gone with him. Or was his invitation some kind of ruse, along with everything else? Surely it was already too late by then? The kind of complicated financial shenanigans he was up to would have taken months, maybe even years, to organize and implement. That's certainly what the investigators thought when they questioned me—over and over again—about the days leading up to Richard's disappearance.

"How many suitcases did he leave with? What did he pack? Did he have any cash lying around the house that he might have taken with him?"

I really didn't know. I honestly couldn't say. Though I'd spent each waking hour—and so many sleepless ones—raking over every last ember of memory. But all I could come up with was that he seemed mildly upset that I'd forgotten to pick up his dark blue suit from the cleaners the day before he left.

"Why do you think that was?" the investigator from the DA's office asked me, leaning forward with his mini-recorder.

"Because it was his favorite?" I replied.

"This isn't anything to joke about, Mrs. Hyatt," the FBI agent told me. "This is an extremely serious act of criminal fraud that took a hell of a lot of thought and planning. We have good reason to believe he had help. And we are looking into every aspect of your and your husband's life and finances. So if you want to save yourself a lot of heartache down the pike, you might as well tell us everything you know right now."

But even if I did know something about what Richard had done, there was nothing anyone could do about saving me from heartache. The whole thing unfolded in the confusing, slow-motion way of so many disasters. First, he didn't call me when he landed in Hong Kong. Then his assistant at LRH phoned to ask what had happened in London.

"What do you mean? I thought Richard was going to Hong Kong."

"He was, but he never made his connection in London. We thought maybe he'd taken ill? John Burbank's e-mailed me three times this morning. Richard's already missed the first session."

He was going to end up missing all of them. And a lot more than that. Our anniversary. His daughters' graduations. Their engagements. Marriages. He simply walked away from everything. He disappeared into thin air. But not without siphoning off—in an apparently brilliant and brazen series of money transfers—nearly two hundred million dollars from LRH's three largest clients. Richard's firm tried hard to keep a lid on what had happened, but that ended up only making matters worse. When the press learned about the "cover-up," they tore into the story with a vengeance.

They smeared Richard's reputation and LRH's shocking lack of oversight and transparency all over the business pages and Internet. It was horrible.

And then it got worse.

The article made the front page of the *Wall Street Journal* a week after Richard went missing:

LRH FRAUDSTER HAD FEMALE ACCOMPLICE

Her name was Ilsa Nilsson. She was an account executive working with Richard in Assurance Services, and several named sources within the company offered the opinion that they were having an affair.

"She was always in his office."

"They used to sneak out to lunch together."

"You could just tell by the way he looked at her."

According to the *Journal*, she disappeared the same weekend that Richard had; a brother claimed she was "planning to hook up with a friend in London." A photo of the two of them sitting together at some LRH function from a year before soon surfaced on the Internet. There was Ilsa with her high Nordic cheekbones and swan neck, gazing adoringly at my husband. And Richard, a bottle of beer in his hand, facing the camera with an embarrassed grin.

❦

"Be kind, for everyone you meet is fighting a hard battle," Plato purportedly said. Those words resonated with me when I first happened upon them a year or two after Richard vanished. At least, I thought, I wasn't alone.

Well-meaning people told me it was time to move on. As though I could simply walk away—just as Richard had.

By then I was getting ready to sell the house in Westchester to pay off legal fees, and both of the girls had had to apply for scholarships and student loans. By then I'd finally come to realize that what had happened wasn't some kind of gigantic misunderstanding. I'd stopped waiting for the phone to ring. Or the front door to open. I no longer heard footsteps on the stairs at night. Richard wasn't coming back. I sometimes wondered if he was even still alive. I imagined him dead—with her, of course, it had to be with her—in a car crash, drowned, a suicide pact. Not that I really wanted him to be dead. No, in fact, I actually preferred that he still be alive—so that I could kill him myself. With my own bare hands.

The worst thing, of course, was the self-doubt. Had I actually married a sociopath—or did he slowly change? Had Richard ever really loved me—or had he been deceiving me with consummate skill for more than twenty years? In the beginning, I clung to the belief that our marriage had been real. His love sincere. I knew in my heart that this was true. It *had* to be! Something—gambling, blackmail, bad investments—had forced him to take these crazy, desperate measures. But as the various investigations continued and no such evidence surfaced, I was slowly forced to relinquish even that possibility of solace. The questions continued in my mind, though. Back and forth. Old ones. New worries. Was Ilsa the first? Or had he been cheating on me from the very beginning? Everything we did, every word he said, became suspect. Shadowy. Full of double meanings. Shifting perspectives. I was fighting a hard battle.

It didn't help that so many people assumed that I must know something about what my husband had been up to. I was interviewed by the FBI, the DA's office, and the SEC on and off, more times than I can remember.

"Your neighbors claim you two were very, very close," one of the FBI agents informed me. "In fact, everyone we've spoken to says that."

What should have been a compliment became a curse. And it was impossible to even begin to explain any of this to my daughters. At first I assumed that Franny, who was still living at home when it happened, was taking the brunt of it. She complained about the constant disruptions, the satellite vans parked in front of the house, and the snide comments from her high school friends, but there was something in her essentially sunny and even-tempered nature that helped get her through. Olivia, on the other hand, had always been more introspective and self-critical. She'd also been more of a daddy's girl than Franny. I didn't realize just how hard the whole thing was on her until she came home for spring break that first year.

"I don't understand why you didn't even *try* to stop him," she told me tearfully one night. "Why you just . . . let him go like that."

"But, sweetie, I didn't know—"

"Mom! Please! It's *me* you're talking to. You *had* to have known somewhere deep down inside. If he'd gotten himself into some kind of a financial mess, we should have helped him work it out. We should have *been* there for him, rather than forcing him to run away like that. God, he must have been so ashamed! You know it's true. Why else would he have abandoned us like that? Just left us—without a word!"

❧

How long can you go on hashing over the same questions—without finding any answers? Whatever Olivia and Franny might have felt or believed about my role in their father's disappearance, they understood that I, too, was in a lot of pain. They were just beginning their lives. Mine, however, already half gone, had been totaled. Later on, after they graduated from college, started working, fell in love and married, the emotional turmoil surrounding their father's deception stopped taking center stage in their hearts. And after I moved up to the Berkshires, I saw less of them. So when we got together, we worked hard to make things go smoothly. Eventually, we stopped talking about what had happened. It had become, in time, something dark and threatening that hovered beneath the surface of our lives. Something that you could manage to ignore if you just kept your gaze on the horizon.

I thought it was better that way. Even Gwen, who had moved in with Franny and me during the worst of the scandal, learned to leave well enough alone when it came to my missing husband. I got short and snappish with her whenever she asked how I was "feeling about everything." Though the fraud investigation was still officially open, as far as I was concerned the case was closed. That is, until I began to work for Mackenzie.

❦

I was up at his house most days after he gave me the job. I worked alongside Peter Welling and his crew the week they tore up and rebuilt Mackenzie's hillside. It was the beginning of May, but a late-spring rain had washed through the region the day before. The property looked buried in mud, though I could see the new contours forming behind the metal pilings that Peter's crew was jackhammering into the muck.

"Tell me this is all part of the plan," Mackenzie said, materializing next to me on the top of the rise. I was wearing mud-splattered rubber boots and a hooded slicker. He was carrying an oversized black umbrella, which he held over both of us as we looked down on the earthmovers crawling up the hill.

"It's all part of the plan," I assured him. "Don't worry. This is definitely the before shot."

"Well, I suppose it's too late to start second-guessing you now. I don't go in for that sort of thing anyway. What's done is done." I glanced up at him. His usually animated face looked a little slack.

"We're building a garden here," I told him. "I think maybe this time *you* need to lighten up."

"You're right!" he said with a quick bark of a laugh. "Bad day on the market. But the sun will come out tomorrow, right?"

"I hope so. I'm expecting a couple of tons of Vermont blue slate to be delivered. Those trucks have got to make it up the driveway."

"I was talking metaphorically, Alice. But I kind of like your literal response. Is that how you always handle bad news? You just roll up your sleeves and get practical?"

Though I felt the question was a little personal, I thought I heard genuine interest in his tone.

"I've never thought about it in quite that way. But, yes, of course, hard work is good therapy."

"Which explains, I guess, why Green Acres is doing so well. It's your way of coping with what happened?"

"No, not at all! I really love what I do," I told him. "It has nothing to do with my husband."

"If you say so," he replied, his gaze moving back over his ravaged hillside. "I guess I'm more of a cause-and-effect kind of person."

❦

After that, whenever he was in residence, he made a point of coming out and finding me at the end of the day. If the weather was decent, he invited me up for a drink on the deck to watch the sunset. I got more confident and relaxed as the groundwork for the gardens began taking shape below us. And as I grew more comfortable in his presence, I found myself challenging him about fracking and what his multibillion-dollar corporation was doing to the land.

"Natural gas burns cleaner than any other form of fuel," he told me during one such discussion, "releasing less CO_2 into the atmosphere. As far as I'm concerned, it's win-win: cheaper energy that's actually better for the planet."

"You know perfectly well that fracking's an environmental disaster! The methane that's released from all those natural gas wells you've been drilling is more than a hundred times more powerful a greenhouse gas than CO_2." I'd been reading up on the subject and was a lot better informed on the issues than when we'd first met.

"And I think you've been drinking that clean-energy Kool-Aid, Alice. It's ridiculous how gullible you liberal bleeding hearts can be! Do you want to know who's behind a lot of the antifracking press you take on such faith? Rich, entitled people who don't want their beautiful country estates disturbed by poor neighbors who are hoping to lease their land and keep their farms going."

"Good luck with that after their groundwater gets poisoned!"

I think we both looked forward to these arguments. He had a quick mind and a deep understanding of his business. Did he actually believe in what he was saying? I don't know. I sensed he liked to conduct these sparring sessions with me because in fact he was a little lonely. There was something isolated about him—just as there was with me. We'd both seen too much of the world for our own good. He would bring up the subject of Richard from time to time, and I tried my best to take it in stride. I didn't want him to see what a hard time I still had with the whole thing.

"You never know about people, do you?" he said at one point when we'd been talking about my husband.

"No, you don't," I replied, though I'd once thought I could know. I would have sworn on my life that I'd been in a happy, loving marriage. For the first time in quite a while I felt my heart contract with pain, and I didn't like the feeling.

"So how do you deal with it?"

"You can't," I said, looking up from my drink to meet his gaze. "Some things never get resolved. You have to just learn to put them behind you and move on."

"Oh, Alice," he said, shaking his head. "Who do you think you're kidding? You're never going to be able to put something like that behind you."

7

❦

I decided to wait to tell Gwen about Mackenzie's charitable foundation until most of the construction work on the property had been completed. I needed to be absolutely sure that Mackenzie was pleased with how things were progressing before getting my friend's hopes up. I also wasn't ready to deal with her reaction. I knew she would want to meet Mackenzie—and pitch him—and I had to put my own concerns first. But I was aware that only a trickle of contributions for the Bridgewater House capital campaign had come in over the winter and spring—and that Gwen was feeling pretty low.

One Friday afternoon in late May, Mackenzie arrived by helicopter just as I was getting into my car to leave. He called to me as he started down the steps from the helipad above the tennis courts, and I waited for him in front of the bank of garages.

"You should see all of this from up there!" he told me, pointing to the sky. "The place already looks amazing—like Machu Picchu, for chrissakes!" We'd planted fast-growing grass around the retaining walls and walkways, and I could imagine how the hillside might resemble—at least from the air—that beautiful terraced city built by the Incas. His enthusiasm was infectious, though I'd come to realize that his spirits could just as easily swing the other way. He'd hinted that his moods were often market driven. Obviously he'd had a good week business-wise.

"We start putting in the trees and shrubs on Monday," I told him.

"Fantastic!"

Gwen was waiting for me in the Green Acres office when I got back from the site. We were heading out to the Triplex Cinema in Great Barrington for our usual Friday-evening dinner and a movie. I decided to finally fill her in about the Mackenzie Project as I drove the back way through Alford, the greening hills aglow in the soft light of early evening.

"Are you fucking kidding me?" she said, turning toward me in the front seat.

"No, really," I said, smiling. "It's for real. The official mission is to save and protect endangered horticultural spaces. It's a private charity—Mackenzie doesn't want the whole world beating a path to his door—so you wouldn't have found it in the standard foundation listings."

"And however much he pays you—he donates that same amount as a matching fund for our region?"

"That's right."

"This is incredible! Why didn't you tell me before?"

"Because it seemed a little too good to be true. This whole experience with Mackenzie feels like that. You wouldn't believe how much he's pouring into these gardens, Gwen. Next week I'll start putting in some of the most exquisite plantings money can buy."

"When do I meet him?" she asked, her eyes shining. "How do we do this?"

"I was thinking that it's probably better if he doesn't know we're best friends," I told her. "It would look a little conflict-of-interesty. But the Bridgewater gardens really are the perfect fit with his charity's mission. I thought I would just hand him one of your brochures and the capital campaign plan—and let him know that his foundation has an opportunity to do something really worth-while right here in Woodhaven. What do you think?"

"It's totally brilliant!" she said. "Oh, God, Alice! This could be it! This could turn everything around for me."

❦

Mackenzie had been in such a good mood on Friday, I decided not to wait. Gwen equipped me with a binder of printed material and a cover letter over her signature. I drove it up to Mackenzie's house on Saturday morning.

"He's at some hearing in town," Eleanor told me when she answered the door. "I think he'll be gone a while. I'd be happy to give that to him, if you want to leave it with me."

"Thanks. I think it's self-explanatory. But ask him to call me if he has any questions."

I picked up my paper and muffin at the general store, and then dropped by the post office for my mail. I was climbing back into my Subaru when Tom Deaver called to me from across the parking lot.

"Alice Hyatt! Wait up a minute."

I felt my pulse quicken. There was an eagerness to his stride that made it clear he had something he wanted to ask me. I watched him approach and thought, not for the first time, what an attractive man he was. The male of the species barely registers with me these days, so I took this opportunity to try to analyze what it was about Tom that made him seem different. He wasn't particularly tall or broad or physically forceful, though he was pretty fit for someone who was probably hitting fifty. His dark brown hair was a little long for my taste, but his face was open and kind, his skin roughened from a lot of time spent outdoors. And there was something about the way he moved—a kind of inner grace—that caught my attention when I saw him around town. I liked his voice, too. It was one of those melodious, self-assured baritones you often hear on public radio.

"Wind power promises to be a great alternative to fossil fuels," he'd said during a program I'd attended at the library a few months back. Tom was an environmental writer and activist who ran the Clean Energy Consulting Cooperative. The talk, titled "The Future of Wind," was part of a regular series the library presented promoting local experts and authors. "And we're in the perfect position right here in Woodhaven to test its tremendous potential to dramatically change our relationship to the planet. . . ."

Tom's proposal to mount several wind turbines on Powell Mountain had been causing a lot of local controversy. Some people were all for tapping the energy savings that wind power could generate. Others, mostly those who lived near the mountain, worried about the noise the turbines purportedly generated as well. I'd stopped by the lecture to try to get a better sense of what was involved, but Tom's talk had run long and I'd had to leave before the Q and A session got under way. Still, I remembered feeling impressed by how impassioned and committed he was about the project. It occurred to me that, without really realizing it, I'd been giving Tom Deaver a lot of thought.

"Hi, Tom," I said, smiling as he came up to me.

"I just don't believe it!" His voice was shaking.

"What?" I asked. Something was clearly wrong.

"You're actually *working for* Graham Mackenzie?" he said.

"No, I don't work for him—not for his company," I said, thinking Tom must have been misinformed. "I'm just designing a garden for his new place."

"Where the hell do you draw the line?"

"What do you mean?"

"How can you in good conscience allow yourself to have anything to do with a man like that? Someone who destroys the land for a living!"

"I . . . I'm running a business," I began to say, but then I realized that Tom had repeated back to me almost exactly what I'd accused Mackenzie of at our first meeting. "Listen, initially I had some reservations, too. But once I got to know him better—"

"No," Tom said, shaking his head back and forth as if he couldn't bear to hear what I was saying. "No—not *you*, Alice. I really thought better of you. I don't know why, but for some reason I thought you cared about the environment. I thought you had some integrity."

"I do care," I said, stung by his indictment. "I care very deeply. The garden I've created incorporates solar power and recycled materials. All my designs are—"

"What difference does any of that make? You're still working *for* a man who stands for everything we're *against*. I'm just stunned you don't seem to get this."

"You must not know him very well," I said. I was tempted to tell him about the Mackenzie Project, but I had to remind myself that Mackenzie had made it clear he wanted to keep the foundation under wraps. "He's really remarkably knowledgeable about landscape design."

"Oh, is he?" Tom said, taking a step back and looking me over. "And Hitler painted watercolors!"

He turned on his heel and walked away without giving me a chance to respond. Not that I could have. He'd left me speechless.

❧

Later, though, and in the days ahead, I thought of any number of comebacks. From the reasonable: *I try not to judge other people based on what they do for a living, but rather on how they act in their daily lives—and Mr. Mackenzie has been a perfect gentleman.* To the downright petulant and furious: *Who made you the boss of me?* But no matter what I came up with, I knew that none of it would be convincing enough to change Tom Deaver's mind. Or his downgraded opinion of me. And I began to realize that how he viewed me mattered more than I cared to admit.

No, not you, Alice. I really thought better of you. . . . So he'd had me in his sights—or at least in his peripheral vision—just as I'd had him in mine. *For some reason . . . I thought you had some integrity.* And he'd liked what he'd seen. At least until now. It was interesting how our argument had suddenly brought him into sharp focus for me—and to the forefront of my mind. What I knew about him, though, could fit on a sticky note. He'd been widowed about five years ago, after his wife suffered through an almost decade-long series of cancer treatments.

"That man's a saint," Brigitte, our postmistress, had confided to me one Saturday right after I'd moved back to Woodhaven. Tom had just left after buying stamps in front of me in line. "Never complains. Always has something nice to say—and him with his wife living at home in hospice care for almost a year!" A few months after this encounter, Gwen told me that Tom's wife had finally passed away.

"That's the kind of man I want at my deathbed," she'd said. "Apparently he held her in his arms as she breathed her last. I'm going to give him a year—then I'm going to pounce."

Gwen hadn't followed up on her threat, though, which was unlike her. I kidded her about it from time to time.

"He's fair game now," I'd told her when we saw him shopping

at Guido's with two of his teenaged children a couple of years after his wife had died.

"Yeah, he's pretty tempting, isn't he?" Gwen said as we watched him surreptitiously. He was wearing jeans and a battered baseball cap. He was standing in front of the meat counter, and the butcher was laughing at something he'd said. "But there're those four teenage kids to contend with. I think I'm going to wait until they're out of the house."

As far as I knew, the Deaver children were in college now, though I think I'd heard the oldest one had already married. It was only recently—around the time of Tom's lecture at the library—that I became vaguely aware I didn't have my eye on Tom Deaver for Gwen's sake, but for my own. Not seriously, though. I was through with men. But theoretically, if I ever was to get involved with anyone again—which I wasn't—I'd want him to be someone like Tom. Thoughtful. Committed to a job he really believed in. Making a difference in the world. That he looked damned good in jeans and had a voice that made my mouth go dry was definitely a plus. But I knew now that I'd clearly blown it with him before I had to worry about dealing with any of these fantasies in a real way. And when I asked myself if I would have refused to work for Mackenzie because it might have improved my chances with Tom, the answer was an unequivocal "no."

❧

"Guess who called me," Gwen said, her voice on the phone sounding girlishly breathy.

"Tom," I said. It was a week after my run-in with him, and the whole bruising business was still taking up way too much of my time and attention.

"Who?"

"Tom Deaver. Didn't you want him to—"

"What? No—Graham Mackenzie! He called me at the office about half an hour ago and we talked. And talked. We just hung up. He's coming by later this afternoon to see Bridgewater House. The timing couldn't be better. The place looks run-down as hell, but this is the perfect time of the year to show the gardens. The peonies and lilacs are blooming."

"Don't forget to mention to him that they go back generations."

"I won't. I've been working on my pitch ever since you told me about his foundation. I've got it down chapter and verse. And I'm going use everything in my power to persuade him that the Bridgewater House gardens deserve his funding dollars."

"What do you mean by *everything* in your power?"

"Well, I think he might be susceptible to some of my physical charms, don't you?"

"You've got a great story, Gwen. You don't need to oversell it."

"What are you implying?"

"I think you know what I mean," I told her. Gwen was an unabashed flirt. She was certainly attractive enough to sit back and let men come to her, but that just wasn't her style. And though I hated to admit it, sometimes I found the way she threw herself at guys—especially those who had something she wanted—a little embarrassing. All too often Gwen took up with wealthy married men. And these relationships always followed the same basic and usually very brief dramatic arc: euphoric opening, tumultuous intermezzo, abrupt denouement. The fact that several of Gwen's lovers had offered to leave their wives for her—and that she'd turned them down flat—had convinced me that my friend preferred the excitement these liaisons provided over the men themselves.

"No, I think you better spell it out," she replied.

"Okay," I told her, undeterred. I decided she really needed to hear what I had to say. "I think you should approach Mackenzie in a businesslike manner. He strikes me as the kind of man who doesn't need much persuading when it comes to certain things— like your physical charms. And you don't want to end up mixing business with pleasure. You don't want to come across as unprofessional, do you? This is just too important."

"Perhaps you'd like to come over and chaperone?" she asked, but I could hear the irritation behind her glibness.

"No, of course not," I said. But I lied. I was responsible for bringing the two of them together. My needy, impulsive best friend and an entitled, volatile man. Had I done something I would come to regret? All sorts of alarm bells began to go off in my head.

8

❦

*T*he June issue of the *Woodhaven News*, our local monthly, carried a write-up on the special meeting at the town hall that had been held on a Saturday morning at the end of May to discuss Tom Deaver's wind power initiative. The last paragraph of the story read:

> After a series of unfortunate exchanges between Mr. Deaver and Mr. Mackenzie, who represented the Powell Mountain Homeowners Association, the chair of the planning board was forced to abruptly adjourn the session. The selectmen would like it known that all such forums should be kept cordial and in the public interest, and that personal disparagements and inappropriate language will not be tolerated. The Wind Power Initiative has been put on indefinite hold.

No wonder Tom was upset when he saw me at the post office that day. He'd just come from what was clearly a bruising confrontation with Mackenzie, not to mention dashed hopes for his project. It changed nothing, I knew, but it helped explain his anger, and

I was able to gradually stop obsessing so much about what had happened between us. I had plenty of other things on my mind.

Gwen, for instance. And Mackenzie. The two of them separately. As well as the possibility of the two of them together. Gwen had dutifully reported back to me after Mackenzie's visit to Bridgewater House. The meeting had gone well, she told me. He'd seemed interested in the project. He thought the property was indeed beautiful and deserved to be preserved. Gwen felt hopeful that they could work together. Mackenzie had requested that she submit a formal grant proposal.

"And?" I asked.

"What?"

"Well, what did you think of him? You asked me the same question a couple of months ago, remember? Would you say he has a soul or is he just all about making the big buckaroonies?"

"He seems very nice," Gwen said. *Nice?* That was such a namby-pamby word—not part of Gwen's usual vocabulary at all.

"What's going on?" I asked her.

"Nothing. I don't know what you're talking about."

"Yes, you do! What really happened with Mackenzie? You're being cagey. You're hiding something."

"And *you're* being paranoid. And, if I may say so, more than a little insulting. I know perfectly well what you were implying when you told me not to be unprofessional. You were worried I was going to act like a fool in front of your big-deal client. Plus you have no real faith in my ability to make this campaign a success. You hurt my feelings, Alice. If I was hiding anything—I guess it's that."

If she'd meant to put me on the defensive, she'd done a good job. I apologized, and we got off the phone soon after. But the following Friday morning she left a voice mail saying she wasn't going to be able to make it to the movies that night. Something had come up. The same thing—whatever or whoever it was—came up again the week after. I called her a couple of times, but kept getting bounced to her voice mail. I decided to let it go—and let her make the next move to get back in touch. I was relieved to think that I was the problem, and that my worst fears hadn't materialized. At least, I hoped that was the case. I wasn't able to gather any collaborating evidence from Mackenzie.

Though I was spending almost every waking hour at his house these days, I hadn't actually seen him since the day he stopped me in front of the garages. Our early-evening idylls on his deck had come to an abrupt end. But I assumed he was in residence because his helicopter was there, and I would occasionally hear his voice behind his office door when I came in for one of Eleanor's lunches or snacks. Sometimes Mara would join us as well. Eleanor had issued her and Danny a standing invitation to drop by for meals anytime they wanted. But most days Mara and I were too busy for more than a store-bought sandwich wolfed down on the run. I was overseeing the installation of the most complicated and expensive project of my career while Mara was almost single-handedly running Green Acres in my absence.

"Mrs. Bostock wants you to call her," Mara told me one morning in early June as I was heading out to the site.

"Can't you follow up on that?" I asked. Brook Bostock, one of our wealthiest clients, was generally easygoing, but she tended to chatter on. I didn't have time for that today. Damon Fagels was due at Mackenzie's in less than an hour to start mounting the wrought-iron fixtures.

"She's called three times," Mara said. "She wants to talk to *you*. She asked if you were ever here these days."

"Okay, I'll try her on my cell later," I said, pushing open the door.

"And Vera Yoland called again."

"Again?" I asked, turning around. Vera Yoland sat on the board of the Berkshire Botanical Garden and the Berkshire Natural Resources Council, was past chairwoman of the Lenox Garden Club, and had her fingers in just about every important horticultural pie in our area. I'd been introduced to her half a dozen times since moving back to Woodhaven—at gardening events and benefits—but she seemed to make a point of staring right through me. I'd seen her be gracious and charming to those she wanted to impress. I was just someone she clearly felt she needn't bother with. Whether that was because she knew about the fiasco with Richard or because she simply disliked me for myself alone, I couldn't say. That Vera Yoland had called me—twice—seemed unbelievable.

"Yeah, the first one's with the messages I left for you yesterday," Mara said, "right there beside your phone."

I closed the door and went back to my desk. It was covered with stacks of mail and message slips. I knew that Mara would be troubleshooting any really serious problems, but I could tell from sorting through the many "While You Were Outs" that I needed to step in soon and handle some of these matters myself. Sal Lombardi had called twice over the last week, which was odd because we usually dealt directly with his caretaker. I found Brook Bostock's messages as well as those from two other regular clients. And there in Mara's looping hand was Vera Yoland's name and number. She lived in one of those meticulously restored Victorians in Lenox. Her gardens, which had been featured in *Martha Stewart Living* a few years back, had been maintained for decades by Coldwater Landscape Design. Could Vera be thinking of making a change?

I was running late, but my curiosity got the better of me. I picked up the phone and dialed Vera's number. She answered on the second ring.

"Oh, yes! Alice! Thank you so much for getting back to me!" Her emphatic patrician voice carried across the room. Mara looked over and frowned. "I've been hearing such absolutely amazing things about the gardens you're putting in for Graham Mackenzie!"

"Thank you," I said. "It's an enormous undertaking, but I think he's pleased with how things are coming along."

"Someone told me he insisted that everything be finished by the end of June. Can that be possible? What an incredible task! You must be laboring away like Hercules!"

Vera Yoland's laugh was high, brittle, and, it seemed to me, a little nervous. She must have been aware that she'd been rude to me and was now anxious about approaching me to take her gardens on. Six months ago I would have jumped at the chance. After my experience with Mackenzie, though—and the joy of creating something totally new and original—the prospect of maintaining Vera's staid English-style property seemed less than thrilling. But the sweet revenge of having her ask—after treating me so dismissively in the past—was pretty delicious.

"That's the deadline," I told her. "And I'm doing everything in my power to honor it. Graham Mackenzie is *such* a generous and supportive client. It's actually been more like a collaboration—and I think the outcome is going to be pretty spectacular."

"Oh, how marvelous! That's just what I was hoping to hear! And you're feeling pretty confident about that end-of-June completion date?"

"Yes, though we're not nearly there yet. I'm still waiting for shipment confirmation on some—"

"Oh, that doesn't matter!" Vera said breezily. "We'll come in and help fill in any holes you might have with mulch or annuals. Every garden we include gets a little free face-lift right before it's shown."

"*We?*" I asked, suddenly confused.

"The Garden Conservancy, dear," Vera explained. "Didn't I make that clear? I told your girl yesterday that I was calling about Open Days. I'm one of the regional representatives. Everyone's been talking about the Mackenzie property, and we decided that we wanted to feature it that first Saturday in July as the kickoff to the entire summer season. It will be such a coup! We're expecting a huge turnout. I know it's going to be a tremendous draw and we . . ."

An Open Day. The Garden Conservancy wanted to show my garden during an Open Day! These self-guided tours through the most beautiful private gardens in the country had been initiated several decades ago by the prestigious Garden Conservancy and since then had grown into some of the most anticipated social events of the summer. Having your garden chosen was the equivalent of being nominated for an Academy Award. The recognition alone was a tremendous and extremely coveted honor. It was something that would ensure the ongoing success of Green Acres. I felt so giddy I had to sit down.

"Tried any number of times . . ." I vaguely heard Vera continue. ". . . must really finalize things immediately . . . already so late in the game . . . press releases . . . the housekeeper has tried but . . . hoping you might intervene . . . can't move ahead without his permission . . ."

I finally realized what Vera was trying to say.

"You want me to ask Mr. Mackenzie for you?" I said.

"Yes, if you would. He's not answering my calls. I've tried to make it clear to him in the voice mails I left who I am and what the Garden Conservancy represents. But then it occurred to me that Mr. Mackenzie might have no idea how special it is to have his home selected for an Open Day. He travels in such different circles than the rest of us—nobody on our board has ever actually met him."

"I'd be happy to ask him," I said, my heart still racing. I felt a surge of goodwill—to Vera, to the Garden Conservancy, to life it-self. I'd been through hell, but I'd persevered. And this, I knew without a shadow of a doubt, was my reward. What a tremendous boost this was going to mean for my business—not to mention my ego. I'd been so right to take the job with Mackenzie! A part of me couldn't help but wonder what Tom Deaver would think when he learned that the esteemed Garden Conservancy had chosen to rec-ognize my work in such a wonderfully public way.

"What was *that* all about?" Mara asked when I hung up the phone.

"I'm guessing you've never heard of Open Days," I replied. "Or you would have hunted me down and made me return that wom-an's call yesterday."

"You're right. So what's the big deal?"

But after I explained about the Garden Conservancy and the honor of being chosen for an Open Days tour, Mara just shrugged.

"Is this going to mean you spend even *more* time over there? Because I've got to tell you, things are really beginning to get to a breaking point around here. I'm not sure how much more I can handle on my own."

"Don't worry," I told her, shuffling the messages she'd left me into a workable pile. "I'll take these with me and make a lot of calls on my cell. I'll try to get back in time to go over some of your con-cerns, okay? But you're doing a wonderful job! And—if everything works out the way I think it will—you should start planning what you're going to do with a very nice bonus."

❦

I wasn't able to get in to see Mackenzie that day. Eleanor told me he was on a series of extended conference calls and could not be inter-rupted.

"But it's very important news," I told her. "And I know he'd be happy to hear it! I'll be here pretty late—so if he happens to become free later—just give me a shout, okay?"

"It would be lovely to give him good news," Eleanor said. "At the same time, I'd prefer not to have my head bitten off. I promise to come get you, though, if he ever comes out of that office again."

Damon had trouble fitting the wrought-iron railings into some of the stonework, and he had to do a lot of resoldering. Late in the afternoon, we had to call Nate back in to discuss changing the slope of the flight of steps leading down to the pool below the waterfall.

"It's too much of a grade," Damon said. "Too steep for kids and anyone who's not in great shape."

"Yeah, but how many people are actually going to be using it?" Nate said. I could tell he was irritated about having his work called into question, especially by someone he didn't report to. He'd done a massive amount of stonework in record time and had assumed he was through with the project. "I saw this more as a kind of maintenance area, you know?" We were standing on a shadowy rise by the empty oval pool that indeed I'd envisioned being looked at primarily from above. I'd had no plans to cultivate the glade other than keeping the undergrowth trimmed around the pool.

"I'm just saying," Damon replied, shrugging. "But if you don't care about code, it's fine with me."

"I'll tell you what worries me more," Nate said. "That exposed area up there. This is some kind of a drop, man. I'm thinking you need to put a railing or something around the mouth of that waterfall."

I looked up at the cliff towering above us.

"Nate's right," I said after a moment. "I was hoping for an unimpeded view, but it's really too dangerous to leave like that. Especially considering all the people—" I stopped myself, realizing that

I was about spill the news from Vera before Mackenzie had agreed to it.

"All what people?" Damon asked. They both turned to look at me.

"Okay—please don't breathe a word of this because the client hasn't signed off on it yet, but we've been selected to kick off Open Days this year."

"No fucking way!" Nate said, laughing.

"Fantastic!" Damon agreed. As artisans who depended on the gardening trade for a lot of their custom work, Nate and Damon knew that this was a big win for them, too. After that, they quickly agreed to make the changes and additions they'd both suggested, and we were able to call it a day before evening descended altogether. I stopped by the house on my way home, but Eleanor told me Mackenzie was still holed up in his office.

"That man's going to work himself to death," she said, shaking her head.

❦

The office was dark by the time I got home, but Mara's beat-up Corolla was still in the drive, and I noticed the lights were on in the greenhouse. I walked across the lawn, where the first of the summer's lightning bugs were drifting upward through the humid night air.

"Mara?" I called as I entered the small greenhouse that my grandfather had built more than fifty years ago and that I now used primarily to store trays and hoses. Two years ago I'd added an extension: a much larger commercial steel-framed and polycarbonate model, which was where we nurtured our seedlings and housed the tender perennials and shrubs over the winter. Mara was at the far end of the addition, her back to me. About half the trays were empty now after several hundred of the sturdier annuals we'd grown had found their way into our clients' gardens over the last several busy weeks of planting. We were waiting another few days before putting in the more delicate varieties.

"Mara?" I said again as I started down the center aisle toward her.

"Oh!" she said, whirling around.

"Sorry if I scared you," I said. "You're working awfully late."

"Yeah, well," she said, wiping her hands on her jeans as she came down the aisle to meet me. "The plants needed pinching back. They were getting really leggy." She looked tired.

"Listen, I'm sorry," I told her. "We ran into a lot of problems today and I didn't get to those calls. But I promise to do it first thing tomorrow. And I'll also try to give you more of a hand in the office."

"It's okay," she said. "The way I acted before? I think I was just embarrassed I didn't know about Open Days."

"Don't be silly," I said, surprised and touched that she would admit this to me. We walked out together, switching off the overheads and leaving what she had been doing unfinished.

"No, stuff like that is really important," she said as we walked back along the drive toward her car. "It's the kind of thing I need to know if I'm going to make it in this business."

I felt another wave of pleasure at hearing her declare that the job mattered to her. That she saw it as her future. I knew that I was forcing Mara to work hard, but I also believed that I was giving her a great opportunity to learn a trade from, quite literally, the ground up. It was so difficult to know what she was thinking and feeling most of the time. But I felt a chink had opened between us—and that for just a moment or two I was able to see into her heart.

9

I ran into Gwen at the farmers' market two days later. I'd dropped by to pick up something to eat on my way back from the site. It was nearly five o'clock and I hadn't had lunch. Worse, I still hadn't been able to meet with Mackenzie. And the couple of morning hours allotted to planting a semicircle of weeping cherries had turned into an all-day ordeal. I'd hoped to use some of my Green Acres workers that I'd recently been pressing into service at Mackenzie's, but Mara had put her foot down, saying they just couldn't be spared at such a busy time. So I had to rely on the less than cooperative crew the nursery sent. The afternoon had evaporated without my realizing it, and I was starving. Then I heard Gwen's voice behind me at the Bread of Heaven stand.

"Where've you been hiding, stranger?" she said.

"What?" I asked, turning around. She was wearing a sleeveless jersey minidress, oversized sunglasses, and a wide, innocent smile.

"I've been trying to reach you," she told me.

"Really? You couldn't have been trying very hard."

"What's the matter? You look a little frazzled."

"That's because I am. Mackenzie's missing in action and I have a lot of things I really need to talk to him about."

"I'm sorry," she said.

I hated to do it, but I couldn't help myself.

"Have *you* heard from him?" I asked.

"No. Not lately," Gwen said. Which could have meant she'd last seen him two weeks ago—or just yesterday. At least she had the decency to keep her sunglasses on and not try to look me in the eye. What the hell was she up to? But I was pretty sure I knew, because this wasn't the first time Gwen had suddenly dropped out of my life without explanation. In fact, it had become a pretty good indicator that she had embarked on another one of her clandestine affairs. *Here we go again!* I thought. It was her choice, of course, and in the past I'd forced myself not to be too judgmental about some of Gwen's more dubious romantic decisions. But now I suspected her behavior was coming between me and my client at the worst possible moment. And this after I'd handed the Mackenzie Project to her on a silver platter! How could she be so selfish and unthinking?

At any other time after not seeing Gwen for such a long stretch, I would have insisted that we sit down together and catch up. But as it became my turn at the Bread of Heaven queue to place an order, I realized I'd lost my appetite—not only for a sandwich but for my friend's company as well.

"Sorry," I said, stepping out of line. "I've got to run."

"Is everything okay?" Gwen asked.

"I'm working night and day to get this garden done on time," I told her. "So if you happen to see Mackenzie before I do, please let him know we really need to talk."

❦

I'd stopped answering Vera Yoland's calls. A full week had gone by since she'd spoken to me about the Open Day event, and it was now only three and a half weeks before the proposed date itself. Press releases needed to be written and sent out, brochures and tickets printed. As agonizing as it was to watch this opportunity slip through my fingers, it was becoming increasingly clear to me that I had no choice but to turn down the greatest professional honor of my life.

The project itself, however, was coming together beautifully. I'd pushed my suppliers hard, dropping hints that exciting news about my work for Mackenzie was in the offing. As a consequence, I was expecting a shipment of the last of the specimen trees—a dozen black-barked river birches—that afternoon. As I waited in the driveway for the delivery, I looked down and saw Mackenzie below. I'd yet to walk him through the nearly completed garden rooms, but there he was, pacing back and forth across the sundial terrace as if it had been in his possession for years. I shielded my eyes against the afternoon sun, watching him stop, turn, and walk back the other way. His head was down. He seemed unaware of his surroundings. He appeared to be talking to himself. It took me a moment to realize that he was on a hands-free phone.

It had been several weeks since I'd seen him, and I was shocked by the change in his appearance. Even from this distance, I could tell he'd lost weight. He moved slowly, hunched over a little, as though in some pain. I'd been so preoccupied with my own concerns that it hadn't occurred to me that Mackenzie might not be just overwhelmed by work—or distracted by a new love affair. He'd always seemed so much bigger than life to me. It was unsettling to think that he could actually be ill.

The delivery truck arrived, and I spent the next hour or so overseeing the planting of the new birches at the northern edge of the property. The whole time I was working, however, I also had my eye on Mackenzie as he moved restlessly around in the garden below. He remained on the phone, occasionally shaking his head. His tone seemed subdued. Not once did I see him laugh.

After the crew left, I debated about what to do. Though I longed to approach him about the Open Day—in fact, this was probably my last chance to do so—I couldn't imagine interrupting him during what was obviously a serious call. But he solved the dilemma for me. He stopped in midstride, looked up the hill at me, and—almost as though he'd read my mind—waved me down. Then he continued pacing.

". . . I'm not sure how many more times we're going to have to go over this," he was saying as I approached. He nodded vaguely to me, and went on: "I've talked to your lawyers. You've talked to my lawyers. Your lawyers have talked to my lawyers. Listen, Sal, the point is, your team had its shot at due diligence. Six fucking months of it . . . Okay, but that's your problem now, isn't it? Do you really think bringing in even *more* lawyers is going to solve anything?"

Mackenzie turned and crossed the terrace again, walking right over the beautiful stone-and-iron compass mosaic that Nate and Damon had laid into the pavement. I doubted he even noticed it.

"Take this to the press?" he cried. "Go on! Be my guest! You have my absolute blessing to look like a total fool. No, I'm not gloating. You've got to know how sorry I am about what's happened."

He turned back in my direction, shaking his head.

"So why not shut up for a minute and listen to what I have to say? Right, I realize that, but I really am trying to help. Okay. The best thing you can do—in fact the *only* thing you can do as far as I'm concerned—is to just suck it up and take one mother of a write-down. Yes, I understand. But you know what I think? You'll be roughed up in the market for a week or two, but then you'll bounce right back. No, really. Sure. Me, too. Yeah—I wish."

He stopped pacing and stood with his back to me, looking out over the valley. I didn't realize the call had ended until he said to me without turning around, "Word of advice, Alice: never do business with friends."

I'd heard him mention "Sal," and wondered if he'd been talking to Sal Lombardi, whose calls I'd tried to return earlier in the week. But Sal's wife, Gigi, had told me her husband was down in the city and she had no idea what he might have wanted. Though Mackenzie's comment almost begged the question, I decided not to ask him if he was referring to his neighbor. The last thing I needed was to get caught in the cross fire between two of my most important clients.

"I hope everything's okay," I said, walking over to him. Up close, I could see how the weight loss had further loosened his jawline. And there was a new pouchiness around his eyes that made him look older and somewhat sad.

"No, actually, it's not," he said. "I've hit some pretty choppy water, Alice. And after years of smooth sailing I'm afraid I've lost my old knack for coming about."

I didn't know what to say. Should I try to commiserate? Or offer solace? Here we stood in this man-made paradise he'd paid me an enormous sum of money to create for him, and I was pretty sure that he was barely taking it in—let alone deriving any pleasure from it. And I was surprised at how much that bothered me. How much it mattered that he should enjoy our great shared endeavor. I'd known when I took on this project that I wanted to prove something to myself. Now I realized that I'd been hoping to prove something to Mackenzie as well. I wanted him to feel that he'd been right to believe in me. That I'd done him proud. I longed to hear the old excitement in his voice. *What I'm hoping for is something totally*

unexpected and unique. The fact is I want you to create the most
beautiful garden in the Berkshires for me.

"You're right," he muttered, as though I'd actually been speaking to him. "Enough of this! Self-pity is such a ridiculous waste of energy. So, Alice," he said, turning to face me. His gaze was hooded and weary. "I understand you've been trying to get hold of me." I knew that Eleanor had been attempting for days to get him to respond to my repeated requests. Was it Gwen who'd prompted this sudden willingness to talk?

"Yes," I told him. "Something's come up that I think you're going to like. At least I hope so. Because, in my world at least, it's a pretty big deal. . . ."

❧

I was sure that my news about the Open Day would shake Mackenzie out of his slump, but he seemed to just absorb it into his general unhappiness.

"So I agree to let the public come traipsing through here," he said, "and they trample all over the flower beds and have their little dogs pee on the bushes. What exactly do I get out of it?"

"Recognition," I said, my heart sinking. This was hardly the response I'd been counting on, and his peevishness surprised me. I was aware that he could be bullying and demanding, but this was the first time I'd ever known him to be small. "A chance to show off what you've done. This is an amazing accomplishment. Everyone's talking about it."

"Oh, Christ!" he said. "The thing is, this isn't the optimum moment for me to be showing anything off. I hope you didn't go and promise that Yoland woman anything. I got at least two dozen different messages from her. You'd think people would start to get it when you don't call them back!"

"Of course I didn't promise anything," I said, affronted. "Though I might have given her the wrong impression about how you'd react. I'm sorry—I assumed you'd be pleased."

"Don't get all martyrish on me, Alice," he said. "I have enough on my plate right now without having to deal with your tender feelings."

"I'll live," I told him, though in fact I was bitterly disappointed. It was my garden, too, I wanted to remind him. But the truth was that without his money neither of us would have been standing there, surrounded by beauty and utterly miserable.

"I'm not sure *I* will," he said. "Along with everything else, I feel like absolute hell. If we're going to continue this, do you mind if we find a place to sit down?"

"Of course," I told him. "But would you like me to give you a quick tour of the gardens first? There are benches down there by the waterfall. Do you think you can make it that far?"

"Well, let's give it a try," he said, and then, surprisingly, he held out his arm. He might have done it to help steady himself, but it felt more like an act of gallantry to me. And so we set off at a leisurely pace . . . across the sundial garden . . . down the steps to the miniature lily pond . . . along the walkway covered with flowering wisteria . . . up to the newly planted birch grove surrounding the Buddhist shrine . . . down the curving staircase to the perennial beds, where rosebushes had already started to climb up the retaining wall . . . and along the colonnade of lime trees. He moved with some difficulty, but his mood seemed to lighten with every new garden room we entered.

"Beautiful," he said, running his hand over one of the wrought-iron railing knobs that Damon had shaped into a perching bird.

"Ah, I love that smell," he said, breathing in the sharp aroma of freshly clipped boxwoods.

"Of course, the hedges still have to fill in a good deal," I told him as we stood in the rounded terrace where the boxwoods were to be trained to form a waist-high spiral maze. "You won't get the full effect for another few years."

"In the meantime, that fountain gives this area the focus it needs," he told me. "I love the way you have water trickling or splashing at every turn. I noticed it in the plans, of course, but I didn't realize how soothing it would be."

"Well, that's the point, isn't it?" His praise was beginning to work its old magic on me. "A garden should be an oasis of serenity and reflection. A place to commune with—how did Lincoln put it?—'the better angels of our nature.'"

"Or to grapple with the devil, as Eve might have put it," he said as we started down the short flight of steps to the largest terrace with its wide-open vistas. The redirected underground brook rushed through its stone channel and cascaded over the ledge. "In any case, you're to be congratulated, Alice. This is magnificent."

"Thank you. We've a number of things left to do. One of them is to install a railing around that waterfall. I know we talked about having an infinity view—but the drop-off now is just too dangerous to leave it the way it is."

"It's a pity," he said as we walked across the flagstones to the verge and looked over. Water thundered down the sheer rock face. Mist rose from the pool below. "But I see what you mean."

"The benches are over there," I said, pointing to the alcove under the stand of weeping cherries.

"That's okay, I'm feeling better now," he said, looking out over the valley to the distant mountains. "It's really incredible what you've accomplished, Alice. You've actually moved rivers—like Le Nôtre did for the Sun King at Versailles. It's amazing what money can buy, isn't it?"

"When it's put to good use," I said. "The way you've done here. And with what you're doing through your foundation."

He didn't respond right away. He just stood there, gazing out, lost in thought.

"This Open Day business means a lot to you, I take it," he said finally, his eyes still on the horizon.

"Yes, it does," I replied, looking over at him. I didn't want to pressure him, but at the same time I couldn't lie. I knew him well enough to know that he wouldn't have wanted me to either. Whatever else he was, whatever problems he might be facing, he was a man who preferred hard facts and unpleasant truths to more-digestible alternatives.

"Goddamn it . . . ," he muttered. I got the sense he was talking to himself rather than to me. The whole time I was with him that afternoon, in fact, I'd felt he had been carrying on some sort of interior argument or debate whose answers kept eluding him.

"Oh, what the fuck, Alice," he said after a moment, in his familiar combative tone. "Let's just go ahead and do it!"

10

Vera Yoland was thrilled, of course. We talked a number of times over the next couple of days about copy for the press release and the self-guided tour brochure she was having designed as a handout for attendees.

"And I'll need a simple black-and-white map with legends of the gardens," she told me. "Is that something I should talk to Mr. Mackenzie about?"

"No," I said. "He asked me to handle all the details." In fact, he'd phrased it a little differently. *You sic that Yoland woman on me again and all bets are off!* "I'll e-mail you a plan as an attachment later this afternoon. And I'll give you my edits on the press release then as well."

"That's lovely, dear. But I really feel I should talk to Mr. Mackenzie myself. I've been getting queries from some of the local newspapers about his company. And I thought he might perhaps be kind enough to clarify a few—"

"I'm sorry," I lied, "but Mr. Mackenzie is tied up in business meetings all this week. He specifically told me he can't be disturbed and asked that I handle everything on his behalf. Is there someone in particular you'd like me to speak to?"

"Oh," Vera said, obviously disappointed. "Let me get back to you on that."

I assumed the subject was closed—until a few days later when Mara told me we'd gotten a call from a reporter at the *Berkshire Herald*.

"I tried to help him," she told me, "but he wasn't interested in the garden or the Open Day. He wanted to know a lot of stuff about Mackenzie's businesses."

"That's ridiculous," I said. "Why would we know anything about MKZEnergy?"

"That's just what I told him. But he didn't seem to want to take my word for it. He said that Vera Yoland had promised him you would call him back and go over his questions."

His name was Jeff Isley and he'd left a cell phone number, which I took with me to Mackenzie's later that morning. I was there to troubleshoot the installation of the underground watering system, but the company seemed to have everything well in hand, so I tried Isley's number. Reception is often spotty in the mountains and, though the call went through, it was dropped after a couple of rings. I tried again, but without success, and decided to wait until I could get to a landline.

I'd forgotten all about him when my own cell rang about an hour later.

"Hi, it's Jeff Isley. Returning your call." There was static on the line, but I could hear him well enough.

"Yes, you wanted to speak to someone about Graham Mackenzie's garden?"

"The garden. The man. The fact that his company's stock price has fallen another seven percent since Tuesday. And that there's word on the Street that MKZ's desperate to raise cash."

"I'm a landscape designer," I told him. I understood now what Mara meant about Isley's attitude. "I don't know anything about the business side of Mr. Mackenzie's life. But I'd be happy to talk to you about his garden. What would you like to know?"

"How much did it cost? I think his shareholders would be interested in hearing that while their investment in MKZ is in free fall the CEO of the company has had no compunction about ramping up his extravagant lifestyle."

"Do you have any interest in the garden or the Open Day event? If not, I'm going to have to hang up."

"Wait, sorry, hold on. I do have a couple of questions I think you can help me with. But you're right—I'm not writing a piece just about the garden. I'm actually doing a feature profile of Graham Mackenzie. He's one of the wealthiest and most controversial residents in our area, and I think our readers would like to know more about who he is and what he's really like. Can you give me your impressions of him?"

I didn't trust Isley. It seemed clear to me from things he'd already let drop that his "profile" of Mackenzie was going to be a hatchet job. I'd realized by now, of course, that my client was having financial problems. In fact, I was pretty sure it was affecting his health. It made me furious to think how quickly the media had smelled trouble and started sniffing around for blood. Isley's tone and approach reminded me a lot of the relentless scrutiny my daughters and I had faced after Richard's disappearance. It was clear why Mackenzie had originally hesitated about agreeing to the Open Day. He knew perfectly well that the Jeff Isleys of the world were lying in wait. I also realized why he'd agreed to go ahead with it. *This Open Day business means a lot to you, I take it.* He'd done it for me, even though it could very well mean more trouble for him.

"He's a very generous human being," I told the reporter. "And he has a real passion for gardening—and garden preservation. In fact, I have to say he's one of the most knowledgeable clients I've ever worked with. I feel that this garden—which you really should make an effort to come out and see on Open Day—has been a true creative collaboration and, in many ways, Graham Mackenzie has been my inspiration."

"Wow," Isley said. "Do you have any idea how totally opposite your take on Mr. Mackenzie is to that of most people I've spoken to about him?"

"No, I don't. You asked for my opinion—and that's what I've given you."

"And I can quote you on that? That Mackenzie's been 'an inspiration' for you?" His tone was laced with sarcasm, and I knew I'd been right. He was determined to damage my client's reputation. I didn't care if mine was the only positive voice in Isley's entire article. In fact, I'd be proud of it.

"Absolutely. You can quote me as saying Graham Mackenzie's a very generous human being as well."

❦

I'd hoped after our initial tour—and Mackenzie's obvious enthusiasm for what I'd shown him—that he might make himself more available to me. But my creative collaborator remained behind closed doors during the final days leading up to the garden's opening. And I missed him. A good deal of the pleasure I'd taken in working for Mackenzie had to do with enjoying his company. As I oversaw the final touches—the outdoor lighting, the Tuscan terracotta urns planted with annuals and trailing vines—I felt let down. I'd hoped to be sharing all of this with him. And I kept turning over in my mind what Isley had said about the negative opinion others had of my client. How his stockholders might be upset to learn about the personal expenses he'd been racking up. I decided I owed it to Mackenzie to tell him about what the reporter was up to. A couple of days after my conversation with Isley, I told Eleanor I needed to speak with her boss. I'd tracked her down to the kitchen where she was making a pot of tea.

"He's not up to it," she told me bluntly. "He didn't even get out of bed this morning. Though it doesn't keep the man from working. I don't think anything can."

"I hope it's nothing serious," I said.

"He's having trouble keeping food down," Eleanor told me. "And he's getting these dizzy spells. It's the high blood pressure—and all this business pressure. He lives on that damned phone. I just wish he'd break down and see a real doctor."

"Real? In what way?"

"Mr. M's a big believer in natural medicine. Vitamins, herbal supplements. Red yeast rice extract for the cholesterol. That sort of thing. Which has been fine until now because he's mostly been as healthy as an ox. But since the market took a dive—and whatever else is going on—he's been one big walking complaint. I've been doing what I can about the stomach problems with diet. I thought these tisanes might help." Eleanor glanced down at the pot that was steeping on the counter. "But I'm beginning to think they're only making matters worse. And Mr. M won't listen to me."

"Do you want me to try? I know some good local physicians I could recommend. And I really do need to talk to him. I have to warn him about something."

Eleanor looked at me and frowned.

"More bad news is *not* what he needs right now. You got your way about the Open Day. I think you should just leave Mr. M alone until he can sort out some of these other problems and get back on his feet."

I was surprised by Eleanor's vehement tone and by the fact that she obviously counted me among her employer's long list of worries. It bothered me that she thought I'd pushed Mackenzie into agreeing to the Open Day event. I wanted to explain to her that it was an honor for him, not just for me. Anyone who knew about the prestige of the Garden Conservancy would understand that. But I decided to just let the matter drop. Eleanor was being overly protective of Mackenzie, I realized. She'd always struck me as more emotionally invested in her boss than perhaps was normal for an employee. I remember the pride she took in first showing me the house. Her thinly veiled dislike of his difficult ex-wife. The fierce way in which she guarded his privacy.

"Well, please let him know that I hope he feels better soon," I told her. "And that—if he's up to it—I'd really appreciate a moment of his time."

"Will do," Eleanor said, transferring the pot to a tray. But it was pretty clear she meant *will not.*

❦

"I hope you're planning to bring Danny with you tomorrow," I told Mara the morning before the grand unveiling. I'd stopped by the office to touch base with her on my way to the site. As I sorted through the stacks of mail and messages, I realized that things had started to pile up again. Among the dozens of "While You Were Out" slips, I saw that Sal Lombardi had finally returned my call. And Isley had phoned. Twice. I crumpled up the reporter's messages and tossed them into the wastebasket.

"Where?" Mara asked. I glanced over at her to make sure she was kidding. She returned my look with a blank stare.

"Oh, come on, Mara!" I said. "You know perfectly well what's happening tomorrow!" Though she'd apologized about her initial response to the Open Day news, in fact, she'd made it increasingly clear to me over the last few weeks that she considered my proudest professional moment nothing much more than a distraction. She continued to complain that I wasn't around enough. She objected so often to my using our regular Green Acres crew at Mackenzie's that I finally stopped asking for their help. Or hers. It really bothered me, though, that she couldn't see how important the event was for our future. I'd told her just the week before how it was going to do more good for our reputation than any amount of advertising or publicity.

"It's bound to bring in new business—and just the kind we want. Wealthy, top-tier clients who understand the value of the Garden Conservancy imprimatur."

"Oh, that's just great!" she'd said sarcastically. "We can't even take care of the ones we already have."

Now, however, she chose not to respond at all, turning her back to me as she swiveled around to her computer. Suddenly, I'd had enough of her attitude.

"Let me put this another way," I said as I walked to the door. "I *expect* you to be at Mackenzie's tomorrow to help with the tour. It's the perfect opportunity to meet potential new clients—and make a good impression. Feel free to bring Danny, if you like."

"Do you have any idea how much I already have to do around here?" she replied. "I was hoping to finally get to the accounts tomorrow. We're almost a month behind as it is."

"I'm sorry, but I think I've made myself clear," I said as I left. I didn't slam the door, but I didn't close it gently behind me either.

❧

I was scheduled to give Vera Yoland and Lisbeth Crocker, another regional representative, a walk-through of Mackenzie's gardens that afternoon. I warned Eleanor ahead of time that they'd be coming.

"I don't think Mr. Mackenzie would particularly like to run into them, so he might want to stay inside."

"Don't worry," she told me. "I don't think he'll be going out today."

"Oh, dear," I said, "is he still in bed? I hope he's going to feel well enough to participate tomorrow."

Eleanor gave me a hard look.

"I hope he's going to feel better, too. But I wouldn't get your hopes up—and I certainly wouldn't try to pressure him into it."

"Of course not," I told her, once again taken aback by her attitude toward me. Where was this coming from? Could it be Mara? Despite the long hours she was putting in at the office, I did occasionally see her and Danny visiting with Mackenzie's housekeeper. I knew Eleanor doted on Danny and that—for whatever reason—the two very different women appeared to have formed a close bond. I could easily imagine them sharing their mutual dislike of the Open Day event and what they both seemed to view as my unhelpful preoccupation with it.

Vera and Lisbeth, however, made me realize that my excitement was not at all misplaced. If anything, their enthusiasm for the garden rivaled my own.

"This is absolute heaven, Alice!" Vera exclaimed as I led the two women through the garden rooms. We'd stopped halfway down the corridor of lime trees and were looking out over the rooftops of Woodhaven and the rolling farmland beyond. From where we stood, we could see two male volunteers roping off a freshly mowed field at the base of the mountain. This was where the guests would park. The Conservancy had arranged for a couple of vans to transport attendees who couldn't make the long hike from the parking area up the steep driveway to the house. The three of us had spent the last hour discussing other logistics for the following day: the best place to set up the sign-in table, where to serve refreshments, how many volunteers they'd recruited and where I'd like to see them placed.

"Of course, most people will want to ask you their questions," Lisbeth said. "But we're expecting quite a crowd, so we will have experienced gardeners on the grounds who can pinch-hit."

"That's great," I said. "My assistant is quite knowledgeable, too."

"And will Mr. Mackenzie be putting in an appearance?" Vera asked.

"Well, I hope so . . . ," I said. Vera and Lisbeth exchanged a look. Vera seemed poised to say something more, but then hesitated. She pursed her lips and looked down. For a moment, a certain uneasiness hung in the air—a question, a doubt—but I chose to ignore it. Instead, I repeated in a somewhat forced upbeat tone: "I really hope so! But we'll just have to see. Mr. Mackenzie has so many demands on his time these days."

❧

The lights were on in the office when I got back, though it was nearly eight thirty. I felt a pang, remembering how I'd left things with Mara.

"You're still here?" I asked as I pushed open the door.

She looked up from her desk, which was cluttered with files and ledgers.

"We've got a problem," she said.

"What is it?"

"Nate called before. The bank stopped payment on our last check to him."

"That's strange."

"I've been looking up our account online. I know I should have been keeping a closer eye on all this, but I've just been so busy with other things."

She sounded so apologetic and upset, I felt bad. After tomorrow, I'd be able to take some of these responsibilities off her shoulders.

"We all make mistakes, Mara. We'll just issue him another—"

"No, we can't. We've exhausted our credit limit. That's why I didn't realize what was going on. But for the last week or so, the checks have been eating into our overdraft protection. Nate's was the first one over the line."

"But that's crazy. I deposited Mackenzie's last payment to us days ago. We should have tons of cash on hand."

"That's just it. I've been getting e-alerts from the bank, but I thought they were routine, so I didn't bother to open them."

"E-alerts? About what?"

"Mackenzie's check," Mara told me. "It bounced."

Part Two

that

11

$\mathcal{I}$ didn't sleep very well ..at night. I knew there had to be a good explanation for Mackenzie's check not clearing, but the slipup was still pretty unsettling. I'd spent thousands of dollars recently on my client's behalf—more, much more, than I could possibly cover on my own. Most of my regular suppliers had offered me extended payables schedules, but I would need Mackenzie's money very soon to satisfy all the bills that were coming due. I kept waking up and going over the situation. There couldn't be any doubt that Mackenzie was good for the money. Jeff Isley had mentioned a cash crunch at MKZEnergy. That's all this was, I decided. The man was worth many millions of dollars, I reminded myself as I finally started to drift off to sleep again. . . .

I had a confused and fragmented dream about Tom Deaver. We were alone together in some great forest, and we kept trying to reach for each other through the undergrowth and tree branches, but our outstretched hands never quite joined. But, oh, how I longed to touch him! How I yearned to feel his strong arms around me, comforting and reassuring me that everything was going to be all right.

I woke up with a start. It was still dark at six thirty. But at this time of the year, the sun should have risen about an hour ago. I got out of bed and pulled back the curtains. My backyard—the garden, the hemlocks, the path leading out to the barn—all seemed to have disappeared! My own reflection stared back at me from the whited-out window. It took me a disoriented moment or two to realize that the morning was socked in with fog. I listened to the radio while I hurriedly showered and dressed. The inversion, most prominent in low-lying areas, was supposed to burn off by midmorning.

I realized that driving was going to be dicey, but I wanted to be up at the site by eight o'clock since Damon Fagels had told me he planned to install the wrought-iron railing around the waterfall about that time. Ever since Nate had pointed out the danger posed by the drop-off, I'd been obsessed about getting some kind of protective barrier up in time for the Open Day. Of my long list of concerns about the event, this one had worked its way to the top. I'd actually had a dream a few nights back that I was falling from that very spot—and I'd woken up in a panic, my heart pounding. Now, as I started to drive through the heavy mist, I felt a similar sort of anxiety set in. The fog made the most familiar structures—the stand of spruces at the bottom of my drive, the outlines of the Cabots' farmhouse—seem misshapen and somehow ominous. Visibility improved slightly as I made my way through town and then up Mackenzie's driveway. Though the mountain was still shrouded when I reached the top, I could make out Damon's van parked in front of the garages, and I heard the sound of hammering—metal on metal—coming from below as I got out of my car.

The gardens were eerily beautiful that morning—otherworldly, dreamlike. But because I couldn't seem to shake the sense of dread that had settled over me, there was something a little nightmarish about the stone wall that suddenly loomed into sight—and the slippery feel of the railing as I moved warily down the steps. Everywhere, too, was the sound of invisible water: dripping, flowing, splashing. The fog thickened the farther down I went. I followed the muffled sound of voices and hammering, shuffling along the balustrade to the final short flight of steps that led to the waterfall garden.

". . . do you think I should do?" I heard Nate say. I hadn't expected him to be at the site, too, and for a moment I was pleasantly surprised, assuming he'd volunteered to help.

"Well, if it was me, I'd call her on it right away," Damon said. "I can't begin to guess how much she'll be clearing out of all this. And to think of the way we both busted our balls to get things done! But why would she jerk you around like that? It just doesn't make—"

"Hello, there!" I called out. The two men slowly took shape as I moved toward them through the murk. They were gripping a wrought-iron frieze of birds and butterflies that curved around the promontory. They stood on either side of the channel of water that rushed between. The stream flowed through the middle posts of the frieze and disappeared over the mountainside.

"Alice," Damon said, his tone suddenly subdued.

"Oh, Damon, that's just beautiful!" I said, coming up to him and reaching out to touch the railing.

"No, don't!" he cried. "The cement's not set yet."

"Sorry," I said, taking a step back. I realized now that the two of them were holding the railing in place. Though I couldn't see their faces that clearly, I could sense their unhappiness. "Listen, Nate," I said, turning to him, "Mara told me about your call last night. We're going to sort this thing out. There's nothing to worry about."

"There better not be," Nate said. "I mean, if you or Mr. Mac-kenzie had any problem with the quality of my work, I'd expect you to say something. But stiffing me like this is really—"

"It was a *mistake*, Nate," I said. "You've done an amazing job. Both of you have. And you'll see later that I've included your names, numbers, and Web sites in the brochure that's going to be handed out during the tour."

"That's very nice," Nate said. "But what I need right now is to get *paid*, okay? I can't tell you how many other jobs I've blown off over the past two months to get this work finished for you. In fact, this is all I've been doing most of the spring and summer so far. I've been waiting on that check to pay my fucking mortgage, Alice! This is no joke. I need that money to survive."

"And you're going to get it!" I told him, trying to keep my tone upbeat and unconcerned. But I could feel the morning closing in around me—heavy and claustrophobic, like the fog itself. I needed to talk to Mackenzie, I realized. And I had to get to him right away—before Eleanor arrived for work at nine. Expressing my thanks again for everything they'd done, I left Nate and Damon to finish the installation and headed back up through the gardens. A hazy orb of sun swam overhead, and I could feel the heat of the day starting to radiate through the mist. As I climbed the last flight of steps to the sundial garden, the house suddenly emerged through the drifting fog: enormous, gleaming, substantial as an ocean liner. Now I could make out the garage banks rising up the hill behind the house, and beyond that the horse stables and corral, tennis courts and helipad. The sight of all this—solid proof of Macken-zie's tremendous wealth—lifted my spirits. His bad check had to have just been the result of careless bookkeeping, understandable when you considered how much else he had on his mind.

Still, I was happy to see that Eleanor's car was not yet parked in its usual spot. I quietly climbed the stairs leading up to the side deck. From there, I could see the mist rising in columns above the town and valley, and though the gardens below were still blanketed, I knew that as soon as the sun cleared the tree line the fog would start to burn off. The gardens should be perfectly visible by the time they were opened to the public at ten.

One of the sliding glass doors to the great room stood halfway open. A curtain fluttered against my face as I stepped inside. The enormous space was dim and cool and still. Though I'd been in the house many times over the last few months, I'd rarely had an opportunity to venture much beyond the kitchen area. I had no idea where Mackenzie slept or where I might find him at that time of day. But I decided my best bet was to check his office, which I knew lay at the end of the corridor to my left. I was halfway down the hallway when I heard Eleanor's voice: "What do you think you're doing?"

I froze.

"What's it to you?" Gwen said. Their voices were coming from a room not five feet up the hall to my left.

"Does he know you're here?"

"Mind your own business."

"It's my business to look after that man."

"And you think I'm harming him somehow? I'm getting sick and tired of you treating me like I'm up to no good."

"Oh, I know what you're up to."

"Listen, Eleanor, what I'm giving Graham is a whole lot better for him than all those tinctures and infusions and whatever you keep pushing on him."

"You're a leech. Just like all the rest of them."

"Who the hell do you think you are? You're the maid, for chrissakes! You're the chief cook and bottle washer. And if you think

Graham's going to be happy when he learns that you've been talking to me this way, you'd better think again."

"He's not well. He's under a tremendous amount of strain. And you're not helping matters by barging in here at all hours of the night. You're right—I am the maid. I make the beds. I wash the sheets. So I have a pretty good idea what you've been doing."

"Oh, give me a break, Eleanor! Graham and I are two consenting adults. We're simply enjoying each other's company."

"Where is he, then? And how did you get in here? Why are you going through his things?"

"I'm just looking for—but why the hell do I have to explain myself to you?" I heard something being dropped—or tossed—and then footsteps. I flattened myself against the wall as Gwen walked out of the room, down the hall away from me, and out the front door.

Eleanor was always so self-possessed that it actually took me a moment or two to make sense of the odd, strangled sound coming from the room nearby. But when I did, it was with a mixture of embarrassment and pity. She was the kind of woman who took pride in being in control. For someone like Eleanor, crying wasn't a form of release—it was an admission of failure.

❦

She didn't see me when she left the room a minute or two later. I retraced my steps to the deck and took it around the front of the house to the kitchen entrance on the other side. By the time I slid the door open and called, "Good morning!" Eleanor was already at work and seemingly composed.

"Hello," she said, pulling an apron on over her uniform.

"I didn't hear you drive in."

"I left my car down in the parking area and walked up," she

said, as she began to rinse some dishes in the sink. "Figured you might need some extra spaces up here. Lord, that was a climb, though."

"Thanks, Eleanor," I told her. "For coming early and helping out. I know how you feel about all this and I'm sorry. I know you have a lot on your mind, and so does Mr. Mackenzie. But I found out last night that the second half of his payment to me—a very large check—didn't clear. My own checks have started to bounce because of it, so you can understand how upset I am. I *have* to talk to him, Eleanor. Now. Before all this starts."

"I came in early to talk to him, too," she said, picking up a wineglass and starting to dry it. "You're not the only one with problems. You're not the only one who's upset. But he's not in his bedroom. And he's not in the office. I don't know where he is."

"Listen, I have to ask him—," I began to say just as the doorbell chimed. Eleanor threw down her dish towel and walked out of the room to answer it. I heard the distinctive voice of Vera Yoland in the foyer, and I realized there was very little chance that I would be able to resolve my financial situation with Mackenzie before the Open Day event began.

12

It turned into a beautiful day. The evaporating early-morning mist left a sheen on the gardens, making everything look fresh and inviting. The moist surfaces helped to highlight the mastery of Nate's stonework—the grays and mossy greens of the ten-foot retaining wall behind the climbing roses looked particularly striking—and added a shimmer to Damon's magical wrought-iron creations. Vera and Lisbeth manned the sign-in table that we'd set up on the portico in front of the house. The plan was for them to direct visitors to start the tour in the sundial terrace, which was where I'd decided to take up my position; from there I could see and point out the salient features of most of the other garden rooms.

Mara asked if she and Danny could cover the Buddhist grove. I assumed she wanted to be there because it was the farthest away from the center of activity—and other people. It was nice to see Danny again, though he ran right past me to Eleanor, who was helping to set up refreshments on the deck, and gave her a big hug. By nine forty-five all the other volunteers had arrived and had taken up stations around the gardens. At ten o'clock sharp, two of the white vans the Garden Conservancy had leased for the day crested the top of the driveway and pulled up in front of the house.

Within minutes I was greeting guests, fielding questions, accepting compliments, and, as discreetly as possible, handing out my card. Most people who attend Open Day events have a serious interest in gardening and are eager to talk about their own gardens and share their experiences. Fairly early on, the sundial terrace grew so jammed with visitors who wanted a few minutes of my time that Vera came down, clapped her hands, and announced, "We've gardening experts all around the property, so please let's not congregate in one place!"

I kept looking around for Mackenzie and thought I spotted him about an hour into the event, dressed in summer whites and surrounded by guests, on the lime tree colonnade. I waved, but I don't think he saw me. Sal Lombardi and his plump, vivacious wife, Gigi, came through.

"This is just fabulous!" Gigi cried, enfolding me in her warm, perfumed embrace. "I'm overwhelmed with garden envy! But I'm so thrilled for you, Alice! This is your moment."

"Everything good?" Sal asked, leaning in as he shook my hand. Balding and linebacker broad, he had a weather-beaten face and a reputation for being a cutthroat venture capitalist. But he'd always been protective of and thoughtful toward me, especially after he learned about Richard's disappearance and my subsequent struggles.

"I couldn't be more thrilled," I said, and in fact, at that moment, it was true. My earlier fears and money worries seemed to have burned away with the rising temperatures and clearing views—and I felt buoyed by all the praise and the growing crowds.

"We need to talk," he said. "Give me a call on Monday."

I saw Mackenzie's ex-wife, Chloe, pull up in an open convertible, despite the fact that the volunteers below had been expressly instructed not to allow any cars up the driveway. I could all too easily imagine how *that* conversation had gone. It wasn't until Chloe got out of the car and was crossing the parking area to the front door that I saw her son, Lachlan, was with her. Had he been lying down in the backseat of the car? Asleep, perhaps? With his stubble of beard and untucked shirt, he looked particularly unkempt.

"Wait! You can't go in there!" Lisbeth said, jumping up and blocking the way when Chloe swept past the sign-in table. "Only the gardens are open to the public."

"We're not *the public*," Chloe announced before leaning over and whispering something in Lisbeth's ear. Whatever it was, Lisbeth shrank back, giving Chloe room to push around her and through the front door. Lachlan sauntered past the sign-in table without a word and followed his mother into the house.

"Well!" I heard Lisbeth say to Vera as she took her seat again. Both women were wearing wide summer hats decorated with flowers, and for a moment their heavily bedecked brims formed a single spray as they conferred. These Open Day events seemed to inspire the wearing of decorative headgear—fanciful floral affairs for the women, boaters and Borsalinos for the men. And because Gwen loved wearing hats, I was sure I kept seeing her in the crowd as well. Standing under the weeping cherries in a sheer pink dress and matching cloche . . . or was that her climbing the steps to the birch grove sporting a wide-brimmed straw sun hat and tiger-striped Capris? She would drift out of view as my attention became diverted by new visitors and fresh questions, but Gwen's presence in the garden—and in Mackenzie's bedroom earlier—continued to circle in the back of my mind.

There was no question any longer that she and Mackenzie had

embarked on some kind of an affair. Eleanor had accused her of "barging in here at all hours of the night." And Gwen herself had proudly claimed that she was "doing him a lot more good" than Eleanor's natural remedies, and that she and Mackenzie were "simply enjoying each other's company." Which, if Mackenzie hadn't been ill and in the middle of a financial crisis, I might have been able to take more at face value. But the last time I'd seen my client, he seemed so sapped of vigor and in such physical discomfort that it was difficult to imagine him sexually active—especially with someone of Gwen's high-octane disposition. Perhaps it was because they both seemed intent on hiding their relationship from me, but I found myself wondering if something *else* was going on.

But what exactly? Maybe they were actually coming to care about each other, and all they wanted was a little privacy. Though it seemed several lifetimes ago now, I could still remember what it felt like when I first fell in love with Richard. How the desire to be alone with him became an almost physical requirement—my body aching until I could be held in his arms again. Just being in his presence made me feel more deeply alive than I'd ever been before. How wonderful it would be, I thought, if Gwen had found her match at last—and Graham Mackenzie had given himself over to the smart, fun-loving, and generous person I knew my best friend to be.

Much later it struck me, how I'd been thinking about love—and the dream I'd had the night before—when I saw Tom Deaver walking down the steps toward me. He was wearing a blue-and-white-striped shirt and chinos. His shirtsleeves were rolled up to his elbows, exposing deeply tanned and well-muscled forearms. He smiled when he saw me. It was a down-turning, tentative grin that melted away any residual resentment I might have been harboring from his outburst several weeks back.

"Hey, Alice," he said, coming up to me.

"I'm kind of surprised to see you here," I told him. "I mean, how can you in good conscience allow yourself to step onto the property of someone who destroys the land for a living?"

"Oh, please," he said, shaking his head and looking away, "I can be such an incredibly pompous ass sometimes! I came to apologize. But now that I'm here—I have to say, I'm just totally blown away by what you've done."

"Thank you," I said, feeling myself flush with pleasure. Of all the compliments I'd received that morning, his gave me the greatest boost, and I was momentarily lost in the intensity of his gaze. His eyes were green flecked with gold, a kaleidoscope of shifting depths and eddies. I'd managed to put him out of my mind over the past month or so, but seeing him again made me realize that—despite our differences—I was still very drawn to him.

"No, really," he said. "I think these are the most beautiful gardens I've ever seen." His gaze was saying other things as well, it seemed to me. Or was I just wishing it to be so? I found myself having a hard time looking away. It occurred to me that it couldn't have been easy for him to come that morning. Despite the bitter exchange he'd had with Mackenzie and the implosion of his Wind Power Initiative, he'd still managed to overcome his pride and put his anger on hold. Had he really done it because of me? Something unsaid—and perhaps unsayable—hung between us. The silence was starting to lengthen uncomfortably.

"Have you visited here before?" I asked finally.

"No," he said. "Not unless you count hiking on the mountain when it was still undeveloped. Even then, these were the most spectacular views in the county."

"I'd be happy to show you around later—," I began to say just as someone tapped me on the shoulder.

"You're the landscape designer?" an elderly woman asked. She was accompanied by a friend about her own age, and they were both clutching copies of the Open Days catalog. She pointed to a shaded area nearby. "I wanted to ask you what the dark reddish brown plant is over there under the buddleias."

"It's chocolate heuchera," I said.

"You mean coral bells? No, I don't think so," she told me. "I've never seen that variety before. I was just saying to Lily that it must be a—"

"I'll catch you later," Tom said with a smile as the woman continued to tell me my business. I run into this a lot. Gardening enthusiasts often turned into zealots who, like baseball fanatics or wine collectors, prided themselves on an encyclopedic grasp of their beloved subject's minutiae. I watched Tom out of the corner of my eye as he worked his way across the terrace, stopping from time to time to say hello to the many people he seemed to know, and I felt a surge of anticipation. *I'll catch you later.* I wasn't sure whether he meant it literally and intended to stay around for my guided tour—or not—but I knew that something had been righted between us.

❧

It was nearly noon when I decided I needed to take a break and grab a glass of the lemonade Eleanor had set out for visitors on the deck. But when I got to the table I saw that the several large glass pitchers were empty. A couple of ice chips floated in a half inch of water at the bottom of the insulated bucket. It was hot now, and I could tell that the guests who were milling around on the deck were hoping for something cool to drink. I picked up the empty pitchers and made my way around to the kitchen entrance. The inner glass door was open, and I could see and hear into the kitchen area through the screen.

". . . that's all I'm asking for," Eleanor was saying. She was facing Chloe across the butcher block island. Lachlan was sitting at the table, scrolling through his cell phone messages.

"Not my problem," Chloe said. "And what in the world makes you think I have any influence over what Graham does anyway?"

"I'm—I'm desperate," Eleanor said. "I'm asking you—no, I'm begging you. My son put his life savings into MKZEnergy because of what Mr. M said. And everything I have—*everything*—is tied up in that company."

"Well, welcome to Mackenzie World," Chloe told her. "I can't believe you were naive enough to accept Graham's claims without checking into them first. He's a salesman, for heaven's sake! And unfortunately, he's the kind who tends to believe his own sales pitches."

"But what am I going to do? What can I tell my son?"

"Tough luck?" Chloe said. "I don't mean to sound callous, Eleanor, but how do you expect me to help you at this point? Everyone knows it's buyer beware when it comes to investing. I've got enough money troubles of my own right now—plus I have Lachie to worry about."

"But he promised me—"

"Oh, spare me! I have no idea what Graham might have promised you—he promises the world to everyone he meets. Now where the hell is he? He made us come all the way up here for this goddamned boondoggle. You'd think he could somehow manage to put in an appearance."

I backed away from the screen door, still clutching the pitchers. I didn't want to think about what I'd just overheard. *It wasn't meant for my ears,* I told myself. *It has nothing to do with me.* I felt my mental focus narrow, blocking out Chloe's words. I had things I had to attend to. Thirsty visitors. I was halfway aware that I was operating on a kind of automatic pilot. I just knew I had to keep moving. There was a spigot at the bottom of the steps just beneath the deck, and I decided that I would fill up the pitchers with cold water from the tap. I was halfway down the side steps when I heard raised voices on the hillside below me.

Then I heard a scream. A long, high, piercing scream. And then another. I hurried back up the steps and over to the railing. A group of people was clustered at the edge of the waterfall terrace, looking down.

"Call 911!" I heard someone cry. The kitchen door slammed behind me.

"What's going on?" Chloe asked as Eleanor and Lachlan followed her out onto the deck. I didn't bother to answer.

I ran. Hoping it was nothing. A slip. A turned ankle. *Please don't let it be anything serious,* I prayed. A crowd had gathered at the overlook by the time I reached the terrace.

"What happened?" I asked, pushing my way to the front. There was a group of people below, clustered around something white on the ground. I saw Tom running down the stone steps that Nate had so recently rebuilt.

"Okay, the paramedics are coming," he said. "They told me not to move him. Back up and give him some air."

It wasn't until a couple of people had edged away as Tom suggested that I saw who it was. He was flat on his back. His right arm was flung over his face, but there was no mistaking the silvery hair. Tom knelt beside him and gently pulled his wrist between his own fingers, feeling for his pulse.

"Hold on," I thought I heard him tell Mackenzie. "Just hold on now."

13

❧

$\mathcal{B}$y the time the ambulance arrived, the terrace was jammed with onlookers.

"Who is he?"

"What happened?"

"Someone said it's the owner."

"I heard he just collapsed."

"It's the heat."

"It's a heart attack."

"Move back, people!" an EMS worker cried, pushing through the crowd as two others ran behind him with a stretcher. I stood by the waterfall, clutching the wrought-iron railing, and watched as the paramedics rushed down the steps and over to the group surrounding Mackenzie. I saw that Chloe and Lachlan had joined them. They both seemed remarkably composed. Chloe stood off to the side, arms crossed, looking on silently as the paramedics crouched around her ex-husband. It was hard for me to see what they were doing, although one seemed to be administering CPR. I saw Lachlan approach Tom, who had moved away from Mackenzie when the paramedics arrived. They exchanged a word or two, with Tom nodding in agreement to something Lachlan said.

My eyes welled up with tears as the EMS workers lifted the stretcher bearing my client and started the cautious climb up the stone steps. Though Mackenzie was strapped down, the workers were obviously trying hard to keep the stretcher level. I could see them straining under the weight, the sweat pouring down their faces. Chloe, Lachlan, Tom, and the rest of the small group followed behind. It looked all too much like a funeral procession to me, and I felt a chill run through my body.

"Tom!" I called, hurrying over to him. "How is he? What happened?"

"I don't know," he said. "But it could very well be a heart attack. I'm going to drive the wife and son to the hospital. They don't know the way."

"That's kind of you," I said. But I wasn't surprised that he'd volunteered to help. He seemed to me the sort of person you could count on in a crisis. And one who would know the right thing to do.

"Do you think we should call things off here?" I asked him.

"I'm not sure, Alice . . . ," he said, but then I think he realized that I was at a real loss. "But if it was up to me? Yes, I think I would. He might—I'm afraid he might be in pretty bad shape."

"But he was breathing, right?" I asked. "You could feel his pulse?"

"I think so. But I'm not a doctor. Listen," he said, touching my arm. "I'll let you know if I learn anything more, okay?"

"Thanks," I said. My heart ached as I watched him follow the paramedics. What a disaster! For Mackenzie. For the Open Day. And, yes, also for me. My problems seemed to be coming to a head. What was I going to tell my employees and suppliers now? As I walked up through the sunlit gardens to find Vera, I felt sick with worry. And guilt, too. All I could think about were my own concerns while Mackenzie's life could be hanging in the balance.

"Oh, what a shame!" Vera said when I told her that I thought we should cancel the event. "We're having such a wonderful turnout. I think we might actually be setting a record." She turned and looked down at the many people who were still wandering through the garden rooms. The hush that had fallen over the crowd when the EMS team arrived had lifted now. Most of the guests didn't seem to realize that it was Mackenzie who'd been taken away in the ambulance. I heard someone roar with laughter.

"I'm sorry," I told her, "but I don't think we have any choice. I very much hope Mr. Mackenzie will recover quickly. And then we could reschedule later in the summer."

"I'm afraid not," Vera said. "The rest of the season is writ in stone at this point. What a pity, Alice. You've really done a superior job here. Oh, well. But I think you're probably right; best not to appear insensitive. Lisbeth and I will tell the volunteers to start asking the guests to leave."

"Thank you," I said. We'd been talking in the driveway. As I watched her walk back to the sign-in table I heard a crunch in the gravel behind me.

"You're Alice Hyatt, right?" Though he sounded familiar, when I turned around I didn't recognize the middle-aged man standing there. He had a bushy salt-and-pepper mustache and a big stomach. It took me a few seconds to place the voice.

"Jeff Isley? The *Herald*?" I said.

"That's right. I'm grateful you told me about this," he said, taking in the gardens and views. "It's pretty incredible. Any chance you could spare a few minutes? I've been trying to get hold of you for days."

"Yes, I know," I said.

Isley shook his head. "Look," he said, "I'm just trying to figure out why you'd want to go to bat for someone like Mackenzie. You know he's going to end up screwing you just like everybody else."

"That's none of your business," I said. "And now, if—" I was about to tell him to get lost when I saw Mara hurrying along the driveway toward me with Danny in tow.

"Is it true?" she cried as she came up to us.

"I was about to come find you," I said. "We're telling everyone to leave."

"Oh, God!" Mara said. Her face was drained of color. "Is he dead?"

"What's going on?" Isley asked.

"Come into the house with me," I told Mara, turning my back on the reporter. "Let's find Eleanor."

🍎

I could hear Sal Lombardi's voice in the living room when we came into the entrance hall. I started down the corridor in that direction, but Mara didn't follow me.

"We'll see you in the kitchen," she said, taking her son's hand and heading the other way.

"Okay," I told her.

Sal, Gigi, and another couple I recognized as Mackenzie's wealthy neighbors down the mountain were sitting on the leather sectionals in front of the wall of windows.

"Hello, Alice," Gigi said as I approached. "Eleanor invited us in after the ambulance left. We were all just wandering around in total shock! God, what a horrible thing to happen to you on your big day."

"Any word on how he is?" I asked. I supposed it was Eleanor who had served them the glasses of wine they were drinking.

"Not yet," Sal said. "You look like you could use a drink. Do you want one?"

"Thanks, but no," I said. I realized it was probably inappropriate for me to ask one client about another client's finances, but I couldn't help myself. I had to know. "Listen, is it true that Mr. Mackenzie's business is in real trouble? There's a reporter here from the *Herald* who's been hounding me about a story's he doing on it."

"Just like every other business reporter in the world," Sal said. "It's that jerk Isley, right? Does he know about Graham?"

"I think he does now."

"Well, there goes the rest of my investment."

"Honestly, Sally," Gigi said, "you make it sound like all you care about is money."

"Isn't that why you married me?" Sal said with a laugh. But he wasn't smiling when he turned to me. "The answer to your question, Alice, I'm sorry to say, is yes. MKZ's a house of cards at this point. It's collapsing as we speak."

"And once the market hears Graham's in the hospital," the other man added, "I bet those shares are really going to tumble."

"Not that they have all that much further to go," Sal said. "Damn Mackenzie! He brought this on himself. I just hope the bastard gets a chance to learn from his mistakes."

I left them to their drinks. Mackenzie's drinks, really. But who was I to begrudge them a little solace? No, what stuck in my craw was the fact that Sal, who seemed to have taken a beating in some deal with Mackenzie, could talk about it so calmly. He could even laugh! Unlike me, Sal had money to burn. Sal was a savvy investor who had no doubt evaluated the risk factors inherent in doing business with Mackenzie. Unlike me.

❧

Mara and Danny were sitting at the kitchen table. Eleanor was on the phone.

"... but that's all I know. .... Well, go ahead and call the hospital, then. .... No, I certainly will not!"

Eleanor hung up with a bang and said to Mara, "What nerve! I can't believe that woman—" She must have seen Mara looking past her to me as I came through the doorway. Eleanor stopped herself and turned around. Her eyes were bloodshot and her lips puffy from crying.

"Have you heard anything?" I asked Eleanor.

"No," she said. She walked over and sat down beside Mara, who lifted Danny onto her lap.

"Hey there, big boy," Eleanor said, kissing the top of Danny's head. Her cheeks were wet with tears.

"What did Mr. Lombardi say?" Mara asked. Her face was splotchy, as though she, too, had been crying. Which seemed odd to me. As far as I knew, Mara didn't particularly care for Mackenzie; I wasn't certain she'd ever actually *met* him. And yet she'd seemed terribly distraught—in fact more emotional than I'd ever seen her—when she first came up to me and Isley on the driveway. Perhaps, like me, she was worried about how we were going to deal with the bad check if Mackenzie was seriously ill.

"They were talking mostly about MKZ," I said, sitting down across from Mara. "How the stock's in free fall. And apparently the news about Mackenzie is only going to make matters worse."

"And Mr. M told me this was the time to buy," Eleanor said, shaking her head. "He told me that he shouldn't really be giving me a tip like that, because some people might think it was insider trading, but that MKZ had never been better priced. And that big things were going to be happening at the company."

"When was this?" I asked her.

"The beginning of the year."

"And you invested a lot?" Though I already knew the answer, I didn't want her to realize that I'd been listening in on her conversation with Chloe earlier.

"Yes, but the thing is—" Eleanor took a deep breath and continued. "I told my son, Derek, about it. I was so proud that I could share something so important with him. I wanted him to know I wasn't just Mr. M's housekeeper—that he really valued me. Derek didn't tell me until yesterday—when he first realized the stock price was sinking—that he cashed in his 401(k) so he could get in on the deal. And he's got a young family to support."

We sat there in silence for a moment. Then Eleanor said: "I just can't believe Mr. M would let this happen to me! I know he'll do something to help when he hears how much I lost."

"I'm sure he will," I said. I was counting on the same kind of miracle from him.

"Because, you know, he really is a *good* person," Eleanor went on. "He's always been so generous to me. He put me on full benefits right away. He always gave me a nice holiday bonus. And I always felt he appreciated who I was and what I did for him. I felt he cared. No, I *know* he did. People just can't fake that sort of thing."

I wasn't about to tell her, but I knew all too well that people could.

14

*S*al stopped by the kitchen on his way out to say good-bye.

"You'll call me when you get word—right, Eleanor?"

"Of course, Mr. Lombardi."

After we heard the visitors leave, Eleanor got up from her chair with a sigh.

"I guess I should get some lunch on the table," she said to Mara. "Do you and Danny want to stay?"

"Sure," Mara said. I hadn't been invited, but I was too upset and nervous to sit still anyway.

"I need to get back to the office," I said. I knew I had to keep moving and working—anything to keep from dwelling on the situation. But it was painful to drive along the top of the gardens on my way out. Had it really been only a little over four months since I'd first seen these half dozen sloping acres? I'd invested so much time, energy, and imagination into them! And so much hope. The Open Day had come to seem the ultimate proof of my worth, not just as a landscape designer but as a person. Where did that leave me now?

When I got back to the office, I decided to spend the rest of the afternoon sorting through the accounts. Once I got a better grip on what we actually owed, I was certain I'd feel less panicked. Green Acres was a solid, going concern, I told myself. I wasn't about to let one bad account—no matter how big—undermine that. I'd forgotten, though, that Mara had upgraded and moved the accounting software to her computer. And I didn't realize until I tried to log in at my own computer that I could no longer access the books from there.

I moved across the room to Mara's desk and sat down. Because she'd arranged her area so that the back of her terminal faced me, I rarely had the opportunity to see her screen. It was filled now with a montage of photos. Family photos, I assumed, because there was Danny and a young woman, around Mara's age, who looked a lot like her except that she was smiling in almost every frame. And there was a shot of a good-looking man in his late twenties and an older man standing in front of a ranch-style house flanked by willow trees. It cheered me to think that Mara and Danny were part of a larger family, even if Mara never alluded to it.

I was able to find the accounting software easily enough, but it was password protected. I tried numerous name and number combinations until I finally hit on "Danny829"—I knew his birthday was coming up at the end of August—and found myself looking at an unfamiliar accounting setup. I wandered around in the system, clicking on different tabs, trying to locate the most current receivables statement, and feeling increasingly frustrated. I was relieved to look up and see Mara and Danny coming down the path to the office. But that feeling didn't last long.

"What's going on?" Mara cried when she saw me at her desk. "What the hell are you doing?"

"I was just trying to look at the accounts," I told her. I could tell she was incensed, but I was pretty angry, too. I got up from the desk. "Don't yell at me like that. This is *my* office."

"I thought I could count on a little privacy around here," Mara said, softening her tone. I sensed she was making a concerted effort to get her feelings under control. She turned back to her son and said, "It's okay, sweetie. Why don't you run out to the garden and see if you can find some more of those caterpillars? You know where to find their special house, right?"

Danny looked from Mara to me. It must have been a pretty unsettling day for him.

"I hear they sometimes turn into butterflies," I told him.

"Yes," he said, nodding. That seemed to reassure him, and he left, the door slamming behind him. Mara and I took a moment to watch him make his way across the lawn to the old greenhouse and then reemerge a moment later carrying a big plastic jug.

"Sorry," Mara said, walking past me to her desk and sinking into the chair. She ran her hands through her hair. "Listen—I'm just really stressed about what happened."

"I can tell," I said. "Are you okay? You look exhausted."

"I am," she said. "I'm living with a three-year-old. I've been putting in ten-hour workdays. And now I'm scared shitless my job's going to go up in smoke."

"Don't worry," I told her. "I know we'll be able to work this out. I think Eleanor's right: Mackenzie would never leave us in the lurch. He may be tough, but I think he's loyal. I think he takes care of his own."

"You think?" she said sarcastically. "The truth is you didn't really know a damned thing about him when you took this job on."

"Please, there's no point in arguing," I told her. "We really need to work together right now. For starters, could you please print out the latest statements for me? Then maybe we can sit down and try to figure out how we're going to manage."

❦

It was worse than I'd thought. Convinced that Mackenzie's second and final payment was covering me, I'd spent freely with several firms I'd never worked with before and whose terms were more rigid than those of my regular suppliers. Invoices from a nursery in Oregon, a high-end garden furniture company in North Carolina, and a rose grower in Ontario were all overdue. Bills were also starting to come in from local vendors. These were the very garden centers and nurseries I needed to be on good terms with if I hoped to stay in business. And I didn't have the money to pay any of them.

"Maybe we could try to speed up our receivables?" I asked Mara, running my eye over the list of our regular customers. There were a few who occasionally required past-due notices, but in general our clients kept pretty current.

"How? By billing ahead?" Mara asked. "I don't see how we can do that without setting off alarms."

"You're right," I said. "I was just thinking out loud. The last thing we want is for word to get out that we're in trouble."

"That might already be happening," Mara said. "Damon kind of cornered me this morning. He asked me if he could get paid in cash for the waterfall railing."

"Did he say why?"

"No—and I didn't ask. I didn't commit, of course. I told him I'd have to talk to you about it first."

"Thanks. But you're right: he knows what happened. Nate told him about the bounced check. I guess there's no way we're going to be able to contain this thing. We need to get cash flowing again—fast."

"Don't worry about paying me for now," Mara said.

"That's ridiculous. Of course I'm going to—"

"No, you've been really generous with all the overtime this summer. Danny and I are good for now."

"That's kind of you, Mara, but I'll find a way to pay you."

"I'm not being kind, just realistic. We've got to pay the crew first. We lose them, and we're really sunk."

❦

Mara and Danny left about an hour later. We hadn't solved anything, but at least I now understood the extent of the problem. And it was daunting. Green Acres had been wrung dry in terms of money—and at the worst possible moment. Mackenzie had to come through, or I was going to have to start liquidating my retirement fund. Or consider mortgaging the house. Which would not only break my heart but put at risk a promise I'd made to my father years ago.

❦

"You know, your great-grandfather built this place," he'd told me the summer before he died. That was the year my dad started repeating himself and living more and more in the past. I'd heard the story many times before about how dapper Walter Childs, a New York City lawyer, broke a leg during a fishing trip in the summer of 1901, and was laid up in the rural backwater of Woodhaven for a few weeks. He stayed in a boardinghouse run by my soon-to-be great-grandmother's family and quickly fell in love with the young woman who helped take care of him. After they married that Christmas, Walter took her back to the city to live, but soon discovered that his new wife yearned for the wooded hills of her childhood. So Walter built her the eyebrow Colonial farmhouse not far from the Heron River site of his accident. The family spent

every summer there for the rest of their lives. Just as his eldest son—my grandfather—and his family did after him.

"One of my first memories was selling raspberries out there by the roadside," my father told me—again, hardly for the first time. "Summer of '38. Nobody had any money. My father had lost his job in the crash and we'd moved up here from the city. The bank was trying to foreclose on the house, but my mother and father were determined to keep that from happening. There was my mother, who'd been born wealthy, with maids and chauffeurs in New York City, putting up jam! My father grew vegetables. And all of us kids did our bit, helping out in the garden and running that fruit stand."

"I know, Dad," I told him, only half listening.

"No, you don't!" he said, his voice rising. "You have no idea what it was like! You'll probably never know what it feels like to be in danger of losing everything you have! But if you do, Alice, you've got to promise me something."

The doctor had told us that it wasn't good for my father to become upset. And I'd been spending a lot of time that summer trying to deal with these sudden outbursts.

"Of course, Daddy, I'll do whatever you say," I told him.

"No, I mean it, Alice," he said, his voice suddenly forceful and clear. He looked me in the eye. "I'm going to leave this place to you when I die because you're my only child, but it really belongs to our family. To those who came before—and those who'll be coming after. Promise me you'll never let it go, okay?"

I was married then. To a wealthy, successful man. We owned a big Cape Cod in Westchester and a vacation condo on Sanibel Island in Florida. The idea of needing to sell the old family farmhouse in the Berkshires seemed far-fetched, to say the least.

"Yes, of course," I told him without a second thought. "I promise."

❦

It was almost dark when I decided to call it quits. I'd been over the statements so many times the numbers were starting to run together. I was just shutting down Mara's computer when I heard a knock on the screen door.

"Alice?"

"Tom!" I said, startled. He'd never been out to my house before, as far as I knew, and the barn was tucked back in the woods behind it. Not the easiest place to find.

"I didn't mean to frighten you," he said. "I was going to call you, but I thought it would be better if I came over."

"What—?" I began, but then I knew. I heard it in his voice. "Oh, no, please . . ."

"I'm sorry," he said, letting himself in. I remained behind the desk, unable to get up, searching his face for some sign that I was wrong. But his gaze was solemn. "I've been at the hospital all afternoon with Chloe and Lachlan. No one would talk to us for the longest time. I kept trying to get information from the nurses or from anyone in authority, but it was like I was asking for state secrets. A doctor finally came out and talked to us. I'm sorry, Alice, but he didn't make it."

"Oh, God," I said, trying to take in the news. Mackenzie— always so much larger than life—gone. It was inconceivable. "But— what happened? Was it his heart?"

"I think so," he said. "A massive heart attack, probably. They'll be doing an autopsy. Chloe told me that his cholesterol and blood pressure had been out of control for years. And that he didn't take care of himself. Apparently he had some issues with mainstream medicine."

"I know," I said, taking a deep breath, trying to calm myself down. I felt panicky, my heart racing. I'd gambled everything on

Mackenzie—without even realizing it. Everything I'd worked so hard for since Richard had disappeared. All those hours, weeks, years making myself over, learning a new trade, building the business. All to be undermined by another charismatic man! But it wasn't love that had blinded me this time—it was pride. In my talent. In Mackenzie's approval. In the glittering promise of the most beautiful garden in the Berkshires. What a fool I'd been!

"Are you okay?" Tom asked. "I'm really sorry—I know how much you admired him."

And I had. I'd been drawn to his magnetic self-assurance. To that booming laugh. His keen mind. And, of course, the exuberant ambition he put into our shared endeavor. I'd never really seen the ruthless side of Mackenzie that Tom knew. Nor had I ever sensed that he was the kind of man who, as Chloe said, "promises the world to everyone he meets." I'd believed in him. I'd convinced myself that our relationship was special. And that he regarded me as someone exceptional. Like him.

"Yes, I'm okay," I said, getting up from the desk. But once I was on my feet, I felt sick to my stomach and dizzy. I held on to the back of the chair as the realization of what had happened—and all that I'd lost—swept over me again. I bowed my head. I shut my eyes. My head was spinning. Somewhere, I heard Tom call my name. Then I felt his strong arms around me, holding me upright.

"Alice," he said, pulling me close. I found myself resisting at first, then giving in to his embrace. Everything in my world had gone wrong. And at the same time, this—Tom's body against mine—felt so right.

15

*

$\mathcal{G}$wen called me first thing the next morning. I was still in bed, though I'd been awake since before dawn. Thinking. Worrying. Cycling through the events of the day before. Anxiety weighed on my heart. Even the memory of Tom's arms around me the night before couldn't dislodge it.

"Did you hear?" Gwen asked in a small, frightened voice.

"Yes, I did," I said. "It's awful, isn't it? How are you holding up?" I'd been so overwhelmed by my own concerns, I hadn't given any thought to what Gwen might be going through.

"Not so well," she said. "Can I come over?"

"Sure," I said, sitting up in bed. "I'll make us some breakfast."

I got dressed and went downstairs to the kitchen. Some people—like Gwen—need to eat when they're upset; others—like me—lose their appetite. But I've always found that the act of cooking steadies my nerves. The world just seems less formidable when I have a spatula in my hand. By the time Gwen arrived, the smell of bacon filled the downstairs and I had a stack of pancakes warming in the oven.

"Hey, there," she said, walking right over to me and giving me a big hug. "Oh, God, Alice, this is so awful!"

"I know," I said, hugging her back. Then I started to set things out on the wide-planked kitchen table. I had the French windows open to the backyard, and a gentle breeze ruffled the paper napkins. In an attempt to add a little cheer to the sad morning, I'd cut some fresh roses and lady's mantle and arranged them in a silver urn in the middle of the table.

"When did you find out?" I asked her as I sliced bananas and strawberries into a cut-glass bowl.

"I had to pry it out of that damned housekeeper," Gwen said, pouring herself a cup of coffee. She leaned against the counter and watched me as she talked. "I kept calling the house yesterday when I heard what had happened. God, she's so possessive! And kind of scary, like Mrs. Danvers in *Rebecca*. But who else could I call? The hospital wouldn't talk to me because I'm not family. It was awful. Being so worried and then having that woman treat me like such crap! When I called for about the tenth time, early in the evening, she was blubbering—which is how I learned about it. I've been out of my mind ever since."

"Okay," I said. "Sit down and have some breakfast. And then I really need to hear what's been going on with you and Mackenzie. Am I right in thinking that you two were involved—and not just professionally?"

"What a sweet euphemism, Alice," Gwen said as she took a seat across from me and started to pile food onto her plate. "*Not just professionally!* But, yes, of course, you're right. Though I know you warned me against it. Even before I met Graham you told me I should watch my step. But what was I supposed to do? I mean, from the very beginning we had this amazing connection!"

"I thought so," I said, watching her dig into the pancakes I'd served her. "And I'm not surprised, really. I think I knew when I introduced you two that something like that might happen. Oh, Gwen! What a damned shame. I'm so sorry he's gone! For everyone's sake—but especially yours. You must be heartbroken."

She nodded her head as she continued to eat. She might be devastated, but it wasn't affecting her appetite.

"That's better," she said as she stirred sugar into her coffee. "I've been wanting to talk to you about Graham and me, but I just didn't feel right about it. It still seemed so new—and so special. I wasn't ready to share it yet. I don't think I've ever really felt this way before. Protective, I mean. About the two of us."

"I understand," I told her. But though things might very well have been different between her and Mackenzie, the truth was that Gwen had always kept her love affairs to herself. I'd grown accustomed to her disappearing from my life for weeks, sometimes even a month or two at a time, when caught up in one of these grand passions. And then coming back and—often hilariously—dissecting her ex-lover's character and foibles with me once the relationship began to unravel. As they all inevitably did.

"Graham was such a wonderful man . . . ," she said. "God, what passion—and generosity!"

"Yes, I know," I said, but I found myself not really wanting to hear any of the intimate details regarding their relationship.

"So you think this might have been the real thing?" I asked her instead.

"I'm having a hard time thinking about it in the past," she said, gazing out the French windows into the sunlit morning. "He still feels so present! You know, I feel like he really cared about me for who I am. There was definitely something going on between us. But now I guess I'll never know if it would have lasted. Goddamn it!" she said, shaking her head. Her eyes filled with tears.

"Oh, Gwen," I said, reaching across the table for her hand. My friend wasn't a weeper. In fact, I couldn't recall the last time I'd seen her cry.

"I'm a real mess, Alice," she said, the tears rolling down her cheeks.

"Of course you are! Go ahead and cry. Who gives a damn what you look like? You should be letting your feelings out. It's horrible that this has happened to you! It's so unfair."

"I mean, I'm *in* a real mess," Gwen said. "I don't know what to do."

"What do you mean?"

"Gr-a-ham," she said, stuttering a little as she tried to pull herself together. "Graham understood how much Bridgewater House meant to me. . . ."

"I'm sure he did," I said. Gwen wiped her eyes and blew her nose on a paper napkin. She took a breath and continued on in a steadier tone.

"And he loved the place, too, especially the property. He saw how significant it was historically—and the amazing potential it had if it was fixed up properly. In fact, it was his idea to turn the stables into a museum and learning center."

"That's great," I said, studying my friend as she looked down at the napkin that she'd wadded up in her lap. She seemed lost in her thoughts—and they clearly weren't happy ones. "So? Was he going to contribute to the capital campaign?"

"No," she said, looking up and meeting my gaze. "He promised to underwrite the whole thing."

"What? But isn't that almost—"

"A million dollars," she said, nodding. The tears began to flow again. "When we first got together, he was only interested in making a generous gift. But the more I told him about my ideas for

Bridgewater House, the more excited he got about it, too. He began to talk to me about how it could be turned into this museum and research center for local history—one that would bring scholars in from all over the country. Then he began to envision the place becoming a kind of cultural gathering place for the town, too. A beautiful historic setting for holding parties and lectures and concerts. One night when he came over to the house, I took him out to the old stables and he just fell in love with the building! You know how it has those great big old sliding doors and soaring ceilings. *This is it!* he told me. *This is going to be the Bridgewater House Museum and Research Center.* And he made the pledge right on the spot. Though he insisted it be anonymous."

"That's wonderful," I said, but Gwen looked so downcast that I knew already where this was heading. "I hope you got that in writing."

"Not really," she said. "I mean, of course, I drew something up for Graham to sign, but—things began to get more serious between us. And then he began to have some business setbacks. It just didn't seem right to press him."

"So—you only have his word?"

"He told me he was talking to the Mackenzie Project staff— that he was getting the ball rolling. I'm sure he did. I mean, you don't make that kind of promise to someone you—someone close to you—and not follow through with it, right? He knew how much this meant to me, Alice! He knew my career basically depended on it, really."

"No, it doesn't!" I told her. "Mackenzie's contribution would have been great, but you're going to make the Bridgewater House restoration come together one way or another—even without it."

"Well, that's not the only thing at stake anymore," she said. "When I told Larry Wadsworth—he's the Bridgewater board chair—that I'd made the capital campaign goal nearly a year ahead of schedule, he was just floored. The next day he called me and asked if I'd be interested in heading up the Commonwealth Historical Commission. The CHC, Alice! It's my dream job! But I've got to get Mackenzie's money for Bridgewater House first. I've just got to."

"That might be a problem," I told her bluntly. It seemed to me that we'd drifted pretty far from the shock of Mackenzie's death to concerns about my friend's career. I couldn't help but wonder just how much Mackenzie's passing meant to Gwen after all.

"Why?"

"His business problems were really escalating. Listen, I wasn't going to burden you with this today, but you might as well know the truth: his last check to me bounced. And it was for a lot of money."

"Oh, no!" Gwen said, her eyes wide. "Oh, shit."

"Exactly," I told her. "And I have a bad feeling that his creditors are already lining up. Sal Lombardi did some kind of a deal with Mackenzie recently and he made it pretty clear that he got badly burned. And Sal said something about the MKZ stock tanking if word got out that Mackenzie had fallen ill. God knows what will happen to the company now."

"This is awful! Are you going to be okay?"

"Well, you better believe I'm going to fight tooth and nail to get what I'm owed. But, you know, I'm thinking . . . Mackenzie's not-for-profit might very well be protected if the company itself goes into bankruptcy. I'm sure I remember hearing that when Lehman Brothers went down in 2008 they had a big charitable arm that couldn't be touched. You should look into that. Maybe Sal could help you—he's still chair of the Bridgewater House board, isn't he?"

"Yes," Gwen said. "Though he hasn't been all that active since . . ."

I'd forgotten. How in the world could I have forgotten? Perhaps because it had been one of the briefest of Gwen's many short-lived affairs. It had started about two years ago, though, as usual, I didn't hear about it until Gwen put a stop to the business a few months later. Sal had fallen for her hard, which was never the best approach with my friend. He offered to leave his wife, to set Gwen up in a luxury co-op in Manhattan, to give her whatever she wanted—but the more he pressed her, the less interested she became. She was finally able to end things by pointing out how inappropriate it was for a board member to fraternize with an employee. She could easily get fired. That helped salve Sal's ego a little. Though Gwen had confided to me that he'd wept when she told him they were through.

"Listen, let me ask Sal for you," I told her. "I won't get specific. I was going to approach him anyway for advice about how to get my money. And it would be a natural thing for me to bring up the charity. It was one of the main reasons I agreed to work for Mackenzie in the first place."

"Thanks, Alice. That would be great. But, yes, I think it would be better if you kept my name out of it."

❧

Gwen stayed for another hour or so, and the conversation turned back to her and Mackenzie. She revealed little bits and pieces of their time together. They met mostly at night, apparently, and rarely seemed to leave the house.

"We're both such night owls," she said, slipping into the present tense. "And we both get so hungry in the middle in the night! Graham makes a terrific omelet, by the way. *Made*, I mean, of course, damn it."

"He was sick for the last couple of weeks, wasn't he?"

"Yes, he had some kind of a stomach thing. I think it was all tied up with his business troubles. The last few nights I saw him, I don't think he slept at all. He'd prowl around the house or work in his office. Sometimes he'd even go out and wander around in your garden."

"Weren't you worried about him?" The last time I'd seen Mackenzie his physical deterioration had really shocked me.

"He told me it was nothing serious," she said. "He didn't like to talk about his health, or anything personal like that. He told me he lived for today. He said that he thought we were kindred spirits in that way. We kept it pretty light, Alice. But that doesn't mean it wasn't real."

"Of course not," I said.

"He made me laugh. Which is just about the most wonderful thing one person can do for another. Don't you think?"

❧

Even by the time she left, I still wasn't sure whether it was Mackenzie's death or the possible loss of his funding that had forced Gwen to expose her more vulnerable side to me that morning. She tends not to get emotional, though I've always suspected her tough-girl persona to be something of an act. But she's definitely not the kind of person who gives her heart easily. As far as I knew—and I knew pretty much everything about Gwen—she'd yet to give it fully to anyone. So I could understand her shock if, having finally fallen in love, death suddenly robbed her of that hard-found happiness. If that's what had actually happened.

Gwen often revealed things to me obliquely or after the fact. In truth, our friendship had never been the particularly gushing, tell-all kind. I suspected that Gwen, like me after my marriage collapsed, didn't always trust her feelings. But though we tended not to confide every little thing to each other, we never held back for very long about the truly big things. I knew that eventually I'd learn what was behind Gwen's tears that morning. It seemed to me that there was more than just frustration in her voice when she said, *I've got to get Mackenzie's money for Bridgewater House!* There was also fear.

16

❧

"$\mathcal{H}$i, Brook, it's Alice."

"Who?"

"Alice Hyatt from Green Acres."

"Oh, my goodness! How *are* you? I heard the news about Graham Mackenzie. I was hoping to get to your Open Day, but I had an event in Williamstown and I didn't get back down here until late afternoon. I'm so sorry—it must have been just horrible for you!"

"Yes," I said. I was on my fourth client call of the morning, and they'd all started out more or less this way. "It was pretty shocking. A heart attack, apparently. He was under a lot of stress."

"So I heard," Brook Bostock said. "Did you see the article in the *Wall Street Journal* this morning? Michael pointed it out to me at breakfast. Apparently they had to stop trading Mackenzie's stock yesterday because it dropped below some per share price limit. The poor man. I met him a few times at parties and fundraisers up here, and he was always so charming! But I'm sure you got to know him a lot better than me. It must have been exciting working with him on that garden. I've been hearing from everyone what an absolutely stunning . . ."

I loved Brook, but she could talk your ear off. I let her ramble on, only half listening, while I ran my eye down the list of clients that Mara had drawn up for me. These were the ones who had either called repeatedly for me and/or complained during the last month or so when I was so wrapped up at Mackenzie's. This round of phone calls was an attempt on my part to make nice and, hopefully, drum up some additional work. But in every case so far, my efforts only seemed to prompt a lot of questions about my late client.

"I've heard so many things, Alice. What was he really like?"

"I understand he sank millions into that house. Was it amazing on the inside?"

"Is it true the Fed is launching an investigation into his business dealings?"

"What's going to happen to the gardens now, do you think? It would be a shame not to have them cared for, after all your hard work."

This last one was from Brook, and it was typical of her thoughtfulness. Brook and Michael Bostock were among my first customers. She'd hired me originally to enlarge their fenced-in kitchen garden, but had been so pleased with the results that she'd given me carte blanche to reimagine all the landscaping around their beautiful Arts and Crafts home on Willard Mountain. We became friendly, if not quite friends. I'd convinced myself that it was better for professional reasons not to get too close to my clients; though, in truth, I was also determined to keep the emotional complications in my life to a minimum. However, if I had to choose one person on my roster to confide in, it would probably be Brook Bostock. I knew she'd been through some tough times herself, and I appreciated her confidence in me. She'd sent a number of important referrals my way over the years.

"I really don't know what's going to happen to it now," I told her. "Mr. Mackenzie's death has left a lot of things hanging, I'm afraid."

"But you're okay, right?" Brook asked, perhaps picking up something in my tone I hadn't meant for her to hear. "He didn't leave *you* hanging, did he?"

I was tempted to tell her. For a moment I hesitated, torn between my sense of professional propriety and my aching need for sympathy.

"I'll be fine," I said at last. "I was actually calling because I know you tried to reach me a couple of times recently. Did you and Michael decide to move ahead with the patio landscaping we talked about earlier in the year?"

"I'd forgotten all about that, actually," Brook said. "No, I was calling to let you know that I'd put a little bug in Vera Yoland's ear about featuring Mackenzie's garden in the Open Days program. But obviously, you got the word."

"I had no idea I had you to thank for that! How generous of you, Brook."

"Oh, please, you know how I feel about Green Acres. And I'm glad you reminded me about the patio. Sure, let's get going on that. It would be great to have it ready by the end of the summer. We're planning a big party for my sister-in-law's fiftieth over Labor Day weekend."

❦

Though I was grateful to Brook, the additional work at the Bostocks'—as well as a couple of other projects I was able to scrounge up—couldn't begin to dig me out of the financial hole I now found myself in. Only the money Mackenzie owed me could do that. And I didn't feel right about pursuing payment until after his funeral.

"Eleanor told me the ex-wife and the son are planning a service in Atlanta," Mara reported to me the Monday after Mackenzie's death. "But the body still has to be released by the coroner."

"What's the holdup?"

"I don't know. The ex isn't telling Eleanor anything. Though Eleanor's totally convinced she plans to sell the house and get rid of the help. Apparently the ex and the son both hate the place."

"Well, the Mackenzies are divorced, and unless he named Chloe as executrix—which I sincerely doubt—she won't have much of a say in what happens to his estate. The whole thing will probably be tied up in probate for months."

"We can't wait months to get that check reissued."

"I know, but we have to at least wait until Mackenzie's in the ground. It's indecent to go after the money until then."

"The man fucked us over. *That's* indecent."

We went around the question a few more times, but I was adamant. I was also convinced that I wouldn't have to put off demanding what I was owed much longer. But I was wrong. On Wednesday there was still no news about the burial. There was, however, a major investigative piece on the front page of the *New York Times* business section, under the headline THE DOWNFALL AND DEATH OF A FRACKING KINGPIN.

It prompted the two calls I was most dreading.

❧

Both of my daughters inherited their father's head for numbers. By the time they were acing their algebra quizzes in junior high school, they'd already left me far behind in the mathematical dust. I could balance a checkbook, of course. But until Richard's disappearance, I'd felt no need to get involved in the financial side of our life together. My husband was a professional number cruncher, after all. So when it fell to me to try to make sense of the endless bills, policies, checking accounts, and investment statements he'd left behind, I found myself struggling to interpret what seemed to me a foreign language.

"What's a SEP IRA? Why do they have to use all these ridiculous acronyms?" I remember complaining to my younger daughter, Franny, sometime during those first, nightmarish months after Richard left. At that point I was moving papers randomly around the dining room table at night, making different piles, hoping that everything would somehow just fall into place if I hit upon the right arrangement.

"It's a kind of retirement account, Mom," Franny said, looking up from her homework. "Everybody knows that. What are you doing? Do you need some help?"

"No, I'm okay," I lied. "I'll work this out somehow. But it all seems like such a jumble!"

"Here, let me take a look," she said, pulling her chair closer to mine, and within half an hour, she'd reorganized the stacks of paper in a way that clearly made sense to her. Though she must have realized it was all still pretty much a mystery to me.

"It's good Daddy put everything in your name, too," she told me. "And that he paid the mortgage off. Things could be a lot worse, I guess. But I think that maybe I should work out a little budget for you—and a list of what bills need to be paid when. This is all stuff you really should know anyway. It's no big deal."

It was Olivia who came right out and said what Franny had probably been thinking. My elder daughter was home from college for the summer, and by then it had become clear to us that we were going to have to sell the house to stay afloat.

"How can you *not* know what the place is worth? Or which bank held the mortgage? God, Mom, it's like you were living in a fog all those years! No wonder you had no idea what was going on behind your back. You didn't even know what was happening right in front of your nose!"

Her criticisms hurt—all the more so because I knew they were true. I vowed then to take charge of my financial situation. Learn what I needed to know to keep on a sound footing money-wise and start making smart decisions. I took a few seminars and read some books. My eyes continued to glaze over a lot of the time, but I managed to pick up the basics. Though I had to admit, none of it really interested me. Not the way it did Olivia and Franny, who both began to follow in their father's footsteps professionally, Olivia as an analyst at Morgan Stanley and Franny handling the accounting for a boutique advertising agency in SoHo.

I think they were both concerned when I announced that I was starting my own small business. In the early days of Green Acres, they checked in with me frequently, quizzing me about how I'd set up the books, what software system I was using, whether I had all the tax consequences under control. When they came to visit, they spent more time poring over my ledgers than they ever did admiring the growing portfolio of gardens I was creating and maintaining around the area. For them, Green Acres was all about the numbers. And gradually they began to relax and believe that somehow or other their clueless mother was managing to make a success of things. I didn't talk to them about it very often. I knew they wouldn't much care that Sal Lombardi had hired me to design his pool garden. Or that Brook Bostock loved what I'd done with her front border. But when Mackenzie gave me the commission to design the most significant new garden in the Berkshires in years, I couldn't help myself. I had to crow a little.

"It's a fabulous piece of property," I remember telling Olivia when I first got the job. "About twenty or so acres on the top of Powell Mountain. And the sky's the limit in terms of budget."

"Who is this person again? Graham Mackenzie? That name rings a bell for some reason."

"He's the third-largest natural gas producer in the country."

"Oh, my God! He's that fracking guy! I've read about him, Mom. He's supposed to be a real wheeler-dealer. Super-successful, but leveraged to the hilt. I read somewhere that he has more questionable subsidiaries than Enron."

"He didn't hire me to do his books," I told Olivia, upset that she was acting like such a wet blanket. Why couldn't she just congratulate me—and let me enjoy my good news? Unfortunately, though, that was Olivia's way. My older daughter's glass was always half empty. The reaction I got from Franny—usually so optimistic and encouraging—surprised me much more.

"Be careful," she said when I told her about the size of the project. "My agency took on a major new client this winter and it's almost capsized us. The billings are so much bigger than we're used to, we've been forced to cut some commission deals with the media. Thank God we have all sorts of guarantees written into the contract. Make sure you get that, too, Mom. You can never be too cautious."

I'd originally hoped that Olivia and Franny would be able to attend the Open Day celebration. For me, it represented the pinnacle of my success. The ultimate proof that the financially incompetent housewife whom my husband had discarded, whom my daughters had worried about and pitied, had been able to redeem herself. But their busy lives had kept them in the city—and away from the resulting disaster. Thank God. I kept meaning to call them in the days following Mackenzie's death, but I continued to find reasons why I should put it off. What was the point in talking to them until I knew something definite about the funeral? Or until I had some word about my money situation? Or until . . .

"Mom!" Olivia said, her voice shrill on the other end of the line. "I just finished the *Times* piece on Mackenzie. This is your client, right? And he's *dead*? He *died* at your big opening day? He's all you've been talking about for the last four months—and you didn't think to call me and tell me the news yourself?"

"I'm sorry, honey," I said. "But it's been so chaotic—"

"I bet!" she said. "This is just incredible. It's pretty clear the man was nothing but a crook! I can't believe you allowed yourself to get involved with him. I can't believe you were so *proud* of the work you did for him! What is it about you that makes you drawn to these cheats and liars . . ."

She stopped herself before I did it for her. It had been years since she'd made even a passing reference to her father. I think that, of the three of us, Olivia had been the most damaged by his betrayal. She certainly was the first to claim to have put the whole thing behind her, slamming the door on the past. I was shocked to learn, a week before her wedding, that she hadn't yet told her fiancé, Allen, about what had happened. *Why should I?* she'd told me. *Daddy has nothing to do with who I am now. Nothing!* It had taken me until then to realize that she wasn't just ashamed of what Richard had done; she was terrified by it. If someone she loved and admired had turned out to be such a monster, then whom could she trust? Including herself.

"I'm sorry you had to learn about this the way you did," I told her. "I should have called, but—honestly—I knew you'd be upset, and I had enough on my plate. Mackenzie's death and business problems have complicated things for me—and for Green Acres."

"Complicated? In what way?"

"He owed me money. A lot of it."

"Oh, Mom . . ." Olivia sighed. I would have so much preferred that she yell at me the way she had earlier. Because in the slow exhalation of her breath I heard her opinion of me shifting . . . changing . . . deflating.

Olivia must have called Franny as soon as she hung up with me. Ten minutes later my younger daughter was on the phone.

"Mommy? Are you okay?"

"Yes, Franny. I'll be fine."

"But this money situation—how bad is it?"

"I don't really know yet."

"But you did make him sign a contract, right? You have something in writing that will stand up in a court of law?"

I thought of the day I presented my plans to Mackenzie. The moment of triumph when he turned to me and said, *It's perfect! Absolutely fucking perfect! I knew you could do it!* How he'd reached so casually into his desk drawer to pull out his ledger and write me the biggest check I'd ever seen. After that, it seemed ridiculous to have him sign anything else. I didn't use contracts at Green Acres. It wasn't that kind of business. I usually just called and gave my clients an estimate of what any given project would cost, and then sent in the bill when it was finished. I'd never had a problem in the past. But Franny and Olivia existed in a different world, one where verbal agreements were no doubt considered antediluvian.

"Mom . . . are you still there?" Franny asked.

"Yes," I told her. "I'm here." But where I actually stood I really couldn't say.

17

❦

*Y*ou learn a lot about people when you're in financial trouble. Mara, for instance. I was both touched and taken aback when she said I didn't need to pay her until I got our money problems sorted out. What a selfless gesture, I thought, from someone who was usually so curt and detached. Her behavior continued to impress me in the days following Mackenzie's death—days that stretched into nearly a week with nothing resolved about Mackenzie's funeral service. Apparently, for reasons that weren't at all clear, the medical examiner was refusing to release the body to the family for burial.

"Eleanor says the ex-wife is reading everybody the riot act," Mara told me the Friday after Mackenzie died. "The hospital. The coroner's office. Eleanor, even. Like she has anything to do with this. What a b-i-t-c-h!"

It felt strange, after spending almost every waking hour at Mackenzie's for so many months, to have no direct communication with the household. If not for Mara's relationship with Eleanor, I wouldn't have had a clue what was going on. That the two women continued their unlikely friendship, even though the link that first brought them together had been broken, intrigued me.

"So you've seen Eleanor?" I asked.

"We talk on the phone," Mara said. "She asked me and Danny over for lunch tomorrow. She doesn't like being alone at the house. It's depressing for her now that Mackenzie's gone—and she doesn't know what's going to happen to her."

"It's kind of you to go," I said.

"No, it's not," Mara said. "I *like* going. She's good people. And she's great with Danny. He just loves her."

Though the way to Mara's heart was obviously through her son, I couldn't help but wonder what else moved and motivated her. I remembered the stricken look on her face—and her terrified *Is he dead?*—when she learned that Mackenzie had been rushed to the hospital. Had she cared about him more deeply than I realized, or did the crisis perhaps remind her of some other similar event in the past? Her behavior since his death had seemed a little unusual as well. Though she remained acerbic and short-tempered, she'd never been more helpful. In fact, she seemed to be going out of her way to be of use, coming in early and working late, keeping track of the crews, getting the bills out on schedule, fielding the queries about payment that were starting to mount, and, in general, freeing me up to make calls to current clients and potential new ones. She even brought me a few leads.

"You might want to follow up on these," she said, handing me a creased copy of the Open Day handout with three names and numbers written in her careful schoolgirl hand on the back.

"Who are they?"

"People I met at the Open Day. I talked to them about Green Acres. You know—what we do, how we work."

"Mara! You actually pitched them? That's great. But then maybe you should handle these yourself."

"No way," she'd said, turning back quickly to her computer. "That's not what I'm good at."

But just what Mara was capable of remained an open question in my mind. I realized that something had shifted between us since Mackenzie's death. The crisis had brought us closer together, the way bad times often will. But it was more than that. Mara had become invested in Green Acres to a degree I'd never sensed from her before. I felt we shared a mutual determination to get our business back on track. And that, in fact, it had now become *our* business.

Other people, however, were less helpful. Less understanding. Nate had been particularly persistent, calling every day, leaving increasingly angry messages. I finally paid him and our summer crew out of my personal checking account. I gave Mara a handwritten check as well.

"Just so you know, I'm not cashing this now," she said. "And give me a list of everything you're paying with your own money. I'll record it as a loan to the company. And we'll reimburse you as soon as we get things straightened out."

Her matter-of-fact tone—so different from the semihysterical reactions I'd received from my daughters—cheered me more than I could say. She seemed so determined. It was almost as if she had no doubt, at least none of the sleepless dread that I was experiencing, that we'd pull through this.

❧

The Lombardis' pink stucco mansion, which Sal had named Lombardi Oaks, was located down the mountain from Mackenzie's. It featured multiple turrets, towers, balconies, parapets, and mullioned windows, and seemed to have been designed by the same architectural firm that came up with Cinderella's castle for Disney World. It was, as far as I was concerned, a real hodgepodge, but Sal was enormously pleased with it. It was clearly, in his mind, a symbol of his success. He spoke frankly about his hardscrabble background. He was proud to be self-taught and self-made, a rough diamond in the venture capitalist world that was so densely populated with Ivy League types.

"I work by my gut," he told me when I first came to know him. "I'd trust my instincts over all the spreadsheets and P&Ls in the world. Numbers can be manipulated and massaged, but not a person's character. And I like to think that I invest in people, Alice, not companies."

Sal and Gigi had been Green Acres clients almost from the moment I'd opened my doors. I'd first met Sal during a fund-raiser at the Berkshire Botanical Garden, one of the many not-for-profit organizations in the area that he supported financially. Though the tickets were pricey, I'd decided that attending would be good for my fledgling business. But, not wanting to go alone, I'd asked Gwen to attend the gala with me. I should have realized it at the time, of course, but when Sal first struck up a conversation with the two us he wasn't really all that interested in Green Acres. He glanced from me to Gwen as he swirled the ice around in his tumbler of scotch, nodding as I tried to soft-sell him on my services. But his gaze lingered on Gwen as I nattered on. Until Gigi found us, that is.

"I like what Alice here was saying about using sustainable materials in her landscaping work," he told his wife, surprising me a little. It seemed to me he'd been only half listening to my spiel, but I would come to realize that he didn't miss much. "What do you think about having her give us a proposal on the pool project?"

Gigi nodded and smiled, scrutinizing the three of us as if trying to puzzle something out.

"Whatever you say, darling."

After Gigi led Sal off to their table for dinner, Gwen said to me, "Man, does she have *him* on a short leash!"

"What do you mean?"

"Oh, come on, Alice! Can't you tell? He's a player. Didn't you see him mentally undressing us? What's happened to your sexual radar?"

"I've no use for it anymore," I said. "And if he was mentally undressing anybody, it was you, not me. But I sort of liked the guy."

"Who's saying I didn't?"

It was true that I wasn't as attuned as I used to be to sexual atmospherics, but that didn't mean I was oblivious to them. I kept my antennae up when I was around Sal over the weeks and months that followed as I worked with him and Gigi on the pool garden. But I didn't get the sense that he was on the prowl. He and Gigi seemed devoted to each other and their three grown children. And they were both at the giddy, adoring stage with their first grandchild, pressing their latest iPhone photos on me whenever the opportunity arose. The only hint I got of any extracurricular interests on Sal's part was when he asked me for a personal reference for Gwen.

It was a couple of months after the Botanical Garden gala and Gwen had put her name forward as a candidate for the executive director position of the Woodhaven Historical Society. Though it seemed a bit of a stretch to me, Gwen had made the case that her varied backgrounds in real estate, sales, and management, as well as her extensive knowledge of the area, made her exceptionally qualified. And apparently she'd been able to sell the board on this idea, as she'd managed to land on the short list of candidates. She'd also mounted a major charm offensive and rallied every important person she knew in the Berkshires to write a letter on her behalf.

"It's now down to me and some dullard from Boston with an MFA in historic preservation," she'd told me. "But if they primarily want somebody who can go around shaking the money tree for Bridgewater House, they really need to go with a local. Someone who knows where all the wallets are buried. Sal Lombardi's head of the search committee. So put in a good word for me, okay? I gave him your name as a reference."

Sal's questions about Gwen were, at first, circumspect and by-the-book. Was she reliable? Hardworking? Trustworthy? Did she seem to me to be a self-starter? Then they drifted into more personal territory. How long had I known her? Was her character all that it seemed to be? Of course, I answered all these queries with glowing affirmatives. And then he threw in the kicker. Was she . . . *married*?

"What?" I asked.

"I was just wondering if she was—well—you know—really settled down in this area," Sal said, stumbling over his words. "I mean, I'd hate to hire her and then have her leave for some more glamorous post elsewhere in a year or two. And I always find that married—"

"She's not," I said, putting him out of his misery. Or had I, unintentionally, caused him more heartbreak than the poor man deserved? Because, though I was now alerted to the fact that he was attracted to Gwen, I had no idea at that point just how smitten he was with her. And I was never sure how soon after that their affair started—or if it had already begun. I didn't want to think that Gwen had willfully used Sal's interest in her as leverage to get the job. But in less than six months after taking the position, she'd spilled the beans to me that they'd been romantically involved. And that he was ready to get a divorce—anything!—to keep her in his life.

"He's a real sweetheart," Gwen had told me. "But it's over for me. I'm just not attracted to him anymore. He was a mess when I told him. He's such a macho kind of guy, but he cried like a baby. Then he pulled himself together and told me not to worry about the job. That this wouldn't affect our professional relationship. He'd deal with it. You know, Alice, remember when I told you I thought he was a player? I was wrong. He's not. He told me that he'd never cheated on Gigi before this. And I believe him."

I never let on to Sal that I knew what had happened. In the last couple of years I'd been in social situations with both him and Gwen, and only the closest of observers would have suspected that they'd ever been more than colleagues. Gwen had no trouble being breezy and upbeat, but I thought Sal acted different in her presence. He stood erect, shoulders back, eyes straight ahead, like a soldier at attention. And that's what he was in a way, I suppose: a man still at war with his feelings.

❦

Though when I went to see him a week after Mackenzie's death, he seemed very much at ease. He greeted me at the front door and led me through the elaborately furnished downstairs. So different from Mackenzie's understated taste, the interior design style of Lombardi Oaks was oversized and overstuffed: enormous tufted chairs and couches, ornately carved wooden tables and breakfronts, gilded mirrors.

"Gigi's at Kripalu doing her yoga thing," Sal told me as he showed me into his study. "She said to say hi. But I wanted to talk to you alone anyway. Take a seat. Care for a drink or anything?"

"No, I'm fine," I said, sitting down opposite him on a velour-covered couch that enfolded me in its cushiony embrace. "All I want is your advice."

"Shoot," he said.

"Mackenzie's final check to me didn't clear," I told him. "It was a big one—half of what he owed me. I have bills coming due from all over. I have no idea how to go about collecting the money, Sal. Who do I talk to? Where should I call?"

"I wish I could tell you," Sal said. "I've been asking myself the same questions. Graham screwed me, too, as I think you've gathered by now. He sold me a bill of goods on one of his subsidiaries. Turned out to be smoke and mirrors. I'm taking a real bath on it. It's going to seriously hurt my profit picture next quarter."

"I'm sorry to hear that," I said, but at least he had a profit picture to worry about.

"And I'm sorry to hear about you," Sal said. "I was the one who recommended you to Graham. Believe me, I never would have sent you his way if I'd had any idea what he was really like. He fooled me, Alice. And he fooled me good. I knew his reputation, of course, but I like to decide for myself what someone's made of. And he convinced me that he was something of an entrepreneurial genius. That he'd figured out how to turn natural gas production into gold. And I bought into it. But Graham has always been overleveraged, and when the gas glut began to escalate earlier this year—in no small measure due to MKZEnergy's spectacular growth—the share price plummeted. The whole business started to collapse under the weight of all that debt. He was a victim of his own success. And it looks like we're both victims, too."

"How can you sound so calm about it?"

"I'm not," Sal said, shifting uncomfortably in his chair. "I'm actually furious. I was duped. I was made to look like a fool—very publicly. Losing the investment is one thing—having my reputation take a hit is another. And he knew what he was doing when he sold me that piece of crap. He knew exactly what he was doing. The worst thing about it all is that I thought we were friends. I really *liked* the man. I enjoyed his company. I hate his guts now, but I'm still going to miss him."

"So there's nothing we can do? We just kiss the money goodbye? It seems so unfair!"

"Well, I'll probably write most of it down as a tax loss," Sal said. "You'll have to get in line with all the other creditors. My guess is there'll be some kind of a class-action suit. You could join that. But even then, you're only going to recoup pennies on the dollar. I'm sorry. I wish I had better news."

"Is this why you've been calling me?" I asked. "You wanted to warn me about Mackenzie's financial situation?"

Sal's gaze slid past me for a moment, focusing on something across the room.

"Yes," he said, but then he shook his head. "No. No, I'm sorry, it was something else. But it doesn't matter anymore. Listen, Alice, if I'd had any idea what you were facing, I would have tracked you down in person to let you know."

"Thanks," I said, getting up to leave. And then I remembered what I'd promised Gwen. "You know, there is one other thing. Mackenzie told me he would put money into his charitable fund—something called the Mackenzie Project—if I took on his landscaping job. He pledged to put in dollar for dollar what he paid out to me in services. What happens to that money now, Sal? Am I right in thinking that his creditors can't legally touch it?"

"Why do you ask?" Sal said, sighing a little as he pushed himself out of his chair. He was still such a burly, vital man that it was easy to forget he was a grandfather and probably hitting seventy soon. But I thought he looked every bit his age as he lumbered to his feet at this moment.

"It was a big reason I agreed to take the assignment on," I told him. It wasn't a lie, though it wasn't exactly the truth.

"I see," he said. "I was wondering, because I learned recently that an anonymous donor has given Bridgewater House an enormous donation. Enough, actually, to cover the costs of the entire capital campaign. Your friend Gwen made the big announcement at the last WHS board meeting. A good thing, too, because I know some of my fellow board members were beginning to wonder if Gwen was up to the job. I just hope she got all her *i*'s dotted and *t*'s crossed on this one. I'd hate to see anyone disappointed."

As I said, Sal Lombardi didn't miss much.

"You didn't answer my question," I said as he led me to the front door.

"Well, it's a yes/no kind of answer," Sal replied. "*Yes*, in general, charitable organizations cannot be attached during bankruptcy proceedings. At the same time, I happen to know that Graham made Chloe chair of the Mackenzie Project to keep her busy and out of his hair. Do you think she's going to honor Graham's pledge to Bridgewater House? It's only a guess on my part, but I'm afraid that's probably where the *no* comes in."

18

❧

I was impressed by Mara's suggestion that we carry the business expenses I was paying for out of my personal checking account as a loan to the company. It made me think. Why shouldn't I apply to the bank for a loan myself? I had a friendly relationship with Sherry Genzlinger, the manager of our local Barrington Bank branch, who'd been more than helpful when I first set up my Green Acres account there several years back. She was an avid amateur gardener, and often pumped me for professional advice about her roses. She loved David Austins in particular, despite their sometimes fickle and withholding nature in our hardiness zone.

When I stopped by the bank that Monday morning, Sherry was on the phone. She saw me hovering outside her door, waved me into her small, sunny box of an office, and nodded at the gray molded plastic chair facing her desk. I took a seat.

"Well, this is a nice surprise," she said with a smile when she finished her call. "What can I do for you, Alice?"

Though I'd convinced myself that everyone I saw these days knew what a mess I was in, Sherry's welcoming unconcern made

me realize she was oblivious to Mackenzie's—and now my—
financial troubles. I filled her in as briefly as possible.

"Oh, dear," she said, clicking the top of her ballpoint pen nervously up and down. "That's a very large sum of money. Shouldn't
you have . . . ?" But she let the question trail off when she saw my
expression.

"I've never had any problems with receivables in the past," I
told her. "And I was recommended to Mr. Mackenzie by a long-
time client. It was my most important commission so far. But I got
wrapped up in having it be a success, and I just didn't think about
how much money I was laying out until it was too late. Yes, I
should have done a lot of things differently. I realize that now."

"And you say you can't get through to anyone at his company?"

"It's all just 'Leave a message after the beep,' and I've tried every extension I could find. Nobody's gotten back to me. MKZ
headquarters is in Atlanta, and I read that they're planning a massive restructuring and layoffs. The last thing anybody probably
wants to deal with right now is their former CEO's personal expen-
ditures."

"You've tried his wife?"

"His ex. Her phone's unlisted, but I don't think she's going to
be of much help in any case. She called the gardens a waste of
money and a boondoggle."

"Have you considered legal action?"

"Yes, and I'll go that route, of course, but I need a cash infusion to get me through in the meantime."

Sherry frowned and put down the pen.

"What did you have in mind?" she asked.

"A business loan of some kind. Whatever you can suggest. I
figure I'll need about—" I named a sum that made her wince, and
I quickly tried to soften the blow. "But, as I explained, I will be

seeking legal recourse. I *will* get this money back. It's just a matter of time."

"That may be so," she said, "but that's not going to wash with our loan officers. What sort of collateral do you plan to offer?"

"Green Acres," I said, sitting up straighter in the uncomfortable chair. "It's been growing every year since its inception. I've an excellent roster of clients, including some of the best properties in our area. My staff is well trained and hard—"

"Alice, please," Sherry said, holding up her hand. "Let's be practical. Your equipment is leased. Your business has no bricks and mortar, nothing *tangible*, in terms of assets. And you're already carrying debt. We can't very well repo your client list if you don't make the interest payments."

"But I've been doing business at this bank for *years*," I told her, despising the whine I heard in my voice. No, I was *not* going to humiliate myself or look pitiable! As I stood up to leave I said in a more conciliatory tone, "Look, I'm sorry. I know you would do something if you could. And it's been good just talking to you."

"Wait," she said. "Hold on. What about a second mortgage or a home equity line of credit? You own your place free and clear, right? I'm sure we could fast-track the paperwork for you, Alice. I'd see to it."

"Thanks," I said. Though I knew it made sense, the idea also made me sick to my stomach. I could hear my father's beseeching *Promise me you'll never let it go!* I'd already stumbled so badly. But mortgaging the family homestead felt to me like the ultimate failure. I shook Sherry's hand and said, "I really appreciate your help. Let me think about it."

❧

It was Mara's idea to send back many of the outdoor lights, urns, fountains, and other fixtures I'd purchased for Mackenzie's gardens.

"After all, *he* didn't pay for any of it," she pointed out, "*you* did. Everything was ordered in your name, and I bet a lot of these places accept returns. You'll at least be able to recoup part of the money that way."

"Yes, you're right," I replied, but the idea made me uncomfortable for some reason, and I put off doing anything about it.

"Listen, you've got thirty days to return most of these items to your suppliers," Mara pointed out a few days after she first made the suggestion. "I put together a list of what we can ship back, and I called around. If we get everything packed and out of there this week we can save a bundle by sending the stuff UPS Ground."

"Thanks," I said, running my eye over the list Mara had compiled. "Let me think about it."

"What's there to *think* about?"

"Let me be!" I snapped, folding the list in half and stuffing it into my shoulder bag as I left the office. Though I appreciated Mara's help, I didn't appreciate being nagged. I had too many other things on my mind, I told myself. I knew that wasn't really the problem, of course. But I was fed up with trying to deal with everything, including my own failings, and I wasn't in the mood for self-reflection.

I'd planned to run errands in Great Barrington, but instead of making the right when I got into town, I found myself taking the familiar left turn up Powell Mountain Road. I hadn't been back to Mackenzie's since the Open Day. That was almost two weeks ago now, a period of time that seemed to have been warped by the emotional fallout of my client's death. In some ways, it felt like years since I'd last driven up the winding roadway through the lush and lovely woods. At the same time, the awfulness of what had happened was still far too fresh in my mind. I parked in front of the garages. Eleanor's car wasn't in evidence, and the house had a closed-up feeling—drapes drawn in the windows facing the parking area, a soggy pile of newspapers moldering on the steps. The dahlias and petunias in the large terra-cotta pots flanking the portico, left unwatered for far too long, had collapsed into a snarled nest of shriveled flower heads and stalks.

It wasn't until I walked around to the steps leading down to the sundial garden, though, that I realized just how quickly nature had worked to reclaim its own. The grass, which hadn't been mowed in almost two weeks—and this at the height of summer—had shot up at least half a foot in some places and had started to invade the terraces. Weeds were creeping into the flower beds, strangling some of the tender perennials and insinuating themselves among the roots of the newly planted shrubs and specimen trees. Crabgrass flourished in the crevices of the walls and pathways. As I walked down the steps, I saw a stack of faded Open Day programs wadded together under a bench. An empty plastic cup—swept by the breeze—skittered across the deck. Clearly, no one had cleaned up after the Open Day event was canceled. Everything had been left—just as at Pompeii—the way it was the moment catastrophe struck.

I continued on down through the garden rooms, each showing signs of neglect: the roses in need of deadheading, the boxwoods raggedy with new growth, the fountain dry as a bone. I remembered the sense of oppression that weighed on me the fogged-in morning of the event. But what I felt now was even more unnerving. As my footsteps echoed on the flagstone walkway I had the distinct feeling that I was being watched. But by whom? And from where? When I reached the waterfall terrace I turned around and surveyed the house, which I could see in its entirety from that vantage point. But the wall of windows stared blankly out over the valley. Determined to get hold of myself, I resolutely approached Damon's beautiful wrought-iron railing and looked down.

Someone had turned off the pump, and now the water just trickled over the ledge and dripped into the pool below, which had filled with leaves and other debris. The little glade was choked with weeds. But there was nothing about the sun-dappled scene below to indicate that a man had looked death in the face there. And this was probably the last thing Mackenzie saw, I realized—a canopy of green, a mild blue sky, a cloud passing leisurely overhead. Even with Open Day visitors strolling around on the grounds above, it was a peaceful, solitary place to die.

I bowed my head, trying to finally accept what had happened. Because that was why I'd come, I realized now. Not just to face the fact that Mackenzie was gone for good, but to start to come to terms with the need to dismantle the gardens we'd built together. That I'd created from scratch—and poured my heart and soul into. That I'd been so proud of. Too proud, of course. Chloe was right, after all. The project was a boondoggle and a waste of money. Mine.

I sensed something behind me and whirled around. It was Eleanor, dressed in her perfectly pressed uniform, looking as terrified as I felt. She had a kitchen knife in her hand, which she slipped into her apron pocket when she saw who I was.

"What are you doing here?" she demanded.

"I—we—" I felt around in my shoulder bag for the list Mara had put together and pulled it out. "We're planning to return a lot of these garden fixtures. I was just looking around to see how much work would be involved."

"You should have alerted me!" she said, still clearly upset. "I saw someone walking around out here—and I didn't know what to expect. I keep thinking that . . ."

"I'm sorry. I didn't mean to scare you, Eleanor. I didn't realize you were still coming in every day."

"Yes," Eleanor said. "I'm cleaning the place from top to bottom. And I'm keeping an eye on things. Someone has to. People hear a big house like this is sitting empty—and bad things start to happen."

"You thought I was an intruder?" I asked, trying to understand why she was so distraught. She kept looking around nervously, as if expecting someone—or something—else to suddenly emerge from the shadows. Her mood was infectious, and I couldn't help turning and looking behind me, too. The wands of the weeping cherries shifted in the breeze, but that was all.

"I keep thinking I see him," she said.

"See who?"

"Mr. M," she said, putting her hand over her mouth as if the words had escaped of their own volition. "I know he's dead, of course. I *know* that. But I'll be up there, working in the kitchen or vacuuming the living room, and I'll look out the window—and see—I'd swear I'll see—" She closed her eyes, fighting back tears, as she shook her head quickly back and forth.

"Let's go up to the house, okay?" I said, taking her by the elbow. She let me lead her back up through the gardens to the deck. We entered through the kitchen door, which stood open. The top-of-the-line appliances gleamed in the late-afternoon sun. Plates and glasses were arranged neatly on the shelves. The tile floor looked recently buffed. But the fruit bowl stood empty. And there was no whiff of the comforting cooking smells that usually permeated the room.

Eleanor went over to the table and sat down. I followed, pulling out a chair across from her.

"What were you planning to do with that knife?" I asked her, nodding at her apron.

"I don't really know," she said with a rueful laugh. "I guess I just needed something to hold on to. It makes me feel safer. Or at least a little less scared."

"Mara told me you don't like being up here all by yourself," I said. "And I don't blame you. Why do you keep coming in?"

"I have a job to do," she said simply. "I know that sounds crazy. Especially because I'm not getting paid anymore. But I wouldn't feel right leaving Mr. M in the lurch. And I couldn't just walk away from his beautiful house. I intend to close this place up properly. Though I know that's crazy, too, because he left me in such a bad way. Just the way he did you and Mara. It's all so hard to understand, isn't it? I mean, he was such a wonderful man! So generous and thoughtful. But at the same time, he was such a— well, he didn't tell the truth, did he? About his company and my savings. I've lost everything. My retirement. My investment in his company. And my son lost everything, too."

"I'm sorry," I told her. "I know how you feel. And it *is* hard to understand. But we just have to keep trying. I'll tell you what, though—I'm pretty sure walking around with a knife in your hand is going to do you a lot more harm than good."

On my way out, I took one last look at the hillside I'd come to know so well. The sun had slipped behind the clouds, and the distant mountains were backlit with an orangey, otherworldly glow. I remembered looking at this same view with Mackenzie. Had it really been only a few weeks back? It seemed like decades ago now. I'd taken him on a tour of the nearly completed gardens, and he'd told me: *It's really incredible what you've accomplished, Alice. You've actually moved rivers—like Le Nôtre did for the Sun King at Versailles. It's amazing what money can buy, isn't it?*

It was amazing, too, what money could destroy. Or the prospect of it, anyway. I thought of the many lives that Mackenzie's death had undone. Mine. Mara's. Gwen's. Eleanor's and her son's. In the last moments of his life had Mackenzie's thoughts flashed on us, and the countless employees and shareholders whom he'd let down? Because he must have known that it was over. That he was never going to be able to come through on the many inflated promises he'd made to all the people who depended on him. Who believed in him. Who, like Eleanor, still kept seeing him out of the corner of her eye. Torn about what to feel toward him. Unwilling to pass final judgment on him. Unable to let him go.

19

❦

Olivia and Franny came up for their annual summer visit at the end of July. As usual, my daughters took the week off from work to spend what Olivia called "quality time" with me. Their husbands would be joining us over the coming weekend. In the past, I'd try to clear the decks during their vacation, but this year I really needed to keep working. Along with all the usual demands of managing a landscaping business at the height of the season, I was doing everything I could to drum up new clients. Complicating matters, Mara and I had run into a lot of problems and complaints about the fixtures we'd tried to return. Very few of the suppliers wanted to reimburse us for the full price of the items, and I had to threaten a couple of times to take legal action. An empty ploy, as I didn't have the wherewithal to hire a lawyer.

The worst thing, though, was dealing with all the dunning calls from the various nurseries and garden supply outfits I owed money to. Mara and I tried to let most of these go directly to voice mail, but occasionally I'd find myself talking to some irate supplier who'd managed to get through to me directly: "You're ninety days past due. We're putting you on credit hold. Don't even *think* about ordering from us again."

"Yes, I know," I would respond in my most soothing tone. "I'm sorry, but I'm owed a lot of money myself and I'm afraid I won't be able to pay you until—"

But nobody seemed to care that I, too, had been stiffed. That was *my* problem. One that, as the weeks passed, seemed further and further from any sort of resolution. Though I continued to pay my workers out of my personal account, my little nest egg was almost tapped out. I'd looked into cashing out my retirement plan prematurely, and discovered that I would lose easily a third of it to the IRS if I did so. I was waking up in the middle of the night routinely now, going around and around with all this. I'd get out of bed exhausted before the next demanding day even began. And it got harder with Olivia and Franny under my roof, because I was determined not to let them know just how bad things really were.

"Oh, don't worry. I'm working that out," I told them vaguely the night they arrived from the city and asked me for an update on the Mackenzie situation. I was so happy to see them—my beautiful, vibrant, successful daughters!—that for those first few hours at least I was able to put my problems aside. They'd come up for a much-needed break from their own work and worries, and that's exactly what I planned to give them. If I wasn't able to be with them every minute, so be it. Though I initially tried not to let them know that I'd be tied up pretty much the whole time they were visiting.

"Let's go up to Williamstown tomorrow and see a play!" Franny suggested over a late supper of gourmet goodies they'd brought with them from the city. Unlike me—or perhaps because of me—neither of my brainy daughters had really learned to cook. They survived on takeout in the early years of their professional careers, then both had the good sense to marry men who knew their way around a kitchen.

"We could have lunch at the Clark and then go to a matinee," Olivia said. "What's playing now, Mom?"

"I've no idea, sweetie. This is my busy time, remember? I'm afraid I'm going to have to pass on the matinee, but I could meet you on the way back for dinner. There's a new place in Lenox I've been wanting to try."

In this way—skipping their day trips and shopping excursions, but having ready suggestions about what the three of us could do together at night—I was able to juggle work and my daughters' expectations through most of that week. Thursday evening we planned to have a picnic supper at Tanglewood and listen to the concert on the great lawn. I'd promised to make my mustard-and-herb fried chicken—a childhood favorite of my daughters—and had every intention of heading back to the house around four thirty to start cooking. But right around that time Mara, who had been placing an order with Finari's, our local garden center, put down the phone and said, "You'd better pick up. Ted wants to talk to you."

Ted Finari, founder and owner, was one of the good guys of this world. He was the first to extend credit to me when I started my business, and had been a booster of Green Acres ever since, often sending new business our way. We were on ninety days payables with him and, at this point, only a few weeks in arrears. But I still picked up the phone with a sinking heart.

"Hey there, Alice," he said. "I'm sorry to bother you, but I've been hearing some kind of troubling things around town. Is it true you got screwed by that fracking billionaire?"

"Yes, I'm afraid so," I said, glancing across the room at Mara. She was pointing at her watch, and I remembered that she'd asked to leave early, too. She and Danny were helping Eleanor get ready for a tag sale she was hosting in Pittsfield on Saturday. Eleanor was giving up her own small one-bedroom apartment to move in with her son. I nodded at Mara, waved toward the door, and watched her leave as I listened to Ted's reply:

"Oh, man, what a scumbag! What's this country coming to that a guy like that can screw over honest, hardworking people? Where are the laws, for chrissakes? Where's the accountability?"

"I've been asking myself the same thing, Ted," I told him, hoping that I was wrong, and that he'd just called to commiserate.

"I mean, first Madoff, and then AIG and all those too-big-to-fail banks! It's really infuriating! I get so pissed off just thinking about it—" As Ted continued to rant and rave about the injustices of our current brand of capitalism, it began to occur to me that he was stalling. He was embarrassed and uncomfortable about coming to the point.

Finally, after another few minutes of this, I asked him, "Is there a particular reason you called, Ted?"

"Yes, there is," he said with none of his earlier bluster. "Oh, shit! I'm sorry, Alice, but I can't keep carrying you. We've got plans to expand the center next fall and the bank is asking for all sorts of assurances before they agree to financing. My accountant warned me that they'll be going over our books with a fine-tooth comb. I've got to have everything current."

"And by 'current,' you mean . . . ?"

"I'm really, really sorry, but I've got to put you back on thirty days," he said.

He did sound sincerely apologetic. For all the good that did me. In many ways, Finari's Garden Center was the lifeblood of my business. We bought almost all our regular stock from them, and this was one of our bigger months for ordering plants and shrubs. Even including the new, expensive nurseries I went to for the exotic plantings I used at Mackenzie's, I owed Finari's more than any other single supplier at this point. If I couldn't manage to pay them, Green Acres wouldn't be able to keep going.

"I understand, Ted," I told him. "I don't know what's going to happen here. I'm swamped with debt because of all this. But thanks for helping me out as long as you did. I really appreciate it."

"Damn it, Alice! I wish things could be different."

"Me, too," I said, hanging up the phone. I sat at my desk and dropped my head into my hands. I was too exhausted to cry. I'd run out of excuses. I knew I had no choice now. I'd have to call Sherry the next day to begin the process of mortgaging the house—and put in jeopardy one of the things I cherished most in my life.

I have no idea how much of the conversation Franny actually overheard. But, obviously, it was enough. The screen door slammed as she came in, and she walked right up behind me and began massaging my shoulders. It was something she used to do to comfort me during the bad times after her father left.

"I thought so!" she said. "I told Olivia you were still in trouble. It's that damn Mackenzie guy, isn't it? Why didn't you tell us?"

"Why do you think?" I said. "I'm thoroughly ashamed of myself. I feel like a fool and a failure. Your sister's right. There does seem to be something about me that's drawn to cheats and liars."

"Leave it to Olivia to go straight for the jugular," Franny said. "Well, at least I know what's happening now. I was beginning to think you were mad at us for coming down so hard on you after that *Times* piece ran." She patted me on the arm and said, "Okay, you, up and out of there. We need to get back to the house and let Olivia in on all of this. And I mean *all* of it, Mom. I think we both deserve to know *exactly* where things stand, okay?"

❧

We never made it to Tanglewood that night. We sat down around the kitchen table and I told them the whole story. But this time I didn't sugarcoat the facts or hold anything back. I made it clear that I knew I'd let my pride and ambition trample all over my better judgment. I pointed out how I'd ignored a number of important warning signs that Mackenzie was in trouble and untrustworthy. How I'd recklessly spent an enormous amount of money that wasn't even yet in my possession. I was as hard on myself—and as honest—as I could be. And when I was done, I sat back with a sigh and waited for the recriminations to start.

Instead, Olivia reached across the table and squeezed my hand.

"I'm sure you have every reason to be proud of that garden," she said. "I don't think you should lose sight of that, okay? That you created something really amazing."

I'd been fine up until then. But my tough-minded, highly critical older daughter's kindness took me completely by surprise. My eyes filled with tears.

"Thank you," I said as Franny handed me a napkin.

"That said," Olivia went on, "it's pretty clear Green Acres is teetering on the edge of collapse, and you've got to do something immediately to shore up the financial structure."

"Wouldn't mortgaging the house make the most sense?" Franny asked. "Aside from this mess with Mackenzie, you've got a very viable business going, Mom. Interest rates are still pretty low right now. What's the problem? Is it that you're worried about making the payments? It seems to me you could swing them pretty easily."

"No, that's not it," I said. How could I explain this to my practical, hardheaded offspring? I took a deep breath, and decided that I had to at least try:

"I know you don't remember your grandfather all that well. You were still only girls when he died. But that last summer when we were all up here together, he made me promise him something. . . ."

They were silent for a minute after I finished. Franny was the first one to speak.

"But taking out a mortgage doesn't mean you're going to lose the house, Mom. That could only happen if you defaulted on the loan. It seems to me that a mortgage is a really sensible way of tapping into all the equity that you've built up in this place over the years."

"I know," I said with a sigh. "You're right, of course. I'll—"

"No, I understand," Olivia said. "It's not about equity. It's about family—and what Granddaddy said. This place doesn't belong to just you—it's a part of all of our lives. And you don't feel right about cashing in on it."

"Exactly," I said, looking across the table at my older daughter, who was full of surprises suddenly. Olivia and I had often been at odds with each other over the years. It felt especially good to discover that we both felt the same way about something I thought was so important.

"I'm going to talk to Allen," Olivia announced. "Goldman's having a good year, and he's been promised a big bonus. And I've got some non-retirement money kicking around. Between the two of us, I'm sure—"

"No, between the four of us," Franny said. "Owen and I aren't exactly hurting either."

❦

By the time my sons-in-law arrived for the weekend, it was settled. I didn't ask the details of who gave how much—all I knew was that a sum covering what Mackenzie owed me was being wired into the Green Acres business account and would be available the following

Monday morning. I was touched and relieved and more grateful than I could ever say. I insisted on calling it a loan, though, and paying the going interest rate on the amount. I was still horribly embarrassed about getting myself into such a mess, but I was proud of my daughters for behaving with such maturity and compassion. They were all the proof I needed just then that I wasn't a complete failure in life.

To thank them I went all out and made an elaborate dinner on Saturday night. We ate in the dining room, setting out the heirloom silver and using the frail, paper-thin linen that had been in the family for generations.

Allen, who bought wine with the same discrimination and skill with which he purchased equities, opened a bottle of vintage Bordeaux. He held up his glass and said, "To the future!"

"Hear, hear!" I said.

"And to family!" Franny added, smiling across the table at Olivia. It occurred to me that they'd gotten on particularly well with each other that week. I'd witnessed none of the little episodes of sibling rivalry and jealousy that so often erupted when they spent more than a couple of days in close quarters. Despite my problems, it was one of the nicest vacations I could remember in a long time.

"No, you sit," Olivia said when I started to get up to clear after the main course. "Franny and I will get the dessert." But a few minutes after they disappeared into the kitchen, I remembered that I hadn't turned on the coffeemaker. I got up and followed them through the swinging doors. They were standing side by side at the kitchen sink, rinsing dishes.

"When are you going to tell her?" I heard Franny ask.

Olivia whispered something in reply, but I couldn't make it out. I guess it was because the last few months had brought so much heartache and disappointment, but I immediately jumped to the conclusion that something was wrong—and that they were keeping it from me.

"Tell me what?" I demanded.

"Mom?" Olivia said, turning around. "I thought we agreed that Franny and I would do the cleaning—"

"What's going on?" I said. "What don't you want me to know?"

"It's nothing bad," Franny said, laughing.

"Actually, it's something very, very good," Olivia said. "Allen wanted to open a bottle of champagne when we announced it, but who cares?"

"What? Oh! Don't tell me . . . ?"

"Yes, Mom," Olivia said, beaming. "We're having a baby. You're going to be a grandmother."

20

❦

Though I'd always hoped that my daughters would have children of their own someday, Olivia's news thrilled me in a way I really hadn't anticipated. It instantly recalibrated my priorities, and made me realize how, immersed in my own problems, I'd allowed myself to ignore the important things in life. Like the miracle of life itself. And the unbreakable bonds of family. I had a harder time than usual saying good-bye to everyone on Sunday afternoon. I hugged Olivia to me before she and Allen got into their car.

"You'll take good care of yourself, right?" I told her. "You know you have to eat regularly and take plenty of folic acid and—"

"Your daughter's already the leading expert on prenatal supplements," Allen told me as he opened the passenger door for his wife. "If we're going to beat the traffic, we'd better get going."

Franny, Owen, and I waved them off as they started down the driveway, and Allen gave a farewell honk as he made the right onto Heron River Road.

"It goes by so fast, doesn't it?" Franny said, turning to me. Owen started to load their suitcases into the trunk.

"Too fast," I said. "And I could kick myself for wasting so much of it on Mackenzie." I felt so sad! I had to work hard to keep a smile on my face, but Franny picked up on what I was feeling anyway. She's always been empathetic, but after Richard left, she became even more acutely attuned to my moods.

"You know what I think, Mom?" she said. "It's time for you to put that awful man behind you. I just hope he won't affect how you feel about *all* men. It seems to me there are some pretty nice ones kicking around up here."

I knew she meant Tom Deaver. They'd met him when he dropped by the house late Friday afternoon, unaware that I had visitors. He had a gallon-size ziplock bag full of ripe tomatoes with him.

"I thought maybe you could use some nourishment," he said, holding up the bag and looking past me to my daughters, who were hovering in the hallway behind me. I introduced everyone and invited Tom in for a visit.

"No, I can't stay," he said, glancing from me to Franny and Olivia. "I was just checking in. But it's nice to meet you both. You know, I realize this is going to sound really hokey, but as far as I'm concerned the three of you could easily pass for triplets. Anyway, here are some tomatoes for your dinner. I've got so many coming in right now I don't know what to do with them."

Before Tom was even halfway down the driveway, Franny poked me in the ribs and giggled.

"He was flirting with you, Mom!" she said. "*Triplets?* You know, that really was hokey, but he was able to pull it off somehow. He has a kind of boyish, endearing Jason Bateman vibe going."

"Yeah, with maybe a little Dennis Quaid macho swagger thrown in," Olivia added. "Not bad for a middle-aged guy. Who *is* he?"

I tried to brush my daughters' questions aside, but they were persistent, and before too long I found myself telling them about the selfless way Tom had handled his wife's illness and early death. About his Clean Energy Consulting firm. And the Wind Power Initiative that Mackenzie had helped shoot down. How, despite that, he'd stepped up and done what he could when Mackenzie collapsed during the Open Day event.

"He came by here later that night to tell me Mackenzie hadn't made it," I said.

"Later? How late? And what's that look on your face?" Olivia demanded.

"You're blushing," Franny said. "I knew it! You've got a thing for this guy. Well, I've got to say, I like the sound of him. Plus he grows his own tomatoes. That's hard to beat."

❦

After Franny and Owen left, the house felt empty. I usually don't mind being by myself. My disastrous marriage cured me of the need for intimacy. And the fear of loneliness. Over the last half dozen years or so I'd come to realize that I really enjoyed my own company. But Olivia's announcement had stirred up all sorts of maternal and nostalgic feelings in me. It brought back vivid memories of my own pregnancies—and the joy and excitement of young motherhood. Along with all that, of course, it brought back Richard. I could still never think of him without pain. And I resented the way he remained embedded in my life, tangled up in all my memories. Every happy moment that I'd shared with him was now tinged with anger and regret.

It was still light out at seven thirty. I poured myself a glass of white wine and wandered outside in my bare feet. The grass was cool and lush, the shadows lengthening across the lawn. I loved this time of day in the summer, when the crickets are tuning up in the underbrush and the birds are calling back and forth to one another.

Good night! Good night! I sat down in one of the old teak chairs facing the long back border and watched the first of the fireflies drift across the patchwork of bleeding hearts, Shasta daisies, and echinacea. How lucky I was to be able to hold on to all this! How grateful I was that my children could help me out the way they had. What a relief not to have to worry any longer about how I was going to cope. And yet . . .

I couldn't seem to shake my melancholy. It was more than that, really. It was a helpless sense of time passing—and of regret. About the mistakes I'd made in love. And now with work. The misjudgments for which I had only myself to blame. Just when I was convinced I'd finally gotten my life back on track, I'd stumbled badly. I'd nearly lost everything again. It frightened me how close I'd come.

"Alice?" I heard Tom call from the front of the house. I got up quickly and walked around to the front yard. He was looking through the open screen door, the light from the hallway spilling out onto the porch.

"I was in the back," I said, climbing the steps. "My family left a little while ago. Would you like to come in and get something to drink—and then join me outside?"

"Yes, thanks, I would," he said. I pushed open the door, and he followed me into the house. As I led the way down the hall to the kitchen, I could sense his gaze taking me in. I had on a pale pink sleeveless linen sundress, wrinkled from a day of wear. But I knew that it showed off my well-toned arms to good effect and contrasted nicely with my summer tan. I had my shoulder-length hair up in a clip, though strands had escaped and curled around the nape of my neck. I wasn't sure if it was me—or the effect he had on me—but I thought I looked pretty good. Hardly one of Tom's triplets, but still womanly and attractive. Which was not something I'd felt about myself in a long time.

So I was surprised—and disappointed—by what Tom said when we took our seats outside on the darkening lawn.

"I'm afraid I'm once again the bearer of bad news," he told me. "Or at least upsetting news."

"Oh, dear," I said, turning to look at him in the fading light. "What is it?" He had a profile that wouldn't have looked out of place on a Roman coin: high forehead, aquiline nose, strong chin. But he seemed distant and distracted.

"I'm friendly with Harry Corbett, who's in the district attorney's office," he replied as he stared unseeing out over the wildflower field. "Apparently, they received Mackenzie's autopsy report, and something's not right."

"What do you mean?"

"Harry told me they're going to be opening up a homicide investigation into what happened."

"What? That's crazy! Mackenzie had a heart attack. We were both right there."

"Yes, I know," Tom said. "And I've been going over it again in my head. That's certainly what the EMS guys seemed to think. And that's what the doctor at Berkshire Medical Center told us. I was with Chloe and Lachlan when they heard the news. I'm absolutely sure the doctor said he thought Mackenzie's heart 'just gave out.'"

"But now they think it *wasn't* a heart attack? What was it, then?"

"I don't know. The DA's keeping a tight lid on whatever the autopsy findings are—but something's obviously wrong."

"Wow," I said, trying to make sense of Tom's news. I'd already adjusted my thinking to the idea that Mackenzie had died because of heart problems. And it seemed to fit with everything I knew about him: the high blood pressure, his distrust of mainstream medicine, the severe financial pressure he was under. I couldn't help it, but I didn't want to be forced to imagine a different—and possibly suspicious—scenario. I was ready to put Mackenzie's death and all the bad things associated with it behind me.

"You must have been there pretty early that morning," Tom said. "Did you see anything that seemed odd to you?"

"No," I said, but then I remembered the eerie sensation of making my way down through the gardens in the heavy mist. "Though—I know this is going to sound a little weird—I did *feel* something. The mountain was all fogged in, and I was upset because Mackenzie's last check to me didn't clear. I hadn't slept well, worrying about how I was going to get paid. So maybe it was just my own anxiety, but I felt something ominous in the air."

"That's awful about the money," Tom said. "Did you have the chance to talk to him about it?"

"No, I didn't. Nobody seemed to know where he was. In fact, I didn't see him until much later on—maybe halfway through the morning. He was dressed in white, talking to some people not that far from where he collapsed."

"I don't remember seeing him at all," Tom said. "At least, not until I heard that scream and went down to see what had happened. Well, obviously, we're not going to solve this ourselves. Harry told me they'll be sending out detectives to interview everyone who might have any information. I imagine they'll want to talk to you, Alice."

"That's fine," I said. "I'm an old hand at that sort of thing."

Tom took a moment to think about what I'd said. I could feel him glancing over at me. Finally, he asked:

"You mean . . . because of your husband?"

So he knew. Though I didn't like the fact that he'd heard the gossip about my failed marriage, I was relieved that I didn't have to explain the whole thing all over again. And yet I also realized that

I wanted Tom to know what had happened from *my* point of view. How it had blindsided me. How it had altered my once trusting and compliant nature. But mostly, I think I wanted him to understand the person it had forced me to become.

"Yes, that's what I mean," I said. "Listen—would you care to stay for dinner? I've all sorts of delicious leftovers from the weekend. It would be very easy to throw something together for us."

"I'd like that, Alice," he said. "I'd like that a lot."

❧

We had cold chicken and a variety of salads and the rest of the white wine. We ate at the kitchen table.

"Should I light the candles?" he asked as I put out the plates and silverware.

"Sure," I said.

"It's so hot tonight," he said after we took our seats across from each other. "Maybe you could turn the overheads down a little?"

I turned them off and opened the French doors. We ate by the light of the flickering candles. At first we didn't say much. I think the romantic atmosphere made us both suddenly feel a little awkward and shy. But then he asked me again about Richard, and I began to tell him the whole dreadful, complicated story. It's one I've always struggled through in the past, groping for the right words and emphasis, but there was something about Tom's straightforward questions and obvious concern that made this particular telling easy.

"The case is still open. Periodically, I get calls when a new investigator comes on board or some fresh piece of evidence crops up, but nothing ever comes of it. I know they've given up on actively trying to find him—or I guess I should say *them*."

"How do you feel about that?" Tom asked, looking at me from

across the table. His gaze was warm and curious. "Does it still upset you?"

"No," I said with a rueful laugh. "It infuriates me! I can't abide the idea of the two of them living in the lap of luxury on some exotic island off their ill-gotten gains! But you know what's kind of funny? Richard never really enjoyed lazing around on vacation. I just hope he's going stir-crazy wherever he is!"

"You can laugh about it, though," Tom observed. "That's good. And your daughters seem to have turned out wonderfully. That kind of thing can really tear a family apart. My own kids went through a bad time when Beth was so sick. My youngest is still really struggling to find his path in life."

"How many children do you have?"

"Four altogether," he said, looking down into his half-filled glass. "Beth had a hard time conceiving when we first got married. We finally decided to adopt two sisters from China. Then—as so often happens, apparently—Beth got pregnant a year later. So we had three all under the age of five. But it worked out great. Lily and Rose are in their late twenties now, both doing basic research in Boston. Peter's with Apple in Cupertino doing something in content management—something way beyond my grasp. Timmy was the surprise, coming along a year or two before Beth was first diagnosed. He got the brunt of it—and he's the one I really worry about. He dropped out of U Mass last fall and is working at some divey restaurant in Amherst. One week he's going to be a cartoonist. The next he's planning some indie film. But he's just drifting, really."

"I guess we never stop worrying," I said. "Even when they're doing great." I was about to tell him about Olivia's big news, but he went on.

"The trouble is Timmy just doesn't *listen*! He lives in his own little world—convinced he's some kind of great artist. But it's all just magical thinking as far as I'm concerned. He has no idea how to deal with reality. How to behave like an *adult*. I get so angry with him! I keep trying—" But he stopped himself in midsentence, shaking his head.

"I'm sorry," he said, smiling at me in that self-deprecating way I'd come to know and like. "I'm venting. Which is incredibly rude and selfish of me after you've been so gracious. I just haven't been able to talk to anybody about all of this in a while. At least not somebody who listens as well as you do."

"Oh, please, no apologies needed," I said, getting up and starting to clear the table. "It's a relief actually to hear about someone else's problems for a change."

"That damn check!" he said, standing as well. "I hope it hasn't affected your business."

"It could have," I told him honestly. "But my family's helping out. Which I'm both enormously grateful for and terribly ashamed of."

"It's hardly your fault. And from what I've read, you're not the only one Graham took to the cleaners."

Tom helped me load the dishwasher and hand-wash the wineglasses. For some reason, doing these simple domestic chores together felt more intimate than anything else that had passed between us that evening. I was suddenly overly aware of him. He was a couple of inches taller than me. So when he turned, put down the towel, and drew me into an embrace, I had to reach up to put my arms around his neck. It felt so natural—and at the same time electric with sexual tension. What was I doing?

"This was nice," he said, leaning over and brushing his lips against mine. Then he kissed me for real—but slowly, gently. I held back. Though my body ached for more, the rest of me wasn't ready. But it was wonderful just to feel desire again—something I'd long thought was behind me—and perhaps even better to feel desirable.

He left soon afterward, but his presence lingered on while I closed up the house and headed upstairs to bed. Despite Tom's disturbing news, I fell asleep that night with a smile on my face.

Part Three

21

The story was on the front page of the *Berkshire Herald* Tuesday morning under Jeff Isley's byline: MACKENZIE DEATH RULED SUSPICIOUS. Isley obviously didn't have any more information than Tom had, but the reporter managed to stretch the piece by adding rehashed segments of the article he'd written soon after Mackenzie's passing. Though Isley had mercifully left my name out of the original story, I was horrified to come upon it toward the end of his new, lengthy feature.

Due to his outspoken advocacy of the practice of hydraulic fracturing, which helped him amass what had once been a considerable fortune, Graham Mackenzie could be a polarizing figure in our area. Several local environmental groups have criticized the danger "fracking" poses and the aggressive tactics Mr. Mackenzie's company MKZEnergy used to obtain lease agreements from landowners in states that permit gas drilling along the Marcellus Shale. In the past several months, as MKZEnergy's share price plummeted,

Mr. Mackenzie also came under attack for overleveraging his company and underreporting its many problems.

Locally, however, Mr. Mackenzie was not without his supporters. Alice Hyatt, proprietor of Green Acres and the landscape designer who created Mr. Mackenzie's lavish garden, had only words of praise for her employer. Shortly before the Open Day event during which Mr. Mackenzie collapsed, Ms. Hyatt called him "a very generous human being. He has a real passion for gardening—and garden preservation. I feel that this garden has been a true creative collaboration and, in many ways, Graham Mackenzie has been my inspiration."

Though unconfirmed, rumor has it that Mackenzie's sprawling multimillion-dollar mountaintop estate will soon be on the market. The house has been shuttered, and the gardens partially dismantled. Driving past the site on a recent afternoon, this reporter was reminded of the similar fate of Xanadu at the end of *Citizen Kane*. The mystery surrounding Mr. Mackenzie's death has all the makings of that rags-to-riches-to-rags-again classic, and will certainly be just as fascinating to follow as the story unfolds.

"What a piece of crap!" I said out loud, though I was alone in the kitchen. I tossed the newspaper into the trash. Yesterday, after I confirmed that the wired money had come through, Mara and I had mailed out a large number of checks. But it would take another day or two for the payments to reach their recipients. In the meantime, my already angry suppliers would be further put off by my out-of-date comments quoted in Isley's front-page story. When the phone rang, I half suspected it to be one of them.

But it was Gwen, finally returning my call from the day before.

"Have you heard the news?" she asked.

"Yes, that's why I tried to reach you."

"What do you think it means?"

"Your guess is as good as mine. I was told that the DA's office is trying to keep the autopsy report under wraps."

"I need to talk to you," Gwen said.

"How about dinner? I've got—"

"No, *now*. I really need you. I'm at work. How soon can you get over here?"

Gwen was not an alarmist. She was not a taker. I couldn't actually remember the last time she'd said she really needed me—or anybody else, for that matter. I stopped by my own office first and left a note for Mara. Then I drove into town and bought two tall coffees and some muffins at the general store. A needy Gwen would probably also mean a hungry Gwen. Thirty minutes later, I pulled into the parking area behind Bridgewater House, where Gwen worked during the summer months. From mid-October to early May, when the unheated and weather-beaten old estate was uninhabitable, she operated from her modest Cape just outside of town.

The Woodhaven Historical Society might well have had grand plans for the complete restoration of Bridgewater House, but the place was currently in a pretty sorry state of disrepair. The three-story white clapboard structure—originally Colonial with Federal and Victorian additions and embellishments—had visible signs of serious problems: flaking paint, crumbling brick, a fantail window missing panes. But I knew from the architectural report Gwen had commissioned that its unseen structural problems were even more serious. The stone foundation had eroded, and dry rot was setting in. I was careful to watch my step as I climbed the rickety stairs at the back of the house that led up to Gwen's improvised office area. The little suite of rooms with its whitewashed walls and wide-planked floors had been the servants' quarters originally. Gwen's desk, an elaborate golden oak affair that she'd borrowed from the estate's extensive furniture collection, was the only note of ostentation in the otherwise simple and utilitarian setup.

When I pushed open the door I saw Gwen's laptop sitting open on the desk, surrounded by papers, books, and stacks of file folders. But the room was empty.

"Gwen!" I called, putting the coffee and muffins down on the desk. "Hey, Gwen! Where are you?" Silence. I'd never actually ventured beyond Gwen's work area when I stopped by Bridgewater House in the past, and I wasn't sure where else to look for her. As far as I knew, the main part of the house was closed to visitors, the electricity turned off, and the furniture under protective sheeting. I opened one door to find a walk-in closet stacked with boxes of Woodhaven Historical Society letterhead, note cards, and mugs. I tried another, which opened to an ancient tiled bathroom with a pull chain toilet and a rust-stained sink. It also had a small window that offered a partial view of the backyard. The windowpanes must have been original; they were dimpled and wavy in the way that old glass can be. So the glimpse I caught of my friend— hurrying from the stables to her car—seemed distorted, as though she was moving underwater. She stashed something—a cloth bag? a rolled-up shirt?—in the trunk of her car before turning back to the house.

"Coffee! You're a saint!" she said, closing the door behind her as she came in. "God, what a horrible morning!"

"So you read that asinine article? I could strangle Isley for quoting me like that."

"Where? In the *Examiner*?" Gwen said, prying off the plastic top from her coffee as she sat down behind the desk. "No, I haven't seen it. I got a call from a state police detective first thing this morning. Before I'd even brushed my teeth, let alone had a chance to read the paper. He's coming by here later this afternoon to interview me."

"They're not wasting any time," I said.

"You didn't give him my name, did you?"

"What? No—I haven't spoken to anybody yet. I just heard that the police were going to start getting in touch with people who knew Mackenzie."

"But why am I on the top of the list? The detective told me that he wanted to ask me about my 'relationship' with Graham. Who would have told them about that? Who else knew?"

"Well, let's think," I said, pushing the bag of muffins across the desk. But Gwen ignored it. "Eleanor might have said something. She was probably one of the first people they talked to. I bet they interviewed her yesterday and she told them about you then."

"You're right! Of course. That bitch. Well, I'm going to deny there was anything—anything romantic—between us. It was just a professional relationship. Plain and simple."

"Gwen, you can't do that. This is an official investigation. A homicide investigation. You can't lie about something this important. You could find yourself in serious trouble."

"I'm in even worse trouble if I tell the truth," she said. "I can't have the whole world knowing about Graham and me! Especially in light of his anonymous pledge to Bridgewater House. I think I might be able to survive as executive director if I come clean about Graham being the anonymous donor. Everyone knows now that MKZ's probably heading for bankruptcy. But I'll be totally sunk if my conflict of interest comes out."

I was on the verge of reminding Gwen that I'd warned her about that very thing. She'd jumped down my throat when I told her to watch her step with Mackenzie. If she'd listened to my advice, she wouldn't be facing this crisis now. But I held my tongue. How many people had tried to warn me, too, about Mackenzie?

"I bet Eleanor's already told them about the two of you," I pointed out. "She's the housekeeper. She was right there. She would know, wouldn't she?"

"Yes, and I think she's also half nuts. She turned against me with such a vengeance when Graham and I first got together. I don't know what was wrong with that woman—whether she was jealous or just overly protective. But I promise you, she used to look at me with absolute hatred in her eyes. It was scary."

"That said . . . she's still telling the truth about you and Graham being involved."

"It's her word against mine. No one else knows about it."

"Actually, that's not true."

Gwen looked over at me. She put down her coffee.

"You? Would you really say anything—if I asked you not to?"

"It's not just me," I told her, avoiding a question I wasn't sure I knew how to answer. "I think Sal caught wind of it. I already told you what he said about Chloe running the foundation. But I didn't tell you that when I asked Sal about the Mackenzie Project he hinted that he knew it was Mackenzie who had made the big pledge to Bridgewater House. And he seemed worried. About you. About what was going to happen to this place without Mackenzie's pledge. I don't know for sure, but there was something about his tone of voice that made me think he also knew something was going on between you two. Or at least suspected."

"Sal would never do anything to hurt me," Gwen said.

"That's not the point. What I'm trying to tell you is that you can't control the situation. Any number of people might have seen you going to or coming from Mackenzie's late at night. For what?

A meeting about his *pledge*? You can't bluff your way out of this, Gwen."

"Just watch me."

"What? Watch you go to jail? You could be convicted of obstructing justice if they find out you're lying about Mackenzie. I know what I'm talking about. Please—just be honest about what happened, okay?"

She shrugged in reply. She had no intention of listening to me, I realized. She calmly reached over and opened the bag and began to peel off the waxy paper cup from a blueberry muffin. She'd always been so damned headstrong! So sure of herself. And it had always been a trait I admired. Until now.

"Where were you when Mackenzie died?" I asked.

"I'm sorry?" she said. "What is this? A practice run before I get grilled by the police?"

"I'm just curious. I'm pretty sure that everyone else I know who was involved with Mackenzie was at the Open Day event. I thought I saw you in the crowd once or twice, but I wasn't sure. Were you there?"

"No, sorry," Gwen said, brushing crumbs off her fingers. "I didn't make it. Graham and I walked through the gardens together a number of times, though. Haven't I already told you how fantastic I thought they were, Alice? You did an incredible job."

"Where were you, then?" I persisted, aware that Gwen was avoiding my gaze.

"Home," she said, taking a sip of coffee. "I got up late—then I just lazed around."

I didn't enjoy catching her in a lie. At the same time I was hoping it would teach her a lesson. Make her realize what a mistake it was to think she could skirt the truth.

"I happen to know you were in Mackenzie's bedroom around eight thirty or so. I was at the site early that morning to check on some final details in the garden. I came up to the house after that, hoping to talk to Mackenzie about the check that didn't clear. I didn't mean to eavesdrop. But I couldn't help it. You and Eleanor were really going at it."

"So what?" Gwen asked. "So what if I was there early? I left right after that. I went home and, like I said, spent the rest of the morning lazing around."

"Gwen! You just totally changed your story! Don't you see how suspicious that makes you seem?"

"To whom?" Gwen asked, looking me straight in the eye. "Do you suspect me of something, Alice?"

"Just idiocy," I said. "I've been through this kind of thing before, remember. I can't tell you how many times I was interviewed after Richard disappeared. How many times they made me go over every little detail of our lives together, especially those weeks just before he vanished. You don't know what that kind of scrutiny is like."

"You got through it," Gwen said.

"But I had nothing to hide."

"I don't either," my friend insisted. "Not really. Not anything that did anyone any real harm. I'm just trying to protect my career. My future. And I think you'd do the same thing, Alice, if you were in my position."

22

*

$\mathcal{B}$ut what I'd told Gwen about not suspecting her wasn't quite true. The news that Mackenzie's death was under investigation—and that he might actually have been murdered—had started to change the way I thought about everyone who'd been close to him. And I couldn't help but find Gwen's self-serving reaction to his passing—as well as her decision to lie to the police—deeply troubling. Mackenzie's reneging on his pledge gave her a motive, and her being at his place the morning he died gave her the opportunity. On the other hand, she was my dearest friend, and I just couldn't imagine her killing her lover—no matter how angry and upset she might have been. Besides, it seemed to me that other people had much more obvious and pressing reasons for wanting Mackenzie gone.

Chloe for one, whom her ex-husband had been about to cut off without a dime. Lachlan for another—and for the same reason. Or, perhaps, the two of them working together. I'd heard the bitter way that Mackenzie, Chloe, and Lachlan spoke to one another. There was certainly no love lost among the three of them. And if Mackenzie was eliminated before Lachlan lost his inheritance, there might very well be a lot to gain.

Then there was Eleanor. She fed and cared for Mackenzie. She had daily access to his house. She knew his habits intimately. She'd trusted and admired him, and he'd paid her back by ruining her and her son financially. And she was so tightly wound emotionally. It wasn't hard to imagine her snapping under extreme pressure, losing control, lashing out.

There were others, too, though they seemed more far-fetched to me. Tom, for instance, whose wind project Mackenzie had stopped dead in its tracks. And Sal, who'd obviously lost a bucket-load of money to a man he'd once considered a friend. Plus Sal had loved Gwen, but had been forced to sit by and watch her fall under the spell of a powerful rival.

It wasn't until the next day that I realized there was another person I hadn't considered whom some might feel belonged on the growing list of suspects.

❧

I knew and liked Ron Schlott, Woodhaven's chief of police. He was a genial, hail-fellow type who was a couple of years younger than me, a son of the man who'd been the police chief when I summered in Woodhaven as a girl. The family seemed to have a tradition of public service; Ron's brother, Brian, headed up the town's highway department. Ron was jowly and big-bellied, his police belt riding low on his overburdened hips. He knocked on the door of Green Acres around eleven o'clock the following morning. With him was a compact, balding man wearing wire-rimmed glasses and a blue blazer.

"Hey, Alice," Ron said when I opened the screen door. He turned and nodded to the man at his side. "I'd like you to meet Lieutenant Vincent Erlander. He's the state police detective in charge of the investigation into Graham Mackenzie's death. You got a few minutes?"

"Sure," I said, opening the door wider for them to come in. I asked Mara to bring out some folding chairs from the storage area. We set them up in front of my desk, and Ron and the detective took their seats.

"I'd like to talk to you, too," Erlander said as Mara started back to her side of the room.

"I'm not going anywhere," she told him, sitting down at her computer, which effectively blocked her from view. Erlander turned in his chair and narrowed his eyes in her direction, but then turned back to me and opened up a well-worn leather-bound notebook.

"Okay, just some basics to start," he said, clicking on a ball-point pen, then taking down our names, addresses, phone numbers, nature of our work, years in business, etc. Mara contributed her information from behind her terminal without missing a beat, but at the same time continuing to click away at her keyboard. This clearly irritated Erlander, who struck me as somewhat humorless and short-tempered. A couple of times I noticed Ron shift unhappily in his chair when Erlander was particularly brusque.

"When did you first meet Graham Mackenzie?" Erlander asked after he'd completed the background questions.

"Sometime in mid-March," I told him. "I don't remember the exact date."

"March twentieth," Mara volunteered. "Your appointment was for four o'clock."

"Mackenzie's been in the area for a year or two," Erlander pointed out. "But this was the first time you'd come face-to-face with him?"

"Yes. We traveled in somewhat different circles. He called to talk about a business proposition."

"His housekeeper called, actually," Mara corrected me. "Eleanor. But you've spoken to her already."

"Do you think you could manage to come around and join us?" Erlander said. "I prefer not to have to communicate with a disembodied voice."

"All the schedules and stuff are on my computer," Mara replied. "I'd just have to come back here anyway to look things up."

Erlander shook his head silently as he jotted something down, but he continued without further debate.

"I take it this meeting was to discuss putting in the big garden?"

"Yes," I told him. "He offered me the job that evening."

"From what I understand, it was a pretty sizable undertaking. A real coup for your business—especially considering how small and relatively new it is."

"That's right."

"And you liked the man, too—am I correct?" Erlander asked, pen poised as he looked across at me.

"I take it you read the *Examiner* article," I noted drily. "I offered that opinion before I knew about my client's many financial problems and possibly underhanded dealings. But, yes, for most of the time I knew him, I was impressed by Mr. Mackenzie. He was full of life and enthusiasm for things that mattered to me. He was very knowledgeable about landscape design and supportive of my work. It was hard for me not to like him."

"And he must have been pretty impressed with you, too," Erlander said. "From what I understand it's quite an honor to have a garden selected for an Open Days event. That was a real feather in Graham Mackenzie's cap."

"No," I said. "He didn't want to do it at first. I think that his business problems were beginning to catch up to him by then. He probably knew it wouldn't help his public profile to have all this expensive new landscaping on view when his company was doing so badly."

"Really?" Erlander said. For the first time, I think what I'd told him didn't jibe with the impression of Mackenzie he'd already formed in his head. "So why did he go ahead with it?"

"I'm not sure, but I think he did it as a favor to me."

"That's a pretty big favor, if your assumption is correct."

"Well, actually, we'd become . . ." I hesitated, not wanting to overstate the case, but I couldn't think of a better word. ". . . friends. Or at least friendly. We had some things in common."

"He knew about your husband, then?" Erlander asked, turning over a new page in his notebook. "You two talked about what happened?"

"I can't imagine what that has to do with—" I began to object. I already felt that Erlander's questions had become overly personal, but this one seemed particularly intrusive and embarrassing. Though I was well aware that everyone in town knew what Richard had done, no one ever broached the subject. I noticed that Ron had taken a sudden interest in his fingernails.

"It's a simple yes or no question, Mrs. Hyatt," Erlander replied. "Did you or did you not talk to Mr. Mackenzie about your husband's disappearance?"

"Yes," I told him, my temper hanging by a thread. "I did. But I don't see what any of this has to do with your investigation."

"Really? I find that surprising. Your husband perpetuated a massive financial fraud and then vanished. Mr. Mackenzie is being investigated for possible fraudulent activities and has met a suspicious end. As far as I'm concerned, that kind of coincidence requires at least a question or two."

Was he hoping to get a rise out of me? Or was he just naturally snarky and insinuating? I couldn't tell, but I knew it wouldn't do me any good to get in an argument with him. Erlander reminded me all too clearly of the agents and detectives who'd swooped down on me after Richard's disappearance and worked me over hour after hour, day after day. I was so vulnerable and terrified then. I had no idea how to deal with that kind of pressure. But when I wept and protested—or when I let them see how angry their endless questions made me—it only made matters worse. Sensing my fear and shame, they would redouble their efforts, no doubt convinced they could wring something out of me after all. I knew enough now to try to answer Erlander simply and clearly. To attempt to show no emotion. I reminded myself that as a police investigator, he was sanctioned by the state to pry into whatever subjects he deemed necessary, no matter how out of line I thought they might be.

"Yes," I said, folding my hands in my lap. "I see your point."

"Well, thank you," he said with a tight little smile. "Now, perhaps you could tell me when you first discovered that the check for the second half of Mr. Mackenzie's payment to you didn't clear?"

"How did you hear about that?" I demanded.

"*When* did you first learn about it?" Erlander asked again, as if I'd just said something he didn't understand.

I glanced across the room to see Mara peeking around the computer screen, but she moved back out of sight when I caught her eye.

"The day before he died," I said.

"I understand it was for a lot of money. You must have been pretty upset. Did you try to contact Mr. Mackenzie about it?"

"Yes," I told him. "Of course I was upset. I went to his place early on the Open Day morning to oversee the installation of the railing around the waterfall. I decided to go up to the house afterward to ask him about the check."

"You were right *there* that early? Right above the pool?"

"Yes, but the whole mountain was fogged in. I couldn't see ten feet in front of me." Then a shiver went down my spine. I once again felt that ominous sense that had overtaken me as I made my way through the mist that morning. "Are you telling me that Mackenzie was already down there? That he was there the whole time?"

"I'm not *telling* you anything," Erlander says. "I'm *asking* you about your whereabouts that morning. Do you remember seeing anything unusual?"

His aggressive, almost accusatory tone was tinged with excitement now. I was telling him something he didn't already know. And it was something important. He'd stopped writing and was leaning forward in his chair.

"No. But, as I said, it was hard to see. I spoke to the contractors who were putting in the railing for a few minutes. And then I went up to the house."

"What time was that?"

"Around eight thirty or so."

"And what happened then?"

"Mackenzie wasn't there. His housekeeper didn't know where he was." Erlander hadn't asked me who else might have been there, just what had happened, so I decided I didn't need to mention that I'd overheard the fight between Gwen and Eleanor. "The volunteers from the Garden Conservancy arrived soon after that, and we started setting up for the event."

Erlander went back over my early-morning visit to the garden a few times, obviously trying to jog my memory about what I had seen. But I'd already told him everything I could remember. I explained what Nate and Damon had contributed to the garden design, and Mara supplied Erlander with a printout, including contact information, of every subcontractor and supplier who'd worked at one time or another at Mackenzie's.

"Anyone you know of who had a beef with your client?" Erlander asked.

"Plenty of people stood to be hurt by his business problems," I replied, "as I'm sure you already know. And others had reservations about his 'fracking' practices, which he was a great proponent of. But I can't imagine that either of those things would be reason enough to kill him—if that's what happened."

"If indeed," Erlander said, swinging around in his chair to face the back of Mara's computer. "And what about you? Anyone you know of who had a problem with Mr. Mackenzie?"

"Nope," Mara said.

Erlander waited, still turned in Mara's direction, as if he expected her to add something to her terse reply. After a moment or two of silence, he swiveled back around to me.

"Okay," he said. "What can you tell me about digitalis?"

"What?" I asked, uncertain if I'd heard him correctly.

"Di-gi-tal-is," he said. "What can you tell me?"

"Well, it's a tall spikey plant with fingerlike flowers," I replied, trying to make sense of this line of questioning. "Its common name is foxglove. If grouped properly, it can be a nice choice for a garden border. But I find it often doesn't last more than a season or two in our climate zone."

"Did you use it in Mackenzie's garden?"

"I don't think so," I said, frowning as I tried to remember. We'd been forced to make several last-minute additions to fill areas where some of the late-blooming perennials had not yet leafed out. But digitalis would not have been my first choice. "No, wait—

maybe we did. Mara, didn't we end up planting some in that shady area behind the tennis court?"

"I don't know," she replied.

Erlander closed his notebook and got up. As he started to move toward the door, Ron rose as well.

"Thanks for your time," Ron said, shaking my hand warmly. "You'll call us if you think of anything else? You have our cards, right?"

"Yes," I said. They'd handed them to me when we first sat down.

While Ron and I said good-bye, Erlander waited in front of the screen door, looking out across the peaceful, sunlit morning. Then he turned back to me and asked, "Isn't digitalis considered toxic?"

"Well . . . yes," I told him.

"So don't you think it's a little dangerous to use it in a garden you know is going to be open to the public?"

"Not at all!" I replied, unable to keep the annoyance out of my voice. "Hundreds of plants are considered toxic. Hollies, lupines, lily of the valley, wisteria . . . The list goes on and on. We wouldn't *have* gardens without them."

"But it *is* dangerous."

"For heaven's sake, yes! But only if you ingest it."

23

❧

$\mathscr{I}$ had a meeting that afternoon with one of the potential clients Mara had lined up at the Open Day. Their place was over in Monterey, so I had to take off right after Ron and Erlander left. The house was a rambling nineteenth-century white clapboard beauty with wide porches and a lovely view of Lake Garfield. The owners, two scientists who seemed oblivious to the news about Mackenzie's death (thank heavens), wanted me to help them rethink their overgrown long front border which had deteriorated into a wild tangle of rugosa roses and tumbling fieldstones. By the time I left, we'd agreed that I should draw up some designs and an estimate, and that we'd meet again in a week or two. I liked the couple and came away with a good feeling about the project.

I stopped in Great Barrington on the way home to do some shopping and didn't get back to the office until nearly six. Mara was already gone, so I didn't have a chance to talk to her about the interview with Erlander until the following morning.

She arrived an hour later than usual, the screen door slamming behind her. She walked over to her desk without so much as a glance in my direction.

"Everything okay?" I asked.

"Bad night."

"I hope nothing's wrong with Danny. You know, you can always call in and ask for a day—"

"Danny's fine," she said, cutting me off.

I'd become so used to Mara's moodiness that I didn't think twice about her attitude. We worked in silence, both of us busy at our computers. I was scheduled to meet with Brook Bostock that afternoon to show her my AutoCAD plans for the new terrace garden, and I decided to go over the designs again page by page, thinking through how I was going to present them. I'd forgotten all about Mara until she abruptly announced, "That detective called me at home last night."

"Who—Erlander?"

"Yeah. He said he had some 'follow-up' questions for me and wanted to arrange a time to come over. But no way was I going to have that man snooping around my place! I told him I'd just prefer get it the hell over with. So we did it on the phone."

"Hadn't we already covered everything here?" I asked her.

"No," Mara said, getting up and coming around to lean against the side of her desk. She folded her arms over her chest in what seemed to me a defensive posture. I remembered her hostility earlier, and it dawned on me that she was angry about something. "He had me on the phone for over an hour. Thank God I got Danny down before he called."

"I'm sorry, Mara. What in the world did he want?"

She stared at her feet for a moment or two, though I sensed she wasn't really seeing the black-painted toenails or the worn leather ankle bracelet.

"He told me I shouldn't talk to you about any of this," she said, looking up and meeting my gaze. "I wasn't supposed to even mention that he called me behind your back."

"Okay," I said.

"Like I wouldn't tell you? Just because he told me not to?" She snorted derisively and shook her head.

"It's totally up to you," I said to her, trying to keep my tone nonchalant, though I was dying to know what they'd discussed. "I don't want to get you into any sort of trouble."

"Yeah, well, I think I can handle that. He hardly asked me anything about myself. And he really didn't even ask that much about Mackenzie and the Open Day. It was actually all about you. Like did you ever talk to me about your husband? Did you tell me about him running away with all that money, and some babe? Did you ever get calls from overseas? Any suspicious e-mails? One question after the next—bam, bam, bam—all about you and your marriage."

"And? What did you tell him?" I asked, trying to figure out what Erlander was up to. It was Mackenzie who had been murdered, so why all this interest in Richard?

"That you didn't tell me *anything*!" Mara burst out. "The first time I heard about any of this was yesterday. I mean, what's that all about? I felt like—I don't know—like a real idiot. And even worse, I don't think Erlander believed me. Of course he thought I knew. I mean, we've been working together for almost two years now."

"Oh, Mara," I said, finally realizing what was wrong. She was hurt. "I'm sorry. I thought you'd heard. Everyone in Woodhaven seems to know. They're just too polite to say anything."

"Well, I'm not all that friendly with people in Woodhaven. I come over here to work, and that's all I have time for. And anyway, I'm not one of those types who sits around gossiping, okay?"

"I know that. I'm—"

"What—like you didn't trust me?" Mara said. "Like you thought I didn't know how to keep a secret? Well, you don't know me very well, that's for sure."

"No, you're wrong!" I said, getting out of my chair. I came around to stand in front of my desk, too, hoping to make the point that we were equals. This was important, I realized. Mara needed and deserved a full explanation. "Of course I trust you. Probably more than almost anyone else I can think of right now. And I count on you so much—more than I can say. I'm sorry if I never told you about Richard. I honestly assumed you'd heard about it elsewhere. It's something I have a hard time talking about, frankly. It was so horrible! It ruined my life. I had to start all over again after it happened. And I guess more than anything else I just wanted to put it behind me. Haven't you ever felt that way about anything?"

She looked at me for a moment or two. Then she nodded.

"Yes," she said. "I've felt that way."

"And I thought I was so happily married," I said as I began to tell the story one more time.

❦

"I'm sorry," Mara said when I had finished. "That really sucks. But you know what? I think you're a whole lot better off without him. Look at what you've been able to do on your own! I bet you never would have started Green Acres if you were still some suburban housewife."

"You're right," I told her with a smile, confident that things were okay between us again. And I was beginning to realize how much that mattered to me these days. It was true what I'd told Mara about my counting on her. I'd also come to respect her opinion. "So what do you think Erlander was after—asking you about all this?"

"Obviously he thinks there's some kind of connection between your husband's disappearance and Mackenzie's death."

"I'm the only connection that I can think of," I said.

"Yeah," Mara said, "I'm afraid so."

"What's his theory, then? That for some reason I helped my husband and his lover abscond with the funds and then—having developed a taste for crime—turned around and murdered Mackenzie because he stiffed me?"

"You could have murdered your husband and his girlfriend, too," Mara pointed out. "I mean, didn't they, like, disappear off the face of the earth? Nobody knows what happened to them or all the money they stole, right?"

"That's true!" I said, laughing. "And honestly? I probably would have if I'd had any idea where to lay my hands on them!"

"Listen . . . ," Mara said, hesitating briefly before she continued. "You know, maybe this really isn't anything you should be joking about. I mean, sometimes things can come out sounding one way when you really mean for them to sound another. And this Erlander guy? I think he's actually sort of serious about you as—well—as a suspect. He asked me a lot of questions about your whereabouts during the Open Day. And what your reaction was when you heard about the check bouncing."

I stared at Mara. "And what did you tell him?"

"Only that you seemed kind of upset," she replied. But I could tell by the look on her face that she recalled just as vividly as I did how I had responded when she told me the news that night.

❧

I'd gotten back late that evening after showing Vera and Lisbeth around Mackenzie's garden for the first time. Their enthusiasm had really buoyed me, and I was flying pretty high. But when I saw that the lights were still on in the office, I'd felt bad. I'd been awfully heavy-handed with Mara that afternoon about helping with the garden tour the next day, and I decided I needed to tell her I was sorry. But she insisted on apologizing to me first—something about a check we'd written to Nate that hadn't cleared our account. After some back-and-forth between us, she finally got around to explaining to me why.

"Mackenzie's check. It bounced," she told me.

"What do you mean?"

"Just what I said," Mara replied slowly, no doubt aware that I needed some time for the bad news to sink in.

"All of it? The whole thing?"

"Yeah. That's the way it works."

"But—it has to be a mistake, right? Some sort of oversight on Mackenzie's end? He'll just have to issue us a new one."

"It was returned for lack of funds over a week ago," Mara said grimly. "And nothing's happened yet. I wouldn't hold my breath."

"Well, he has to pay us, Mara!" I said. "He'd better pay us! If he doesn't come through with that money, I'll kill him!"

❦

It was so hard to tell with Mara, but I sensed some sea change in her attitude toward me after our conversation about Erlander's questions—and Richard. It might have been my imagination, of course. Occasionally, though, I would catch her looking at me. Weighing something. She'd glance away whenever I caught her at it. But it made me feel uneasy. And sad. Could she *really* think I had something to do with Mackenzie's death? Surely she knew me better than that! And yet I realized she felt I hadn't been forthright with her about my husband. So I suppose she had every reason to wonder what else I might be keeping from her.

And it wasn't just Mara. When I walked into the post office later in the week, I felt a sudden hush fall over the little lobby, and I guessed they'd been talking about the murder. And me, too, perhaps. I knew from Gwen that Erlander was making the rounds, interviewing everyone who'd been at the Open Day or who knew Mackenzie in some other capacity. According to Gwen, her own interview with the detective had gone just the way she'd wanted. Apparently, she'd laughed off his questions about rumors that Mackenzie and she were more than friends.

"I told him Mackenzie was way too old for me!" she said, batting her eyelashes.

"Oh, God, you flirted with Erlander?"

"Well, it worked, didn't it? Before he even brought it up, I told him I knew Mackenzie's pledge was in jeopardy because MKZ is in such a financial mess. He didn't question me very closely, so I didn't have to tell him *when* I found out. He seemed a lot more interested, actually, in asking me about you."

"About what?"

"Your history. The whole business with he-who-must-not-be-named. I asked him what in the world that had to do with his investigation."

"Oh, thank God, Gwen!" I told her. "At least I'm not the only one to wonder why he's pursuing that line of questioning. What did he say?"

"That he makes a policy of looking under every rock. The truth is, I don't think he has any idea what or who he's looking for, under rocks or not. And how smart can the man be if he still hasn't figured out about me and Graham?"

"I wish to hell you'd tell him the truth. It would look so much better coming from you rather than—" But I stopped when I saw Gwen shaking her head. "Damn it!" I said. "And I *have* been totally honest with him. I have nothing to hide, and look what's happening! Erlander's going around town stirring up people's suspicions about me. I hate this!"

I knew it was irrational, but I really was afraid. I couldn't shake the sensation that malevolent forces were at work. That somehow it was possible I could be held responsible for Mackenzie's death. And I was beginning to understand Erlander's reasoning. The victim had died in a garden that I designed. I'd admitted to being steps away from the scene of the crime. Mackenzie owed me a great deal of money, putting my hard-earned success and independence in jeopardy. Along with all this, I knew that there were too many unanswered questions about my past. Huge sums of money gone missing. The accused parties disappearing into thin air. But what disturbed me more than anything else about the situation was that Richard's crimes should somehow end up making me—the person he'd most wronged—look guilty.

24

🍎

When Tom Deaver called late Friday afternoon he seemed to be making an effort not to appear to be asking me out on a date. He mentioned in passing that he'd been invited to a political fund-raiser for a local state senator at a private home in Richmond the following evening. Then he casually suggested I might want to come along.

"I hear the gardens are pretty incredible. It's at Hal and Suzy Fremont's house. Do you know it?"

"Oh, yes! That's the place with all the amazing stonework, right? I covet that wall every time I drive by."

"Good. It's just cocktails and elbow-rubbing. It would be great if you could make it. I usually avoid this kind of thing like the plague. But the senator's been really supportive of clean air energy projects, and I want to stay in his good graces."

I took a ridiculous amount of time deciding what to wear. The Berkshires are generally pretty casual, but this was a party at one of the fanciest homes in the area. I needed to avoid overdressing, while at the same time I knew it would be a mistake to look too informal. I eventually settled on a summery silk sheath with a flowy hem that swirled around my calves, and classed it up with high-heeled sandals and a double strand of freshwater pearls.

"You look very nice," Tom said matter-of-factly as he opened the door to an ancient VW Beetle convertible and helped me in. I thought he did, too. He was wearing a white sports jacket and a blue oxford-cloth shirt, open at the collar. His dark brown hair was tousled from the drive over, making him appear more carefree and relaxed than he usually did.

"I only drive this on special occasions," he told me as he worked to get the VW into gear. "And when it's not raining. The ragtop's pretty much a sieve at this point, and the transmission's ornery as a mule. But there's something sort of cool about pulling it up alongside all the Infinitis and BMWs."

There was something kind of glamorous about it, too, I thought, as we drove through the lush green countryside. Or maybe I was just enjoying the pleasure of being in the company of an attractive man again. Tom lent me his comb when we arrived at the Hendersons' and waited patiently as I did what I could with my windblown hair.

"I give up," I said finally, putting away my compact.

"I lied before when I said you looked nice," he told me, his hand closing over mine as he took back his comb. "I promised myself not to press my luck tonight. But I have to tell you—the truth is you look pretty wonderful."

Tom's saying so made me feel I actually did. And I found myself walking on air as we made our way across the lower field, where the cars were being parked, through an apple orchard, and then up several flights of beautifully laid blue slate steps before reaching the back of the house with its expansive views westward of open meadows and rolling hills. The terrace was framed with clipped boxwood hedges, roses, and wrought-iron tripod trellises woven with flowering clematis. Waiters moved through the crowd carrying trays of champagne and canapés. A jazz trio played unobtrusively in a corner of the living room, which, like the gardens and the rest of the house, was elegantly and expensively decorated. What looked to me like a David Hockney watercolor hung above the white marble mantelpiece.

I was touched that Tom introduced me to the many people he seemed to know as "Alice Hyatt, the wonderful landscape architect." And then, if someone seemed to show an interest in pursuing the subject with me, he would wander away to talk to another guest for a few minutes. Though I'd worked rooms before, I'd never had such a willing and discreet accomplice leading the way. By the time we left the party, after a gracious pitch by Suzy Fremont for the senator's reelection campaign, I'd accumulated a number of excellent leads.

"You're a terrific front man!" I said, laughing as we walked back down to the car.

"Only if it's for something I believe in," he told me. Though we hadn't discussed it beforehand, when he said he felt that he "owed me a dinner," I happily acquiesced. I liked the easygoing, spontaneous way things seemed to be developing between us. We ended up at a family-style Italian place in Pittsfield where the proprietor recognized Tom right away and seated us in a quiet back corner.

"I used to come here a lot," he said. "It's a great place when you have a slew of noisy children on your hands."

Tom knew the menu by heart. He ordered dinner and wine for us both.

"Do you miss those days?" I asked after the owner had poured our glasses of Chianti and walked off with the menus.

"Oh, sure, when the kids were young—and Beth was still

okay," he said, looking out across the busy room. "But later? No. It was pretty rough, honestly. I was juggling too many things and none of them particularly well."

"Why do I think that's just not so?"

"Well, that's kind of you," he said. "Everyone thought I was such a saint. Dealing with the kids. Caring for Beth at home. But the truth is . . . I was so deeply angry most of the time. At Beth. At how that damned disease was taking everything away from her when she still had so much left to give. And how it was totally taking over my life. The anger was kind of like my own disease, you know? Eating away at me from the inside."

"Oh, I know all about anger," I told him. "And I agree. It can eat you alive if you don't watch it. I still have to work every day not to let that happen. But time helps. It really does. I think I'm maybe a little further along in the recovery process than you are."

"No," Tom told me with a quick laugh, "I think you're just further evolved than me on every level."

I didn't mind the more somber turn our conversation had taken. There were very few people I could talk to openly about what had happened with Richard. And, more to the point, what had happened to me because of it. I felt bad that Tom was still dealing with what seemed to me a lot of unresolved feelings. At the same time, his own struggles made mine seem less lonely. I took comfort in the thought that we both had faced—and were still grappling with— some serious heartache. The dinner was good, though I ate very little. I was far more interested in what Tom was saying—and what he wasn't. I caught him looking at me speculatively a few times.

"What?" I asked finally, over coffee.

"Oh—well . . . ," Tom said, obviously embarrassed. "I just wondered how your interview with Detective Erlander went. I take it he talked to you."

"And I take it he talked to you about *me*, right?" I asked. "Don't worry! I've heard from a number of people that he's been going around asking questions about my checkered past. It's so crazy, though. I can't imagine what he really thinks Richard's disappearance has to do with Mackenzie's death. My friend Gwen says he told her that he likes to look under every rock."

"I think it's more that he's grasping at every straw," Tom said. "He pulled the same kind of thing with me. He uncovered a number of blog posts I'd written over the last couple years for a Web site called EcoCrisis.org. I did a lot of research into the bigger gas producers, including MKZEnergy. I didn't have a lot of good things to say."

"And exactly what does this have to with the investigation?"

"Well you might ask!" Tom said, shaking his head. "As best I can figure out, Erlander seems to think that Mackenzie blocked my wind power initiative to get back at me for the negative coverage. I'd like to think that was the case, honestly. But I kind of doubt Mackenzie ever even heard of EcoCrisis, let alone felt my pieces would have any serious impact on his business. No, he didn't give a damn about *my* views. All he cared about was making sure *his* precious vista remained unobstructed."

"And so? Erlander suspects you killed Mackenzie because he killed your initiative?"

"That's my guess," Tom said. "I checked in with my friend in the DA's office after that to see if I should take any of this seriously. He said that Erlander's known to be a very thorough investigator. And because Mackenzie's death is so high profile he's under a lot of pressure to get things right. He's been down to Atlanta twice to interview Chloe and Lachlan. He's got people doing background checks, combing through MKZ's business records. They're talking to everyone who had any sort of dealings with the man—including your friend Gwen."

"Oh?" I said. "What about her?"

"You knew, didn't you?" Tom asked, signaling for the check. "About Mackenzie promising to underwrite the Bridgewater House restoration, then backing out when his business started to tank? Seems like everyone had some kind of grudge against the dearly departed over money."

Though I pretended to shrug off Tom's revelation that Erlander knew about Mackenzie's broken pledge to Gwen, it actually worried me almost as much as the news that he obviously still had me in his sights. Though Gwen herself seemed unconcerned, I knew just how wobbly her alibi was—and that, if forced to, she intended to commit perjury. But when I called her the next day to tell her what I'd learned, she quickly sidestepped the subject.

"So you and Tom went out on an actual date?" she said. "I should be jealous. I thought we had him earmarked for me."

"Did you hear a word I just said, Gwen? Erlander knows all about the pledge. He knows you have a motive for killing Mackenzie. And I bet you anything he's going to be looking a lot more closely at your relationship."

"So?" Gwen said. "Like I told you, if he digs anything up, I'm just going to say it's idle gossip. Hearsay. Jealous old biddies angry that they're not getting any. Speaking of which, how was he?"

"What?"

"Tom, for heaven's sakes! What's he like in bed?"

"We—we haven't gotten that far," I told her. "Not everybody hops between the sheets on the first date."

"That's true. And I'm just going to ignore the aspersions you seem to be casting in my direction. The fact is, though, you've gone way too long without a little carnal pleasure in your life. Don't you think it's about time, Alice?"

It was a good question and one, in fact, that I'd been struggling with. Tom had made it clear—though in a gentle and gentlemanly way—that he was ready. But I just couldn't seem to let myself go any further than the lengthy kiss we exchanged. I was attracted to him. I respected him. I knew him to be a kind and caring person. But something was holding me back.

"Once burnt, twice shy?" Gwen asked.

"I guess so," I said. "Plus I've got a lot of other things on my mind."

"Well, just don't wait too long," Gwen said. "Speaking from experience, I can tell you that if you see anything that looks remotely like happiness—grab it."

25

❦

Gwen had been planning the benefit at Bridgewater House for several months. She insisted that it be held at the house itself despite its current state of disrepair.

"I think it's important to get people to come in and actually *see* it," she explained when she stopped by my office a week before the event to run her catering choices by me. "I know it's looking a little worse for wear right now, but it's really lovely in its own way—and so full of history. I think people need to *feel* that—to come to know its place in the town and the family who lived there for so many generations. It's the only way potential donors are going to form an emotional attachment to the house and want to invest in its future."

"You've really been thinking this through," I told her, impressed by her reasoning.

"I have no choice! This is my one shot this summer at drumming up some attention and support. After Graham made his pledge, I was planning to have the evening serve as a big celebration. *Hooray! We've reached our goal!* But now—without that—I've got to

find other people who are willing and able to step up and contribute in a major way."

"How are the RSVPs coming?"

"Okay," she said, but I could hear the disappointment in her
voice. "I've got about forty commitments, but a number of the
heavy hitters still haven't responded. And the board isn't really
helping. I was hoping they'd reach out to their wealthy friends in
surrounding towns and bring in some fresh blood. But it's like pulling teeth to get them to do anything! They were all so gung ho
when I first talked about the benefit, promising me all sorts of support. But now? Since I told them I'm not getting Graham's million,
I feel like they're blaming *me* for the money not coming through."

I remembered what Sal had said about how some members of
the Woodhaven Historical Society board were "beginning to wonder if Gwen was up to the job." And I was worried about what this
latest turn of events would mean for her future as executive director. I realized that she'd made a mistake by announcing Mackenzie's gift before she actually had it in hand. And it had been wrong
for her to get involved romantically with a donor, though I believed
only myself and maybe Sal knew about that side of the story. But at
least she'd been able to land the huge pledge in the first place, even
if it didn't pan out. It seemed unfair that the board wasn't behind
her. As far as I could tell, my friend was going all out to make the
campaign to save Bridgewater House a success.

"Let me see your invitation list," I told her. "I could do some
follow-up calls this week if you'd like. And I'd be happy to let my
clients know about it. Most of them support the Botanical Garden
and other historic Berkshire estates. I'm sure some of them would
be interested in helping to preserve Bridgewater House and its
gardens."

"Would you?" Gwen asked. "Oh, Alice, that would be so incredibly wonderful!" If I didn't know her better I would have suspected there were tears in her eyes.

"Of course," I said. "And maybe Tom can give me some additional names. He seems pretty tied in to philanthropic circles up here. I bet he'd be willing to lend a hand."

Over the last couple of weeks Tom and I had been seeing a lot of each other. We'd explored the gardens at Ashintully. Driven down to the Cobble in Ashley Falls and climbed Hurlbut Hill with its stunning views of the surrounding countryside. I was touched and pleased that he suggested excursions he knew would appeal to me. Though I was still not ready to head into the bedroom, we tended to end up after these outings on my living room couch in increasingly more horizontal positions. He began to call me just to talk. We'd fallen into the habit of chatting every night after dinner, catching up on our days, making plans for the upcoming weekend. When he phoned that evening and I told him about Gwen's dilemma, he volunteered right away to get word out to his extensive contacts about the benefit.

❦

Our phone calls and e-mails obviously did some good. By the time I pulled into the driveway at Bridgewater House on Friday night the parking area behind the house was filled. I had to back out again and find a place in the ranks of cars that were lining either side of the road. It helped, too, that it was such a beautiful late-summer night, the warm, still air alive with the music of crickets and tree frogs. I saw Brook and Michael Bostock ahead of me as I walked along the ten-foot-high yew hedge that screened the estate from the road. I called out to them, and they stopped and waited for me to catch up.

"Thanks so much for coming!" I said when I reached them.

"I'm glad you told us about it," Brook replied as we made our way down the potholed driveway. "I've always loved the look of this place from the outside. It's great to hear they're planning on fixing it up. Especially the gardens. Once the weeds start in, these wonderful old borders just don't stand a chance!"

Handsome and reserved, Michael usually let his wife do all the talking, but he spoke up now. "Are you involved with the group that's behind this, Alice?"

"A good friend of mine is the executive director."

"Let them know I'd be happy to help out with the woodwork restoration when the time comes."

"That's terrific," I told him, knowing how much it would mean to Gwen to be able to include Michael Bostock Fine Wood Designs, an award-winning maker of custom furniture, on her list of pro bono donors.

"Isn't he the best?" Brook asked, taking her husband's arm as we started up the wide front steps to the wraparound porch, a late-nineteenth-century addition that featured elaborate gingerbread ornamentation. But even in the softening glow of twilight it was obvious that the balusters were chipped and peeling.

Though Gwen had told me about her plans for decorating the formal front rooms for the evening, I was still pleasantly surprised by the magical effect she was able to create by festooning the ceilings with thousands of tiny white blinking lights swathed in gauzy white bunting. She'd cleared most of the furniture from the rooms, which helped emphasize their spacious dimensions as well as the stately multipaned windows and wide-planked floors. The downstairs was filled with well-dressed people, several of whom I didn't recognize. So the board of directors had come through after all, I thought, corralling their friends from nearby communities.

I saw Sal and Gigi surrounded by others from the group of

wealthy homeowners who had helped develop Powell Mountain. I remembered Gwen complaining that these were the sorts of people who tended to "throw all their money at Tanglewood and at Shakespeare and Company and totally ignore this historic gem right here in their own little town." I was delighted that she would finally have the opportunity to try to enlist them in her cause. And I was pleased to see Vera Yoland and Lisbeth Crocker from the Garden Conservancy, both of whom I'd asked to come, along with several more of my Green Acres clients. I thought it was smart of Gwen to invite folks from the local community as well, including Ron Schlott and his wife.

I was just sorry that Tom, who'd been such a help with the arrangements, wasn't going to be able to make it. He'd gone down to stay with his youngest in Amherst for the weekend.

About half an hour after I arrived, Sal Lombardi welcomed everyone with a brief speech and then turned things over to Gwen. I thought her pitch was just right—full of interesting anecdotes about the house and gardens, the Bridgewater family and their descendants. She pointed out the historic and architectural significance of the estate. She talked about the plans that the architect had drawn up for the restoration project, and encouraged everyone to take a closer look at the blueprints that were displayed on a table nearby. Then she paused and looked out over the crowd with her brightest smile.

"Just think what it must have been like two hundred or so years ago. On a warm summer night very much like this one, with friends and neighbors gathered in this lovely house for a celebration. A wedding, perhaps, or an important anniversary. Can't you just hear the voices and the music and the laughter? It all lingers on somehow in these rooms, don't you think? All that history. The life of the town of Woodhaven. Our town. Please—won't you join me in helping to keep this beautiful and unique home alive? Join me in restoring it to its rightful place at the heart of our community. For our enjoyment and deeper understanding of our past. And for our children and all those who will come after us."

The applause was warm and, I thought, heartfelt. But before it had quite died down, I heard a woman behind me say, "You'd never guess what a shameless little hussy she is."

"Really?" another woman whispered. "No, I wouldn't. She seems so smart and together."

"Well, watch her now as she starts to work the room," Gigi Lombardi replied, because by then I recognized her voice. "She's going to go around to all the wealthy older men in the crowd and flirt with each and every one of them, like some queen bee collecting pollen."

"Actually, I don't think the queen ever collects the—"

"Oh, who cares?" Gigi said irritably, cutting off her companion. "I don't trust her. I don't trust any woman who uses her sexuality to get what she wants. And I especially don't like one who's so intent on working her wiles on my husband. Look, there she goes now."

Dismayed, I watched as Gwen sidled up to Sal with a flute of champagne in each hand. Though he at first shook his head, she laughed and pressed one on him and then clinked her glass against his. She leaned in and whispered something in his ear, her hair brushing his cheek. Poor Sal! He nodded at whatever she was saying, red-faced, a glazed look in his eye.

"My friend Trish Moorehead serves on the WHS board with Sal," Gigi continued. "She says that as far as she's concerned Gwen Boyland only got the position because she played up to all the men on the board. Including Sal, who—and I say this with love—is a total sucker for a pretty face. Gwen called him this week and begged him to bring all our well-connected friends with us tonight.

I could hear her wheedling little voice halfway across the room! I know Trish really wants her out, and so do all the other women on the board. She's barely raised fifty thousand for the restoration campaign so far, though she promised everyone a big pledge was coming in. Well, let me tell you . . ."

I moved discreetly away before I could overhear any more. I was equal parts annoyed with Gigi for spreading such ugly gossip and upset with my dearest friend for giving her every reason to do so. I spent the rest of the reception making nice with the other guests and talking up the restoration project, but my heart had gone out of the evening. I lingered after the others started to leave, helping the catering staff police the rooms for empty plates and glasses.

More sad than angry now, I noticed Gwen on the front porch talking to a tall, balding man sporting a floppy bow tie. She kept touching his arm to make her points and stood on tiptoe to give him a kiss on the cheek when he finally took his leave. But she seemed drained when she walked back into the house.

"You're such a good pal," she said, coming up to where I was loading the last of the wineglasses into their carrying racks. The caterers were lugging their equipment out to the van.

"Whoa, don't take that away," Gwen said, grabbing a half-empty bottle of wine from a passing tray. She then turned to me and said, "Stay and help me finish this?"

"Okay," I said. "Are we celebrating or commiserating?"

"A little of both. It was a much better turnout than I expected at first, thanks in no small part to you and Tom. But after printing and mailing the invitations and adding up all the catering costs, et cetera, I figure I netted maybe four thousand dollars."

"That's nothing to sneeze at, Gwen."

"Yeah, but it's a drop in the bucket in terms of the campaign goal. I don't know what else to do. I was hoping this party would jump-start some serious interest in the project, but I didn't pick up that vibe when I made the rounds. Did you?"

"No, I picked up on something else, though."

"Oh?" Gwen said, turning to me.

"You've alienated all the women on your board because you're such a—and I'm merely quoting here—'shameless little hussy.'"

"What? Those crazy old bags. They're just jealous!"

"This isn't the high school prom, Gwen!" I snapped. "Or a beauty pageant. It's not about who's the prettiest or most popular girl in the class! And you know what makes me really angry? You gave such a great speech. You put together a terrific presentation. You were so confident and persuasive. And then you ruined it all by vamping around the room afterward."

"That's pretty harsh."

"Well, I'm sorry, but it's time you heard this. You're not a teenager anymore. You're a competent, capable, and mature woman, and you need to start behaving like one. Frankly, I think you'd get far better results if you stopped acting so desperate."

"It's not an act," Gwen said, draining her glass. "I wasted too much time thinking Graham was going to come through for me. If I don't raise at least half the money for the restoration by the end of this fiscal year, I know the board's going to replace me. I'm forty-eight, Alice! My mortgage is under water. My 401(k) is a joke. So, yeah, I *am* kind of desperate, okay? I have to use everything I've got to make this happen!"

"And I'm telling you that you've got a lot more going for you than your looks. Start using your head. Rethink your strategy. Figure out a way to get the board—especially the women—back on your side."

Gwen held the wine bottle up to the light. It was empty.

"You're right," she said with a sigh. She walked over to the table where the plans for the building restoration were displayed, put the bottle down, and shuffled the blueprints together. She started rolling them up. "I need to rethink a lot of things. I'm beginning to realize just how hard Graham's death hit me. I've been feeling so down—and vulnerable. It's great you and Tom are getting together. But, honestly? It makes me feel that much more alone."

"Come on—you could have your pick of men! All you have to do is crook your little finger."

"Yeah, maybe," she said, turning to face me. "But I'm worn out. I'm getting too old for all these games. I want someone who really cares about me—someone I can trust. And—well—you might as well know: Sal's been asking to see me again."

"Oh, no, don't go there, Gwen!"

"I think I have to," she said, closing her eyes. "I'm tired—and I'm afraid. Sal's always been so loving toward me."

"You almost broke his heart last time. It isn't fair! And it isn't the solution. You'd just be using him. You told me yourself that you weren't attracted to him anymore. It would be cruel. It would be—"

"My damned decision!" she said, her eyes flashing open again. "I really resent it when you get all high and mighty on me, Alice. I hate it when you tell me what you think I should do. Because what you just don't seem to understand is that I'm not *like* you. I don't have your education or your inner resources. I don't have your drive and determination. And I don't have a well-off family waiting to bail me out if I fail. *This* is all I have," she said, circling slowly around on tiptoe, arms curved above her head, like a little girl in a ballet class. "And it's not going to last forever."

26

❦

"You're being maudlin and ridiculous," I told Gwen when she complained about losing her looks. "And you're wrong about not being determined. Who was it that stood up to that bear the summer we first met? I'll never forget how you faced off against him! You've always been fearless, Gwen. And self-reliant. *That's* who you are. You'd be utterly miserable living off a man. And you'd make Sal miserable, too."

"Stop lecturing me!" she snapped. "Even in your darkest hour, I never told *you* what to do. I was just there for you. I heard you out. I passed the tissues. I poured the wine. What I did not do was dispense any sort of judgment. And that's what I need right now. A real friend—not a life coach!"

"I will not sit by and watch you throw away everything you've worked so hard for."

"Well, I'm afraid you're going to have to do just that," she said. "We're done here."

Gwen and I don't usually let our differences of opinion get in the way of our friendship. We argue, of course. Things can get pretty heated between us, but we've never allowed the bad feelings to hang there for very long. Until that night.

"I think you're making a terrible mistake," I told her as I drew my bag up over my shoulder.

"Yes," she said. "You've made that abundantly clear."

I knew she'd call me over the weekend to apologize. She'd wake up the next day, think over what I'd said, and realize that I was right. It might take her a little while to admit it, I told myself on Sunday afternoon when I hadn't yet heard from her. Gwen could be so stubborn! But on Monday morning when she still hadn't gotten in touch, I realized how serious the situation was. It was inconceivable to me, but my oldest and dearest friend seemed to be giving up. On her independence. Her future. The very essence of what made her such a unique and wonderful human being.

How had this happened? I knew she'd been going through a rough stretch since Mackenzie's passing, but I couldn't remember her ever sounding so down and defeated. Not to mention deceitful: lying to the police and rekindling an affair with someone she no longer loved. This wasn't the Gwen I'd known and admired most of my life. What was really going on? I kept turning over in my mind one particular thing she'd said: *I'm afraid*. But of what? Whom? What wasn't she telling me? For the first time since I learned that Mackenzie's death had been ruled suspicious I felt my confidence in Gwen's innocence start to waver. After all, I'd learned the hard way about being too trusting. I'd learned in the cruelest way possible that thinking you know someone, even someone dear to you, doesn't always mean you do.

❧

With all this on my mind, I arrived at the office on Monday in a foul mood. Mara seemed more withdrawn than usual, too, though it was hard for me to tell what her true emotional baseline was anymore. The closeness we'd shared when we were first dealing with the Mackenzie mess was gone now. I wasn't quite sure why, but I could definitely say when it had ended: the night Erlander had called her at home and told her about Richard's disappearance. I couldn't believe she would actually suspect me of foul play, but she was certainly acting as though she did. When I caught her eyeing me surreptitiously later that morning, I finally snapped:

"What? Is there something you want to ask me?"

"No," she mumbled, looking down at her keyboard.

"Is there something you feel we should be talking about?" I tried again. I was fed up with whatever cat-and-mouse game she was playing. When she didn't answer, I found my all-too-ready temper coming to a boil. "What the hell is it, Mara? Don't you think I see you staring at me with those—"

"Hello? Excuse me?" Chief Schlott asked, pushing open the screen door. One of his deputies, a young officer with a buzz cut whom I knew only by sight, came in after him. "I knocked, but I guess you didn't hear me." He looked from me to Mara, then back to me again. "Sorry to interrupt."

"That's okay," I said, though I felt embarrassed at being caught in the middle of a harangue. I knew I had a reputation around town for having a short fuse. It went back to those early, trying days when I'd first relocated to Woodhaven and was forced to rethink my entire life. I was pretty curt then. And demanding. I kept most people at arm's length. Relations improved when folks got to know me better, but I think Erlander's recent round of interviews had unfortunately jogged a few memories. I could almost hear people thinking . . . *I always thought she had something to hide . . . Surely she must have at least suspected what her no-good husband was up to . . . I heard she learned Mackenzie owed her a ton of money—right before he was murdered. I bet she really lost it then!*

I got up from my desk and came around to shake Ron Schlott's hand. But then I saw the piece of paper he was carrying. He held it up in the air between us.

"This is a warrant, signed by a judge, to search the premises of this place of business and the attached greenhouses. Just to make this official, Alice, I need to inform you that I'm Chief Ron Schlott of the Woodhaven police force and this is my deputy, Niels Halderman, who will be helping me with the search."

"A search warrant?" I asked stupidly, though the evidence was right in front of my face. "What in the world are you looking for in here?"

"I'm sorry, Alice," Ron said. "I really can't go into that. May I have your permission to start?"

I glanced over at Mara, who was staring back at me, open-mouthed.

"Of course," I said, mystified. The whole thing felt as melodramatic and unreal to me as a made-for-TV movie. "Search away! If you're looking for a blunt object, there's a nice heavy maul in the tool area in the back of the barn."

"What?" the deputy gasped.

"She was only kidding!" Mara cried, rising halfway out of her chair. "She doesn't mean anything by it. She didn't do anything wrong!"

"It's okay, miss," Ron said as he started across the room to the double doors that opened to the back of the building. "No one's accusing Mrs. Hyatt of anything. And I recognize a joke when I hear one."

❧

I knew I had nothing to hide. At the same time, I felt anxious and conflicted as Ron and his deputy moved methodically through the converted barn. I watched their progress through the long sliding window that separated the barn from the office area. They were running gloved hands over the mowing equipment. Taking down and closely examining every shovel, rake, and hoe. Looking around and behind the forty-pound bags of fertilizer and grass seed. Though these were just workaday items—and the bigger machines on lease—the search still felt like an invasion of my privacy. And no matter what Ron claimed, there was an implicit threat in what they were doing. They were obviously looking for something that might implicate me in Mackenzie's death.

I pretended to be busy. Mara did as well, scheduling an appointment for me with one of our clients. Checking in on a worker who'd been out sick. She was still on the phone when Ron and the deputy emerged from the barn. They appeared to be empty-handed.

"I've got to head back to the station now," Ron told me, "but Niels is going to stay on and finish up here."

"Fine," I said, relieved that Ron obviously didn't think the rest of the search was worth his efforts. The whole thing was such a waste of time! I got up and walked him out the door.

"Sorry about all this," Ron said quietly as we watched his deputy cut across the lawn to the greenhouses.

"I assume that if you found anything incriminating you'd have had me in handcuffs by now."

"I'm afraid I can't dis—"

"Oh, I know, Ron," I said. "You're just doing your job."

I went back into the office and tried to do mine, but I couldn't concentrate. *What in the world was Erlander up to?* For surely, this whole thing was his idea, and he would have had to have something specific in mind in order to get a judge to sign his warrant. As I was mulling this over, Mara's cell phone rang.

"What?" she said, picking it up. "Oh . . . no! When did it start? How bad is it?"

She sounded upset. My first thought was that Danny's babysitter was on the line and something had happened to Mara's son. I knew Mara hated to have anyone pry into her private life and disliked taking personal days, but I was determined to give her the afternoon off if she needed it. Typically, though, when she glanced up and saw that I was looking her way, she spun around in her chair to face in the opposite direction. Though she lowered her voice, I was still able to make out snatches of her side of the conversation.

"But why didn't you . . . I wish you had . . . of course we will . . ."

Then a loud crash and tinkle of glass coming from the greenhouse made me forget all about Mara's worries. I sprinted across the lawn to deal with my own.

Niels was sprawled at the far end of the new extension with three of my antique bell jars in shards around him. These had been my grandmother's and, though I rarely used them in the garden these days, I treasured their pretty domed shapes and cut-glass handles. To keep them safe, I had arranged them on a strong aluminum shelf above one of the long seedling trays. In the summer season we used this area for drying and processing herbs and flowers for the teas, extracts, and potpourri that I'd been selling for the last couple of years at the Berkshire Botanical Garden's Holiday Fair.

"What the hell happened?" I demanded as I made my way down the aisle toward Niels. I noticed a thin trail of blood trickling along his jawline.

"I'm sorry," he said, attempting to sit up. "Those things just came down on me."

"I very much doubt that," I told him. "Don't move. You'll only cut yourself more. I'll get a broom and try to clear this mess up."

It took a while. There was glass everywhere. The bell jars had obviously hit against the hard aluminum counter edge as they came down and shattered into what seemed like literally a million pieces. Except for the cut on his cheek and a few scratches on his palms, Niels was fine.

"I'll have you know those bell jars were antiques," I said as I swept around him. *What an unnecessary loss!* I thought, my anger building again as I whisked a portion of my family's past into the dustpan. "Irreplaceable antiques."

"I'm sure the county will pay for any damages," he told me.

"Do you have any idea what the word 'irreplaceable' means?"

"I'm *sorry*, okay?" he said. He was obviously one of those people who went on the defensive when he was found in the wrong. Bullies did that, it seemed to me, and I didn't like bullies.

"What in hell are you looking for?" I demanded. "It's ridiculous to have you creeping around behind my back, destroying my property! Just tell me what it is you want, for heaven's sake. I'll help you find it!"

"That's okay," he said, getting to his feet and gingerly dusting off his pants. "I already did." It was only then that I noticed he'd been lying on top of a big black plastic bag. Whatever was in it appeared to be squashed beyond recognition.

"You did?"

"Yes, thanks," he said, picking up the bag. "Sorry about your jars."

I walked slowly back to the office after he'd left, trying to figure out what the deputy could have carried off with him. There was nothing much in the greenhouse this time of the year. The annuals had all been planted. It was far too early in the season to start bringing in the tender perennials for the winter. I didn't actually spend much time out there myself these days. Mara had taken over most of the watering, maintenance, and cleaning. Perhaps she'd have some idea what the deputy might have found.

"Mara?" I called as I opened the screen door. But she was gone.

27

❦

*M*ara didn't come back that afternoon, and she didn't phone in. It was unlike her to leave early without an explanation. I remembered the alarm in her voice when she took the call on her cell right before I was forced to run out to the greenhouse. I wondered again if something had happened to Danny. When she didn't come into work the next morning I began to really worry. I checked in with a few of our crew members, but none of them had heard from her since the day before either.

"And she was going to let me know about someone else taking over for me next Monday," Todd Franey said. "I've got to go to my cousin's wedding in New Hampshire with my folks."

"We'll work something out," I told him, jotting down a reminder to myself. Before I hired Mara, I used to handle all these details on my own. I'd grown so used to her dealing with the crew—all the scheduling and new hires—that I realized I hadn't even met a number of the people who were now listed on our weekly work sheet.

When lunchtime came and went without any word from her, I

decided I had to do something. I knew what a private person she was, but she seemed pretty much alone in the world. She never mentioned family or friends. The only incoming calls I ever over-heard were from Danny's sitter. She'd never even given me her cell phone number. I dug out the personal information form I'd asked her to fill out when she first took the job, but there was no home phone number; the only thing she'd listed on it was an address: 34 East Meadows in neighboring Columbia County. I looked it up online and was able to locate it on Google Maps, but I still couldn't find a number to call.

I activated the office answering machine and closed up shop. It took me about half an hour to get over to the area where East Meadows should have been, according to Google, but I couldn't find any sign or street bearing that name. It was one of those badly zoned parts of the county; an adult video outlet stood not twenty feet from an abandoned motel. After driving back and forth along the forlorn stretch of highway a couple of times, I pulled into a run-down gas-station-cum-convenience-store and asked for directions.

"You talking about the trailer park?" demanded the twenty-something girl behind the counter. She had tattoos snaking down both arms and a silver stud in her lower lip. She was clearly put out that I'd interrupted her intense scrutiny of the *Us* magazine that sat open in front of her.

"I'm not sure," I said. "Is that what East Meadows is?"

"Only one I know of," she said, turning a page. "Down the road about half a mile. Turn right on Guyer's Lane." She glanced up, gave me a hard look, and said, "So you buying something or what?"

I grabbed a roll of mints from the candy rack, paid her, and got the hell out. The first stretch of Guyer's Lane, a dirt road, was oc-cupied by a junkyard specializing in used auto parts. There was a huge mound of tangled mufflers and another of hubcaps, glinting in the afternoon sun. Remnants of what had once been a working farm rose up the hill behind this jumble: a graying eyebrow Colonial with plastic sheeting in its windows, a derelict barn, and a roofless milking shed.

The road was potholed, following the edge of a field that had long since gone to seed. Goldenrod nodded above a thick carpet of overgrown weeds. Rusted barbed wire clung to the collapsing split rail fence. Over a small rise, the lane gave out abruptly onto a roadway that circled through a trailer park that had obviously been there for some time. Porch extensions, vegetable gardens, and aboveground swimming pools lent most of the small plots a homey, settled-in feeling, though there were a few trailers with rusting exteriors and boarded-up windows. In front of one of these paced a skinny dog, tied to an outdoor utility post, who barked frantically as I passed. I circled slowly, looking for number 34, which Mara had listed as her address, but very few of the house numbers were visible from the road. I was halfway around the circle for the second time when I noticed a white single-wide with a sunflower growing beside the door. I recognized the chipped clay pot, which was now dwarfed by the nearly six-foot plant. This was the sunflower, then just a seedling, that I'd given to Danny so many months ago. Someone—no doubt Mara—had secured it with string to a downspout. There was no driveway as far as I could see, so I parked the car in the grass in front of the trailer.

The yard was a neat, carefully organized, outdoor paradise for a small boy. There was a miniature trampoline, a waist-high plastic pool in which floated three different water guns, a rope swing that seemed designed to deposit its cargo onto a well-padded pile of dry leaves. Wooden slats had been nailed to the maple tree that housed the swing, and halfway up its twenty-foot height sat a rudimentary plywood fort with an oversized umbrella for a roof. I knocked on the trailer's aluminum doorframe, though I didn't expect to get a response. Mara's car wasn't there, for one thing. And someone had lowered all the blinds on the inside. I knocked again, and waited, debating about what to do.

"Nobody's home there!" called a female voice from across the way. I turned around. An overweight blonde was sitting in a lounge chair inside a screened porch tent next to her trailer. "You're looking for Mara, right?"

"Yes," I said.

"They pulled out this morning," she said. "You're welcome to come over here. I'd get up, but I've just done my nails and I don't want to mess up my handiwork." I crossed the road to her. "That's the grand entrance," she said, nodding at a zippered door. I undid it and let myself into the surprisingly spacious and welcoming outdoor room. A brightly colored fake Oriental rug lay on top of wall-to-wall indoor-outdoor carpet. There were two lounge chairs, a small couch with a lively assortment of throw pillows, a round glass table upon which sat a jug of iced tea, an open box of Milano cookies, and a plastic caddy stacked with nail polishes and all the accoutrements for a mani-pedi.

"I'm Shelly. Sorry, but I'm not going to shake," she said, holding up both hands, fingers spread. Her nails, at least an inch long, were a vibrant turquoise. "Help yourself to a drink—and a cookie."

"Thanks," I said, pouring myself a glass of iced tea and taking a seat on the couch, which I realized too late was a glider. I slid halfway off it as it shot out from under me, my drink sloshing across the rug.

"Oops!" Shelly said with a laugh. "Sorry! Should have warned you. But most people who drop by know this place like it was their own. We're a pretty tight little group here. Don't get too many strangers out this way."

She couldn't have been more cordial, but at the same time I heard the question behind what she was saying.

"Mara works with me," I told her. "Over in Woodhaven. She left early yesterday and didn't come in this morning. I got worried. I don't have her cell number. All I have is this address."

"You're the gardener?" Shelly asked, looking me over skeptically.

"I own a landscaping business," I told her. "Mara's been working with me for almost two years."

"I know," Shelly said. "Because I've been taking care of Danny for almost two years now. What a great kid! We had such a ball together! Oh, boy, am I going to miss him."

"You mean they've left?" I asked, looking back across the way at Mara's trailer. "For good?"

"Well, I've got a feeling there's nothing exactly good about it. But, yeah, I don't think they're coming back."

"What happened?"

"Hell if I know," Shelly said, blowing on her fingernails. "Mara came home in the middle of the afternoon yesterday. She seemed real upset. She asked me to keep my eye on Danny over here while she took care of some stuff. I asked her what was up, but, like always when I asked something she didn't want to hear, it was like talking to a brick wall. Then I realized that she was cleaning out the trailer. Throwing a lot of stuff away. I couldn't help myself—I went over there with Danny and asked again what was going on. I don't know what the deal is with her, but I know she's got one hell of a chip on her shoulder. The thing is, though, I've been taking care of Danny for a long time now. It's really not about the money. I love that kid, and I know he cares about me. I don't think I was out of bounds wanting to know was going on, was I?"

"No," I said, hearing the unhappiness in her voice. "I don't think you were."

"Well, that makes two of us," Shelly said, shaking her head. "Because she told me to keep my damned nose out of her business. Like I was some stranger, snooping around! She grabbed Danny and kept working. She started loading up the car late last night, probably after Danny was asleep. They left real early this morning. I guess she'd hoped none of us would be awake to see them take off. She gave him a Popsicle to distract him as she drove out. I know that's why she did it. So he wouldn't see me waving good-bye."

"What makes you think she's not coming back?" I asked, looking across the road again. "She left all of Danny's toys."

"That's stuff me and Al donated," Shelly said. "Stuff I never had the heart to throw away when Luke—that's our boy—outgrew it. And anyway, she stopped by and told Pete—he's the owner—that she was going. When he explained to her that he couldn't give her back the deposit because she hadn't given him any notice, she told him where he could put it. What a potty mouth! And right in front of her nephew!"

"Nephew?" I asked. "Danny's her son."

"Is that what she told you?"

"Well . . . ," I said, trying to remember if Mara had actually ever told me that was the case. If not, she certainly let me assume it was so. I'd referred to Danny as her son more times than I could count, and she'd never corrected me.

"Well, she told *me* he's her nephew," Shelly said. "Whatever the hell's going on with her, I can't believe she'd lie about something like that."

"But he calls her Marmy," I pointed out. "Don't you think that's a baby name for Mommy?"

"Nope. He meant Mara," Shelly said with conviction. "Danny

told me a couple of months ago that he missed his 'mommy.' I asked him where she was and he told me she was in bed—and then he burst into tears. I didn't feel right pushing him for more information. And he never mentioned her again. I'm pretty sure he wasn't supposed to tell me even that. He looked real guilty after he'd said it."

I tried to make sense of Shelly's revelations, but nothing seemed to add up. I'd thought of Mara as such a strong, capable, and loving single mother for so long, it was almost impossible for me to suddenly picture her in this changed, more distanced role. And why would Mara want to keep Danny's real identity a secret from me?

"So it wasn't you who called Mara on her cell at work yesterday?" I asked.

"Nope."

"Whoever it was said something that really upset her. I think that's why she left so fast." I got up to leave myself, after thanking Shelly for the iced tea and the conversation. She got to her feet, too.

"Listen," she said, holding open the netted door and then following me out, "I know I came down pretty hard on Mara just now. I'm just real hurt that she took Danny away the way she did. But I'm also real worried about the two of them. They seem so alone in the world. And she seems to be in some kind of trouble. I'd do anything to help them, honestly. If you manage to get in touch with her, would you tell her that for me?"

"Of course," I said. We were two very different women, leading very different lives, but we felt the same way about Mara and Danny. And that made it seem like we had a lot in common.

❧

It was late afternoon by the time I got back to Green Acres, and the answering machine was blinking. I ran through the messages.

Three from crew members checking in about their schedules. Two from clients. One from Ted Finari asking if I wanted to participate in his "Putting Your Garden to Bed for the Season" annual seminar at the garden center. At first I thought the last message was a wrong number. It had come in just a few minutes before I returned.

"Hi, it's Sarabeth at the hospital. Sorry to call here, but I can't seem to get you on your cell. Please give me a call back as soon as you can. It's—it's important." She left a number with a 570 area code.

I was about to delete it, but then something made me listen to it again. It was the little stumble on "it's important" that gave me pause. Whoever Sarabeth was, she had something to say that was making her nervous. I dialed the number.

"Oh, you *are* still there!" she said before I had a chance to say hello. "I'm so glad I could catch you before you left. I'm sorry. I'm really so very, very sorry, Mara. But Hannah—she's gone."

"I'm not—," I tried to say, but Sarabeth ran on.

"Once the infection started to spread there really was very little that anyone could do. Jack asked me to call. He's just too—"

"I'm sorry." I finally interrupted the woman's babble. "But I'm Alice Hyatt, Mara's employer. What is this about? What's happened?"

"Oh!" Sarabeth cried. I heard muffled voices in the background. Then a clattering sound. Then silence.

28

🍂

I put the phone down and walked across the office to Mara's computer. The screen filled with the same montage of photos I'd first stumbled upon the day of Mackenzie's death: Danny and the young woman who looked so much like Mara, smiling into the camera. The handsome, twentysomething man standing next to an older man in front of a ranch-style house flanked by willow trees. For the first time I noticed the edge of a barn behind the house and a swath of cornfield. I located Mara's iPhoto software, opened it up, and started to scroll through her library of photographs. Most were organized automatically by date. There were many shots taken around the ranch house, and these showed what seemed to be an extensive farm with outbuildings and a big red barn. In a photo dated four years ago, Mara and the other woman, who was obviously pregnant, stood with their arms around each other's waists beside a pickup truck.

Then I found a folder of photos marked "Events." These weren't just dated; someone had labeled most of them as well. There were numerous shots of what looked like typical family occasions—

cookouts, Thanksgiving dinners, birthday parties. I stopped on one of a gap-toothed Danny, his face smeared with chocolate, sitting on the lap of the woman who looked like Mara. It was labeled "Hannah and Danny on his 2nd birthday." Hannah . . . who I realized now had to be Danny's mother. The "mommy who was in bed." The woman they could do nothing for at the hospital. Who hadn't regained consciousness. Who was gone. Mara's sister.

I felt heartsick for Mara—and saddened by the thought that the world had lost this lovely, laughing young woman whose face looked so familiar. I also suddenly felt like an intruder. I closed iPhoto and pushed back from the desk. I was tempted to shut down the computer altogether. But something made me hesitate—and rethink my qualms about digging further into Mara's private life. Yes, I was upset by what I had inadvertently learned about the tragedy that had befallen her and her family. But still, I sensed that if I turned away now and decided that none of this was my business, I'd be letting Mara down.

For whatever personal and obviously painful reasons, she'd taken on the tremendous responsibility of raising her sister's child. She'd been a loving and unwavering presence in his life during what must have been a very difficult period for them both. And at the same time, despite these other burdens, she'd been a highly effective and loyal business partner for me. With a pang, I remembered her rushing to my defense when I made that crack about the maul during the police search. "It was a joke!" she'd cried. "She doesn't mean anything by it. She didn't do anything wrong!"

Without Mara's determination, I'm not sure I would have been able to make it through those frightening and uncertain days after Mackenzie's death. But it wasn't just that I owed her something. In her cynical and withholding nature I recognized my own wised-up self. I think Mara was actually more like me than anyone else I knew—including my daughters. Both of us had been forced by experience to believe that we were going to have to get through life pretty much on our own. And yet she'd come to my aid in more ways than she would probably ever realize. It was my turn now. I moved back to the computer.

❦

Her e-mails were all business related. So, seemingly, were the document and spreadsheet files. It wasn't until I started to scroll through the Internet sites she'd bookmarked that I found anything that might be considered personal in nature. There was a long list of Web sites related to hydraulic fracturing: newspaper pieces, legal articles, research findings, government resources. She'd even bookmarked a couple of the posts that Tom had written for EcoCrisis .org. Her interest in all this surprised me. I remember the very first time the subject had come up between us—the day that Eleanor had called to arrange the appointment for me to meet Mackenzie— and I'd asked if she thought that fracking was a danger to the environment. "Maybe," she'd replied with a shrug, "but so are a lot of other things."

As I continued to make my way down the extensive list of fracking-related Web sites, it became clear that she'd actually been putting a great deal of time and thought into the question. Many of the bookmarks involved disputes between people who had leased their land in Pennsylvania and the lessee—an hydraulic fracturing company called EnergyCorp. She'd saved dozens of related news articles, legal filings, and YouTube videos. I scrolled up and down through this cache of information, unable to make sense of why Mara would have wanted to save it.

When the phone rang, I reached for it and answered automatically: "Green Acres."

"You're still working!" Tom said. "I tried the house a few times, but you didn't pick up. What's going on?"

I'd been so immersed in what I was doing that I'd lost track of time. It was almost eight o'clock. I explained to Tom about Mara's disappearance, what I'd learned about her and Danny from Shelly, and what Sarabeth had unwittingly revealed to me about Hannah's death.

"I've been trying to dig into things on her computer," I told him. "It's so strange. I've come across an enormous number of bookmarks about fracking. She acted totally uninterested in the issue the whole time I was working for Mackenzie—but from what I see here, I have to say she seems to have actually been almost obsessed by it. I wish I knew when she'd saved some of these links."

"Well, that's easy enough to find out," Tom said. "Do you want me to drop by and help you with this? I take it you haven't eaten yet. I'll pick up something for you from Radicchio's on the way if you'd like."

❦

Tom prided himself on being up on all the latest technology, and he enjoyed demonstrating his prowess in all things digital. After he arrived with some flatbread pizza for me, I pulled up a seat next to his in front of Mara's computer.

"A lot of people don't realize that their viewing history is stored on their computers even after they think they've erased it," Tom said, clicking away at the keyboard. After a moment, he continued: "Yes, you're right. She was keeping tabs on the whole industry: news coverage, lawsuits, the latest research findings. This does seem a little obsessive. And she's been tracking all this for almost a year and a half."

"Really?" I said, leaning forward to get a closer look. He

started to scroll down the list of sites she'd visited the week I hired her as my assistant at Green Acres. Then he jumped ahead, scanning over the sites she visited the first few months in my employ. "Hold on!" I cried as I saw a link that stopped me cold.

"What?"

"Go back up again—slowly," I told him. "There! Right there. Oh, my God. Can you click on that for me?"

"Okay," he said, giving me a curious glance. "The link's dead. But I'll just cut and paste it in. Here we go—"

It was one of those encyclopedic medical Web sites that covered everything from cold sores to chronic fatigue syndrome, and every disease, remedy, symptom, and side effect in between. The page Mara had saved was titled "Digitalis and Toxicity" and went into minute detail about the uses and abuses of the plant-derived drug. My eye fell almost immediately on the following: *A lethal dose of digoxin, the medicine extracted from the digitalis plant, is considered to be 20–50 times the maintenance dose. In healthy adults, a dose of less than 5mg seldom causes severe toxicity, but a dose of more than 10mg is almost always fatal.*

"What's the matter?" Tom asked, turning toward me.

"Wait," I told him as I continued to scan the page: *Symptoms of digitalis poisoning, resulting from having too much of it in the blood, include: Loss of appetite—Stomach problems such as nausea, vomiting, or diarrhea—Vision impairment—Dizziness and confusion.*

"You're sure she viewed this over a year ago?" I asked Tom.

"Well, yes, this is everything she looked at during that time," he told me, scrolling down the list again. "What's going on?"

"I'm not sure," I told him. "Let's keep going. What else was she viewing?"

More sites on digitalis. Its use in the treatment of congestive heart failure, atrial fibrillation, and other heart ailments. Its history as a plant-derived medicine. How its benefits were first discovered when the leaves of the plant were dried and ingested as an herbal tea. All this followed by a caveat: *The digitalis leaf provides a narrow therapeutic index, requiring close medical supervision for safe use. It is often difficult to recognize the level of maximum therapeutic effect of digitalis without entering the toxic range.*

I sat back. I closed my eyes.

"Hey," Tom said, taking my hand and squeezing it. "Are you okay? Can you tell me what this is about?"

"I'm just guessing, really," I replied, getting out of the chair. My legs ached from sitting for so long, and I had a crick in my neck. I walked across the room and leaned against the front of my desk, trying to put the pieces together. "And this could be a real stretch . . . but I think Mara may have had something to do with Mackenzie's death."

"What?" Tom said. "Did she even know him?"

"I'm not sure," I said. "But she was obviously deeply interested in fracking over a year before I even got the commission. She lied about not having an opinion about it, because all those sites have a decidedly negative bias. She must have opposed it, too. And then— I just remembered—when I first got the call to meet with Mackenzie I told her I wasn't going to go. That I couldn't work for a man who was destroying the environment. But she sweet-talked me into at least talking to him, saying she was curious about what the house looked like on the inside."

"Okay, so maybe she knew more about fracking than she let on," Tom said. "And maybe she wanted you to work with Mackenzie. But it's a huge leap from there to—to killing him, Alice."

"It goes back to something Erlander asked me at the end of that first interview," I explained. "I'd answered all the usual questions—and more than I really thought were necessary about my private life. And then, out of the blue, he asked me what I knew about digitalis. He wanted to know whether I realized that it was poisonous. I said of course I knew—that many, many common plants are. I dismissed the whole thing as another one of his crazy shots in the dark. But then Ron and his clumsy deputy conducted that search here yesterday morning."

"Yes, you told me."

"And the deputy claimed to have found what he was looking for. It was in the back of the new greenhouse where I dry herbs at the end of the season to sell at the Holiday Fair. When Mara first started working here she was even more withdrawn than she is now. I mean, she was abrupt to the point of real rudeness. But she did a good job, and I wasn't looking for a friend, just some competent help. That first fall, though, when she discovered that I dried and processed plants and herbs, she got very interested in learning how to do it herself. I could tell she really enjoyed it—and I liked the fact that she was apparently beginning to appreciate what Green Acres was all about. I eventually let her take over most of that side of things."

"You think she started drying digitalis leaves?"

"Yes, that's what I'm thinking. She might have dried them for an herbal tea that she gave to Eleanor, convincing her it would be good for Mackenzie. But I'm pretty sure that's what was making him so sick the last few weeks of his life—his dizziness, nausea, diarrhea. Those are all side effects of digitalis poisoning."

"Okay," Tom said. "But why in the world would she want to murder him? She had a good job. She was responsible for Danny. Why put her life—and his well-being—in jeopardy? And what's the connection between her and Mackenzie?"

"It has to be something to do with fracking, don't you think? I mean, look at all these hundreds of viewings and bookmarks! Not a week went by when she wasn't checking out the latest news. And she followed all these lawsuits like a hawk. Especially the disputes with EnergyCorp in Pennsylvania."

"EnergyCorp?" Tom asked.

"Yes. That's the name of the drilling company."

"Bingo!"

"What do you mean?"

"I wrote several pieces on the major gas producers for my blog, remember? EnergyCorp is one of MKZEnergy's subsidiaries."

❧

"I want you to call Erlander with this information first thing in the morning," Tom told me after we'd talked the whole thing through a couple of times. We'd gone back up to the house. It had grown chilly, and we were sitting on the couch in the living room having a glass of wine.

"I can't do that to Mara," I told him. "I have to find her first. I need to hear her side of the story. All I have now are little bits and pieces of what happened."

"That's Erlander's job," he said, putting his arm around my shoulders. "Or the police department's. It seems quite possible that Mara did poison Mackenzie. And in a totally premeditated way. She could have been planning this whole thing for almost two years! She could be dangerous, Alice."

I put down my glass. I turned to him.

"I'm sorry," I said, "but I know Mara. She's a good, loyal person at heart. There has to be a rational explanation for this."

"Oh, come on, Alice! We both know that seemingly good people can do really terrible things. I'm sure there is a rational explanation, but I doubt it's one you're going to like. Think about it:

Mara took off in the middle of that search. She must have known what the police were looking for. She's on the run—and I have a feeling that the last thing she wants is you coming after her. Let this go. Let Erlander take over."

"No, it was that call that made her leave," I said, correcting Tom. "I'm sure it was a call from the hospital about her sister. Mara's not running away; she's going home."

"Listen," Tom said, "I know you're worried about her. I know you really care. And it's great to see you wear your heart on your sleeve for a change."

"What do you mean?"

"Sometimes it's hard for me to know what you're feeling," he said, squeezing my shoulder. "Though you've got to know by now how I feel about you. And what I want."

"Tom—," I said, sitting forward. "This really isn't the moment to—" But he pulled me back toward him and into his arms. Then he started to kiss me, but not with his usual gentle consideration. This was real and uninhibited passion, and I felt myself responding to him as I never had before. He began to unbutton my shirt. His hands moved across my breasts, and I could feel my body arching toward him. But my thoughts kept turning back to Mara and the many secrets she'd been keeping from me. How long had she been planning to poison Mackenzie? Why? Where did she come from? How was I going to find her? Because no matter what Tom told me, I knew I had to track her down and get to the bottom of this.

"Alice?" Tom asked as I sat up abruptly.

"Eleanor would know," I said.

"What?"

"I bet she'd know where Mara went."

"Damn it, Alice!" Tom said, pushing himself off the couch. He stood, his back to me. He ran his hands shakily through his hair, visibly trying to get his emotions under control. He muttered something to himself, then turned and looked down at me, his mouth set in a grim line. "I think I've been pretty patient. I've tried to take into consideration what you've been through in your marriage and how you—"

"Oh, Tom, you've been wonderful," I said, chagrined by my behavior. I was also startled by how distraught he seemed. "I'm so sorry that—"

"No!" he said, his voice rising. "No more bullshit! I need you to think about how you feel. I need you to decide what you want. I'm sorry, but I just can't go on like this anymore."

29

🍐

I found Eleanor's cell number the next day in the electronic address book on Mara's computer. My call went straight to her voice mail. I left her a message saying that Mara had disappeared, and that I was worried about her.

"If you know where she might be, or have any information that might help me find her, please give me a call. I just want to help her—wherever she's gone."

It was Friday, always a busy day at Green Acres during the summer, and even busier now that I was all alone in the office. The season was winding down—Labor Day was Monday—and I was fielding a lot of calls from clients who'd soon be closing up their houses for the winter. There were fall cleanups, new plantings, and other end-of-summer projects to schedule. Despite my negligence during the months I'd devoted to Mackenzie's garden, I'd been able to retain almost all of my clients. But I was taking nothing for granted. I couldn't afford to. I was determined to keep Green Acres on an even keel and at the same time start paying back my family. So I made sure to telephone and talk personally—and often at length—to everyone who contacted me. I tried to pick up the phone when it rang, but by midafternoon I was so busy, I had to let a number of calls go into voice mail.

I checked the machine around five o'clock and discovered that Eleanor had left a message asking me to get back to her. When I called, she gave me directions to her place in Pittsfield. I had a hard time hearing her over the high-pitched racket in the background.

"I can't talk now," she said. "Come by in an hour or so. I should be free by then."

The directions led me to a two-family frame house on a tree-lined block not far from downtown. It was a working-class neighborhood. A couple of shrubs or trees sat in front of most of the homes, with the more expansive yards in the rear. A chain-link fence enclosed Eleanor's backyard. I caught a glimpse of a swing set and colorful plastic toys as I parked my car. I followed the shriek of children's voices around the side of the house. There were half a dozen kids, most just toddlers, playing in the makeshift sandbox that took up the back right quadrant of the yard. Eleanor sat nearby on a folding aluminum chair with a baby, deeply asleep, on her lap.

"Hey there!" I said, letting myself in through the metal gate.

"I'd get up," she told me as I approached, "but as you can see, I got my hands full." I sat down in an empty folding chair next to her.

"What you're looking at here," she said, nodding at the children in the sandbox, "is Granny Eleanor's Daycare Center. It started with just my grandkids. But then word got out around the neighborhood. Some days I got almost a dozen little ones to look after—and some of them nothing but trouble. *Lamar!*" she shouted at a boy who'd just pushed another boy backward into the sand. "Stop that right now, or you're going to get a spanking from me. And you know I'm not kidding!" She turned back to me, and said, "I told their mommies that I'm a big believer in smacking fannies. If they don't like it, don't leave 'em with me."

"Good for you," I said. "And it's great you've started your own business. You look a lot happier than the last time I saw you."

She stopped smiling and shook her head. For the first time since I'd known her I thought she looked her age.

"That was a bad time," she said. "A very bad time. I came at you with that knife. I hate to even think about it now. I was not in a good state of mind, and I'm really sorry about some of the things I did and said. Mr. M—well, he was not the person I thought he was. He caused me and my family a lot of pain. But he sure didn't deserve what he got."

"The police talked to you?"

"Oh, yeah. They've been here. Questioned my son, too. They keep sniffing around in our business. I'm pretty sure they're hoping to pin it on one or maybe both of us. We live in downtown Pittsfield, right? Crime capital of the county. We probably fit right into their homicide demographic or whatever. But good luck with them getting anything to stick."

"Don't feel singled out," I told her. "They've been after me as well. They even came and searched my office a few days ago. They told me they found what they were looking for. Whatever it was, I know it was in the area of the greenhouse I use for drying herbs. Though Mara's been doing most of that work for me the last year or so."

Eleanor turned and looked at me.

"I tried to get Mara on her cell after you called," she said. "But her mailbox is full. What's going on? You think she had something to do with all this?"

"I'm not sure," I told her. "The detective asked me about digitalis—and the fact that it can be toxic. I assume the question had something to do with Mackenzie's death. Don't you? Of course, you don't have to tell me, but did Mara make the herbal tea you gave to Mr. M? I remember you telling me once that you thought it might actually be doing him more harm than good."

Eleanor looked away across the lawn. There was a sudden lull in the children's chatter, and I could make out the sound of stop-and-go traffic on Route 7 a few blocks away. Though only fifteen or so miles north of Woodhaven, Pittsfield was another world: urban and gritty, like so many postindustrial New England cities. Eleanor was doing the best she could, but still, being deprived of her job as well as her independence must have been a pretty hard blow. She'd lost so much ground in her life because of Graham Mackenzie. I could sense her debating how far she wanted to get dragged back into the mess surrounding his death.

"The detective asked me the same thing," Eleanor said. "Whether I'd given Mr. M something made with this digitalis plant. I told him I didn't know. Which was the truth."

"But Mara did give you the tea, didn't she?"

"I thought you wanted my help in finding her," Eleanor said, shifting the baby, who was beginning to whimper, into a different position on her lap. "How is this helping to find her?"

"I'm just trying to make sense of what happened."

"Well, I'd do anything for Mara and Danny," Eleanor replied. "And anything to keep them from getting hurt. She's had enough trouble in her life already."

"She told you about her past?"

"No, not really," Eleanor said. "Not about whatever it was that had made her so unhappy. But you didn't need a divining rod to see that she'd been through hell, did you? I assumed it was something to do with Danny's father—a marriage gone wrong, maybe some kind of abuse."

"She's been living in a trailer park in Columbia County," I told Eleanor. "A woman there—the one who took care of Danny when Mara worked for me—claims that Danny's actually Mara's nephew, not her son."

"Is that right?" Eleanor said, looking away again across the lawn where the shadows had started to lengthen. A woman appeared at the side gate and called to Eleanor:

"Sorry I'm so late, Granny. But I'll take those troublemakers off your hands now."

"Hey, Libby," Eleanor said, keeping her seat as the woman let herself into the backyard. I got up to shake Libby's hand after Eleanor had introduced me as a friend.

"Surely you can't be Eleanor's granddaughter," I said.

"Oh, no!" she said, laughing. "We just all call her Granny around here."

Two of the children left with Libby, and shortly after that a father stopped by for Lamar and the baby Eleanor had been holding in her arms. Then Eleanor herded the three remaining children into the house. I got up as she walked back across the lawn toward me.

"I should go," I said. "You've got things to do."

"Wait a bit," she said, waving me back into the chair. She sat down again with a sigh. "I think you may be right about Danny. A couple of times, when Mara was out of earshot, he told me that he missed his mommy. Of course, I told him she'd be right back, but I could tell that wasn't what he wanted me to say. I knew something was wrong—Mara was so secretive and sometimes Danny seemed so scared—but I figured it had to do with the bad marriage. Still, I could tell, she really loved that boy. That's what a mother does, as far as I'm concerned."

"I think you're right."

"Do you know why she had him?"

"No," I told her. "But I got a call for her from a hospital in Pennsylvania yesterday. It sounded like an emergency, so I called back, and before I could explain who I was they told me that someone named Hannah had just died. I'm pretty sure that Hannah was Mara's sister. Danny's mom."

"Oh, that poor little boy! Poor Mara! So she's going home to be with her family."

"She's from Pennsylvania?"

"Yes. A small town in the middle of nowhere, according to her. Honestly, I never could understand why she left. She grew up on a farm, milking the cows and feeding the chickens. I could tell she was kind of torn about the place for some reason, but still, it sounded like a paradise to me. Such a beautiful, peaceful part of the world. But she said that things had been changing there the last couple of years."

"Do you remember the name of it?"

"What do you want with her really?" Eleanor asked, giving me a hard look. "You going to turn her over to the police? I don't know for sure what that girl did or why she might have done it, but I don't want to see her in jail."

"I don't either," I said. "At the same time, it was you who said that Mr. M didn't deserve what he got. Nobody has the right to take another person's life."

"There are all sorts of ways of taking a life," Eleanor replied. "You don't have to kill someone to do it."

30

❦

The town was called Shalesburg, Eleanor told me reluctantly before I left. When I got home that evening, I printed out driving directions from Google Maps. Shalesburg was more than two hundred and fifty miles from Woodhaven, in the heart of Pennsylvania farming country. I decided to get a good night's sleep and make an early start the next day. But sleep wouldn't come. It hadn't put in much of an appearance the night before either. I knew why. Though I did everything I could to push them away, Tom's angry words were keeping me awake. *I need you to think about how you feel. I need you to decide what you want. I'm sorry, but I just can't go on like this anymore.* I must have dozed off finally, because the alarm clock shocked me awake around six o'clock. I pulled myself out of bed, my eyes grainy, my head throbbing.

Though the windshield misted up as I drove through town, it didn't start to really rain until I hit the turnpike, heading west. I turned on the radio to get the weather report, and then kept it on for company. I didn't want to be alone with my thoughts—and Tom's words, which, in my weariness, had taken on a hectoring, plaintive quality. *I need . . . I need . . . I just can't go on. . . .*

But soon enough another voice whispered in my ear, *I'm afraid,* and I found myself brooding again about Gwen. She still hadn't tried to contact me. Had she taken up again with Sal already? If so, was it going to be possible for us to remain friends? I'd actually started to call her the night before to tell her what I'd learned about Mara. I'd been so relieved to think that if Mara had indeed poisoned Mackenzie, then at least my fears about Gwen's involvement were unfounded. But I'd hesitated. I knew there was something Gwen wasn't telling me. Some reason she lied about being at the house the morning of his death. Something that was driving her to make such bad decisions. No, it was Gwen who owed me a call and an explanation, I'd decided. And I'd put the phone down again.

I was well past Albany before the repetitious news cycle began to get on my nerves, and I turned the radio off. After a while, I realized that the *swish, swish* of the windshield wipers was actually having a calming effect on me. I felt the tension in my shoulders start to loosen. It had been months since I'd been more than fifty miles away from Woodhaven. Though this was hardly a vacation, there was something about being on the highway—in steady forward motion, cut off from daily routines and demands—that helped free up my mind. And, as was happening more and more often these days, I found my thoughts turning toward my husband. Not the Richard who'd destroyed my marriage, and almost my life. Not the fraud and the cheat. No, for some reason, the Richard whose betrayal had damaged my sense of trust almost beyond repair had, over the last couple of weeks, started to recede into the background. And the man

I had loved for more than twenty years—my best friend, my passion-ate lover, my daughters' father—had begun to reemerge.

❦

"Wait, no, hold on, let me guess," he said, smiling down at me. He was several inches taller than me and, jammed together as we were in the bar area, I was forced to crane my neck to look up at him. I usually didn't go in for this sort of pickup nonsense, but there was something about him that made me hesitate. He looked more seri-ous than flirtatious, and he had a kind of relaxed, good-natured handsomeness that seemed out of place in a Tribeca watering hole frequented by savvy, up-and-coming Wall Street types. My room-mate from Brown had dragged me there to meet a boy she was dating, and then had melted away with him into the happy hour crowd. I'd been unsuccessfully trying to find my way to the nearest exit when I had—quite literally—run into my inquisitor.

"Guess . . . what?" I asked, surprising myself that I had even responded.

"Kansas," he said, nodding as he gazed down at me. "You're from Kansas. Like Dorothy."

"Oh, you are so not right!" I said, blushing a little. What was this? *I had to ask myself. I was certainly used to my share of come-ons and had learned how to deftly deflect unwanted attention. I would usually never encourage small talk with a stranger in a noisy bar that, just a minute earlier, I'd been intent on leaving.*

"Iowa," he said, watching my reaction, then, "—No, hold on, sorry, but it's definitely an 'I' state. Illinois or Indiana."

"What's with the Midwest?" I asked. "Do I have straw in my hair or something?"

"No, but I see you on a farm," he said. "Or is it a ranch? Somewhere green and peaceful with mountains and—"

"Mountains in the Midwest? Your sense of geography is even worse than your guesswork."

"But I'm getting closer, right?" he asked, undaunted.

What is it about human chemistry? This was certainly one of the sillier conversations I'd had over that busy Christmas break my senior year at Brown, and yet I found myself enjoying it more than any other. Over the noise and under the rather lame repartee, there were far more interesting and exciting questions being wordlessly asked and answered. We lasted another ten minutes in the bar as he worked his way through most of the western and southern states.

"I know what the problem is," he said after he'd tried and failed with both Hawaii and Alaska. "I can't hear myself think. I need someplace quieter to concentrate. There's a nice little Japanese restaurant right down the block. Would you mind?"

I didn't mind in the least. It was utterly unlike me to be so daring and impulsive, but, in the beginning at least, that's what Richard Hyatt brought out in me. I felt carefree and adventurous and fun that night. We laughed a lot, even as we started to trade personal information. He was in the training program at Lerner, Reese, and Hamilton and going for his MBA at Columbia at night. He told me this with obvious pride, though he tried to couch it in a little self-deprecating humor.

"And LRH is paying the freight. I think it's their way of buying my soul. What kind of person would accept a free MBA and then take another job? I'm probably a lifer."

"Well, they must think you're worth it," I said. "That's quite an investment."

"And you?" he asked. "What are your plans post-Brown?"

"This is only going to confirm your first impression of me as a farm girl," I told him, "but I'm thinking of getting a certificate in landscape design. I know it doesn't sound particularly ambitious, *but I've always loved gardening. There's a great program at the New York Botanical Garden, so I could live in the city with my folks and save money."*

"New York! Of course! It's the one place I missed, right? But it's not exactly the garden capital of the world."

"My grandparents have a house in the Berkshires with the most amazing gardens. It's like a second home to me."

He looked at me with what seemed almost like longing, though we'd known each other for less than two hours.

"You're lucky," he said, "to have a place in the world that means so much to you. To have something in life you really want to do."

"And you don't? Accounting doesn't make your heart beat faster?"

"Not really, but making a decent living does. Getting ahead in business does. But that's only so that I can provide for a family someday. I'm sorry, I know this is going to sound like too much information, but the truth is that's all I really want in the world. A family I can call my own."

❧

The rain began to let up around Oneonta. I stopped for gas and a vente cappuccino for the road. A few miles after I got back on the highway, the sun broke through the clouds—almost blinding me— and I had to scrabble with one hand through my bag on the passenger seat for my dark glasses. It still felt odd at times driving by myself. I'd spent so much of my adult life accompanied by Richard and my daughters that even now—after years of being on my own—I could occasionally feel overwhelmed by their absence. One of the biggest mysteries for me about Richard's disappearance was the fact that he'd walked away from us—the family we'd created together and that he'd told me from the beginning he'd longed for most in life. And I'd believed him. It was actually one of the few things about him that I still believed.

He was an orphan, adopted as a toddler by an older couple, but he'd always felt more dutiful than loving toward them, and never at ease in their orderly, modest, mostly silent Maryland home. They died, a few months apart, when Richard was nineteen and a sophomore at Georgetown. He'd sold the house less than a year later and never went—or seemed to look—back. I've often wondered if it was that early lack of connection and identity, of not knowing who he was or where he'd come from, that was behind what happened later. Yes, I'm sure he wanted love and security, but obviously other forces were driving him, too. There had to have been some remote part of him—a cold, closed chamber of his heart—that he kept from us. A place where he nursed his anger and pain, where he made his awful plans. But never once in our entire marriage, even during our last days together, did I sense that Richard Hyatt was anything more—or less—than he seemed.

❦

"Why not come with me?" he asked the night he told me about the company sending him to Hong Kong for the global conference. "It's supposed to be an amazing city. You could explore it while I work—then we could take it all in together at night."

"Oh, I'd love to," I said. "But I just don't think I should leave the girls right now." We were getting ready for bed. I was about to drop my nightgown over my head when I felt Richard come up behind me.

"They aren't girls anymore," he whispered into the nape of my neck as he started to massage my breasts. "And you deserve this. We deserve this. John says he wants to introduce me personally to the managing partners. I'm pretty sure this invitation means a pro-

motion. We can stop in Paris on our way back and celebrate our twentieth in real style."

"Don't tempt me!" I said, turning around in his arms to face him. I let the nightgown tumble to the floor between us. "You know how worried I am about Olivia. And I've got the college tour all lined up for—" But his mouth closed over mine before I could finish, and I felt myself temporarily forgetting everything else but the pressure of his lips on mine. That's all Richard ever had to do—a kiss, a touch, even just a look at times—and I was ready. I don't understand people who are constantly seeking new partners and sexual novelty. For us, all we ever needed was the easy, often hilarious intimacy we shared naturally. The knowing exactly when and where and how to do the right things. After twenty years, it seemed to me that practice had pretty much made that part of our life perfect.

"I hope everyone has as much fun as we do," he told me later as we lay together, spent and happy, on top of the still-made-up bed. "Think what this is going to be like in Paris!"

"Good try," I told him, sitting up on one elbow and taking him in. As far as I was concerned, he had just the right amount of chest hair. Not a dark heavy mat like some of the men I saw in the pool at our country club, but just enough for me to run my fingers through and enjoy its springy give under my touch. He was a little heavier now, smile lines creased his cheeks and forehead, but he still had the same open, boyish good looks that had first drawn me to him. "But not even your very considerable powers of persuasion can change my mind. You go to Hong Kong and wow senior management. I'll stay here, hold Olivia's hand, and take Franny on the tour. Paris can wait another month or two. It's not going anywhere, is it?"

❦

I heard a strangled sob. It took me a few seconds to realize that it was coming from me. Tears were running down my cheeks. I changed lanes, put on the brakes, and pulled off to the side of the road. Then I let go and really wept.

It was Tom, of course. The knowledge that Tom was waiting—that a possible new love was there for the taking—that brought Richard so vividly back to me. I had loved my husband: his mind, his sense of humor and responsibility, his unabashed adoration of our daughters, his very physical presence. I'd loved everything about him—and yet, clearly, I hadn't had the slightest idea who he really was. I realized that I would never be able to get over how wrong I'd been about him—about us. Just as I would never recover from the wrong he'd done me. And yet I knew that if I was ever going to have a chance at happiness again, I would have to try. I'd have to finally leave all the unanswered questions and ambiguity behind. Though Richard had walked out many years ago, the fact was, I'd continued to stay in our marriage. I'd never quite given up. Yes, I'd been embittered. Vengeful. But the very depth of those emotions had kept me mired in this one-sided, damaging, and endlessly bewildering relationship.

And Tom was waiting. But I knew his patience was starting to give way. His anger had startled me the other night. Richard had never really raised his voice to me or the girls. He'd cajoled and kidded—and, yes, sometimes even made love—to get what he wanted. *But what darkness that seemingly sunny nature had disguised!* I reminded myself. Better to be with someone who was honest about what he wanted.

I need you to think about how you feel. I need you to decide what you want.

I thought I knew now. I started the engine. I adjusted the windshield visor against the noonday sun. It was time to move on.

Part Four

31

ℰ

*D*owntown Shalesburg didn't have a traffic light. It consisted of a church, a gas station, and a row of late-nineteenth-century two-story clapboard buildings that had seen better days. There was the Second Time Around consignment shop. The Cut & Dry hair salon. A number of empty storefronts with For Rent signs in the windows. And the Shalesburg Market, which seemed to be the only place open on a Saturday afternoon. I parked in front of it and went inside. I spotted a woman with a small girl in one aisle, but they seemed to be the only people in the place besides the man behind the register. He was in his late fifties, balding, with a face the color and texture of beef jerky. He looked up as I walked over to the glassed-in deli case to the right of the register. A chalkboard on the wall behind the counter listed the day's specials.

"All out of the meatball sub," he told me. "But I can make you up anything else you might want."

I ordered a ham and cheese on rye and watched as the man set swiftly to work. He looked up as he got ready to slice the sandwich in half.

"Pickle with that?" he asked.

"Sure, I'd appreciate it," I told him. "And I'd also appreciate it if you could tell me how to get to the Delaney farm from here."

He shook his head as he tore off a sheet of waxed paper from a roll on the counter.

"Should've known," he said darkly to himself as he wrapped up the sandwich and tossed it and a packet of potato chips into a brown paper bag.

"I'm sorry?" I said, handing him a ten-dollar bill. "I'm just asking where the—"

"You're press, right?" he said, shoving the bag across the counter at me. "Don't you people have any decency? That poor family is going through enough grief right now without the likes of you nosing around again."

"I'm a friend of Mara's," I said. "I've driven all the way over from Massachusetts to pay my respects."

"Oh," he said, hesitating for a moment, but then he seemed to regain his angry momentum. "Well, I've just had it with reporters. These last couple of years have been a total media circus around here."

"Why?" I asked him. "What happened?"

"Thought you said you were a friend of Mara's."

The woman with the child had come up to stand beside me at the counter, waiting her turn.

"Oh, come off it, Verne," she said now. "You have any idea how paranoid you sound?"

"Can't be too careful," he shot back, depositing my bill in the cash drawer and handing me the change. He closed the register and crossed his arms over his barrel chest.

"Mara's been working for me in Massachusetts," I said, turning from Verne to the young woman. "But she didn't tell me why she left."

"We all wondered where she'd gone," the woman said, lifting her basket of groceries onto the counter. Though slim, pretty, and only in her mid-twenties, she already had a worn-down look. "If you can hold on a sec, I'll show you how to get to the Delaneys'."

"Thanks," I said as I walked to the door. "I'll wait for you outside."

❦

"Sorry about Verne," the woman said a few minutes later when she joined me under the awning with her bag of groceries. Her little girl followed her out, intent on ripping the wrapper off a Tootsie Roll Pop. "But he was a buddy of Mara's dad and has taken this whole thing pretty hard."

"Do you mind telling me what happened?"

"No, but let's sit down," she said, moving toward a wooden bench to the right of the door. "I've been up half the night with this one's younger brother." She leaned over to pick up the paper wrapper her daughter had dropped. "Teething!"

"I remember the days," I said.

"Oh, boy, am I looking forward to the time when I can look back, too," she said with a sigh, collapsing onto the bench and closing her eyes. After a moment or two, she straightened up.

"You know what fracking is, right?" she asked me. When I nodded, she went on: "Okay, so Shalesburg was like ground zero for fracking in this area. We got sold a bill of goods from a drilling company called EnergyCorp. They made it sound like the whole thing was a walk in the park. One of those 'make millions at home without lifting a finger!' kind of pitches. Most of the farms around here have been struggling for years, so signing up with the gas company seemed like just the ticket out of trouble. Jimmy Delaney was one of the first to lease his land."

"Is Jimmy Mara's dad?"

"Was. He died a couple of years ago—some cancer that got him in what seemed like a couple of weeks. That was before the accident, thank God, and all the craziness. At least he didn't have to know about that. Probably would've killed him even faster."

"The accident?"

"Yeah. It was really awful. I still hate to think about it. But it's not like that was the only problem we were having. Things were going downhill for months before it happened. The water started turning brown and tasting funny. Trout were dying off. The big trucks they were using to haul the heavy machinery around were tearing up the roads. The countryside was starting to look like a war zone. Then there was some kind of explosion out at the Harney site, and a couple of workers got soaked with the chemical mix they pump into the wells. They rushed them to Community Medical over in Glendale, where Hannah Delaney had just started working as an ER nurse. She was the first one there when they came in, and she ended up getting exposed to a lot of bad stuff."

The young woman shook her head, her eyes glistening.

"Hannah was a year ahead of me in school. She was just the sweetest person, you know? One of the really good ones. Always happens to them, for some reason, doesn't it? She and Jack'd had Danny the year before, and she was already pregnant again. She had some kind of toxic reaction in the ER. Went into shock. They say the workers ended up okay, but Hannah lost the baby—and then a couple of days later she started convulsing. Lost consciousness. Some people say she was brain-dead even then, but Jack refused to give up. Moved right into the hospital room with her, leaving Mara to deal with the farm and Danny. The press poured into this town like locusts. Even that what's-his-name from *60 Minutes* stopping people on the street to ask us how we were 'feeling.' Jesus! I don't blame Mara for wanting to get the hell out of Shalesburg after that. Jack was a mess—and the farm was falling apart. I think she did right to get Danny away from it all, too. So she was making a fresh start in Massachusetts?"

"Yes," I told her. Which was true, of course, but not the whole truth by any means. "I really appreciate you telling me all this. So Hannah was in a coma for—how long?—over two years?"

"Something like that. It seemed pretty hopeless, but Jack never gave up. And he kept hounding EnergyCorp for information about the chemicals. Got a bunch of lawyers involved. He was convinced there was a way of bringing her back if the drilling company would just release details about the kinds and amounts of chemicals they used. At least then the doctors would know what they were up against. But apparently the gas companies are not legally bound to reveal that sort of information—like they're guarding state secrets or something. Pretty pathetic, isn't it? That they get to protect their precious formulas. And Hannah? Who thought about protecting her?"

When we got up, she gave me directions to the farm.

"Tell Mara that Julie Thorndike said hi," she said, grabbing her daughter's hand. "Tell her to call me if she needs anything."

"I will," I said as I headed to my car. "And thanks again."

Though I'd left the store with the sandwich, I'd lost my appetite. I tossed the paper bag into the backseat, started the engine, and continued north, as Julie had instructed me, on the two-lane highway out of town.

❦

A summery haze lay over the rolling hills and fields. I crossed a bridge that spanned a wide, shallow creek, and drove through a stretch of second-growth sugar maples, birches, and hemlocks. I passed a farm with a collapsing silo, a backyard busy with hens, and a handwritten wooden sign that said "F— FRACKING!" in front of the house. A pickup truck sat on its chassis in the middle of an adjoining field, surrounded by grazing cattle. It wasn't until I reached the stop sign that Julie had told me to look for and turned left down the dirt road to the Delaney farm that I noticed how badly the road had deteriorated. Deep ruts and potholes forced me to slow to a crawl, but even then my muffler scraped against the uneven rubble. The shoulders had been filled with gravel at some point, but most of the stones had been dislodged and re-formed into gullies that cut steeply into either side of the road.

After several minutes, the overgrown brambles and shrubs gave way to more-open views of old, lichen-covered stone walls and overgrown fields. Ahead of me through a line of maples, I saw the ranch-style house that I recognized from Mara's screen saver. There were the willows flanking the one-story structure. But the cornfields behind the house that I remembered from the photos were gone. In their place was a sea of mud occupied by a brightly colored army of trucks and pipes and holding tanks. A derrick, tall as a lighthouse, rose above the site. A dozen or so cars were parked along the driveway in front of the house. I pulled up behind the last one in line.

As I made my way across the front lawn, the door suddenly slammed open and a passel of kids in bathing suits spilled down the steps, a red-cheeked Danny in their midst.

"Last one in—!" a young girl in a two-piece screamed as the group raced around the side of the house. The front door stood wide open. I knocked on the frame and waited. I could hear subdued voices inside, and when no one came to the door after a few minutes, I stepped into the small, dark front hall. From there I could see most of the cramped downstairs. The living room was filled with adults holding drinks and plates of food. The dining room table was covered with casseroles, a baked ham, platters of cookies and brownies, and a party-size aluminum coffee urn.

Mara must have spotted me from the kitchen and come down the back hall, because she was suddenly at my side.

"Not here," she whispered urgently, taking my arm.

"I'm sorry, I—" I started to say as she led me back outside.

"Yeah, right, I know," she said, guiding me across the lawn toward the faded red barn. "I called Eleanor this morning to tell her where we'd gone, and she told me you might be coming."

"I'm sorry about everything, Mara," I told her. "I know what happened to your sister. To Hannah. Danny's mom. I'm so very sorry. For you—for your whole family."

"Not many of us left now," she said when we reached a split rail fence that formed a paddock in front of the barn. She turned and looked back at the house. In the backyard, about fifty feet from the fracking site, the children were horsing around in an above-ground pool, jumping off a ladder into the water, pushing each other in. "My momma died when I was fifteen. Then Daddy a couple of years back. Of course I knew it was better for Hannah to go—and I was half praying she would—but still, I wasn't ready. The world just feels so empty without her. The Delaneys used to be a pretty big deal in this town. But that's all over. There's nothing left for us here."

"What about the farm?" I asked.

"What farm? It's a disaster area. You see that water the kids are swimming in? It's trucked in, just liked our drinking water is. They've polluted the groundwater, though they're paying millions of dollars in PR to deny it. Jack had to actually get a restraining order to stop them from pumping after what happened. They claimed they had a legal right! It's all tied up in court now. Lawsuits and countersuits. I've lost track of the whole mess, though

Jack can give you chapter and verse. It's what's keeping him sane, I think. Or almost sane. He barely even said hi to Danny—and he's drinking again. He went cold turkey before Danny was born. Nobody's calling him on it, but it would break Hannah's heart if she knew."

We stood there, watching the kids splashing around in the pool, their high, excited voices floating across the yard to us. After a moment or two, I said, "How did you find out that Mackenzie was building a house in Woodhaven?"

"We got to talk about that now?"

"I think you know that's why I came."

"It was a mistake, okay? Yes, I wanted him to suffer. I wanted to make him pay for what happened to Hannah. Eleanor told me about his heart problems, and I knew the digitalis would make things worse, but I didn't mean to kill him. I really didn't—I wouldn't have been that stupid! I need to take care of Danny. He doesn't have anybody else who can do that now."

"But you came to Woodhaven to track Mackenzie down, right? That seems pretty premeditated."

"Yeah, I know. But the truth is—" She hesitated, turning to face me. "Do you want to know the truth?"

"Yes. Very much."

"Okay," she said, looking out across the work site. "I didn't know what I was doing. I didn't have a *plan*. I just knew I had to do something. I had to get Danny away from this hellhole, and I had to somehow make that fucker pay for what he did to Hannah. I had him on Google Alerts. I saw a notice that he was building some huge place in the Berkshires. I figured it would be easier to get to him there than at his headquarters in Atlanta. By then Jack was already all wrapped up in his legal battles. He barely registered it when I told him we were leaving. I lucked out when I saw your ad in the PennySaver. The only two things I know anything about, really, are farming and computers."

"You took the job so you could be nearer to Mackenzie?"

"Yeah."

"It must have seemed like a miracle when Eleanor called that day."

"Not really," Mara said. "I'd gone up to the house a few times after I started working for you, just looking around. Curious about where the monster lived, you know? I didn't think anyone'd moved in yet. But Eleanor caught me there one afternoon. And I had to think fast, so I told her that I worked for you and that I was just checking out the property, hoping maybe we could do the landscaping. She was so nice—and she didn't suspect a thing. She befriended me and Danny after that. She put in a good word for us with Mackenzie, though I know he double-checked with Mr. Lombardi before letting her put you down on the call list. I feel really bad about how I betrayed her. But I couldn't help myself. I'd do the same thing again if I had to."

"What I don't understand," I told her, "is why you stayed after they started the investigation into Mackenzie's death. You must have known that they'd discovered he'd been poisoned. You were right there when Detective Erlander asked me about the digitalis."

"I was going to leave," she said. "I was going to leave that night, actually. But then Erlander called me at home, remember? He asked me all those questions about you—you and your husband. And I got worried that they'd think you'd done it. Erlander seemed clueless enough to charge the wrong person for the right reason. And I also felt bad about how the whole thing had hurt the business. I wanted to make things right."

She'd stayed out of loyalty. I felt awful about what I had to tell her.

"You need to come back to Woodhaven with me and explain what happened. I'll help you find a good lawyer. I have a feeling that if you're honest about what happened—and why—the authorities will be lenient."

"I can't right now," she said. "I've got to stay for Hannah's funeral tomorrow. But I'll come back after that. I promise."

I looked at her and said, "I'll have to tell them if you don't. I'll have to go to Erlander myself, if you're not back by the end of the day on Monday."

"I'll be there," she said, meeting my gaze forthrightly, but I didn't believe her.

I glanced in the rearview mirror as I drove away. She was still standing where I'd left her, watching me go. It was the last time I'd probably ever see her, I realized. She would take Danny and move on. Some out-of-the-way place where Erlander couldn't find her. Change her name. Invent a new story. She'd done it before. That's what she was going to do now. Start over again—again. Somewhere that wouldn't remind her of the past and everything she'd lost.

That's what I'd do, anyway.

32

🍃

The wreckage of the Delaney farm—and the family itself—
haunted me as I got back on the highway. In my mind's eye I kept
seeing the fallow fields and potholed roadway . . . the ugly tangle
of equipment and holding tanks behind the house . . . the children
swimming and playing within shouting distance of all those pipes
and pumps and toxic chemicals. It was early evening by the time I
took the Woodhaven exit off the turnpike. In stark contrast to the
countryside around Shalesburg, the Berkshires, burnished by the
setting sun and the first red flares of autumn, had never looked
more beautiful.

I loved this bittersweet time of the year in southern New England when the nights have turned chilly and the gardens, though
already starting to die back, are still full of color and texture. The
dense ranks of turtleheads with their gleaming purple helmets. The
delicate, orchidlike sprays of the Japanese anemones. I drove past a
garden where the wide hoop skirts of the hydrangea bushes—white
and otherworldly in the fading light—looked like so many ball
gowns gently adrift on the darkening lawn.

I parked the car by the barn and ducked into the office to check the messages. There was nothing that couldn't wait until morning. I walked up the path to the house, cricket song throbbing in the cool night air as loud and piercing as bagpipes. But the place felt empty to me. The office already seemed so deserted without Mara. And she wasn't the only person I was missing. Gwen still hadn't called. And there was no word from Tom.

With a rising sense of shame, I thought back on the last time Tom and I were together. How selfish and self-involved I'd been! While he'd been so emotionally honest and frank with me. And right about so much. Since Richard's disappearance, I'd prided myself on my independence and self-sufficiency. But I realized now that I couldn't keep sitting on the sidelines of life. What I saw and learned at the Delaney farm that day had opened my eyes to many things. Not least of which being the importance of the fight that Tom had been waging for years. I was ready to join him—and that fight—if he'd still have me.

I decided to wait until the next day to call him. I needed to get some sleep and think through exactly what I was going to say. But I was still as nervous as a schoolgirl when I finally steeled myself to dial his number on Sunday afternoon.

"Alice," he said when he heard my voice. And just the way he said it made me realize that everything was going to be okay.

❦

"I hope you're doing the right thing in terms of Mara," Tom told me after I filled him in on my trip.

"I know I am," I said. "God, Tom, if you could have seen that place! Mackenzie's company ruined a farm that had been in the family for generations—and the whole area is being torn up and destroyed. Hannah Delaney would be alive today if she hadn't been exposed to those chemicals! I can't condone what Mara did, but I sure can sympathize."

"Yes, I know," Tom said. "I'm still worried about your role in all this, though. Letting Mara disappear without telling Erlander. It's taking the law into your own hands. I can see how he might even consider you an accessory."

"Well, no one but you knows that I went to Pennsylvania yesterday. I'm going to call Erlander and tell him what Mara did, but I don't see why I need to tell him *when* I found out. I could just as easily have waited until tomorrow, say, to start wondering where she'd gone. It'll be Labor Day, anyway; no one will be looking for me in the office. I can lie low, keep the answering machine on, and mentally move my trip to Shalesburg forward. Then I could call the police Tuesday morning, after Mara's well on her way."

Tom was quiet for a moment, thinking this over.

"Didn't the family see you?"

"No, I don't think so. Mara hustled me out of the house before anyone noticed I was there. I talked to someone at the store in town, but I can't imagine Erlander's going to track her down. I think this could work, Tom."

"Maybe," he said. "I hope so. You can count on me to back you up if it comes to that. I'm no big fan of Erlander and the way he's conducted this investigation. At the same time, he's obviously putting two and two together now." He paused, then seemed to decide. "The best possible scenario would be for him to learn the truth about Mara's involvement when it's too late to grab her."

"Thank you," I told him. "For understanding and for supporting me on this—and Mara."

"I've seen too many towns like Shalesburg," Tom replied. "I've heard too many stories like Mara's—people whose lives have been devastated by fracking. And it's always the poor and helpless. It's always some desperate farmer just trying to hold on to his land."

"Yes. I see that now. I finally—"

"It's a national disgrace!" Tom went on. "Letting these special interests run roughshod over the law. What you told me about EnergyCorp refusing to release its chemical formula? That's just criminal! And the only people making any real money out of butchering the countryside and destroying innocent lives are the damned Mackenzies of this world!"

I smiled to myself as Tom continued his tirade, though I'd heard a lot of it before from him: ". . . blame an army of high-paid lobbyists . . . total lack of government oversight . . . desperate need to overhaul the whole campaign financing mess . . ." And I would probably be hearing much of it again. At least I hoped so. But I needed to get used to Tom's fiercely held convictions. Not to mention his lack of restraint in voicing them. Richard had been low-key about most of his opinions, political and otherwise. He used to poke fun at people who "clambered up onto their little soapboxes" to espouse this or that cause. I used to agree with him. I used to believe in Richard's "go along to get along" approach to things. Until I saw where that led.

"Tom," I finally cut in, "you're preaching to the choir here."

"Oh!" He sounded startled. Then he said with an embarrassed laugh, "I'm sorry, Alice. I tend to get carried away."

"I've noticed," I told him. "It's actually one of the things I really admire about you. How passionate you feel about these things."

Again he took a moment to respond.

"And certain people, too," he said.

"Yes," I told him. "And those certain people have been thinking—as you suggested. I'm sorry about the way I behaved the other night. I want to make it up to you. Would you like to come over for a special dinner tomorrow night?"

"Yes, I would," Tom said. "Very much. But if you've been on the road all day—as you'll be telling Erlander, remember—I doubt you're going to be in much of a mood to put a meal together. Why don't you come to my place instead?"

"I'd like that."

"Well, let's see if you still feel the same way after you've tasted my cooking."

33

The next morning I decided it would be best to just unplug from the world. My daughters, who usually stay with me over the Labor Day weekend, were busy elsewhere this year—Olivia at her in-laws', and Franny and Owen visiting friends on Long Island.

"Are you sure you're going to be okay on your own?" Olivia had asked me a few days before during one of our regular phone calls. I found it amusing how she'd started to mother me, routinely taking my temperature on Green Acres, the Mackenzie investigation, even my relationship with Tom. Though I don't think she realized it, she was obviously in training for her next job.

"Oh, I'm pretty sure I can manage," I'd told her. "How are you feeling? Morning sickness any better?"

"Finally! I can actually look at eggs in the morning again without gagging. I can't believe you only had to go through this torture for six weeks!"

I was enjoying sharing pregnancy war stories with my older daughter. Being an expectant mother had softened Olivia's hard edges and sweetened her more acerbic tendencies. There was an ease and flow to our conversations now that had all but dried up after Richard left—yet another thing to blame him for. Though we'd touched on it only briefly, I sensed she was thinking about him a lot these days and missing a father's presence in her life. She was calling me more often and talking longer and more intimately than she had in many years.

"So we really don't know *anything* about Daddy's side of the family?" she'd asked the one time we discussed Richard directly. We'd been talking about physical characteristics and wondering if the baby might be a redhead like Allen.

"No," I'd told her. "Your father was adopted, and he never expressed any interest to me in trying to find his birth parents."

"I have such a hard time with that!" she'd said. "How can anybody not care about where they came from? About who they are?" But I understood that what she was really having a hard time with was the fact that half of her genetic makeup—and a quarter of her baby's—remained a total mystery. And she was worried that there were unwelcome genes Richard might be handing down that she couldn't know about in advance and prepare for.

"I think your father never felt loved as a child," I'd told her. "He never felt he belonged. I really believe that did something to him, something that began to affect him more and more as the years went by. Your baby *will* be loved—and he or she *will* belong, so you have absolutely nothing to worry about."

I spent the morning where I'm always the happiest: in the garden. I worked in the long border behind the house—where I couldn't be spotted from the road—weeding, pruning, and deadheading. The warm, dry summer had taken its toll. The dahlias had shot up to almost seven leggy feet, and I had to stand on tiptoe to top off the blooms. The monarda that just a few short weeks ago had been blanketed with butterflies and hummingbirds was now covered in mildew, the once bright red bristling flower heads black-ened as burnt marshmallows. I cut the whole patch down, folded the load into the wagon with the rest of the cuttings and debris, and started across the lawn to the woods where I kept the compost heap, pulling the wagon behind me. I was upending it onto the pile when I heard a car door slam.

Screened by the trees, I watched Gwen walk across the drive, knock on the kitchen door, and then lean over and peer in, shield-ing her eyes against the bright morning sunlight. *Damn her timing!* I thought. Though I was pleased that she'd finally come by, I knew how hard it was for me to hold anything back from Gwen. And what I'd learned about Mara and Mackenzie really needed to be kept under wraps for at least another day. That would be the safest and wisest thing to do. For Mara—and for me. I stayed where I was by the compost pile, not moving.

Gwen knocked again, called my name a couple of times, waited a minute or two, and then started walking back toward her car. But she stopped in her tracks after she'd taken a few steps. Something in her peripheral vision—my bag of gardening tools that I'd left by the border, perhaps?—must have caught her eye and made her turn around. Then she spotted my red plaid shirt through the trees.

"Alice?" she called across the lawn. "Are you *hiding* from me?"

"Of course not," I lied, emerging from the woods and pulling the empty wagon behind me. "I didn't see you until just now."

"Really? I've been knocking on your door and practically screaming your name."

"What's up?"

"Well, it's great to see you again, too."

"Sorry," I told her, leaving the wagon by the border and cross-ing the lawn to her. "I just didn't expect you right now."

"Well, excuse me. I'm obviously interrupting important work here."

"I said I was sorry," I replied. "Can we maybe just start this whole conversation all over again?"

"Oh, who are we kidding?" she said, touching my arm. "I know you're still pissed off at me. And disappointed. I understand why. Let's sit down somewhere and talk, okay?"

"Of course," I said, relieved that Gwen herself would seem to be the main topic of conversation. "Grab a seat under the trees, and I'll get some lemonade."

❦

"I want you to know that I really took what you said about me and Sal to heart," she told me after we'd settled into the Adirondack chairs under the willows. "I may not act like it all the time, but your opinion means more to me than anybody's. At first, I was really hurt and mad about how hard you'd come down on me. But then I began to remember the good things you'd said. That I was competent and capable, and that I needed to find a way to get the board back on my side."

"I'm sure it wouldn't be all that hard if you tried."

"Well, I gave it a lot of thought," she said, "and decided you were right, that the problem was the women on the board. I've been handling them all wrong. The truth is, it's mostly the women who do the heavy lifting. Who get things done. So I sat down and reworked the strategic plan that I inherited when I took the job, reorganizing the restoration into three different phases—and lengthening the construction process by another year. That way, rather than having it look like we were way behind in our fund-raising, I made it seem that we were more than halfway to our goal for Phase I."

"Pretty clever," I said. "But don't you think they'll see right through that?"

"Oh, they did, all right!" Gwen said. "I invited the women on the board, and every female mover and shaker I could think of in the area, over for tea at Bridgewater House last Wednesday. I told them that I needed their advice. That I really believed in Bridgewater House, and I wanted more than anything to make the restoration a reality. But that I thought we'd maybe been setting ourselves up to fail. Maybe we should spread out the fund-raising schedule, and also come up with some real incentives for people to make major gifts. Gigi Lombardi sniffed and said she thought that was *my* job, and if I couldn't handle it, then maybe someone else should!"

"I can't believe you included her in this, Gwen! I warned you about her. She's out to get you."

"I knew that, and I decided it was best just to look the tiger in the mouth—in this case, one wearing bright red lipstick. I said that of course I'd step down if that's what the board wanted, but first I hoped they wouldn't mind looking over some of my ideas. I put the new plan up on PowerPoint and walked them through it while they scarfed down éclairs from Lenox Patisserie. And then I showed them my mock-ups of all the naming possibilities. I'd taken a lot of photos and airbrushed in the engraved marble plaques to make everything look real."

"What plaques?"

"The Trish and Maurice Moorehead Front Parlor . . . The Tifton Family Keeping Room . . . The Gigi and Salvatore Lombardi Dining Room . . . Well, you get the idea. I have to say, the photos did look pretty spectacular and I had them blown up into these easel-backed posters that they could take home with them. 'Just to live with the idea a little,' I suggested. They all just sat there, primly sipping their tea, totally noncommittal. I considered handing in my resignation after they all left."

"But?"

Gwen sat back in her chair and took a long drink of lemonade, swirling the ice around in her glass before continuing.

"The phone rang about an hour later. Gigi wanted to know why she couldn't have the front parlor. It was the biggest and most important room in the house, and she felt that she and Sal deserved it because he was board chair. Then Linda Tifton phoned to say she didn't like the marble plaque. It looked too much like a tombstone. Perhaps something in gilded wood would be more elegant? And did we have to call it the 'keeping room'? Did anyone even know what that was anymore? I got more than $75,000 in pledges by the end of the day!"

"That's great, Gwen. See? I *knew* you could."

"But wait—this is what I really wanted to tell you," Gwen went on. "Sal and I had arranged to spend the weekend at a little B&B in Vermont. He gave Gigi some cock-and-bull story about a business trip, and we drove up together Friday night. We were both real quiet in the car. I kept thinking about how I'd pulled the campaign out of the fire and how great it was that Gigi had come through. I began to think about how I actually kind of *liked* her. Sure she'd shown her claws, but it was only because she really loved Sal and wanted to save her marriage. So what the hell was I doing? When we got to our room, I told Sal I was so sorry but I just couldn't go ahead with it."

"And?" I asked.

"And you know what? He was so relieved! I think he'd just been worried about me, honestly, and wanting to help out in some way. He said he still loved me and always would, but that he really didn't want to break up his marriage or hurt Gigi. We had a good laugh—

and then a good cry. He slept on the couch, and we came back down the next day, his meeting unexpectedly canceled."

"Oh, Gwen! I'm really proud of you for the way you've dealt with all of this."

"Yeah, well, it took me long enough to learn how to stand on my own two feet. And now that I have, I have to say I'm looking back with a lot of regret on how I handled things with Graham. I wish I'd listened to you then, too. You were right that I never should have gotten involved with him."

"Sometimes the rules don't apply," I told her. "Not when your happiness is at stake. You said you felt an amazing connection with him. I understand you wanting to pursue that—wanting be with him. Sometimes you have to listen to your heart and everything else be damned."

"Yeah, sometimes. But this wasn't one of them," Gwen said, setting her empty glass down on the grass. She rose and stretched and then perched on the arm of her chair, looking down at me. "I may have pretended otherwise. I may have even let myself believe we had something going for a little while. But underneath it all, I knew the truth. Graham was a lot of fun, but that was all it was ever going to be, Alice."

"Okay," I said, uncertain why she looked so upset. "So you've figured out how you really felt about him. At least you don't have to worry that you lost the one great love of your life, right?"

"I lost something else, though," Gwen told me. "And it has me really spooked. I keep debating with myself whether or not I should go to Erlander with it—but then I'd have to tell him about my relationship with Graham. And that would jeopardize my job just when things are starting to look up. I try to tell myself it's not all that important, that I should just stop worrying. But I can't help it. I've been waking up in the middle of the night, obsessing about it."

"Why don't you tell me what you're talking about?" I said, re-alizing that this was the real reason Gwen had come to see me. "Maybe I can help you figure it out."

"The truth is, Alice, I was furious with Graham when he died. I'd announced to the board a week or so before that I'd gotten this huge anonymous pledge, but then Graham told me he'd have to put it off for a while. And he was so vague about what was going on and when I could expect it! I finally decided I had to do something to pin him down. I prepared a printed pledge that would have com-mitted him to making good on the money within the year, and I gave it to him the night before he died. But he refused to sign it. We had a fight and he ended up tearing the paper in half. He called me some pretty nasty things—mostly saying that I was only after his money like everybody else."

"Well? Was he right?"

"Honestly? If I were to be absolutely, brutally straight with myself? Probably, yes. I left around midnight and went home and tried to sleep, but I kept worrying about that damned pledge. I didn't want anyone to find it and see what he'd done with it. In the morning I went back up to the house. I was going to lie to him and tell him I was sorry, anything to get the damned thing back. But he wasn't there. The pledge wasn't either. I searched all over his bed-room suite. I was in a real panic! That's when Eleanor came in— and when you must have heard us fighting."

"Where do you think he was during all this?"

"I don't know!" Gwen said plaintively, standing up again. I could tell she felt too restless to sit still any longer. I stood as well, and we started to walk up toward the haying meadow. "He'd been so erratic those last couple of weeks. And he wasn't sleeping well. A couple of times I woke up and found him gone. He'd tell me that he'd been for a walk. He really loved your garden. I think it was the only thing that made him happy in the end. He liked watching the sun rise over the valley."

"So, he might have just gone out for a walk like you said," I told her. "Maybe he took the pledge with him and was thinking about signing it. Chloe or Lachlan probably went through his things at the hospital and tossed it."

"No, that's what's really weird," Gwen said. We'd reached the top of the meadow. From there we could see Powell Mountain rising over the town and Mackenzie's sprawling house near the summit, the wall of windows glinting in the noonday sun. *The gardens must be overgrown ruins at this point,* I thought. Now that I knew how Mackenzie had died—and why—the place looked like an eyesore to me. As ugly in its own way as the torn-up countryside around Shalesburg. What a waste of time and money and property! For a moment, preoccupied with my own thoughts, I lost track of what Gwen was saying.

"I'm sorry?" I said. "What happened?"

"Someone sent the pledge back to me in the mail. Taped back together. No message. Typed envelope postmarked 'Woodhaven.' But why would somebody *do* that? To relieve my mind? Or to put me on some kind of notice? It just feels so creepy! And I know this is going to sound kind of paranoid, Alice, but I feel like I'm being watched. Watched and judged."

34

I knew exactly what I was doing later that afternoon when I showered and put on the black lace-trimmed bra and panties I'd been keeping in the back of my lingerie drawer. Gwen had encouraged me to buy them a year or so ago when we saw the matching pair on sale at the outlet mall.

"What for?" I'd asked her then.

"I think you mean *who* for," Gwen had replied. "Well, you just never know. Maybe it will be like *Field of Dreams*. Buy it and they will come."

I turned around in front of the full-length mirror in my bedroom. Gardening is great exercise, keeping me toned and limber, and my hair was shot through with blond highlights from working outside all summer. All in all, I decided I didn't look too bad for someone who was going to be a grandmother in another few months. I knew Tom liked to keep things casual, so I pulled on a pair of faded chinos and a lightweight cashmere sweater. But I purposely chose clothes that would feel good to the touch and that, yes, would slip off easily. Just as when I brushed my hair up into a loose French twist, I was really thinking about how it would look when it tumbled down again around my shoulders, Tom pulling me closer to breathe in the perfume that I applied with a liberal hand.

I'd been to Tom's house only once before, earlier in the summer when we'd stopped by to pick raspberries. This was when we'd first started seeing each other, and he hadn't asked me inside. I'd appreciated his reticence as well as the glimpse he'd given me of where and how he lived. I was intrigued by the simple but extensive single-story structure he'd designed and constructed for his family, built halfway down a wooded rise overlooking Powell Mountain Brook. He'd planted a large fenced-in garden in the sunny field to the north of the house, with dozens of raised beds and rows of berry bushes and fruit trees. And he'd proudly explained that the house was totally green and off the grid: solar-powered, built with sustainable materials, and including energy-saving lighting, eco-friendly fixtures, and composting toilets.

It was almost dark by the time I arrived, and as I walked down the stone steps leading to the front entrance, I could see Tom working in the brightly lit kitchen, moving from sink to stove, an apron tied around his waist.

He met me at the door with a glass of wine and a kiss. I held the glass at my side while I let the kiss lengthen into something more than just a greeting—and with the promise of more to come.

"Okay," he said, taking me in with a broad smile when I finally pulled away. We were both a little breathless. "Sure you want dinner?"

"How could I pass up seeing you slave over a hot stove in your apron?"

"Actually most of the cooking's done," he said, putting his arm around my waist as he led me down the hall. "I'm at the assembly stage."

"Oh, Tom, this is lovely!" I said when we reached the kitchen, which I now saw opened up on a spacious dining area with a row of floor-to-ceiling windows that looked out over the falls. Outdoor floodlights illuminated the cascading water and the surrounding banks and trees. A long wooden table by the window was set with silverware, cloth napkins, and candles. A jug of giant sunflowers sat on the long butcher block countertop that separated the kitchen from the dining area, and several bottles of wine, a tray of cheeses and crackers, and bowls of olives and nuts were arrayed along its length.

"Hold out your glass," he said, lifting one of the bottles. "You've got a little catching up to do. I had some while I was getting things ready."

I sat on a stool with the glass of wine in front of me on the counter, watching Tom slice tomatoes and shred basil, as we talked about my trip to Shalesburg. His movements were practiced and economical, those of a man who'd single-handedly cooked and cared for four children and an ailing wife for many years.

"Mara told me they planned to hold the funeral yesterday," I told him. "Can you imagine anything sadder? Poor Danny!"

"At least he's probably too young to remember his mother all that well," Tom said, as he whisked together the salad dressing ingredients. "I know this will probably sound a little harsh to you, but from what you tell me, Mara's sister wasn't ever going to get better, right? I don't find it sad, then, that she died. To me, it's a great relief. The family can finally stop hoping for a miracle and start to move on again."

I suspected that Tom was talking about his wife's death, as well as Mara's tragedy, and I appreciated how frank he was about his painful past.

"You're right," I said as we carried the salad bowl, plates, and wineglasses over to the table. We sat, looking out on the brook.

"I'm sure going to miss her, though," I went on. "And Danny."

"So you really don't think she'll be coming back?" Tom asked.

"What for? It would mean facing some really tough questions about what she did. I know she didn't mean to kill Mackenzie. But—though I'm no legal expert—I'm pretty sure she'll be looking at jail time. Who would take care of Danny if that happened? What kind of future would she face with a prison record? There's nothing left for her in Shalesburg. I think it would be better for her just to take off with Danny and try to start again fresh somewhere."

"You make it sound so easy," Tom said. "But once you tell Erlander what she did, don't you think the authorities will be putting on a full-court press to find her? They'll be tracking her phone records, credit cards, you name it. These days, it's harder and harder to disappear into thin air."

"Well, speaking from experience, I know it *can* be done. Even when you manage to walk away with two hundred million dollars that doesn't belong to you. Mara's smart and very savvy with computers. I have a feeling she'll know how to cover her tracks. At least I hope so for her sake."

Tom cleared our salad bowls and then served the main course of grilled salmon, couscous, and green beans freshly picked from his garden. It all looked simple enough, but I could tell that he had put plenty of thought into the meal.

"I just hope you're not sticking your neck out too far for her," Tom said as he took his seat again.

"You mean with Erlander?"

"Yes, though I guess he's going to be feeling pretty relieved to have the whole thing solved for him. He's totally bungled this investigation, as far as I'm concerned. If he'd bothered to look a little more closely into Mara's background he would have discovered the connection between her and Mackenzie himself. Instead, he's taken a scattershot approach, intimidating everyone with his off-the-wall guesswork. He circled back to me the other day, by the way, trying to imply that *I* killed Mackenzie because he'd shut down my wind power initiative."

Tom threw down his napkin and rose abruptly from the table. He walked across the room and grabbed the corkscrew and another bottle of wine from the counter. Though I'd barely touched my own glass, I'd noticed Tom had been drinking pretty steadily over the course of the dinner.

"A little more?" he asked as he took his seat again and started to uncork the fresh bottle.

"No, I'm about ready for some coffee, actually," I told him.

"But I thought we were celebrating," he told me, refilling his glass.

It occurred to me that he might be nervous about what lay ahead. I was nervous as well, though I knew that drinking wasn't the answer for me. I wanted a clear head when I went to bed with Tom. I was looking forward to giving myself over to physical pleasure— something I'd thought I would never have a chance to experience again. And I wanted to feel every single wonderful sensation. But I understood that Tom might be worrying about how well he was going to perform. It must be different for a man, I thought. Much more of a physical test and display of virility. And we were both probably a little rusty. Perhaps he thought the wine was going to give him the courage he needed.

"Didn't Erlander imply something like that earlier in the summer?" I asked, hoping to change the subject.

"Did he?" Tom said. "I guess so. We've been around the issue a couple of times. But he recently got his hands on a video of the meeting Mackenzie and I had with the selectmen that got pretty nasty. He quoted back to me some of the things I'd said that weren't very nice. I admit that I did kind of lose my temper. But we all do at times, don't we?"

"Of course," I told him. "You know what I said to Mara when she told me about Mackenzie's check bouncing? I actually told her I was going to have to kill him if I didn't get the money."

"There you go!" Tom said, banging his fist on the table. "And honestly, Alice? I think I would have understood it if you *had* done it. If my life had been ruined by one swindler and then I'd gotten ripped off by another? I know I'd be in a rage. Who wouldn't be? Who wouldn't need to fight back? Sometimes you have no choice but to act. If I saw Mackenzie standing there looking out over the valley—as if he owned it, as if he owned the whole fucking world?— and all it would take was one little push? I'd have done it myself. He deserved to die. We both know it."

"No, I don't think so," I said, staring across the table at Tom. It seemed to have happened in a split second, though I realized now that he had actually been working up to it for a couple of hours. He had allowed himself to get a little drunk, and now he was spouting a lot of ugly nonsense. "Nobody deserves to die. And nobody has the right to kill."

"Where are you going?" Tom asked as I got up from the table.

"I'm sorry, but I think I better head home." And I *was* sorry. I'd had such high hopes for the evening. Tom had been pressuring me for weeks to take our relationship further. Perhaps, when it got right down to it, he himself wasn't ready. Though I understood his ambivalence, I felt terribly let down and hurt. But I had no intention of sleeping with him in his current condition.

"Why?" he said, looking up at me. "I thought you were staying. I thought we were—"

"No, not tonight," I told him. I didn't want to antagonize him, so I softened the blow with a white lie. "I'm sorry, but I'm just exhausted. These last couple of days have really taken it out of me."

❦

Tom followed me down the hall and out the front door. The cool late-summer evening had turned blustery and colder. Trees groaned as the wind pushed and pulled at their limbs. The stone steps were slick with freshly fallen leaves, and I descended them with care. At one point I heard Tom stumble behind me, swearing to himself.

"Are you okay?" I asked, turning around.

"What?" he called back.

"I'm fine on my own," I told him as I reached my car. But Tom came up behind me as I clicked my key chain, unlocking the doors.

"Why are you going?" he asked.

"I told you, Tom. I'm tired."

"I'm sorry," he said. "I think I upset you." The climb appeared to have sobered him up a little. He steadied himself against the side of my car. But his tirade kept running through my mind as I climbed into the driver's seat and closed the door. I started the engine, but then I lowered the window.

"What makes you think Mackenzie was pushed?" I asked him.

"What do you mean?" he asked, staring down at me.

"I thought he collapsed under the waterfall—in the heat of the day—from the effects of the digitalis. As far as I know, nobody's said anything about Mara pushing him off the ledge."

"You're right," Tom said. He took a step back. "I'm not sure what made me say that. I guess I must have heard somewhere that he liked to look out over the valley from that spot. That's all."

But Tom's vague answer didn't ring true, and I think he saw my puzzled expression as I turned and started to back down the driveway. I felt uneasy as I drove home. Falling leaves tumbled through my headlights and slapped against the windshield. The evening had been such a disappointment. Tom had exposed a side of himself I'd never seen before. And one I hoped never to see again. It could have just been the falling temperatures, but I felt chilled to the bone.

35

✿

I felt too restless and unsettled when I got home to think about going to bed, so I went out to the office and turned on my computer. Tom's outburst over dinner made me think about the town hall meeting he'd mentioned, the one when he'd lost it with Mackenzie. I decided to view the video for myself. It didn't take me long to find a link to it on the town Web site. The video lasted nearly an hour and, by the end, I could see why it had prompted Erlander to circle back to Tom with more questions.

After Tom's lengthy presentation, Mackenzie had very forcefully—and in front of the town officials and a packed room—dismissed the proposal. The video camera was focused on Tom in the front of the room, but Mackenzie's voice off-camera had registered loud and clear.

"This thing is full of holes, full of bluster, and quite frankly irresponsible."

"How can you accuse *me* of being irresponsible?" Tom had demanded, glaring toward the back of the room. "I've been looking into a certain lab that your company used to conduct so-called water testing in—"

"Better watch what you say, Tom," Mackenzie told him. "Think before you start making accusations about something you know nothing about. You keep this up, and I'll make absolutely sure that not only your wind proposal here but every half-baked project your little consulting firm takes on bites the dust."

"Are you threatening me?" Tom replied.

"Don't be ridiculous, Tom," Mackenzie said. "I'm just swatting you away."

"You goddamned son of a—!" Tom shouted as he started down the aisle. But then the video screen froze and I sat there staring at Tom's flushed face, his gaze fixed on Mackenzie with undisguised hatred.

❧

I jumped when I heard the knock on the office door. I hadn't turned on the outside light when I came in, so I couldn't see who was out there. The inside of the office, however, was lit up like a stage set—and I was clearly visible in front of my computer. It was nearly midnight.

"It's only me," Tom called out, knocking a second time.

"I was just closing up," I called back. "Give me a minute to—" But Tom turned the knob and pushed the door open.

"You should be more careful, Alice," he said, closing the door behind him as he stepped into the room. "You really should lock up when you're out here alone working this late."

"I'm closing up now," I told him again as I turned back to my computer and started to shut it down.

"I saw what you were looking at," he said as he came up to stand behind me. "I watched you watching it from outside." I didn't like that he'd been watching me. And I didn't like him standing so close. I swiveled away from him as I got out of the chair.

"Why are you here?" I asked.

"I came to apologize," he said. "I feel awful about how things went before. I'm not sure what happened. But I was drinking before you came, and I guess it all just caught up with me."

"Apology accepted," I said. "Now I think you better go. It's time for us both to get some sleep."

"Did you see the way he tried to sabotage me?" he asked, staring at the darkened computer screen, as though he hadn't heard what I'd just said. "Did you see how he tried to turn everything against me? It was incredible, don't you think? That's what people like him do, you know. Tell whatever lies it takes. Cheat if necessary. Use slander to undercut anyone who tries to stand in their way. Exploit everyone's worst fears. It's all about profits and power for them, but they're able to make it seem like they're the good guys somehow. *Clean gas energy!* It's all such bullshit! But it works! People buy into it. How can you fight something like that? It's just not possible!"

"Let's talk about this tomorrow," I said, taking a step toward the door. "Let's get some sleep and talk in—"

"No," Tom said, grabbing my arm. "I need to talk about it now. I need you to hear me out."

"You're hurting me, Tom," I said, but his grip only tightened.

"I want you to sit down," he said, pulling me back to the chair. "Just sit down and listen."

❧

"He thought he was so powerful!" Tom said, his voice raw with emotion. "He thought he could just go on destroying land and lives for as long as he wanted. He treated my proposal like it was a joke!

Did you hear what he said about 'swatting me away'? I was just a nuisance to him—like a fly. A little speck of nothing."

Tom paced back and forth in front of me.

"Do you have any idea what it feels like? Having your life's work dismissed like that? Brushed away as if everything you'd done was totally worthless? And then to realize that he'd pulled the wool over *your* eyes, too! That you were actually working for him. That was the final straw, I think. I knew I had to get to him. I had to stop him. I had to do something with what I knew about him."

"And what was it that you knew, Tom?" I asked him, hoping the question might slow him down a little. He seemed to be working himself up into another tirade. But this time it wasn't because he'd been drinking, which made his behavior that much more alarming. I wanted to get away from him. I began to calculate whether I'd be able to get around him to the door. Whether I'd be able to outrun him.

"A couple of weeks before the special meeting I started working on another article for EcoCrisis, focusing on Mackenzie and his various companies. I was reading through lab reports on water testing that had been ordered at one particular EnergyCorp site in Ohio that was tied up in litigation. And I discovered some discrepancies in the numbers. Things that just didn't add up. But it wasn't until after the hearing that I decided I owed it to myself to dig deeper. So I drove out to Ohio and spent a day or two poking around. I was able to track down some of the people involved. And do you know what I found? Someone at EnergyCorp had suborned the lab technician responsible for the reports that were submitted as evidence at the trial. He fucking paid this guy off to alter his findings!"

"Mackenzie paid him off?"

"Who knows?" Tom said. "It was one of his people, though. One of his henchmen. But we both know who told him to do it.

Mackenzie pulled all the strings at his companies. He was behind it for sure. And do you have any idea what that means? Do you realize what he might have caused? Hundreds of people could have been sickened! Animals killed! The countryside ruined! All so that he could keep on rolling in his profits. I was able to locate the initial report the lab ran. The real one. The idiots! They didn't even try to cover their tracks. They were so sure no one would bother to question their work. So I knew I had him then."

"You had evidence that Mackenzie was corrupt?"

"Yes, exactly! That's what I'm telling you. I had the son of a bitch—*finally*! So I called him. I told him I had something that I was sure he'd be interested in. That we should meet. He kept brushing me off—*swatting* me away. But I persisted, calling every day or so until I wore him down. I called again the night before the garden opening, and he finally agreed that I could come by early the next day and we'd talk. He said I'd find him in the garden. I walked up from my place. The sun was just rising. As I came up through the woods, I saw Mackenzie standing on that verge, looking out over the valley—over his precious view. I told him what I knew. He didn't bat an eye. He didn't even try to deny it. He just asked me what I intended to do about it. I said that I'd be willing to destroy the evidence and keep my mouth shut, but in exchange I wanted his support for my wind power project."

"But, Tom, that's—" I started to say, but then I shut up. Some part of Tom must have realized he'd resorted to blackmail, but I was beginning to understand that by then he believed that anything he did to bring Mackenzie down was justifiable.

"And do you know how he reacted? The bastard started to laugh! He *laughed* at me! He poked me in the chest with his index finger and said: 'Oh, how the righteous have fallen!' He said what a shame he thought it was that even someone as supposedly holy and pure as me had a price. He kept on laughing until I pushed him off that fucking ridge."

❧

"The fall would have killed him," I said. "*You* killed him. Not Mara. It was you."

"Yes," Tom said, stopping his nervous pacing for a moment and smiling down at me.

Oh, my God, I thought. *He's proud of himself!*

"I checked on him on my way back down the mountain," Tom said. "By then the whole area was fogged in. He was dead. I went through his pockets to see if he had anything on him that would incriminate me—but all I found was a letter of agreement that your friend Gwen had written to him. I mailed it back to her later, just to keep her out of any trouble. You see? I was looking after you even then, Alice. I always take care of the people I love."

"So later that morning at the Open Day when somebody spotted him . . . ?" I started to ask the question but found myself too shaken to continue.

"Yes, I went right down to him," Tom said. "I made it seem like he was still breathing. Like he still had a chance. It was such chaos, nobody seemed to realize I was faking it. People get so frightened around the dead and dying, but there's really no reason to."

"Tom, listen—," I began, but then I hesitated, trying to think of the best way to convince him that he would have to turn himself over to the police. He'd acted impulsively—out of extreme anger—after being ridiculed and humiliated. Surely a case could be made that he'd committed a crime of passion.

"I can see you're a little shocked, Alice," Tom said. "I hadn't actually planned on telling you any of this, at least not so soon. But after you left tonight, I thought about it again. Mara's role in what happened changes things. You can see what an opportunity this is for us, can't you?"

"What do you mean?"

"Erlander obviously suspects that she killed Mackenzie—and the police must have evidence that he was poisoned. Even she believes that's what happened—she confessed as much to you, right? It seems perfect, really, when you think about it. You arranged it so that Mara could get a good head start and a chance at a new beginning. So we don't have to feel guilty about telling Erlander about her. She gets away. And we'll be able to put this thing with Mackenzie behind us and start life together with a clean slate."

I stared at him, appalled. He appeared to have no regrets about killing Mackenzie. He'd kept the truth from me for months, but now, having shared his horrifying secret, he was not only unrepentant but actually thought I would approve of what he'd done. He'd murdered a man. But he was able to dismiss it as *this thing* and then blithely propose that we pin it on Mara. On top of that, he seemed to think that nothing had changed between us. *We'll start life together with a clean slate.* He obviously assumed that I loved and admired him just as much as he did himself. And this was the man I had planned to sleep with just a few short hours ago! I felt sick with loathing. And I was alone with him in the middle of the night, acres from my nearest neighbor.

"Well, of course," I said weakly, stalling for time. I knew I had to get away from him somehow. But at the same time, I knew I had to be careful not to let him see how I really felt about him— or what I was planning. I swiveled in my chair ever so slightly— toward the door. "But didn't you say you thought Erlander would be able to find Mara? That it wasn't so easy to disappear these days?" He'd walked to the far end of the room and was staring through the interior windows into the storage area—his back to me. I slid my chair a few feet closer to the door.

"So? Maybe he does track her down," Tom said, turning around suddenly. He cocked his head to one side as he took me in with that down-turning smile I'd once found so charming. It disgusted me now. "That would be okay with you, wouldn't it? I mean, if they brought her back to the Berkshires and indicted her. If she had to stand trial? You could live with that, couldn't you?"

"Of course," I said, trying to keep my voice steady. I could just make out my reflected image and that of the front door behind me in the interior window. But how far was I from the door exactly? If I used the chair to slide across the room, would I be able to make it before Tom reached me? My heart was beating so loudly I was sure he could hear it.

"What's the matter, Alice?"

"Nothing!" I said, but it came out a strangled cry. This was it, I realized as Tom's expression changed. He started toward me as I spun around in the chair, pushed off, and slid across the room. I tore at the door handle just as Tom reached me, grabbing the back of the chair. I jumped up, releasing the suddenly empty chair, which sent him reeling backward into the office. Then I threw open the door and ran into the blinding darkness.

36

❧

I kept running. The sky had cleared, but the wind was picking up. Stars swirled above me in the moonless night. I slipped on a patch of damp leaves that littered the path—and cried out—but managed to regain my footing. I stumbled on. I heard the office door slam. Tom was coming after me. I had to get up to the house first, I told myself. Lock the doors. Call 911. But Tom could still find a way to break in, I realized. Smash a window. Track me down to the basement or attic, wherever I tried to hide. He knew my house. And he knew me. He'd be able to sense my panic. He'd be able to hear my ragged breathing, my heart thumping like a fist inside my chest. No, better to try to make it to my car. I'd keep running toward the house to throw him off, but then circle back to where I'd parked on the drive near the barn.

Thank God it was so dark. When I got to the kitchen I pulled open the screen door, slammed it twice, and then slipped into the woods behind the house, following the old overgrown cart path that led up to the haying field. I moved as stealthily as I could. The wind, whipping at the branches and gusting through the leaves, gave me cover. Then a light flashed across the lawn and through the trees. The back porch light. Tom must have turned on the outdoor switch. Good. It would illuminate the immediate area around the kitchen door but throw everything else into deeper shadow. I left the cart path and zigzagged through the woods to the drive.

I was more in the open now, but I could make out the pale gleam of my windshield down the road. It was only then—with the car in sight, my escape within reach—that I realized I'd left my car keys in my shoulder bag. Which was in the house. My heart sank. I slowed down. A shadow crossed the lawn, and I started to run again. But I heard something coming up behind me. I panicked. I swerved back toward the house. But Tom was right there. He grabbed my arms from behind and pulled me against him.

"Alice?" he whispered in my ear. "Where do you think you're going?" His voice was so gentle and concerned that for a brief, euphoric moment I thought that I must be waking from a nightmare. I'd misheard. Misunderstood. This was *Tom*, after all. Not twenty yards from where we now stood, my daughter Franny had told me: *Well, I've got to say, I like the sound of him. Plus he grows his own tomatoes. That's hard to beat.*

"It's too bad," Tom was saying. His tone was sympathetic, but his grip was like iron. "I thought we understood each other. I thought we had a future together. And I was willing to overlook so much about you, Alice. I was willing to forgive."

"What?" I asked weakly. "What did you have to forgive me for?" But instead of responding, he suddenly twisted my wrists and yanked them behind me.

"That hurts!" I cried.

"And what about *me*?" he said, pushing me forward. "Do you have any idea how *I* felt when I heard you were working for Mackenzie? *You!* Of all people! I'd had my eye on you for months, Alice. And—admit it—you were thinking about me, too." With my arms pinned at the small of my back, he started to force me down the driveway toward the main road. The back porch light soon faded from view and darkness closed around us. I tripped and nearly fell at one point, and Tom had to haul me back to my feet. After that, I kept stumbling and letting my knees buckle, hoping to slow him down—and throw him off.

"You're right," I said when nothing I tried seemed to work. He just dragged me bodily along beside him. "I did have my eye on you. Then you blew up at me after the hearing and I thought it was over. But you found a way to forgive me, Tom. Are you hoping I'll forgive you, too?"

"I don't need your forgiveness," Tom said. "But I did expect a little appreciation. I thought you were made of stronger stuff, Alice. After what you went through with your husband, I thought we saw the world the same way. Weak or strong. I thought you understood that we have a choice. That you'd learned—and evolved—like me. I was a weakling for a long time—too long—before I realized that I had the power to change. I had the power to make a real difference in this world."

We'd come around a bend in the road, and I saw Tom's pickup truck parked under the trees at the end of my driveway.

"When did you discover this—this power?" I said, thinking my best hope was to keep him talking. It didn't matter what I asked, so long as it directed his attention away from me. All I needed was for his mind to wander for a second or two—just long enough for me to make a move. A narrow but deep gully ran along that section of the drive and I thought that if I could somehow push or trip him into it, I might have a chance.

Concentrating on how I might escape, I missed the beginning of Tom's explanation, but began to focus again when I heard him say, ". . . so I remortgaged the house to pay for the drug treatment. But it wasn't working. She was down to seventy-five pounds, just skin and bones." His voice was so monotone and matter-of-fact, it took me a moment to realize he was talking about his wife, Beth. "She was in pain all the time. And the kids were so damned tired of it all. One night she woke up screaming, begging for more medication. She'd gotten addicted to the morphine. And it made her nasty and paranoid. She looked at me and said, 'I know what you want to do. So do it. Put us both out of this misery.'"

We'd reached the pickup. He pulled some rope out of the back of the truck and started to wrap it around my wrists, tugging hard after each rough turn. It burned, but I almost didn't feel it. My heart had gone cold.

"What did you want to do?" I asked, although I thought I already knew the answer.

"It was what *she* wanted," Tom said as he wound the rope down my legs and around my ankles. "What she begged me to do. What we both knew was the right thing. That's when I realized that I had the power to do it if I dared. It was all in my hands. I'd just never realized it before."

"You killed your wife," I said, the fight going out of me.

"No," Tom told me. "I set her free."

I'd been frightened before, but now I was truly terrified. Mackenzie's wasn't the first life that Tom had taken. I thought back to the times that he had hinted at this. How he might even have been trying to tell me. *Everyone thought I was such a saint. Dealing with the kids. Caring for Beth at home. But the truth is . . . I was so deeply angry most of the time! At Beth. At how that damned disease was taking everything away from her . . . and how it was totally taking over my life. The anger was kind of like my own disease, you know? Eating away at me from the inside.*

He let down the tailgate. I felt so helpless, barely able to move, the ropes cutting into my wrists and ankles. But when Tom tried to lift me up and push me into the bed of the truck, I struggled anyway. I twisted and turned away from him and screamed.

Almost as if in answer, twin beams of light brushed through the woods across the way. A car was approaching from the south on Heron River Road. The headlights swept over us. The car slowed. I heard Tom whisper *"Goddamn it!"* under his breath. We were caught in the glare: a bizarre tableau vivant of human conflict. I cried out again, this time: "Help me, help me!" before Tom pushed me down behind the truck and out of sight. I heard the car braking. *They're stopping!* I thought. *Thank God, they're stopping!* I could make out the sound of rubber on gravel. The tick-tick of an idling engine. And then, with a wave of nauseated disbelief, I heard the tires screech as the car pulled away again and continued down the road. I was too stunned to resist when Tom hauled me to my feet, bundled me into the back of his truck, and slammed the tailgate shut.

❧

As a child, I used to sit outside on summer nights and stargaze with my father, who fancied himself something of an amateur astronomer. He had invested in a high-powered telescope, which he'd set up at the top of the haying meadow, where he would spend endless minutes adjusting and readjusting the lenses.

"Hurry, come look!" he'd cry when he finally got one or another celestial object in his sights. But usually by the time I managed to focus on his find, all I'd see was a hazy blur of light or the far left arc of some planet. I didn't really want to see the universe up close anyway. Instead, I loved to lie on my back looking at the brilliant, unfathomable vastness—all those enormous dying suns and swirling solar systems—and think about how marvelously far away it all was. Light-years away. Millions and millions of miles from us.

My father and those summer evenings returned to me as I was jolted along in the back of Tom's accelerating pickup—cold, frightened, and more alone than I'd ever been in my life. How I longed for the security that had seemed my right as a child! The deep pleasure of my father's company. The sense of connection with something magical and mysterious as we stood together looking up at the heavens. *I see the moon and the moon sees me.* The same night sky that had filled me with such wonder then filled with me anguish now. And regret. The stars, glimpsed between a fleeting jumble of branches and telephone wires, looked down with blind indifference as I thought of all the things I hadn't done. All the mistakes I'd made. Including this last and very possibly fatal one.

Tom.

Where was he heading? What was he planning to do with me? He'd already killed two people and gotten away with it. Though those had been flukes, surely. The first easily overlooked in the confusion of terminal illness and family tragedy. The second complicated by Mara's involvement and Mackenzie's ill health. How did Tom imagine he'd get away with disposing of me? And where? Because I had no doubt now that he intended to do just that. I'd become a serious threat to him. Not just because I could link him to the murders, but because I'd challenged and rejected his whole grandiose and grossly distorted sense of self—*I had the power to do it if I dared!* If he really believed that we shared the same worldview, then he must have been deeply angered by my reaction to what he'd told me. The fear and disgust in my eyes. The fact that I'd run from him. When he'd obviously been expecting me to fall gratefully into his arms.

But I didn't intend to die. I wasn't ready to die. I had a grand-child to welcome into the world in a few months' time. Daughters to look after and love. Friends I cherished. A business I was proud of. Gardens I hoped to build. So many places I wanted to visit. And along with all this, I still had one overwhelming question I needed to find an answer to, a puzzle that, despite the many years I'd de-voted to it, all the numerous false starts and attempts at closure, I realized now I was as far away from solving as ever. Because, as I faced the very real possibility of my death, it was the prospect of never seeing Richard again—his smile, his touch, the voice that would finally explain to me why, *why* he'd done what he had—that was the most difficult to accept.

No! I thought. *I won't let this happen!* I rolled over on my side and started to inch my way painfully around the floor of the truck, searching for anything that might help me break free. I came up against something that felt like a tarp. A roll of what was probably duct tape. And then, just as I was beginning to lose strength and hope, my hands brushed against something cool and dry and coarse. I ran my fingers up and down the side of the thing. Cinder block. Holding it in place with the crook of my knees, I started rubbing my bound wrists up and down one of its rough corner edges. Back and forth, up and down, back and forth.

I'm sure I heard it before Tom did. At first I thought it was just the wind scything through the trees, but then the sound became more distinct. A siren. Maybe more than one. From somewhere be-hind us. Or was it ahead? Then Tom must have heard it, too, be-cause the truck started to pick up speed. Things happened quickly after that. The siren gaining on us. Red lights circling through the darkness. Sirens all around us now. More flashing lights. Tom going faster. My hands suddenly slipping free. A disembodied voice on a bullhorn. "Slow down. Pull over to the side of the road immediately." Tom accelerating. The world in a sickening spin. Screeching brakes. The pickup swerving off the road. Careening into the woods. Impact. Metal shrieking. Me in the air. And then nothing but the brilliant, black, unfathomable vastness.

Epilogue

❧

"That was Franny," Gwen said, dropping the receiver back into its cradle. "They ran into traffic on the West Side Highway. It was all jammed up from the Macy's Thanksgiving Day Parade. They're hoping to get here by three."

"Of course! Just in time to sit down and eat," Olivia grumbled, shifting in her chair beside me at the kitchen table. She was at that point in her pregnancy where she was never comfortable in any one position for very long. We were peeling potatoes. Actually, Olivia was doing the peeling while I lent moral support and did my best to gather up scraps with my left hand. My right was still in a sling. Along with sustaining a fairly serious concussion, I'd fractured my elbow and broken my nose when I was thrown from the back of Tom's pickup. But I'd been lucky. Tom had gone through the windshield, severing his carotid artery; he'd bled to death before the police could pry open the crumpled cab. I'd been lucky, too, in that I didn't know about any of this until I woke up in the hospital the next day. Not only was I spared the horror of Tom's final moments, but because of the concussion, I'd initially had trouble remembering the hour or two leading up to the crash. Though eventually it all came back to me, when I first came to I could recall only a few jumbled moments. But those returned with nightmarish clarity.

"Tom pushed Mackenzie off the ridge," I told Detective Erlander and Ron Schlott when they came to see me in the hospital a few hours after I regained consciousness. "Early in the morning. Before the Open Day even started. Tom killed him. Not Mara. She didn't mean to hurt him. She was only—"

"It's okay. We know," the detective said with surprising gentleness. "Just take it easy. We knew from the autopsy report that Mackenzie died from injuries sustained during a fall."

"So why did you keep after me about the digitalis?" I asked, trying to focus on the two men seated uncomfortably by the side of my bed. "Why that stupid raid?"

"It was a search," Erlander said defensively. "The digitalis poisoning—though not that serious—seemed to point in a certain direction . . ."

"You thought I might have given him a push because the poison didn't seem to be doing the trick?"

"Don't get all worked up," Erlander said. "It's my job to pursue every angle. It takes time. But we were starting to home in on Mr. Deaver. We were just a step or two behind you."

"And I could have been killed while you were out there pursuing your damned angles!" I said, glancing from Erlander to Ron, who looked appropriately abashed. "Did you know he killed his wife, too?"

"What?" Ron said. "No, Alice. She died from breast cancer."

"She would have," I replied. "But I think maybe she was taking a little too long about it as far as her husband was concerned. He told me last night that he'd 'set her free.' I think he must have in-jected her with an overdose of morphine."

"Jesus," Ron said under his breath.

"We will, of course, follow up on this information," Erlander said, his gaze moving from Ron back to me again. For the first time since I'd known him, he looked uncertain. "But why exactly do you think he confided all this to you?"

My shoulder and arm were heavily bandaged. My eyes were black and blue. I had enough stitches in my forehead to pass for Frankenstein. It seemed a little far-fetched to suggest that Tom had been blinded by love.

"I guess he thought I'd understand," I said, suddenly feeling exhausted. I closed my eyes. "Because of the skeletons in my own closet."

A nurse came by soon after that and shooed Erlander and Ron out of the room. I fell back into a fitful medicated sleep. Gwen was in and out. My daughters arrived later in the afternoon. Olivia, who stayed on to help after I was released from the hospital, designated herself my watchdog in terms of the press and the police, denying the former any access whatsoever and the latter only carefully supervised visits. So it wasn't until my second meeting with Ron, who had come to take my statement the morning after I got home, that I finally un-derstood just how close my brush with death had actually been. And, more important, who had saved me. In my confused state, I hadn't given much thought as to how and why the police knew to pursue Tom down that dark country road in the middle of the night.

"Because the 911 call came in on a cell," Ron told me, "we lucked out in terms of backup. The wireless carrier routed it to the highway patrol. And they alerted us as well as a couple of other nearby police stations."

"What call?" I asked Ron, who was sitting on one of my upholstered armchairs in the living room. Olivia and I were facing him on the couch.

"The one from Mara Delaney," Ron said. "I thought you knew. She saw you and Mr. Deaver by the roadside. She stopped, but she had her little boy in the back, and she didn't think she could go up against Deaver on her own."

"That was Mara?" I said, remembering the sweep of car headlights as I struggled to break free from Tom. Mara had come back after all. Just as she promised. And just in time. "But where is she now? Why hasn't she been by?"

"Mom, you're still in pretty bad shape," Olivia said. "We've been telling everyone you need to take it easy for another day or two."

I realized Olivia was trying her best to look after me, so I held my tongue until after Ron had taken down my full statement and departed.

"Mara isn't *everyone*," I told my daughter. "And without her showing up when she did—and making that 911 call—I probably wouldn't be sitting here right now. Could you call her for me and ask her to come over as soon as she's able?"

"I can do better than that," Olivia said. "I'll run down to the office and get her. She insisted on keeping things going while you were out of commission."

I'm not a particularly touchy-feely person, and Mara has always been physically standoffish. In all the many months we've worked together, I don't think we've ever so much as shaken hands. But when she burst into the living room a few minutes later, her face flushed from running, and I stood up in a wobbly sort of way to meet her, she walked right over to me and let me hug her with my one good arm.

"I was so afraid he was going to kill you!" Mara said. "I didn't know what to do!"

"You did great," I told her as she began to cry. "You saved my life. I can't begin to thank you."

Olivia, who had started to follow Mara into the room, stopped, and took us in with a surprised look on her face. Then she quietly backed away.

❦

I made it sound as though Mara would be doing me and my daughters a favor when I asked if she and Danny would consider moving in with me temporarily.

"Olivia should really be getting back to her husband and job in the city," I explained a few days after our emotional reunion. Mara had taken to stopping by for lunch to go over office matters, and we'd quickly regained our terse, no-nonsense working relationship. "And, as you can see," I said, looking down at my arm, which was still immobilized in its bulky cast, "I can't really handle things on my own at this point."

Mara had stared at me across the kitchen table with that intense, unflinching gaze I used to find so disconcerting. I sensed she was trying to figure out if my request was in any way an act of charity—or, even worse, pity. I'd never told her that I'd visited the trailer park when I was trying to track her down, or even that I knew she lived in such straitened circumstances, but I suspected she'd learned as much from Danny's babysitter. I met her gaze head-on.

"You and Danny could have the downstairs suite that we put in for my parents years ago," I went on. "It's roomy and quiet. You'll hardly even know I'm around."

"How am I supposed to help take care of you," she demanded, "if I can't hear you?"

"Oh, I'm sure we'll be able to work something out," I told her.

Though I did initially have my doubts. Since moving back to Woodhaven, I'd managed to convince myself that I was happier on my own. I ate when I felt like it, went to bed when I pleased, watched old movies all night if I wanted to. It was great to be so independent, I'd told myself, so self-sufficient. But my close call with Tom and death had changed me in ways that I was only beginning to understand. With Mara's and Danny's arrival, I began to realize how self-indulgent my solitary existence had actually been. How good it felt to have others around me who demanded my time and attention. We were all a little wary of each other at first, but mealtimes, work, my physical therapy, and Danny's half-day preschool in town soon helped us establish a comfortable, easygoing routine. Danny, who had been shy to the point of muteness around me for so long, slowly began to open up.

By the time Thanksgiving rolled around and my daughters and sons-in-law came up to join us for the long holiday weekend, Danny had turned into a regular little chatterbox. Not just with me, but with everyone he considered a part of his new, extended family. While Olivia, Gwen, and I were working in the kitchen getting the dinner ready I could hear Danny's high-pitched, excited voice in the dining room.

"Nemo is a fish who lives in the ocean," he was telling Olivia's husband, Allen, who was helping Danny and Mara set the table. "But he gets lost and his dad has to go on a venture to find him. . . ."

"An *ad*venture, bud," Mara said. "And you're supposed to be putting the spoons on this side of the knife. Like this, okay?"

"It's great to have you here," I heard Allen tell Mara in a lowered voice. "It's been a big help to all of us."

"Your mother-in-law's almost back on her feet," Mara said. "We should be moving on soon."

It was something I wasn't ready to think about, though I knew the time was coming. Mara was right. I wouldn't really need the sling much longer. It was the emotional support I wasn't looking forward to losing. And Mara's brusque, undemonstrative concern was just the kind of help I wanted. During the few short months of their temporary stay, she and Danny had managed to take up permanent residence in my heart. And I believed the feeling was mutual, though Mara remained as carefully guarded as ever. I'd have to be careful about how I broached the subject of them staying on. Put it on some kind of financial footing, perhaps. Make it seem a mere convenience rather than something a lot more central to my sense of well-being.

"It's going to be another hour or two before Franny and Owen get here," I told Olivia after we put the potatoes on to simmer. "Why don't you lie down for a while? Gwen and I can keep an eye on the turkey."

"Thanks, Mom," Olivia said, getting up with a sigh. "I think I'll take a nap on the couch while Allen watches the game."

"Do you want a little glass of wine to take with you?" Gwen asked. She was uncorking one of the bottles of Côtes du Rhône she'd contributed to the festivities.

"I'm *pregnant*, remember?" my daughter told her.

"I said 'a little,'" Gwen replied. "I can't believe a sip or two is going to hurt you."

"It's not just me I have to think about these days," Olivia replied as she made her way out of the room.

"Oops!" Gwen said with a laugh as she handed me a glass of wine and sat down in the chair Olivia had vacated. "I guess I was being a little insensitive."

"No, Olivia's being *too* sensitive," I said. "I'm afraid this last trimester is not bringing out her best qualities."

"Well, I'm sure it can't be easy for her," Gwen said, raising her glass. "But here's to us. Happy Thanksgiving, Alice!"

"You too," I said as we touched rims. "I feel like I have a lot to be thankful for this year."

"I can tell," Gwen said. "I was worried for a while that the whole mess with Tom was going to turn you against the world again. But it really hasn't, has it?"

"No, you're right," I said, taking a sip of wine. "And I'm not sure why exactly. But getting tossed off the back of that pickup knocked some sense into me. Life is just too short to waste on being angry, Gwen."

"You still have a temper."

"Yes, but I think the bitterness is gone. Mackenzie told me once that what Richard did is something I'll never be able to put behind me. He was probably right. But I think I'm finally starting to learn to live with it."

"Oh, Graham," Gwen said, shaking her head as she looked down into her glass. "I wish I knew how I felt about him. I wish I knew about that damned pledge!"

I'd told Gwen in the hospital that it was Tom who'd returned the unsigned document that she'd prepared for Mackenzie that committed him to his Bridgewater House contribution. And she'd asked me a question I hadn't considered: "Did Tom say whether he'd taped it together? Or had he found it that way?"

"No, he didn't say," I'd told her. "Just that he mailed it back to you."

"Because if Graham had taped it himself," Gwen said, "then I think that would mean he intended to sign it. Which would mean he really did care about me."

We'd gone over this question again and again in the weeks since Tom's death, never getting any closer to an answer.

"Which do you *wish* it would be?" I asked Gwen now.

"You mean, did I want him to love me?"

"Yes," I said. "And did you want to love him back?"

"I didn't used to think so," Gwen said. "I was too obsessed with getting his money, frankly. But the more I think about our time together, the more I miss it—and him. I think we were a lot alike—a little too volatile and greedy, maybe, but also pretty passionate. God knows, he had his faults, right? But something really did click between us. I think we would have fought like cats and dogs. But in the end? I think we would have made a damned good match. So, yes, I think I could have loved him if he'd loved me. But maybe the not knowing—the never being able to know—is what makes it seem possible."

Gwen helped me wash the greens for the salad and get the water jugs filled, then wandered out into the living room, where everyone had gathered in front of the television. I stayed in the kitchen, thinking about what she had said. Occasionally, as the shock and terror of my final hours with Tom began to recede, the actual events of that night would come back to me with absolute clarity. And I could remember the sensation of sliding in my chair across the office floor. Running through the woods behind the house. The feel of cinder block against my skin. The sudden, urgent determination to live. And, at the same time, the sense of finally letting go. The stars swirling above me as I flew into the night. And beneath it all—or above; I wasn't sure which—a sense of profound mystery. Something deep and wonderful that I'd yet to define, let alone begin to understand. Though I knew now how much I wanted to keep trying.

"They're here!" Allen called from the other room. I heard the front door open and looked out the kitchen window to see Allen and Olivia walking across the lawn to greet Franny and Owen. Mara followed them out, along with Danny, who was holding her hand. Then Danny broke free and raced toward the car, excited and happy.

"I'm coming!" I said, though there was no one in the kitchen to hear me. "I'll be right there."

Bleeding Heart

LIZA GYLLENHAAL

This Conversation Guide is intended to enrich the
individual reading experience, as well as encourage us
to explore these topics together—because books,
and life, are meant for sharing.

A CONVERSATION WITH LIZA GYLLENHAAL

Q. Where did the idea for the story come from?

A. Though I don't intentionally set out to write novels about social issues, I do seem drawn to them for background themes. *So Near* involved a child car seat product-liability lawsuit and *A Place for Us* revolved around underage drinking and the Social Host Liability law, which holds parents responsible for what happens in their homes. I've long thought that hydrofracking, especially as it might affect a small, rural community, would be an issue that could contribute to an interesting and tension-filled story. But it wasn't until I decided that I wanted the novel to have a mystery at its heart that I realized how I could work the subject into the fabric of the story. I always think a good mystery is like a Chinese box or a Russian matryoshka doll, where you have one thing hidden inside another and then another. It was fun to create a story with its own little series of nested mysteries—with hydrofracking at the center.

Q. *Is fracking a big issue where you live?*

A. Though western Massachusetts doesn't have much in the way of shale-gas deposits, the possibility of fracking has stirred up some controversy in our area, and a bill banning hydrofracking throughout Massachusetts for at least ten years is currently making its way through the state legislature. Another point of contention, and one I address in *Bleeding Heart*, is wind power. Like almost all alternative energy sources, I think wind power has its pros and cons. There actually was a proposal to mount wind turbines on a mountain not far from where we live in the Berkshires, and it was eventually shot down, though not for the reasons I cite in my novel. But I think the crux of the problem— balancing the need to create green energy against health risks, high costs, and "not in my backyard" concerns—applies to fracking, wind, solar, and probably most alternative energy methods. Though I think it's pretty obvious that I come down on the antifracking side of the equation, I hope I make it clear in the novel that I realize that the issue is complicated and divisive.

Q. *Are you an avid gardener, or did you have to do a lot of research for this book?*

A. The answer is actually yes to both. I am a passionate amateur gardener (see my Web site, lizagyllenhaal.com), but I did end up doing a lot of research on how a professional landscape gardener might go about creating "the most beautiful garden in the Berkshires." Luckily, there are many wonderful resources on the Internet as well as gorgeous gardening books, including *Great*

Gardens of the Berkshires by Virginia Small, with photographs by Rich Pomerantz. I also try to make every Open Day (garden-conservancy.org/opendays) in our area and have been able to visit many private gardens for articles I've written for the Web site Rural Intelligence (ruralintelligence.com). The Berkshires are blessed with some magnificent historic gardens such as the ones at Naumkeag, Chesterwood, Ashintully, and the Berkshire Botanical Garden, which are all open to the public, as well as numerous stunning private gardens. It was a dream come true to create a fictional new garden—one where I had all the money in the world to spend! It's funny, but I can see the garden Alice (and I) designed for Mackenzie so vividly in my mind, it really feels like a place I've actually visited and loved.

Q. The novel is written in Alice's voice and from her point of view. Did you find it difficult or confining to write a whole novel in the first person?

A. I think that Alice is the first central character I've created whose past has made her cynical and somewhat forbidding. My protagonists from earlier novels have all been mostly as Alice described her former self: "I used to be such a nice person. Personable, obliging. My husband, Richard, once jokingly told me after a particularly dull dinner with a business associate of his that I 'suffered fools too gladly.' . . . The truth is, for most of my life, I liked being liked. I'd been raised to be polite and well-mannered. But I think it was also in my DNA." Perhaps it's because I'm getting older and a little jaded myself, but I really enjoyed seeing the world through Alice's eyes. I took vicarious pleasure in having her be irritable and demanding with people, which is something I would never allow myself to be. And it helped that Alice had an earlier life that I could have her look back on and contrast with her current existence and frame of mind.

Q. Where do you write?

A. My husband and I divide our time between Manhattan and a small cottage in the Berkshires. In the city, I usually write in a beautiful old Eames chair that I commandeered from my husband. Our place in the country includes an old horse stable that has become my "writing studio." It still has the old iron stall feeders and leather harnesses on the walls. It remains permeated by a wonderful smell of animal and hay.

When we're in the country, I wake up early and reread and rewrite on my laptop in the house, but in the afternoon I go out to the studio, bolt the door, and start the hard work of writing the next new word, sentence, paragraph, chapter. In the winter I have a fire going in the Jotul stove. In the summer I open the windows and listen to the birdsong and brook nearby. I can watch our family of wild turkeys parading up and down in the old paddock. Other sightings: woodchuck, coyote, fox, and, early last spring, when the trees were just greening out, a big black bear. It was a breathtaking moment when this wall of darkness lumbered right past me—so close that, if the window had been open, I could have reached out and run my hand through the bear's ink black fur.

Q. *Do you have a set writing routine?*

A. I usually wake up early and reread whatever I've been working on. I revise constantly. Then I let the demands of daily life intervene for several hours and pick up again in the afternoon. Most days, I don't hit my stride until three o'clock or so, and then if I'm lucky I get two or three good, productive hours in. I think a lot about what I'm working on when I'm not actually writing: when I'm gardening, for instance, or driving in the car back and forth between the city and our place in the Berkshires. I try to work out problems—a scene I can't get off the ground, a character who refuses to behave—during that two-and-a-half-hour stretch.

A. *What authors do you like? Did any of them influence you in writing this book?*

Q. I read a lot of fiction and poetry, and my list of favorite writers is constantly changing and expanding. In no particular order, I love the fiction of Elizabeth Strout, Hilary Mantel, Allegra Goodman, F. Scott and Penelope Fitzgerald, Susan Isaacs, and Alan Furst, and the poetry of Richard Wilbur, Mary Oliver, Elizabeth Bishop, and Theodore Roethke, to name just a very quick and beloved few. Like so many other readers around the world, I was enthralled by Donna Tartt's *The Goldfinch*. I went back and reread her first bestseller, *The Secret History*, which is set not far from us in the country; it's equally wild and wonderful. When I decided to try to make *Bleeding Heart* something of a mystery, I reread many of my favorite P. D. James novels. I think she's an absolute master of the mystery genre—and just an all-around brilliant writer.

Q. What will your next book be about?

A. *Bleeding Heart* has two separate mysteries at its heart. One is resolved, but the other is left open. I did that on purpose because I want to write at least one more novel about Alice. I really loved writing about gardening and the Berkshires, so having Alice be a landscape gardener in the fictional Berkshire town of Woodhaven is the perfect setup for me. And, as I mentioned earlier, I'm drawn to her acerbic, no-nonsense nature. I'm not sure yet whether the next book will resolve the question of Alice's missing husband, but I think it will again revolve around a mystery. As is often the case when I'm thinking about a new novel, I have just a few vague ideas and characters in my head.

QUESTIONS FOR DISCUSSION

1. What does the title mean? Who in the book has a "bleeding heart"?

2. Do you think Alice was justified in putting aside her principles to work for Mackenzie?

3. Whom did you suspect—and when—of being behind Mackenzie's death?

4. Alice still spends a lot of time thinking about her husband. How do you think her unresolved feelings for him affect the action of the novel?

5. How would you compare Alice's and Gwen's attitudes toward money?

6. Do you think Mackenzie is a crook or just someone whose business takes a bad turn?

7. Alice has a way of misjudging important people in her life, especially men. Why do you think she does that?

8. What is it about Mara that makes so many female characters, including Alice, want to help and protect her?

9. What do you think of Alice's decision not to mortgage the house in Woodhaven even though she desperately needed the money?

10. Alice says that she's happiest and most at peace with herself when she's gardening. Is there someplace—or thing—that gives you a similar sense of well-being?

11. Of all the things that Alice wants to live for in the end, what do you think is most important to her?

Photo by William Bennett

Liza Gyllenhaal spent many years in advertising and publishing. She lives with her husband in New York City and western Massachusetts. She is the author of the novels *Local Knowledge, So Near,* and *A Place for Us*, all published by NAL.